To Jamie,
for your unyielding support throughout the writing of this
book, and always.

Chapter One

The Boy and the Girl

The girl and the boy were being watched; the girl by the boy, and the boy by the Captain of The Scavenger from the bridge of the ship.

The boy, if you could call him that, was tall, ebony skinned, and dressed in the blue and white of the ship's colours. He looked young but had the air of someone you should not trouble yourself to trifle with, nor make the mistake of believing him less wise for his years. After all, like many of the others on board, he was a soldier of the empire. And even though all of them were polite in their duties, turned out well in their uniforms, they would still turn on you in less than a second's notice.

However, today, although the boy was in no mood to fight, his training to resist a conflict was being sorely tested by the girl; like it had been for nearly the whole of the past three months. He had been given the task of chaperoning not only the girl, but her mother.

The mother, who was amiable enough; quiet and pleasant, would go about her day on board following all the captain's rules without any objection. And as he had instructed on the first day these included rules such as: "no passengers are to speak to members of the crew unless permission has been granted by the captain … stay away from the edge of the ship … no wandering above deck on stormy nights … only enter the captain's rooms when specifically invited or instructed to do so … and under no circumstances are you to go fiddling with the cannons, weapons or any explosives on board the ship!"

This was standard procedure and had been explained quite clearly to all crew and passengers of The Scavenger before she set sail. All had adhered bar one! It seemed to the boy that the girl had intentionally gone out of her way to cause trouble, and so what he assumed would be the easy task of chaperoning a mother and her daughter across the seas, had turned into anything but.

For the girl the feeling was mutual. She found the boy's ever presence, even when she couldn't see him, like a shadow she could not get rid of; his shadow invaded her own shadow's space! She had never even wanted to be on the ship in the first place. Nearly four months ago, back home in Vanu, the girl's mother and father had sat her down and informed her that they would be leaving for the capital of the empire. What she did not count on was that only herself and her mother would be leaving; ahead of her brothers and father. Their regiment was still in the process of completing the decampment of soldiers in the Southern Raanian Sea and would follow them some months later. The girl and her mother were left with the task of setting up home in the capital, ready for their arrival.

If the girl was not already upset and angry at having to leave Vanu, the dull task of setting up home, whilst her brothers got out of it, was not helping matters. She was also leaving behind most of her friends. Some had already departed Vanu, but others had yet to leave. It made her anxious as to whom they would find in their new home; she knew full well that most inhabitants of Vanu were not destined for the capital.

Then there was the matter of being on board a ship, and it didn't matter which one. Not only would she be confined in the same place for a lengthy period, away from her brothers, father and friends, she knew she would not do well on board.

Every time she had ever been on a ship; little, big, wide or skinny, she was always very, very ill and being on board The Scavenger was no exception. Nearly three months ago she had been healthy looking, but after nearly a month of being nauseous, another month trying to keep her food down, and this last month finally managing to not be sick, her frame now looked too small, almost gaunt. Even her once olive complexion now looked like it had a tinge of green to it. And although she had finally mastered how to deal with the seasickness, this had taken several weekly visits to the ship's physician, who had her experiment with the likes of drinking salt water and chewing on ginger and cinnamon sticks. The girl had had enough. She was fed up of being cooped up in her cabin or hanging off the side of the ship so instead she set about exploring her new surroundings, and in doing so did everything that the captain had warned the passengers' not to.

At first, she obeyed the rules. After speaking to all the passengers on The Scavenger, she could tell the difference between the military families and the non-military people on board by how they dressed, with their plain but well-cut clothes, or by the way they chose to speak; facts, facts and more facts about politics and the ending of the Five Hundred Year War, and how happy they were to be heading home. They seemed to the girl to always be an optimistic bunch in what was a large and constant nomadic family. This comforted her to some extent, for she too was part of their group.

The boy could see she was in her element; it still amazed him at how children from military families could just seamlessly blend into their surroundings, talking to all men and woman of varying ages and backgrounds with such ease and without scorn from the other party. This was not something he had encountered himself.

The girl then moved onto approaching and talking to the waifs and strays that The Scavenger had picked up from various ports on its journey. These people were much more interesting to the girl. At every port a family or two would depart only to then be replaced with at least one or two lone travellers; or on the rare occasion several got on at once. For instance, at the Port of Kiriso in Maiorban, several soldiers, carrying at least twelve wooden chests between them, boarded. Some of them were officers; their uniforms were black instead of the blue of the ship's crew, also marking them out to be a land regiment rather than a naval one. They towered above all else on board with their black and gold bell-topped shakos adorned with golden speckled plumes, feathered epaulettes to match, and what the girl thought to be a ridiculous number of medals and badges adorned over their left breast pockets. It reminded her of her father's feelings towards soldiers with too many badges: "Amongst them you will find a medal or two for a tour, maybe even a commission, but if they adorn more than that there is a good chance they had polished some General's shoes correctly or took care of his wife for him."

Of this group of officers, one stood out above the rest; he was slightly taller, dusky haired and plain faced but he also looked a lot younger than the others; too young, the girl thought, to be an officer. He had the grace and solemn countenance the others possessed but he did not seem to have the same air of authority surrounding him. He reminded her slightly more of the boy. Coincidentally, the girl had noticed that this officer had a lot of time for conversation with her extra shadow. She had watched them being introduced to each other by the captain, but they either got on so well that they became friends immediately, or the only other explanation she could think of for the ease of their conversation was that they had met before. This was one reason the girl did not approach this officer. Attracting more attention from her extra shadow was not on her agenda, and there was no doubt in her mind that if she did he would join in or tell her off for speaking to an officer without permission. Yet on a few occasions the officer and the girl had caught each other's eye; he would stare straight back at her without any emotion and then, uninterested, turn away. Likewise, the girl was not at all bothered, she could not read the glances he gave her so dismissed him as someone of no information to entertain her out of her boredom.

The girl did finally manage to meet some other passengers whom she took a liking to. At the Port of Oren along the Arinthscar coast a portly man, who on first appearance looked rather grotesque with his swollen belly and pitted purple face, in fact turned out to be very friendly and enthusiastic. He was a man who delighted in telling all the passengers on board that he was on his way to, 'Try out the best wine the empire has to offer, for I have drank the Port of Ornube and Oren dry!'

The gentleman who accompanied him was not so joyous in manner. Tall, slim and extremely pale, almost as white as the belly of the gulls flying above and about the frigate, the girl thought, took to always being a couple of feet behind his traveling companion, but not so far away that he could no longer hear him.

'See here girl,' said the portly man licking his lips, 'I am led to believe by my sources that the royal palace has several underground tunnels that lead to numerous wine stores. They say that the king's wine is the best there is and is so good that it tastes and feels like liquid gold as it trickles down your neck!' He danced the tips of his chubby fingers from the top of his neck down to the bottom, burped and chuckled. 'Isn't that right my Ma-aaan?' addressing his travelling companion, as he tripped and stumbled over his cloak onto the deck. At this display the tall pale man rolled his eyes and walked by the portly man; immobile on his back, his cloak twisted about him.

The girl found many of these instances amusing for a while, but like his pale friend there was only so much one could bear to hear about wine or take in the waft of fermented air blowing in her face.

***

A slight relief from the constant boredom on The Scavenger came when the frigate arrived at another port of call. Just shy of six weeks into the voyage, instead of stopping briefly to let some of its passengers depart, the captain announced:

'Ladies, gentlemen and soldiers. We are stopping in Iscar, the capital port in the Isles of Cairdax. The Scavenger is to restock on supplies. It is twenty-two minutes past eight in the morning; be back on board by three O'clock or The Scavenger shall depart without you.'

To the girl's surprise two of her friends from Vanu, Psychra Lysan and Gunn Ári Ásval, and their mothers Orica and Tyra, were there to greet them. They had left ahead of them some weeks prior to their own departure, and all three of the mothers had kept in contact through letters; the girl's mother having advised the others that they hoped The Scavenger would dock in the many Isles of Cairdax along the way. So it was that the two friends had kept an eye out for the ship; three times a day, every day for the last two weeks, their watch having finally paid off. The six of them spent the best part of the morning walking and talking amongst the market stalls that were dotted in and around Iscar's port houses.

Mrs Ári Ásval tried to reassure the girl about her new home, 'There is nothing to worry about. Yes, it is hard to adjust but you will find friends from Vanu, like us, where you are going also.'

'Besides,' said Mrs Lysan, 'you are going to be living in the capital of the empire. You will not be bored there. I believe that you will be kept so busy you will find there is no time to miss Vanu and your friends, especially once you have immersed yourself into society.' The two women chuckled.

'Yes,' said Mrs Ári Ásval to the girl's mother, 'and I believe your daughter, just as you did, will catch all the young officers' eyes. There will be no time for silly games and nonsense anymore.' Psychra and Gunn laughed at the girl.

'Oh shush,' said Mrs Lysan to her daughter, 'you can stop your laughing. You will not escape the balls and parties either. Your father and I will make sure of that young lady. There will definitely be no more wearing of trousers or playing in the dirt!' Psychra looked disgusted with her mother and Gunn barked a laugh.

'Ha, I think what your mothers are trying to say is that you will be looking to get husbands soon, swanning about in those

ridiculously big dresses and stupid hats! Ha! Ha … Ow!' Gunn
rubbed his head; his mother having just scuffed him.

'You may also hold your tongue young man, if you think that
you can continue as you are. All three of you are in for big changes.
This isn't Vanu now, you know!'

***

When the three mothers briefly left the girl, Psychra and Gunn
alone, having decided to speak to a market stall holder regarding
some shawls he was selling, the other two began to tell the girl of
their new life in Cairdax. This did not make her any more optimistic
about what to expect from the capital.

'Mother has already started making me wear these horrible frilly
things,' said Psychra, as she pointed at the cuffs of her sleeves and
the hem of her dress.

'If you think that's bad,' said Gunn to Psychra, 'at least you
don't have to wear woollen shirts and trousers.' He pulled down
the scruff of his collar to reveal a very red and sore looking rash on
his neck.

'It's too cold in Cairdax,' said Psychra, 'so we can't wear any of
the cotton here. Although, it is hotter in the capital, so maybe you
will be okay with wearing what you are.'

Gunn and Psychra looked on at the girl wistfully. She was
wearing light cotton travelling trousers tucked into some long thin
socks and a short sleeved pale cotton top; items all three would
have worn back in Vanu. The only items of clothing that made her
garb slightly blend in with the others was her large and heavy
travelling cloak; lined with fur, she closely wrapped it around
herself to keep the stiff breeze off.

'Why does anything have to change? Our clothes, our home?
Why did we have to leave in the first place? There is no war, there

hasn't been for years,' said the girl, as she looked around at her two friends' surroundings. 'It's nice enough here, but it's not Vanu.'

The two friends shrugged their shoulders, 'All I know is that we are no longer allowed to have fun,' said Gunn.

'And apparently, we all have to dress like our mothers, prance around at balls and get husbands,' said Psychra, and they all laughed.

The girl imagined Psychra and herself dressed like beautiful birds, lined up on display whilst packs of officers moved along, pointing and chattering amongst themselves as to which one of them they liked the best.

'Or jobs,' said Gunn.

'Well at least you still get some freedom,' said the girl, 'from what the other mothers and girls' said on the ship, Psychra and I get to knit and sew, have several horrible children, and be forever cooking and cleaning!'

'Ha. Yes. Maybe one of you will marry me, then not only will you have all those lovely things to look forward to, but you can spend all your time with me too!' said Gunn, swiftly ducking to avoid the blow of fists from the two girls.

***

As they sat down for lunch, in what were some very shabby tea rooms along the dock, the mothers continued to talk amongst themselves, whilst the girl and her friends' talk turned to the capital.

'I heard from some people who have already arrived in the capital that you can expect quite a welcome,' said Gunn. He stabbed at his piece of cake with his fork, breaking a large piece off before cramming it into his mouth. 'Ugh-par-ent-ney urr wooves and da atts arr at it ugg-in.'

'What?' giggled the girl.

'The wolves and the rats!' said Gunn, having finished off his cake. 'Don't tell me you haven't heard of them?' he rolled his eyes in exasperation, but the girl knew he was savouring the moment to tell all. 'The Wolf King lurks in the shadows, and stalks about the capital, grabbing unsuspecting passers-by. He takes them back to his lair and kills and eats them!'

'No, he doesn't!' scoffed Psychra. 'He doesn't,' she said, reassuring the girl and crossing her arms annoyed.

'What about the rats?' smirked the girl.

'They are just as bad if not worse, especially the Rat King! He lives in the sewers of the city. It's said if you cross him, or so much as look into his eyes, he will remember you, find you out and drag you into the underground tunnels of the city, never to be seen again.'

'Oh, don't be ridiculous!' said Psychra. 'No one wants to know about them, it's all stupid stories anyway, made up to make thieves and murderers look good.'

'No, it isn't, Psychra!' he said, casting a dirty look. Then to the girl: 'It's in all the papers. There have been more arrests in the capital; members of the wolves and the rats. Their leaders call themselves kings,' he smirked. 'I bet they are really fierce.'

'Hardly,' said Psychra, as she rolled her eyes and turned to face the girl. 'It's just these two gangs, they're always fighting and…'

'Gangs? I thought the capital was meant to be a peaceful place?'

'Who told you that?' scoffed Gunn.

'My father, of course.'

'Nowhere outside of Vanu is peaceful, or as beautiful,' said Psychra, 'you only have to look at this place to know that.'

All three of them ate more cake and sipped their teas, pieces of old plaster fell from the ceiling onto their table as horse drawn carriages carrying cargo from the dockside drove by, shaking the building.

'Anyway, you won't be getting involved with stupid wolves and rats!' chirped up Psychra. 'You want to see if you can get an invite to the palace, it's meant to be really beautiful, and the gardens there…'

'Huh, I hear you not allowed in the gardens,' said Gunn.

'…and of course, the royals and Prince Taigor,' said Psychra sighing, having completely ignored Gunn's comment. 'He's meant to be really handsome.'

'Eurgh, why do you care about the Rothians', said Gunn. 'I hear the royals are meant to be really weird. They keep people locked up in their towers and down in the dungeons…'

'No, they don't,' laughed the girl.

'Of course they do!' insisted Gunn, 'and anyway, what else do they do besides sit on their thrones, eating and drinking and having balls whilst the rest … whilst our fathers do all their dirty work for them!'

'Sssssh!' snapped Tyra Ári Ásval at her son. She lowered her voice, 'Be careful what you think Gunn, and be careful about what comes out of that mouth of yours. You don't know who is listening. That goes for all of you. Don't go getting your fathers into trouble.'

'I was only saying what father…'

'Shush … that's enough! Talk about the weather if you have nothing else to say.'

The two girls giggled under their breath, whilst Gunn sulked at the table. The girl felt much better for seeing her two friends and was sad that soon they would have to separate again. Except this time, it could be years instead of months.

***

After they had finished their lunch they all walked back along the harbour front towards the frigate. The clock had started to chime, and the girl and her mother hugged their friends and said their goodbyes before they walked back up the gangway of the ship.

'Write and tells us everything! Especially if you meet the Prince,' shouted a gleeful Psychra.

'Or if you come across the Wolf King, with his huge teeth! And the Rat King, that's if you escape out of his tunnels!' jeered Gunn.

As they ascended the gangway of the ship the girl noticed how few people had re-boarded. There were only two or three military families left and some of the soldiers and sailors had disembarked permanently; it seemed the Isles of Cairdax had been their last port of call.

There were at least one hundred passengers who had not returned and in instead their place was filled with an array of what looked like vagabonds; a mix of young and slightly older boys, who needed a good bath judging by their dirty clothes and not so fragrant odour, and a small party of red coated men surrounding a young woman. The girl thought she did not look much older than herself.

One of the travellers had brushed into the girl but did not turn back to apologise, all she could see was one cold eye, the other was obscured by the brim of his overly large hat. She had an urge to kick him in the knee from behind as she rubbed her right arm but noticed that the remaining soldiers and sailors had also been surprised by the change in passengers. The atmosphere had turned from relaxed and friendly to cold and silent as the officers and crew watched on.

'They are all trouble,' said the portly man to the girl, in slushed hushed tones. She half turned her head towards him to listen, half still turned towards the soldiers and passengers in front of her. 'The people from the Isles of Cairdax,' he continued, after the girl gave him a quizzical look. 'You get all sorts of bad ones from there. Thieves, murderers. The majority of Old Town is made up of them. I would watch your purse and keep your valuables on you whilst they're on board. I guarantee that something goes missing from someone. Or there's a fight, or both.'

'And what about them?' asked the girl.

'Who?' asked the portly man.

The girl nodded in the direction of the six-red-cloaked and black feather hatted men, armed with pistols and bayonets, who looked like they were guarding the girl they were with. The portly man shrugged his shoulders.

'I have no idea. But by the way she dresses it looks like she is destined for the King's Court.' He then hiccupped and slumped in a crumple by the side of the deck.

Intrigued, the girl continued to watch the new comers and the soldiers for a while; both parties disquietly eyeing each other up. But unable to get any more information out of the portly man she disobeyed the first of the captain's orders to not speak to members of the crew and approached one of the Master's Mates.

'Excuse me. Excuse me,' said the girl to the Master's Mate, who looked back at her in alarm, shooting looks between the girl and the officers on board. 'Please. I know I'm not meant to speak to you, but could you tell me who those men are and the young woman they are with?'

'Leave me alone girl,' he hissed, 'you'll get me in trouble.'

'She already has,' came the voice of the boy behind her. 'Move along Vicken, and you,' he said addressing the girl, 'you need to not get these men in trouble. They are trying to work.'

The girl narrowed her eyes at the boy, brushed past him and walked off unsatisfied. Over the next couple of days, she further disobeyed the captain's orders trying to gain more information about these new and unusual passengers. Too curious to sleep, she went up on deck in the middle of the night. The winds were high and the sea rough, but she spotted one of the red-cloaked men talking to the plain faced officer who had boarded at the Port of Kiriso. She tried to listen in to what they were saying but the noise of the weather beating against the ship made it impossible. Slowly, she edged closer, trying hard not to slip on the wet deck but lost her footing and went flying into the black-clothed officer; knocking both him and the red cloaked officer to the floor of the deck. Again, her extra shadow appeared out of nowhere.

'MISS!' he shouted, and it was not out of concern. There was anger in his voice. 'YOU ARE NOT SUPPOSED TO BE ON THE QUARTER DECK IN THE DARK AND IN STORMY WEATHER!'

He grabbed her roughly by the arm, yanked her up onto her feet, shouted back to the officers his apologies, pulled the girl by her arm off the deck and back to the safety of her cabin, slamming the door in her face. Her mother, woken by the commotion, looked even angrier.

The third time she broke the captain's rules happened after dinner in the captain's cabin. The boys and girls her age had been dismissed whilst the wives of officers, including her own mother, stayed behind for after dinner drinks. The girl, making her way back to her cabin, suddenly noticed the young woman who, normally surrounded by her guards but now unaccompanied, was making her way further down into the lower decks of the ship.

The girl wondered why she had not attended the captain's dinner and curious, followed her quietly down the wooden steps and narrow passageways beneath the bridge. She knew they were not meant to be down here, but they were not alone. She stumbled down the wooden steps as the large brimmed hat boy brushed passed her again; ascending the stairs to the deck and flattening her against the hull of the ship. Annoyed by the rudeness of the boy, but undeterred in following the young woman, she glared at the boy and carried on, through several doors, her pace quickening with every step. She stopped abruptly as the portly man's travelling companion came out of a side door to her right. He glared at her and waited until she moved aside for him, stalking off in the opposite direction. The young woman was still in sight, so the girl picked up speed. But as she walked around the curve in the ship the young woman had suddenly vanished.

A large black door loomed in front of the girl, she looked about but there was nowhere else the young woman could have gone. She opened it and stumbled through only to be faced with many big black cannons and weapons; from large bronzed coloured bayonets, guns, swords and sheathed knifes, to large barrels marked with "DANGER" around their bellies. She had entered the gun deck. The bustling crew inside started to shout at her. One voice she recognised instantly above the others, startling her out of her bemusement at the young woman's disappearance.

'MISS!' shouted the boy. 'You are not supposed to be down here! What do you think you are doing? GET OUT!' he bellowed.

The girl ran past him and out of the gun deck, down into the decks below, and through several other doors, then up some ladders, only for the two of them to go straight through a door that was concealed amongst the panels into the captain's chambers. They were met with a startled party of officers' wives, the Captain of The Scavenger and the officers in black, including the younger plain faced officer, all with their wine glasses raised in the middle of a toast. It seemed these officers had joined after her and the other daughters and sons had left the meal earlier.

The girl was not in anyone's good books. Her mother was embarrassed and the captain highly unamused. She was confined to her cabin for a week and then only allowed out under strict orders from the captain that she be accompanied by the boy, everywhere she went, for the remainder of the journey.

***

The now dwindled group of passengers, soldiers and crew, were the final boarders for the last leg of The Scavenger's journey. The frigate continued its way through the slow waters of the Balgon sea, impregnated with giant icebergs; some towering as high as the ship's masts, and across the ever-increasing rough seas of Calpero, before finally entering the calmer, and clearer waters of The Dourbrande Sea. The frigate had been surrounded by sea as far as the eye could see, since the Isles of Cairdax but within the last couple of hours the captain had sighted land, announcing to all crew and passengers:

'Ladies and gentlemen, officers and crew; the Kingdom of Aebra is in sight and we shall arrive at our final port of call shortly.'

The Scavenger was now making her way around the peninsula off the south-east coast, when the boy commandingly shouted at the girl:

'Please! Miss! Come away from the edge. We have nearly arrived in the capital and I don't believe your mother, nor your father and brothers for that matter, would be best pleased that you had come so far and then managed to fall into the sea!'

Her face was hidden from the boy's view, having stood on tiptoe to lean over the side of the ship so she could see the fish swimming below the waves. It reflected the many moons of the world and she rolled her eyes at the disturbance. She had been trying her best to forget that the next stop would be her last and had completely forgotten that the boy was still standing watch over her. Now she wished she could get off the ship there and then as to be rid of the inconvenience when suddenly the captain of the Scavenger, Rost G. Alba, arrived at the boy's side.

'I see you two are still getting on like a ship sinking in the acid waters of the Tyrrscan Sea?'

'Sir … as always,' replied the boy, through gritted teeth.

The girl leaned back in and placed her scuffed boots firmly back on the deck of the ship before turning around. 'Captain Alba,' she said, and bowed her head slightly towards him. 'I did not see you both there,' she smirked at the boy who narrowed his eyes in response, unimpressed.

'Well, you will both get your wish soon,' said Captain Alba. 'Look to the starboard side.' The boy and the girl turned to their right, looking towards the lands of Aebra and its high golden and bronzed cliffs.

'ALL HANDS! Bring her in!' cried the captain to his crew.

At his command the ship's crew went to their stations readying to slow the frigate to dock. As The Scavenger finally reached the tip of the peninsula she became aglow in a mass of bright light. The girl and everyone on board turned sharply back and away from it, shielding their eyes from the sudden glow. The captain laughed as they all opened their eyes again. There were many gasps, then cheering, clapping and a general buzz of excitement spread across the ship's crew and passengers.

As the girl slowly opened her eyes she heard a steady intake of breath. Looking up to see where it had come from she saw the boy steadily eyeing a large black bird flying overhead. Following his gaze, as the bird flew off in the direction of the light, she became distracted by the scene in front of her. To her amazement there appeared a vast city that glistened and twinkled, steeply descending from a high semi-circular ridge, right down to the edge of a bay that surrounded the clear waters of its harbour.

'It must be made of gold,' said the girl, bemused under her breath.

'Ha,' said the boy, 'if only it was. What you see is oro stone.'

'Yes,' said the captain to the boy, 'of course you would remember, having last been here as a small boy. What, eight or nine?'

The boy did not reply, but the girl looked at them both to see if this was true. She had heard that the navy had stopped recruiting small boys for the ships' years before her and the boy would have been born. The two of them did not provide any more on the matter. Instead Captain Alba addressed her instead:

'However, I believe you have never set sight on this beautiful city before? You were born out in the Southern Raanian Seas, were you not?' the girl nodded in reply. 'Well,' the captain said, addressing both the boy and girl, 'welcome back Master Rasia. And to you, Miss Phæ'enor Doven, welcome to Aebra, and the City of Benaghar.'

Chapter Two

A Warm Welcome

It did not take long for The Scavenger to reach the waters of the capital's harbour. Phæ'enor, oblivious to the workings of the ship, was taking in the many buildings in front of her. Golden peaks reflected the light from the sea and the sun all at once, whilst white buildings up high, and many buildings made of the golden oro stone, glistened back at her. And dotted amongst them were shops and warehouses, and the colourful workhouses along the harbourside, with glass glinting in the distance from others.

The city was built in such a way that the many figures of people, moving across and in and out of the maze of streets, could be seen clearly from the harbour. They reminded Phæ'enor of Vanu, where hundreds of colourful little crabs spread out over the island, as the last of the moons of the world appeared in the autumn sky, making their way down to the shoreline to spawn.

Not all the moons had yet gone to sleep here; she could see the largest, Hallumera, and three others, the names of which she could never remember in order, directly above the city. Hallumera could always be seen due to its vast size, but it was day and therefore translucent.

As the ship slowly manoeuvred into the port she could see the city was not as steep as she first thought. Although the ridge at the top was sharp, the descent was more of a long reclining slope than the side of a steep mountain. She looked across it from one side to the other.

'Wow,' she said, stunned.

'Yes,' said Captain Alba, 'the city of Benaghar is built upon the crater of Mount Benaghar.'

'It is a dormant volcano,' Master Rasia half informed Phæ'enor, half accused the captain, who looked at Master Rasia, brows raised.

'But, Sir…?' asked an alarmed Phæ'enor.

Captain Alba, not looking in Phæ'enor's direction, smiled, 'Yes. It is dormant, but there is no need to be worried. The last time it erupted was over three hundred years ago in 1521, at the coming of the moon Feldstar. Yet even then it has only ever erupted to the north side. The lava fills the vast planes on the north side of the mountain instead of the city of Benaghar itself.'

'Are you trying to frighten my daughter Captain Alba?' A slim, brown and dark-haired woman gracefully appeared at Phæ'enor's side. She wore a brightly coloured dress made of silk and sturdy black boots with a summer travelling cloak draped over her shoulders.

'My Dear,' said the woman to Phæ'enor, 'they are but teasing you.' She pointed to the top edge of the city. 'The crater no longer takes the impact of the pressure below it. The last time this part was active the whole mountain side collapsed into the sea.' As she said this she moved her hand from the top and pointed down, directly below The Scavenger. 'You see,' she said, as she looked at her daughter, 'the city lies on the top side while the other half of the crater lies beneath the waters of the city's harbour.'

'Mrs Doven, I see you are ready to depart,' remarked Captain Alba. Mrs Doven smiled, 'I am indeed, and as much as my daughter and I have enjoyed yours and your crew's hospitality, I shall be happy to depart and be back on firm land.'

The Captain returned the smile, 'Well, I suppose this is the last stop for us all, at least for a while.' He surveyed the scene before him; the bustle of people and merchants on the harbourside and movement of ships coming and going into the port. He turned back to them. 'Well, I wish you well and I hope you settle here quickly. I must leave and attend to the command of the ship.' He then turned to his crew, busy with anchoring the frigate.

Phæ'enor noticed the other passengers begin to gather their things. Master Rasia and Mrs Doven checked their own luggage was all there. It was not much, just three large chests and two smaller ones, having discarded their least needed items before they boarded all those months ago. She also noticed that Master Rasia had not added his belongings to the pile. He looked up at her.

'A sailor always travels light, Miss,' he said, and carried on with his task.

The portly man was fumbling amongst his belongings whilst his not so joyous friend looked on bemused by the unorganised activity. To the starboard side the disparate group of travellers from the last port stood idle, bored and waiting, having only one or two pieces of small hand luggage, or like Master Rasia, seemingly none to check. As far as Phæ'enor was aware none of them were travelling together; lone travellers standing near each other but not close enough that you would call them friends or travelling companions. However, directly opposite them, on the portside, Phæ'enor spotted the pale and fair-haired officer, also looking in their direction, quietly studying them. He too must have felt her eyes upon him, for he slowly turned his head towards her. Embarrassed at being caught staring again, Phæ'enor quickly turned away and pretended to be interested in her mother and Master Rasia's conversation:

'Mrs Doven, a message was sent ahead in advance,' advised Master Rasia, he pointed towards several coaches and carriages lined up waiting. 'See there? The one with the two black horses, and blue and black carriage? That is the coach that will take you to your mother's, Ma'am.'

Phæ'enor glanced up at her mother who had muttered under her breath, so as not to let Master Rasia hear: 'Huh, my mother indeed. I think not,' before continuing her conversation. 'Excellent, Master Rasia, that will do for now. We shall let you attend to your own business until captain's orders to leave.'

'Very good, Ma'am,' said Master Rasia, who nodded and left for the direction of The Scavenger's bridge. Along his way he passed the fair-haired officer who was pointedly making his way towards the two Dovens'. Phæ'enor, stiff backed and horrified at him approaching, was about to turn and make her excuses to her mother when she felt a sharp hand grab the top of her right arm.

'Ow!'

'You will stay put, and behave,' hissed Mrs Doven, as the officer finally stopped and introduced himself. 'Mrs Doven, my apologies for not being introduced to you formally, or sooner.' He took off his shako and nodded.

'Officer Nathryn, I am aware of whom you are. My husband advised me to look out for you, as did Master Rasia. Captain Alba also has high praise for your services.'

Phæ'enor was puzzled at the introduction, for she had clearly seen her mother and Officer Nathryn together, along with other guests, within Captain Alba's cabin when being chased by Master Rasia off the gun deck. It showed on her face.

'This is my daughter, and youngest child, Phæ'enor.' As she released her grip on her daughter Officer Nathryn turned to Phæ'enor, smiled and spoke:

'Miss Phæ'enor Doven, a pleasure to be finally introduced to you. I believe you have taken a keen interest in both mine and my men's activities on board?' He half teased, half accused.

Mrs Doven said: 'I do apologise for my daughter's behaviour on board. I am sure she meant no harm and will not behave so again. Phæ'enor, apologise.'

Phæ'enor shot her mother a disgusted look. Then through gritted teeth she said, 'My apologies. It won't happen again, Officer Nathryn.' Without looking at him, Phæ'enor had instead turned her head to the side only to see Master Rasia laughing at her to himself. She narrowed her eyes in response and turned back to Officer Nathryn and her mother.

'Not to worry. I understand we are an odd group of soldiers, from different regiments. However, we were part of a larger group of men attending some of the last meetings to tie up this war, and now we are few with more luggage than we can handle. And between you and me most of it is Officer Farren's collection of seeds and flowers for him to study and draw in his laboratory. The smell of a decaying Atro Hibdaluca flower is unbearable.'

Mrs Doven laughed. Phæ'enor managed a false smile which did not go unnoticed by Officer Nathryn. Just then Phæ'enor was saved anymore of his company; Captain Rost G. Alba had announced for all passengers to slowly disembark. As Officer Nathryn made his excuses to return to his own luggage and men, Master Rasia appeared at their sides with another member of the crew to help. It was Vicken, the Master's Mate Phæ'enor had been told off for talking to without permission. Master Rasia was still reserving a smirk for Phæ'enor, but ready to take their belongings off the ship.

***

As Mrs Doven made her way off The Scavenger, Master Rasia and Vicken followed with the luggage, Phæ'enor trailing behind.

'You best move quicker than that Miss Doven,' Master Rasia called back to her, 'that coach will not wait for you.'

Phæ'enor briefly glimpsed back over her shoulder, most of the passengers had already departed before them but she could not see where the young woman and her guards had got to. Reluctantly, she turned back and, moving a little faster to catch up, slammed into a dishevelled hooded cloaked man, who hurriedly made his way up the gangway. Probably another member of the ship's crew she thought, but she didn't recognise him. Spinning back around she then tripped on something large and grey in her path and went tumbling down the gangway onto the pier. Luckily her mother and Master Rasia had moved swiftly out the way. Phæ'enor, apart from feeling slightly bruised, did not want to get up, knowing that she must look a fool. Master Rasia was probably smirking at her again, along with Vicken and Officer Nathryn.

'Please, take my hand.'

It was not the voice of her mother or Master Rasia. It was much quieter, sweeter, and the hand that appeared in front of Phæ'enor's eyeline was covered with a pale silk glove. Intrigued, Phæ'enor took the hand offered to her and clambered up onto her feet. The grip was gentle, and as Phæ'enor stood up, she was stunned into silence by the owner of the hand in front of her. It was the young woman who had boarded at the Port of Iscar; still surrounded by a red-coated guard, who were watching as their mistress helped Phæ'enor to her feet.

Close-up the young woman was taller than Phæ'enor, by at least a foot. She was also very beautiful, with large pale green eyes that looked even more striking due to the woman's fair complexion and very dark hair. It was almost as black as Phæ'enor's. The girl was clothed in a white lace dress that covered her arms, and drew close-up her neck, a large brimmed hat to match, with very clean black and white eyelet lace boots that disappeared up her dress. Her travelling cloak was red, the same scarlet as her guards.

The young woman smiled enquiringly at Phæ'enor, as though prompting her to introduce herself or say thank you. But still in awe of the young woman, Phæ'enor could not speak. Mrs Doven interrupted instead.

'Excuse me, I am Mrs Doven and this is my daughter Phæ'enor. Thank you for your kind help, Miss…?'

The young woman turned towards Mrs Doven and replied.

'Actually, it's Lady. Lady Quenna Amia.'

There were a few gasps from the small group that had gathered to witness Phæ'enor's little tumble. It was clear that although Phæ'enor did not recognise the name quite a few others had.

'We are so sorry to have troubled you. I am sure…'

'Please, it's no bother Mrs Doven. Why don't you both accompany me on this short walk of the pier,' she replied, with a mischievous smile. 'No doubt your coach is waiting for you, and I can see there is a small gathering of people near mine. I suppose I should make some haste to get to it as well.'

They turned to look in the direction of the end of the pier to see quite a large group of ornately dressed men and women, a much older man in the centre of them, and at least nearly two dozen guards. Although, unlike the crew of The Scavenger, or even Officer Nathryn and his men, these guards were dressed in plates of armour over their breasts, and helmets covering most of their face. Phæ'enor wondered how on earth they could have seen out of them.

Lady Amia giggled and spoke quietly out of the side of her mouth: 'They do look rather ridiculous don't they,' she said, having read the look on Phæ'enor's face. She walked down the pier, arm in arm with the two Dovens. Phæ'enor could see Master Rasia glaring at her from her right as they walked by.

At the end of the pier their small group, along with Lady Amia's guards, Master Rasia and the Master's Mate Vicken, came to stop in front of the large gathered party. A tall, young and white wigged man stepped out in front of the ornately dressed people and slowly bowed his head to Lady Amia. She returned the gesture with a low courtesy. They all followed suit, apart from Phæ'enor who had no idea what was going on and continued to look around and across at them all. Behind, she heard a hiss.

'Miss Doven, follow suit,' insisted Master Rasia.

Phæ'enor realised no one else was rising and that for them to get up she must also do as they had. Trying not to smile at the ridiculousness of the scene before her she slowly curtsied. Everyone then rose from their positions but not one made a comment or a gesture at the lack of interest on Phæ'enor's part.

'Lady Amia, welcome to Benaghar and what I hope will be your new home,' said the elaborately dressed young man. His gold and cream coat reflected the rays of the sun, momentarily blinding those gathered as they looked on.

'Prince Taigor,' replied Lady Amia. 'Thank you.'

The prince bowed in response then spoke again, 'And now I must introduce you to my father, and king,' he half turned back towards the old man in the middle of the group, 'King Rothian, Emperor of Aebra!'

This time Phæ'enor was quick to follow the others around her and curtsied with the rest of the other women gathered, whilst the men bowed deeply. But still surprised to be in the company of the empire's aristocracy and royalty, Phæ'enor turned her head towards Master Rasia, looking at him for confirmation. She was disappointed however. Master Rasia flatly refused to acknowledge her. Instead he, along with Officer Nathryn and the other officers present stood still, not looking at anyone or anything, with their right hand next to their heads in salute.

The prince moved aside as King Rothian moved forward towards Lady Amia. If Phæ'enor thought the others gathered were elaborately dressed they were no comparison with the king. A deep blue cloak made of fur draped to the ground around him, the opening clasped together by a broach of gold twinkling in the sunlight. His crown matched, cushioned by deep blue dyed fur, resting on a wig that looked to have been sewn by silver thread. And beneath all this he was clothed, like his son, from the neck down, in golds and sparkling creams.

'Lady Amia, how happy I am that this day has finally come.'

His voice was deep, steady and kind; unlike the aura surrounding him. Phæ'enor glimpsed the king out of the corner of her eye. Although he was older than the others gathered he did not look frail. He stood tall and proud, solid and strong like an ox. He looked every bit the ruler of the empire. Lady Amia remained in her courtesy.

'Your Majesty, as am I.'

The king smiled and then let out a thunderous laugh of joy, 'Ha, please, Lady Amia, and to all of you gathered here, you may rise! I know my son, Prince Taigor, has already greeted you but now it is my turn. Welcome, welcome all of you to Benaghar! But please, now you must also welcome my future wife and your new queen! All hail Lady Quenna Amia!'

As all gathered, stood and cheered, Phæ'enor stared, bewildered. Lady Amia is to marry King Rothian, but he's so old … and she so young, she thought to herself, as the clapping and screams of delight reverberated around the harbourside. Lady Amia was all smiles as was King Rothian. However, her confusion at what had just happened was noticed; Prince Taigor made his way over to them, whilst others continued to celebrate. He addressed her mother:

'You must be Mrs Doven,' said the prince, 'your husband is an excellent leader and soldier ma'am.'

As Mrs Doven replied in polite conversation, Phæ'enor tried to get Master Rasia's attention again. Still without success she turned back, intrigued by the king and his party, half listening in to the conversation between her mother and Prince Taigor, '…Yes that is correct. Phæ'enor and I will be staying with her grandmother…,' half continuing to look on at the celebrations in front of her and the party gathered by the king's carriages.

Most of the attendees were men, also dressed in wigs and blue and white embroidered tailcoats. They must be royal staff, thought Phæ'enor. The other men present were clearly soldiers but of higher rank than the ones Phæ'enor had encountered so far. They wore red and gold jackets adorned with many golden medals, sachets of stripes, and helmets that had very large plumes of red and yellow feathers poking out the top, which cascaded down past their shoulders.

There was a small party of women, who like Lady Amia, were also dressed in white, except the skirts of their dresses were much more voluptuous in size and the frills rather more excessive in the sleeves. However, amongst them was one woman who Phæ'enor had nearly missed. Covered head to toe in black, she blended into the carriage behind her. A veil of lace covered her face; silk gloves covered her hands, the left of which held a black silk cloth by her side. There was no show of skin or features to this woman. She was only noticeable by the light of the sun catching the dark jewels of her dress.

Phæ'enor's attention was briefly brought back to the others by the king, '…Lady Amia, my Queen, I am sure your journey has been long, and your carriage is eager to present you to the rest of the court…,' She turned back to the woman in black, but she had disappeared. The group started to disperse into their carriages, whilst others turned to walk towards the merchant and shipping houses along the harbourside.

'It is time for us to go to, darling,' said her mother, as she put a hand on Phæ'enor's shoulder and then walked ahead of her.

As she followed her mother, Phæ'enor took one last glance at the royal party to see if she could still make out the lady in black, but in doing so she clocked eyes with another that looked back at her, still and unfriendly. It was a boy, the only one amongst the group; she had missed him at first glance, as he was also wearing blue and white like the staff. He was smaller too; sandy haired and freckled. Standing with his hands behind his back but continuing to move his head, he did not break eye contact as Phæ'enor, her mother and Master Rasia moved passed. Out of nowhere she heard a sharp sound behind her.

'Ssss..!' came the hiss from Master Rasia. The sandy haired and freckled boy glanced at him, looking even more offended than when he had laid eyes on Phæ'enor.

'Move along quick, Miss Doven,' said Master Rasia, raising his voice.

'Why did you hiss at him? ... and who is he?' she said.

'I don't know what you are talking about.'

'But … I just heard you hiss at him … and … and then you both looked at each other like … like …'

Master Rasia brushed passed her, Vicken coming up behind them with their luggage. He did not answer but continued to ignore her, even whilst packing the large town coach with their belongings. Phæ'enor, annoyed, moved away from the coach, and turned to look back at the royal party.

Luggage from The Scavenger was being lifted onto their awaiting coaches. She could no longer make sight of Lady Amia. She must be inside already, thought Phæ'enor. And the woman in black had now completely disappeared. Maybe I imagined her? She thought. However, she could still make out the unfriendly looking boy who was now busying himself with making sure all their party was nearly boarded; King Rothian being one of the last to take his seat in his coach. The only two left on the harbourside were Prince Taigor and Officer Nathryn, deep in what looked like a hurried conversation. Prince Taigor was visibly frowning.

Suddenly, Phæ'enor heard distant, but raised voices coming from the harbour. She scanned the horizon only to see the remaining crew of The Scavenger shouting and running about above deck, with something large and grey running off the gangway; it was a cat. The bird that caught the eye of Master Rasia swooped overhead, gliding in a circle several times. Master Rasia moved behind her.

'What in the worl...' said Mrs Doven, also turning to look back.

In front, Prince Taigor and Officer Nathryn looked towards the ship. Heads peered out of the carriages behind them, whilst everyone else dockside and in the neighbouring anchored ships all stopped to check out the commotion coming from The Scavenger. Phæ'enor's stomach jumped into her mouth as the bird began to screech cries and the men still left on deck started to jump overboard, instead of coming off along the gangway.

Already disembarked crew members, including the Master's Mate Vicken, who was still helping Master Rasia, stopped what they were doing and started to run back to help their ship mates when Officer Nathryn shouted at them:

'WAIT! STOP! YOU SHOULDN'T…'

BANG!

Phæ'enor saw a flash of light; intense heat touched her skin and she felt like she was flying. She caught one last glimpse of the bird soaring overhead, then all turned to darkness.

Chapter Three

No 09, Grand Alboreum Circus

Phæ'enor could hear shouting, screaming and the cries of men and women. People were running all over the place; some across the pier away from the ships, and others, set alight by fire, were jumping into the waters of the harbour. The black bird loomed in the sky, crying out as it watched the madness below. Did the bird order this she thought? It was as though the bird had commanded the ships to burn and was surveying its work from above.

She tried to make her way through the crowd, but the smoke from the burning ships clouded her way. She started to choke, lost her footing and fell to the ground. Bodies of the dead lay like litter; black and tarred, some still smouldering. She crawled amongst them, flinching as now and then she brushed passed a corpse, its dead eyes staring back at her. The heat began to intensify and everything around her caught fire; the bodies engulfed in flame circled around her. The bird flew overhead again as the pier, the carriages, the horses and then more ships started to explode.

BOOM!

'Arrrgh!' Phæ'enor screamed. She awoke, finding herself upright and pouring with sweat. She coughed as she tried to control her breathing. In confusion Phæ'enor looked about her surroundings, she was no longer in Benaghar's harbour. Instead, she found herself in a very blue coloured room. It was mainly in shadow except for the light shining through a gap in the curtains of the window to her right. It cast light onto the iron bed posts, and the blue bed linen, matching the walls. To her left she could make out a loft hatch in the ceiling and below it a small dark wooden table. A robe hung over a chair next to it and a long mirror stood idle in the corner. A small wardrobe stood opposite her at the end of the bed.

The curtains billowed into the room as a breeze came in through the window. Feeling calmer she wiped the sweat from her brow. Looking at the hand she had used she could feel and see herself shaking slightly. She closed her eyes and took a deep breath and thought to herself, I am okay, I am okay. It was then that she realised how much she had sweated. She was damp, all over. The night shirt that she now wore was soaked through, as were the bed sheets beneath her.

Feeling very uncomfortable she gingerly got out of bed, removing the linen that clung to her body. She stood, trying to gain her balance; her legs felt like jelly. She touched and looked down at them, then her arms and then lastly, she touched her face. Only a few bruises and scratches had appeared. She breathed another sigh of relief, only to then remember:

'Mother!'

Phæ'enor, not knowing what to do or where to turn, stumbled around the room and looked for an exit, but managed to bang into the furniture. Unable to see as clear without much light she moved over to the window and drew the curtains fully aside. As she opened them she turned her head away, shielding her face from the brightness of the light. It was still day then, she thought, and although tall, the window was not very wide, so she leant in further to get a better look outside.

There was a tall white building opposite with windows like the one she was peering out of, but no doors; she must be viewing it from the side she thought. As she looked below, a wide cobbled street of grey and yellow stones separated the two buildings. She tried to peer left and right through the window, to get a better view, but could see no more. Disappointed, she leaned back into the room but as she did there came a series of sharp noises.

Tap! Tap!

It was coming from outside. Curious she leaned up into the window again, her face pressed up against it.

TAP!

Phæ'enor flinched in surprise. Nothing had hit her, but she could now make out where the noise had come from. A large stone had landed on the outer sill of the window, a couple of smaller ones lay beside it, and she became aware that she was being watched. Phæ'enor looked across to the window of the building opposite but no one stared back at her. Then she caught movement out of the corner of her eye. Looking up she saw the moon of Hallumera above, the other moons had now gone to sleep, and directly below it a rooftop and the tops of three heads. Faces peered at her from underneath hats, or was it some sort of fur? She could not tell from this distance. Suddenly they all jumped up, the one to the right threw another stone, they all laughed then ran off along the rooftops, disappearing into the horizon.

'Hmm,' said Phæ'enor to herself.

With the curtains now drawn back she turned around. A small narrow corridor led off from the main area of the bedroom. Phæ'enor followed it to its end and opened the dark and heavy wooden door. It took some effort to move it, but it eventually creaked open. Surprisingly, it opened onto a large and brightly lit landing, with a wide staircase spiralling down to the floors below. It was cold outside of her room. She looked back into the blue room and retrieved the robe that hung over the chair by the desk. Putting it on she moved onto the landing immediately outside the room and looked over the balustrade. Phæ'enor could make out another two floors below her and one above.

There were several doors leading off from this landing and Phæ'enor was just about to move off and explore when she caught the sound of voices from below. Mother? thought Phæ'enor again, and she started to swiftly move down the spiral staircase. As she reached the next landing the voices had become louder, but they were not coming from this floor. She moved down the next set of stairs but no longer swiftly. The voices were much clearer now, and as she came to a stop on the last stair, Phæ'enor could hear not only her mother, but at least two or three other women, and a few male voices as well.

'Look, I don't believe there is anything to worry about ma'am…'

'Nothing to worry about? Good gracious man! Do I look like an idiot to you? I may be old, but I've still got my senses, my eyes and ears and I can smell a rat amongst you and your men!'

'Odora!' came the voice of Mrs Doven, 'please calm yourself. I'm sure everything is okay.'

Phæ'enor slowly moved across the black and white chequered floor hallway, towards the voices. It was wide with a large black and glass stained door that loomed up ahead; to the left a large silver gilded mirror; below which stood a dark side table. A small bowl, filled with spilled coins from a velvet purse, glinted in the middle of it. Next to it her dirty and worn travelling cloak had been placed upon an iron coat stand. The voices were coming from another wide black door to the right.

'Ma'am, please, if I may continue,' said a deep male voice.

'Hmm … well, you best be quick about it. I'm starting to lose interest or care for you and your men in my house,' said the other woman again.

'Our house, Odora. Our house!' came Mrs Doven's voice.

'Yes. Well. Officers, please, do continue with what you have to say. I believe our grandmother and aunt would rather be attending to Phæ'enor sooner, rather than later.'

This time the voice came from a much younger woman. Phæ'enor, intrigued to whom all the voices belonged, bent low and looked through a very large brass keyhole into the room beyond. She was out of luck if she wanted to see anything for her view was blocked by dark clothing. Phæ'enor could only assume it was one of the "officers" they were talking to. However, her curiosity was spared the wait when the door was suddenly pulled opened. Phæ'enor, having placed her hands on the door to steady herself, fell into the room and landed at the feet of the person blocking her view.

'Well, it seems you don't have to wait any longer to see your granddaughter, Mrs Jemin.' It was Captain Rost G. Alba of The Scavenger, standing with his hands behind his back, smiling down at her. 'You, Miss Doven, have a habit of falling over, so it would seem.'

Phæ'enor replied with a wincing smile, before turning to another man in the room who had offered his hand to her. Staring up at him she was met with a rather rotund stomach, but very tall and shiny legs; his boots recently buffed. Instead of taking his hand she clumsily got up and dusted herself down on her robes. She did not recognise the man. He wore black like an officer, but he was much older, with grey hair. A rather large moustache dominated his face so all that was left to see of it was his tiny, watery, blue eyes.

'It's the mead, dear.'

Phæ'enor looked to see who had spoken. Sat in a rather large armchair, in front of a large bay window was an old woman. 'His belly, dear?' in reply to Phæ'enor's shocked look. 'That's how the Admiral has a large belly.'

'Odora!' exclaimed Mrs Doven.

'Grandmother!' gasped the other women in the room.

Phæ'enor looked over to see two young women sat next to each other on a red high-backed sofa.

'Oh, shush. We all know Admiral Gull likes nothing better than to drink. Don't you, man? Drinking in the morning, drinking at lunch and dinner. You drink before you see your wife in the evening, and you most certainly drink on the job!'

Phæ'enor looked over to her mother, who now had her head in her hands, whilst the two girls, scarlet in the face, braced themselves for the Admiral to explode in rage. Phæ'enor looked back at the man in front of her, who still facing Phæ'enor but with his back to the others had taken a deep breath, reopened his eyes and turned back to the old woman.

'Mrs Jemin, I shall take my leave…'

'Yes, do!' replied the old woman.

'But, I shall still need to speak with your daughter, Mrs Doven.'

'Yes, of course, Admiral,' replied Mrs Doven.

'WHAT!? Absolutely not, not now, not…'

'Odora!' shouted Mrs Doven at the old woman, 'Phæ'enor is my child and I shall decide whether Admiral Gull here, and his officers', can speak to her…'

'Question her more like!'

'Or not!' said an exasperated Mrs Doven. Then quickly, before the old woman could interrupt again, 'Admiral Gull, Captain Alba and Officer Nathryn…'

Phæ'enor, unaware that Officer Nathryn was even in the room looked around only to see him standing behind an armchair by the large bay window; his uniform had blended in with the dark curtains, camouflaging him. He gracefully bowed at the remaining women in the room. The two girls did the same in reply. The old woman sniffed heavily, looked down her nose at him and turned her head to face the other direction.

'Phæ'enor, darling, please move out the way for the officers,' said Mrs Doven.

At this the Admiral, Captain Alba and her mother exited the room. Phæ'enor listened to their conversation as they moved out into the hallway.

'I think it best that you leave it for a few days,' said Mrs Doven.

'Mrs Doven, I wish I could but the king and Prince Taigor are adamant this be resolved quickly,' replied the Admiral.

Mrs Doven sighed, 'Send a note tomorrow with the best time to call on you. I shall bring Phæ'enor with me.'

'Alone?' enquired Admiral Gull, 'without the grandmother?'

'Alone,' replied Mrs Doven.

As the Admiral was helped into his travelling cloak by a manservant, Officer Nathryn came up alongside Phæ'enor and in hushed tones spoke:

'Your mother is very graceful. Your grandmother, perhaps not.' Phæ'enor did not reply. She had no idea who the old woman was, but she was not aware of her being her grandmother. 'Maybe that's where your father gets his no-nonsense attitude from,' continued Officer Nathryn. Phæ'enor did not know whether to take that as a compliment or an insult. 'I should go. However, I think you and I shall be seeing more of each other. You have a habit of both making trouble, and attracting it, especially around naval Frigates.' Officer Nathryn moved to the door, his travelling cloak swiftly adorned. 'Gooday to you Miss Doven, Mrs Doven.'

He followed behind Captain Alba and Admiral Gull as they departed. Mrs Doven wearily closed the door behind them as Phæ'enor looked on. She smiled as she turned to look at her daughter. Then slowly made her way over and held her tight.

'Are you okay, my darling?'

'Yes, mother. Just … where are we?'

'You are home my dear,' came the voice of the old woman behind her mother.

Mrs Doven rolled her eyes at Phæ'enor, and then composed herself with a polite smile. It was the demeanour Phæ'enor was used to seeing her mother reserve for the other officer wives at balls and when taking tea, whilst they droned on about new fashions, the latest gossip about another officers' wife's entanglement with a younger officer, or how it wasn't long before their husbands got promoted. Phæ'enor had always wondered how her mother's face had not cracked from the pressure of constantly smiling at the nonsense around her. This occasion being no exception, Mrs Doven remained ready, wrinkle and ache free once more.

'Phæ'enor, this is your grandmother, Odora Jemin.'

'Is she?' asked Phæ'enor.

'She is indeed!' replied the old woman affronted.

'Your grandmother, Odora. Your father's mother?'

'Oh,' said Phæ'enor. 'Why do you have different surnames?'

'I remarried after the first husband copped it. Then the second one died shortly after that!' She looked Phæ'enor up and down. 'Still scrawny I see and every bit impertinent. No doubt that is from your mother's side of the family.'

'Excuse me?' said Phæ'enor.

'How old are you now? Thirteen, fourteen years old?' asked her grandmother, ignoring Phæ'enor's reaction.

'I am sixteen, nearly seventeen ma'am,' Phæ'enor snapped back in reply.

'Ha, well you still look like a child. You certainly behave like one too, from what I've heard and seen so far … and …'

'Grandmother! Why don't I ring the bell for some more tea?' came the voice of one of the other two young women in the room.

Looking at them again, Phæ'enor realised they must be twins; almost identical. One had brown hair and blue eyes, the other fair with dark eyes. But they both had freckles on their noses, wore matching attire, white dresses and black boots, and seemed to have the same mannerisms. Both girls noticed Phæ'enor looking. They smiled big and happy grins back at her. Wow, they even have matching teeth, thought Phæ'enor.

'These are your cousins, Phæ'enor,' said Mrs Doven.

'I'm Mimi,' said the fair-haired girl.

'And I'm Simi,' said the darker haired girl.

They both got up with excitement and skipped over to Phæ'enor before grabbing and squeezing her tight. Unable to breathe for the smothering, Phæ'enor stared at her mother, face squashed.

'That's enough girls,' said Mrs Jemin, 'she has only just arrived. I don't want to have to write to her father in Vanu only to say she died from too much hugging.'

'Oh, grandmother,' exclaimed Mimi, 'it is only because we are so happy to see our little cousin after all these years.'

'Yes, we are cousin,' said Simi, still embracing Phæ'enor at arm's length. 'It's been so long since we've seen you. I bet you don't even remember us.'

'Of course she doesn't remember you, idiot! She's never met you,' barked their grandmother.

'Oh, I thought we played together as children?' said Mimi, looking confused.

'I think you were reminiscing about your imaginary friend dear,' replied their grandmother.' Phæ'enor suppressed the urge to laugh out loud. Instinct told her that her grandmother would not approve.

'Oh well,' said Simi, smiling at her cousin, and pulling her by the arm to sit Phæ'enor down on the sofa between herself and Mimi.

'Mr Deke, we require more tea!' called Mrs Jemin, through the open door into the hallway.

There were quick footsteps and a slam of a door in the distance, then more footsteps echoed away until they could be heard no more. Phæ'enor looked from side to side, her cousins smiled at her manically. She looked over at her grandmother, Mrs Jemin. Although a little dumpy around the middle, her face was as sharp as her voice. Her bright blue eyes looked down a long and pointy nose at Phæ'enor; high cheek bones and a chin framed her small mouth and her grey, almost white, hair was severely pulled into a bun on the crown of her head. The pattern of her dress did not help to smooth the hardness of her appearance either; dark grey, almost black, and white thin stripes covered her up to the chin. There was no lace, just a small ruffle that framed her face. Phæ'enor forced a smile.

'Whatever are you smiling at girl?' said a bemused Mrs Jemin, 'you nearly got blown up, it's nothing to smile about!'

'Grandmother!' cried the two cousins.

'Yes, Odora, don't make it out to be as bad at that, please,' implored Mrs Doven. She turned to face her daughter. 'We just took the dying impact of the blast, that's all. We were very lucky that we were no longer close enough to the ship.'

'What did happen? Did anybody get hurt?' asked Phæ'enor, remembering the dead bodies and the ring of fire before she woke.

'Admiral Gull and Captain Alba believe the gunpowder on board was set alight. Unfortunately, the crew that had remained on board to start unloading were killed.'

'Was it deliberate?'

'Yes.'

'But, why?'

'They don't know … but they have been questioning all the passengers, and crew. At least those that survived. That is why Admiral Gull was here earlier, to ask us some questions.'

'Bloody fools,' said Mrs Jemin, 'it was more than likely that one of their more inexperienced sailors accidentally set light to the powder.'

Phæ'enor looked at her mother, she was forlorn and tired. She thought of the crew jumping into the harbour waters and the neighbouring ships being set alight.

'Did anybody else get hurt?'

'No, some of the other ships have damage to them caused by the impact of the blast, but it looks like it was just the crew left that were killed.' This time it was her cousin Mimi who had answered.

'Everyone on the harbourside suffered small injuries, cuts and bruises, that's all,' said Simi. 'It was quite chaotic when we got to you.'

They all fell silent. Phæ'enor could not recall anything from the explosion, only from what she had seen before and that big black bird circling above. The sound of footsteps brought her thoughts back into the room. A door opened and closed out in the hallway, then quicker footsteps and a gentle knock on the door.

'You may enter, Deke,' said Mrs Jemin.

The manservant who had cloaked Admiral Gull in the hallway appeared around the door with a tray full of tea; a young girl, much younger than Phæ'enor, followed him with another tray, this time full of cakes and biscuits before they both disappeared again. The two cousins then poured the tea and, as though they had been waiting for the opportune moment to arise, proceeded to bombard Phæ'enor with questions about Vanu and the journey to Benaghar. They talked at her endlessly for what seemed like hours; about their life in the city, the different clothes she should wear, the fashion houses she should shop at, and the places to be seen to get a husband.

'You'll be wanting a husband I suppose?' asked Mimi.

'What?' said Phæ'enor, spluttering on her tea. 'Why would I want a husband?'

'Well, so you can have children and a family,' said Simi, beaming at her.

'No, no, no,' interrupted their grandmother, 'women don't marry for all that rubbish. Judging by you two, who would want children?'

Phæ'enor feeling a little relived sighed and took another sip of her tea. 'No, you want to marry for the money child. I'll have no grandchild of mine marrying a pauper!'

'Oh, grandmother!' exclaimed the cousins.

They carried on bickering with each other and their grandmother about what type of man a woman should have for a husband whilst Phæ'enor looked to her mother, attempting to catch her eye. Instead, Mrs Doven had closed them, no doubt to shut out the noise of the squabble from her mind.

Phæ'enor, reluctantly turned back to the conversation, but stopped halfway, staring at the net curtains of the window. A shadow had moved across it and had now stopped just outside. No, it couldn't be? Could it? She started to hear the noise of gentle tapping on the bay window, but this time it was not coming from stones being thrown at it. It was more frequent but quieter than the stone throwing from earlier. Phæ'enor looked to her cousins and grandmother to see if they had also noticed but they were still engrossed in conversation about some shop in town:

'Why would you go there, girls?'

'We didn't, grandma. Archä and Mëdez were in the street looking even stranger than usual…'

'Yes, and they were talking to Mr Consta, you know the astronomer…'

'Well, he shouldn't have been. He works for the King's Court. Anyone seen with those two is tainted by association! There's no way he will get a wife once everyone knows…'

'Somehow I don't think Mr Consta is the marrying type grandmother.' The twins looked at each with a knowing glance.

Phæ'enor, turning her attention fully to the shadow, got up slowly, so as not to divert the attention of the party, and moved silently towards the window. The tapping continued, still quiet but less frequent than before.

Tap … tap. Tap. Tap … tap … tap. Tap.

When she arrived at the window she slowly moved the net curtain aside, towards the larger heavy draped ones that had been pulled back to let some light into the otherwise dark room.

'Arrgh!' screamed Mimi.

'Get it away, get it away,' screamed Simi.

Phæ'enor had jumped at their screams and at the enormous bird that was sitting on the outer window sill. Instead of gently tapping, it was now flapping madly against the window. Big black wings and a large red underbelly now blocked the view to the square beyond.

'Move away from the window girl,' shouted Phæ'enor's grandmother.

She had got up, gingerly, but swiftly moved over, pulling Phæ'enor back. With her walking stick she hit hard on the window, scaring it off. The bird hit the window one last time; angrily it seemed to Phæ'enor, before taking flight across the square and over the rooftops.

'What kind of bird is that?' asked Phæ'enor, unnerved still and breathless.

'I hate birds!' said Mimi hysterically. 'I won't be able to go home with that thing flying around…'

'Oh, nonsense girl,' barked their grandmother, 'you are not staying here tonight. Any excuse to stay with your cousin. I have quite enough to feed already. You can both stop whining, right now. No wonder neither of you are married yet.'

'Well that's unfair,' said Simi sulkily.

Phæ'enor's grandmother rolled her eyes and moved towards her chair. She sat down heavily and picked up a large brass bell from the side table to her left. Ringing, Phæ'enor heard footsteps from the other side of the sitting room door then two rapid knocks.

'Enter,' said her grandmother wearily. 'Mr Deke be so good as to escort Simi and Mimi back to Queens.'

'But?' came the disappointed voices of Simi and Mimi in unison.

'But, nothing! You will be escorted back to your home. I've had quite enough of your excitement for the day.'

'But grandma, it is not even tea time yet,' said Simi.

'And that bird is still out there,' said Mimi.

Mr Deke, expressionless, stood there and said nothing. Phæ'enor, although tired of her cousins' conversation felt the need to leave with them. She could do without the incessant talking, but she wanted to know where the bird had come from. It had been there when The Scavenger had docked, there when it had exploded and now it was outside their home. Had it followed her here? She made her decision.

'I'll come,' she said, 'I'm not afraid of birds Mimi, and I'm sure Deke here will also protect you.' Mr Deke, still unmoved remained silent. 'I … I could do with the fresh air as well,' she said after looking at the shocked and curious faces of her two cousins.

'Hmm, you do look rather pale still, dear. Yes, maybe a bit of fresh air and exercise will do you some good. That is a fine idea,' said their grandmother.

'Odora,' exclaimed Mrs Doven, 'she needs rest, not exercise!'

'Mother, I'll be fine, I could do with a walk and I would like to see a bit of the city. After all I didn't get much of a chance when we arrived.'

'Well, that's decided then. Go and get some suitable clothing on,' said Mrs Jemin.

Mrs Doven, exacerbated, looked annoyed at her. Phæ'enor, excited to leave, hurried out of the room and ran up the stairs before her mother could protest further. Several moments later she was back in the sitting room clothed in the only thing she could find in the bedroom; a white lace dress, like her cousins were wearing, but less frilly, the skirt coming just above her dusty and dirty travelling boots.

'You'll need a hat, cousin,' said Mimi, looking less ill at the prospect of leaving, now that there were four of them to fend off the bird than just the two.

'I'll be fine,' said Phæ'enor, brushing her hair to one side.

'Very well. Mr Deke get these two back safely, and you Miss Phæ'enor, best be back before it turns dark. It is not far, and I am well aware of your ability to wonder off at will,' said her grandmother.

'Deke,' said Mrs Doven, 'bring my daughter back safely and swiftly. No detours, Phæ'enor,' she finished sharply, looking at her daughter sternly.

'Yes mother,' said Phæ'enor, and eager to leave she moved swiftly out of the sitting room, across the hall ahead of her cousins, grabbed her travelling cloak from the stand by the door and walked into the sunlit street beyond.

Chapter Four

A Tour of Benaghar

Phæ'enor scanned the blue, cloudless sky, looking for the whereabouts of the big black bird as she continued to listen to her cousins.

'It is lovely and bright outside now,' said Mimi anxiously, 'but it will soon turn dark.'

'Yes, the days will become much shorter and it is not long before the summer ends,' said Simi. Then, turning to Phæ'enor, 'I bet in Vanu you had sun shining down on you endlessly.'

'No, not always,' replied Phæ'enor, 'yes, it was sunny and hot. The days were mostly long but our winters consisted of heavy rains and there was always a period of brisk cold, and terrifying storms from the Raanian Seas. I can definitely remember a few floodings whilst we were there.'

'Oh?' said Simi and Mimi together.

'Well, never our home,' said Phæ'enor, in response to the concerned looks on her cousins' faces. 'My brothers, Phai'thor and Phax'alyn, and father had to move to the north-west of the island to help rebuild the locals' shelters whenever it happened. It was always that side of the island.'

'Help locals?' whispered Simi.

'You mean … you mean … the oth-er-side?' said Mimi, intending to mouth her words quietly but sounding like she could not talk properly.

'What do you mean, the oth-er-side?' demanded Phæ'enor of her cousins.

Passers-by turned their heads at Phæ'enor's raised voice but quickly walked on by as she stared them out.

'Oh, come on cousin,' said Simi in hushed tones, 'why in the world would our cousins and uncle help out the enemy?'

'Oh, you're one of them, are you?' asked Phæ'enor. 'You do know the war is over now, don't you? We no longer have an enemy. There is a treaty between us and the Vanuans, and her allies. We have been helping each other out for nearly a decade now. You can't treat them that way and shouldn't.'

More passers-by looked at the three girls and tutted as they walked away, muttering amongst each other at the noise.

Phæ'enor looked back at her cousins as though they were the two stupidest girls alive. That these were her cousins and how they could not set aside their ancestors' opinions made her even more embarrassed to say they were her family. Irritated by the idea, she made a point to check when she got back to the house exactly how related to them she was.

Offended, Simi and Mimi walked on, noses in the air and mouths pouting in silence until the cobbled streets of Grand Town opened up.

The street had become much wider, stretching down to what looked like a large gate in the distance. Golden white houses and buildings lined either side of it. They were similar to the houses of Grand Alboreum Circus, grand white buildings, but slightly smaller, and terraced all the way down the road.

'It's very pretty here,' said Phæ'enor, awestruck at the size and dazzling grandeur of the place.

Mimi smirked slightly, 'This is Grand Promenade and is just some of what our empire produces; beautiful architecture.'

'Huh, you mean bricks that were cut by Sera slaves in Palestra, then shipped over by Salum soldiers, who work for the Aebran empire against their will, and then constructed by the poor,' stated Phæ'enor in reply to her smirking cousin.

'Oh, please, let's stop this,' cried Simi, 'you have only just arrived, and we are all behaving like we are having some … some sort of school girl squabble; and we are attracting some very dirty looks.' You started it, thought Phæ'enor, as a couple linking arms crossed the road to distance themselves. 'Look, we need to get back before it turns dark. I say we have another couple of hours or so, isn't that right Mr Deke?' Phæ'enor had completely forgotten that the manservant had come with them, having kept a good distance behind. He nodded in reply to her cousin. 'Right, that's settled Mimi, let's take our cousin Phæ'enor on a quick tour of the city. Do you have any coins about you Mimi?'

'Why?' she replied looking confused.

'Well we can't very well walk the entire city in a couple of hours, can we?'

Mimi looked puzzled, 'Oh!' she cried. 'Yes, yes, we can get a carriage from Queens' High Gate.'

***

Phæ'enor followed her two cousins a short distance down the pristine cobbled streets of Grand Promenade, its tall white buildings towering over them. Phæ'enor thought about how much they reminded her of the giant icebergs from the Balgon Sea. It seemed to her that they were becoming more like the size of the houses from Grand Alboreum Circus as they got closer to the gate. Her cousins continued the tour:

'Grandmother's house is situated in the middle of the north-west of the city; part of Grand Town and where all the officers' families live,' said Mimi.

After some time they came to pass many houses that were much smaller in size, and clustered together.

'This is where the lower ranked officers' live,' said Simi.

'And the infantry?' asked Phæ'enor.

'Oh,' said Mimi, 'they live over the other side of the river. Look to your right … just … now!'

However, instead of following her cousins' directions, Phæ'enor had become distracted. They had arrived in a more open area. It wasn't a square, nor did it have much order to it, but Phæ'enor could see much further for there were less houses and more grander buildings. Some made of glass with great domes, some bright gold, others bright and sparkling blues, yellows and reds. There were other buildings that billowed out multi-coloured steam; buildings that seemed to reach into the sky and almost touch it. But to the left, what impressed Phæ'enor the most was what looked like a large entrance, glinting with gold.

'This, cousin, is the leisure area of Grand Town,' said Mimi, bringing Phæ'enor's attention back to her.

'Where everyone comes to socialise and have fun,' said Simi.

'Over there is the large bath house,' said Mimi, pointing to the large golden building topped with a glass dome. 'It is full of amusing waterfalls but the best bit about it is its many hot spring baths. I could do with a nice warm soak now.'

Phæ'enor smiled as she saw the blissful look on her cousin's face.

'Now that one over there,' said Simi, 'is The Grand Tea Rooms.' Phæ'enor looked to see her cousin pointing at the large tall building that was reaching into the sky with its multi-coloured clouds. 'They are not clouds, you know,' continued Simi. 'It's the steam from all the tea.' she giggled. 'It sells all the best varieties in the world that you could possibly hope to find. That's why there are so many coloured clouds.'

'And that gold building, over there, is the heart of the empire,' said Mimi.

Phæ'enor looked at her two cousins', neither of them looked at it as pleased, nor displeased, with it as they were with the others. They just stared at it. It was a very large building, dominating all the others in the vicinity. Its domes and spires stood tall and straight like the soldiers standing to salute in the harbour on her arrival in the city. Phæ'enor thought it looked more like a fortress.

'Is it some sort of castle, or defence?' she asked her cousins.

'Oh, no,' said Simi half laughing. 'No cousin, that building is more like the empire's sanctuary. It's the House of The Brotherhood, where we are watched and looked after from.'

'What? The building looks after you?' asked Phæ'enor bemused.

'Tsht, no cousin,' said Simi, 'it is where everyone goes to worship Tekan, without whom we would not have the empire. Surely you know that cousin? I mean, you of all people, having come from Vanu should know that. The Brotherhood is the be all and end all for us. He gave us the strength we needed, and continues to do so to this day, to help defeat the enemy and become what we have become.'

There were more people gathered in this area, milling about and coming and going from each of the surrounding buildings. Those closest to Simi, nodded and smiled at her in agreement.

'You know you are quite a simpleton little cousin,' said Simi, laughing along with her sister.

'Funny, I thought it was guns, swords, bayonets and gunpowder that won us all the battles and the war.'

'Cousin!' shouted both her cousins in shock. Once again passers-by no longer looked pleased, snootily speeding up as fast as they could to get away from Phæ'enor and the twins. Silence fell between the three of them again. Phæ'enor, realised she had offended and shocked them a little too much, but still having to spend time with them, tried to divert their attention away from The Brotherhood, and changed the subject.

'So, um, you … what is that over there? That statue or …?'

'Oh, that?' said Simi. She had reverted to her chirpy self instantly. A little too quickly thought Phæ'enor but did not question her already strange cousins. They were the simple ones and easily entertained. 'That is one of the main gates within the city, they mark where one area of the city ends, and another begins.'

'It was what I was going to show you before you got distracted by all the buildings here,' said Mimi. 'That one there leads over the Benraeli Bridge and into Parli Town, that's short for Parliament. It's similar in size to Grand Town and is where politics are conducted, and the infantry are housed.'

'Oh,' said Phæ'enor. 'In Vanu, all the military men and their families lived in the same area.'

'Once again cousin, we are not in Vanu. Here the ranks keep to their ranks,' said Simi.

'Anyway, we are not going that way,' said Mimi, addressing Phæ'enor, who had started to drift in the direction of the bridge. 'But you shall see one of the other gates up close in a moment. Come,' and she skipped off down the cobbled promenade, Simi close behind, with Phæ'enor wishing she had stayed indoors instead being dragged about the city by her cousins.

When they arrived, the gate in question lead from Grand Town into an area called Queens High. It was huge. The gate was incredibly tall and very wide, wider than some of the ships in the harbour, thought Phæ'enor. But instead of being impressed or in awe of it, she felt uneasy. The gate was made of iron; black, wide and as tall as the walls surrounding them. She followed the golden oro bricked stone with her eyes; it went on endlessly, bordering this and every other area of the city no doubt. It made her feel small and very insignificant. She turned her gaze back to the gate. At the top was a gold painted iron motif. Phæ'enor could just make out two jaguars on their hind legs, golden teeth barred, and golden eyes of panic, separated by a large figure of a man, standing solemn and still but looking down accusingly. The big cats were speared and being attacked by soldiers either side.

'Isn't it beautiful?' said the voice of Mimi. 'All the gates have a different motif. This one symbolises the defeat of The Namorian Empire by King Conco Indzini.'

Phæ'enor recalled from her father The Namorian Empire was defeated more than sixteen hundred years ago. It was a bloody war that lasted for centuries, whereby soldiers were attacked and eaten by animals. The black jaguar, The Namorian Empires national animal, was used in games to attack captured Benagharian soldiers for sport; they were torn apart, flesh ripped from bones for fun. Still, looking at the iron gate, Phæ'enor was not pleased, it only made her feel uncomfortable.

All three of them and Mr Deke passed underneath the arch of the gate, the guards either side nodding at them in salutation. In front of them appeared smaller buildings but gleaming with the golden stone.

'Now this is Queens High,' said Simi. 'It's full of the most luxurious shops you can find in the whole of Benaghar, and where all the rich, but non-military families live, like us of course.' Simi and Mimi giggled hysterically but soon stopped when they saw the raised eyebrows and unimpressed look on their cousin's face.

'Hmm … well, let's find a carriage,' said Mimi, embarrassed.

'Are you not going to show me around Queens High?' asked Phæ'enor.

'Oh, no, don't be silly,' said Simi, still slightly embarrassed. 'It is only full of more houses. Excuse me Sirs,' she cried to a small group of coachmen, 'we require your services for a couple of hours!' And with that Mr Deke hurried in front of them to acquire their ride.

***

The carriage, a four-seated windowless box, which was extremely uncomfortable, was soon forgot by Phæ'enor. She had even forgotten why she had wanted to come out with her cousins in the first place. Instead, the tour of the city by carriage was greatly enjoyed. First the three of them, and Mr Deke perched above with the driver, travelled swiftly across Queens High and into Kings High, then down into Kings Low. There were many soldiers, sailors and what looked like business men going about their day.

'Here is where the army garrisons are based. You see a lot of ministers and merchants passing through here as well,' Mimi informed Phæ'enor.

As Phæ'enor looked out of the open carriage, she saw many small groups of soldiers and sailors laughing and joking with each other, some striding along in conversation. What must have been parliamentary men and merchants, dressed in serious colours of blacks and browns and stiff hats, were conversing in very terse tones. One was bandying about a handful of paper and got so flustered that several fell out of his hand into the air and flew over the open topped carriage. Phæ'enor could make out a blurred photo of man and the word "WANTED" beneath it and was about to ask if her cousins had also seen it when Simi started talking again.

'It is quite a good area if you want to look out for a husband, but I would go for a Navy man, they have much more money.'

Phæ'enor looked at her and laughed, 'You are obsessed, cousin,' and shook her head heartily as the carriage moved through another gate and over a large wide bridge. To the left she saw the murky blue waters of a river that snaked around a bend and out of view.

'This is the River Nebben. Over there is The Dourbrande Sea,' said Mimi, as she watched her cousin.

'And over there?' asked Phæ'enor, in astonishment at what she had just caught sight of to her right. There seemed to be bridges like the one they were traveling across but further down the river, with at least two or more gate like formations ahead of it. The river seemed to be slowly cascading down towards them and in the far distance beyond was another tall, many turreted building, shining and twinkling in every direction. As she looked there was no mistaking what it could be.

'Oh, that?' said Simi, proudly smiling. 'That is the Palace of Benaghar.' Phæ'enor could not help but smile at its beauty.

'Where Prince Taigor and all the Rothians live,' said Mimi wistfully.

'Ha,' laughed Simi. 'Mimi here is in love with Prince Taigor.'

'So, you like your men powdered and in big white wigs then?' giggled Phæ'enor.

'Oh, yes … what? No! No, I don't, and I'm not in love with him! I'm not cousin … Simi is lying, your lying!'

They giggled at Mimi's protestation all the way into Border Town. Here there was more hustle and bustle of people coming and going from workhouses and large factories on the right. To their left were two to three storey, red and yellow buildings.

'This is where all the ships, and armour are made,' said Mimi, trying to find something to direct the conversation away from the topic of Prince Taigor. 'Of course, there are other workhouses here, and merchant stores, such as raw tea, food, textiles and more from the empire.'

Phæ'enor looked over to the smoking black factories and warehouses. Crates and barrels were being brought up from further down the street, men carrying large boxes between them, some carrying the stock on their heads, sweating under the weight and the heat of the sun.

'Where are all the men coming from?' asked Phæ'enor.

'From the harbourside or course. The Ocean Front area of the city,' said Mimi. 'But you've already seen that.' She finished, nervously looking at her cousin.

Simi stuck her head outside the carriage door window and shouted to the coach driver to change direction. 'On to Newtown, please.'

'But, I don't mind, I didn't get a very good look at the harbour last time…'

'We know!' said Simi and Mimi together.

'Besides we have already seen quite a bit for today and should start making our way back, but not before we show you the shops and markets of Newtown first. They are far more interesting,' said Mimi with excited eyes.

***

Phæ'enor let her cousins' waffle on about the many dress shops, and hat shops, jewellery and shoes shops back through Kings and Queens Low, and on through Queens High, whilst she wondered what had happened that day when she and her mother had arrived in Benaghar only for The Scavenger to explode into flames. What if it had happened at sea? Neither of them or anyone else travelling on it would have survived. But now there were questions being asked, her grandmother had implied they were going to interrogate her, but why? Why would someone want to blow up the frigate, and in a time of peace? What bothered her most was if it wasn't an accident then why do it here, in the harbour? There had been plenty of opportunities over the last three months.

Then Phæ'enor remembered why she had so desperately wanted to come outside with her cousins; the bird. Master Rasia so intent on doing his duty was momentarily distracted by it as it flew overhead. Its large black wings had cast a shadow over the ship, its squawking attracting everyone at the dockside. At first, she thought nothing of the bird's appearance, but why had Master Rasia been so affected by it; was it sounding an alarm? Regardless, what was done was done and she would answer the Admiral's questions, but the bird was now nowhere to be seen.

She felt hollow to think that no one knew what had happened, maybe only the bird knew, but unable to speak, nothing could be done. She was thankful for Master Rasia's insistence that she hurry up down the gangway, and off the frigate. Her father would also be grateful to him. She did not want him to worry, but she knew her mother would have written to him to let him know. And as far as he was concerned the war had ended; no more fighting, no more conflict. To have sent half his family back to peace but to then learn that they had been met with gunpowder and fire, would make him worry for sure.

'Cousin, cousin, look!' cried Mimi with joy, trying to get Phæ'enor's attention. 'We're here! This is Newtown!'

Phæ'enor looked out of the window. The streets were busy with men and women, but not just the military men and women with their fine tailored and plain clothes. There were women wearing bright dresses, feathers, bows and ribbons in their hats that trailed down their backs. Phæ'enor had to look twice at one short woman who looked like she was being swooped upon by a giant bird. It was a stuffed one, perched and fully winged on her hat. Some of the men, not to be outdone, wore multi-coloured stripes, caps and velvet cloaks. The colours swam passed Phæ'enor's eyes.

As the horses pulled the carriage in and up Newtown Promenade, Phæ'enor saw more golden bricked buildings to the left. These were all shops of some sort or another; their windows glittering with merchandise. The carriage began to slow but then jerked suddenly. Phæ'enor and her cousins where thrown forward then back as it came to a stop and the driver and Mr Deke started shouting at someone.

'YOU BLITHERING IDIOT!'

'CAN YOU NOT SEE THAT THIS IS A THOUGHORFARE?

'Absolute idiot that one…'

As the carriage began to move off it turned slowly to the right and as it did so Phæ'enor peered over to see what caused them to stop so abruptly. In the middle of the cobbled street was the slim and snooty travelling companion of the portly drunk on board The Scavenger. He was bent low picking up some sort of metal contraption on the ground. He looked highly dishevelled and was muttering away angrily. Phæ'enor smiled to herself as she turned her attention away from the road, thinking what a change it was to not see him so straight laced and pleased with himself.

However, her smile soon faded when she looked up and all she could do was gape. At the end of Newtown Promenade, there stood two large city gates, side by side. The one to the left could only be described as beautiful. Its stone surround seemed to shimmer in the sunlight as though thousands of stars had been captured in it, and the gate was a deep but bright blue, reaching up to a motif unlike the others Phæ'enor had passed through with her cousins so far. Instead of animals being speared by some gargantuan man, moons and stars and planets spun and twinkled in the wind.

'That is the gate into Hightown, the motif is actually a very large weather vane that interlocks as it closes,' said Simi, who was also looking on. The carriage had slowed nearly to a stop again as it waited for other carriages and coaches to pass by. 'It's a very beautiful part of the city. Up there you will find the largest observatory in the empire, maybe even the world. Hardly anyone is allowed up there. I suppose it is quite a sacred place to some people.'

'Why is that?' asked Phæ'enor, still gazing in wonder. Her eyes had moved passed the gate to be met with a very large golden and blue building stretching nearly the whole of the area and surrounded by an abundance of vegetation that then stopped at another of the city's walls in the distance.

'There are many graves and tombstones of the kings and queens up there. It is said when they die they also look down and watch over us from Hightown. But also, on the other side of the wall is the ridge of the crater, and then passed that the outer city wall.'

'The outer city wall?' said Phæ'enor in surprise.

'Oh, yes. It is said there are miles between the inner-city wall and the outer-city wall; the space stretching right down the mountain side before you can get to it. And even then, the wall is so thick there you would never be able to get in or out,' advised Simi.

'You say "it is said", have you not seen it then, or gone on the other side?' asked a bewildered Phæ'enor.

'Well of course not, cousin,' laughed Mimi, 'we have no need to, and besides why would I want to leave the walls of the city?'

'Not to mention women are not allowed,' said Simi, 'because it's too dangerous for us,' she added at the dumbfounded look on Phæ'enor's face. 'And anyway, it's to keep people out.'

The two cousins giggled. Phæ'enor looked at her two stupid cousins again and thought, this city is a fortress, it may keep some people out, but it was also designed to keep idiots like my cousins from escaping into the wider world, and maybe that was a smart decision.

Her gaze then turned to the gate next to it, but instead of something beautiful, or in keeping with the rest of the gates of the city, this gate was the complete opposite. The only thing that could be said to be of slight resemblance was the height of the gate, tall but in this instance extremely narrow. At the top there were no golden motifs, or intricate gold leaves and flowers twisting about the iron bars. It was plane black iron, no decorations, and at the top wonky iron letters simple spelt out "Old Town." At the foot of the gate stood several city guards, carefully surveying the people in front of it; beyond was a dreary darkness.

'Old Town is not a place for the likes of you or I cousin,' said Simi, 'that's where all the, shall we say, unfortunates of the city live.'

'What do you mean by that?'

'The only good people you will find in there are the market stall holders who come to Newtown to sell their wares,' said Mimi. 'The rest are thieves and murderers. That gate is always guarded to make sure the only people who go in there are the ones that live there.'

'The last time someone from another area of the city went through that gate, they were never seen again,' said Simi.

'You're lying.'

The two cousins shrugged their shoulders. 'Don't believe us then, but trust us, don't try and go in there, the guards will arrest you on the spot.'

'Anyway, there are stories that you can still get in, but by a secret passageway that only the inhabitants of Old Town know about,' said Mimi smiling.

'But it's secret, so if you did find it, there's definitely no way the Old Towners are going to let you back out alive!' laughed Simi.

Phæ'enor shook her head at her cousins' little horror stories and the carriage started to move off again. As they got further into the heart of Newtown colourful shop windows became smaller, eventually turning into market stalls.

Phæ'enor and her cousins got out of the carriage and started to walk amongst the stalls. Some were down the sides of buildings and lining the alleyways, or tightly grouped together in small courted areas. The rest were congregated into a giant mass of stalls in the centre. They varied considerably. There were stalls that sold various trinkets: from bells, tatty books, empty and dirty bottles, old ragged clothes, and broken pocket watches.

There was one stall manned by a blind man who, having sold a very spirited and small exotic looking bird to an equally small and happy boy, proceeded to place the bird in a paper bag, swung it into a spin to twist close the opening, before then handing it over to a now very shocked and upset little boy and his very angry mother. The bird was no longer making a sound.

Then there were the dodgier looking stalls with old and rusty pistols, stalls that sold fierce looking animal traps; ranging from ones small enough for mice to others that looked like traps for giant monsters. One stall's sign read "Children misbehaving? Then try one of these!" only for Phæ'enor to clock eyes on a small neck, wrist and ankle shackle. Wincing she turned away, eager to look at anything else.

It was then she caught sight of many posters, like the one that fluttered over their carriage in Parli Town. The words "WANTED" appeared at the end of every stall. And above each of these, two faces were repeated on every other one. On the first poster a very ugly, droopy eyed man, with skin to match, peered out. His face was full of attitude and underneath it read:

WANTED!

O'scilla Juur:

Known to be the leader of the Old Town Harqs. If you see this man do not approach. Wanted in connection with the following:

It then proceeded to list all the crimes he had committed from stealing, trading in illegal arms, slavery without a warrant, murder and to the improper mixing and use of tea.

'The improper mixing and use of tea?' said Phæ'enor aloud.

'Oh, you're reading the wanted posters are you,' said a disinterested Simi. 'I wouldn't worry about him. He's wanted for every crime ever committed, plus they'll never catch him.'

'Why?'

'Because he lives, and basically runs the whole of Old Town. The city guards are too scared to go in there because everyone there works for him, in some sort of capacity, so he'll never get caught,' advised Mimi.

Great, thought Phæ'enor. She then turned her attention to the second poster. The photo showed a young man, turned to skin and bone. His eyes wide, staring back at her in fear and below this instead of "WANTED" it read:

DO YOU HAVE INFORMATION ON THIS CRIMINAL?
Wolf Canis:

Has been found guilty of the following crimes:
Leader of the gang calling themselves the wolves;
The mixing and selling of tea without a licence;
Being in possession of crown goods;
Being investigated for the demise of His Majesty's Frigate, The
Scavenger.

If you have any information, please come forward.

Phæ'enor looked back at the face of the man staring out at her. This man is the leader of one of the gangs Gunn Ári Ásval was talking about, and blew up The Scavenger? That can't be right, she thought to herself.

'Oh, cousin, do come away. Those posters are old news,' said a now bored Simi.

'But how can that man be the leader of the wolves, and have committed all those crimes? He's just skin and bones, he needs feeding not throwing into a gaol. And how can he have caused the explosion on The Scavenger … he wasn't even on the ship, or near it?' Phæ'enor thought she would have remembered him lurking about the ship.

'Well he is the leader of the wolves and despite his appearance he is quite capable of all those crimes. And whether you believe it or not that includes the explosion. They arrested him the evening it happened, it's in the paper,' said Mimi.

'But what if they are wrong?' The twins shrugged their shoulders. 'Like it says, if you have other information then inform the captain of the city guards,' said Simi.

Phæ'enor, who had gone silent, was still staring at the posters. It seemed odd to her that this man had committed all those crimes. He looked so desperate and ill, and not at all like a criminal.

'Ooh,' said Mimi suddenly, 'come and look at this jewellery.' And she pulled a reluctant Phæ'enor over to the market stall that was laden with colourful wooden bracelets, earrings and rings.

At this Phæ'enor's attention was diverted and she soon forgot about the posters as she was brought back to the abundance of market stalls. The colours, noise and people, crowded her senses blocking all other thoughts out of her head.

As Simi and Mimi were engrossed by the jewellery stand, Phæ'enor's eyes wandered amongst the marketplace. They stopped at a small stall where a hysterical woman was trying to get a large grey, and pointy eared cat away from her goods. It reminded her of the cat she saw the day at the harbourside, just before the frigate had exploded.

'Shoo, shoo!' she screeched, 'get away you horrid thing.' Her stall was full of freshly caught fish.

'I'm so sorry ma'am! Please let me …' came the voice and sudden appearance of Master Raisa. This time he was not clothed in military uniform. Instead, a dark brown cap was tipped over his eyes; he wore a dark jacket and pale shirt, with holes in it, and worn fingerless gloves.

'Get it away from here! It will spoil my fish. What are you doing with that thing anyway? It shouldn't be allowed out!' she screamed at him.

The woman was almost in tears she was so upset, and the commotion started to gather a crowd. Phæ'enor was still half distracted by her cousins excitedly discussing the various shades of green jewellery. So very slowly, Phæ'enor moved away from the stall and her cousins, closer to Master Rasia, his strange large cat and the hysterical fish stall holder.

'Oh, look who it is?' came a voice from out of the crowd.

To the left of Master Rasia appeared an even more ragged looking boy. He wore dirty brown clothes, with a tired and worn travelling cloak, and a large brimmed hat covering one eye.

Phæ'enor recognised him at once as the traveller who had boarded The Scavenger at the Port of Iscar; knocking into her without so much as a polite apology.

'Trying to get your scabby cat here to piss all over the food so you can claim it for yourself?' There was a roar of laughter from more boys, dressed in similar attire, who had also gathered in the crowd.

'Why don't you just piss off O'tila!' shouted Master Rasia, scornfully.

The boy with the brimmed hat lunged at the cat grabbing it by its very long tail. It screamed as he spun it around. By this point Phæ'enor had moved so close she was standing behind Master Rasia.

'Oi!' she shouted, 'let it go!' There was more laughter but the boy O'tila had stopped spinning the cat.

'Why?' he asked, 'do you want it instead?' and with that he threw the cat at Phæ'enor's head. Not surprisingly in a state of panic the cat clawed and scratched her face until she pinched and held it by the scruff of its neck, pulling hard as she could to get it off her. Finally, it released its grip but not without dragging its right claw down the left-hand side of her face. Held by Phæ'enor in mid-air it hissed and growled back at her with disdainful amber eyes, clearly displeased with its situation.

'Miss Doven!' shouted Master Rasia. 'Are you okay?' Then looking at her his expression changed, and he shouted at her instead, 'WHAT – ARE – YOU – DOING –HERE?'

'Trying to help you out!' she shouted back, thinking how rude and ungrateful he was. More laughter reverberated across the market stalls.

'For the love of Tekan, it's a bloody officer's daughter!' shouted one of the other boys.

'That's right,' said O'tila. 'But, not just an officer's daughter. The officer's daughter.' Smirking he looked her up and down. 'Funny, you see being the daughter of one of the most feared captains in the Benagharian Army, and having such a pretty little daughter, you would have thought he would send an actual warrior to look after her.' As he walked over to Phæ'enor, the cat still howling within her grips, he turned to look at Master Rasia. 'Not this pathetic excuse for a soldier!' Silence ensued. 'You see, you need a real bastard to defend a bastard's daughter,' O'tila said menacingly.

But before he could go further Phæ'enor took one look at the hissing cat between her fingers, smiled at O'tila then threw the cat in his face. The market stalls around them erupted into chaos. Fruit and flowers, cages and lamps flew into the air. Fish grew wings and slapped people in the face. As O'tila frantically tried to get the cat off and Master Rasia tried to reclaim it he swung an arm that knocked Phæ'enor flying through the air and into the stall full of animal traps. These did not neatly land back where they had been laid, instead screams of people running away or being ensnared rang out across the stalls. As Master Rasia tried to get Phæ'enor away, O'tila finally managed to fling the cat off his mauled and bloody face. It zoomed passed their eyes, landing instead on Mimi's head.

Having also made their way over to the commotion, the two cousins' high-pitched screams travelled across the market as the cat jumped backwards and forth between the two girls, scratching and hissing. O'tila and his friends started to laugh again but Phæ'enor had had enough.

'MY FATHER IS NOT A BASTARD!' she shouted, as she stormed up to a stunned looking O'tila and punched him straight in the face. There was a moment of silence then all of them, O'tila, his boys, Master Rasia and Phæ'enor flew at each other. Legs and arms swung and kicked, stalls crumpled while some of the crowd jeered, others screamed for all of them to stop.

BANG! BANG! BANG!

The sudden sound of gunshots rang out in the marketplace. All the boys jumped and scarpered, stumbling into the crowd, and over the stalls at the sight of city guards and several soldiers making their way through the upturned stalls. Only Master Rasia remained, standing stock still and staring straight ahead in salute, whilst Phæ'enor carried on hitting an already battered O'tila on the ground.

BANG! BANG! BANG!

Rang out the shots of gunfire for a second time and still she did not stop.

'Miss Phæ'enor Doven!' shouted the familiar voice of Officer Nathryn.

Phæ'enor still determined to show O'tila how much she disliked him carried on punching and kicking him.

'GET-ER-OFF-OF-ME! OW!' screamed O'tila.

Officer Nathryn had no choice. Phæ'enor did not look like she was going to budge any time soon, even the guns sounding off had not stopped her. He put his own gun away, strolled over to Phæ'enor and tried to pick her off the beaten O'tila on the ground. However, realising that it was not going to work he shouted at his men:

'WELL? HELP ME OUT THEN!'

After a few more minutes, with the help of several officers and guards, Phæ'enor was pulled off O'tila, finger by finger, just like the cat, kicking and screaming.

'Take her to the gates and her manservant,' shouted a breathless and now dirty Officer Nathryn to his men. He looked at the two twins, Simi and Mimi, scratched faces and torn clothes. 'And these two can go with you!' Two guards moved the girls' off down the street after a still screaming and angry Phæ'enor. He watched them go for a bit then turned to Master Rasia, who was still in salute. 'AND YOU! Master Rasia, you best report to Captain Rost G. Alba in the morning.' As he turned and walked back away from a bleeding and bruised Master Rasia he shouted back over his shoulder into the crowd. 'The rest of you better clean up this mess! Or you will all be in a cell before the sun sets!'

Chapter Five

The Grand Tea Rooms

Although it had been a couple of days since Phæ'enor's encounter with O'tila in the marketplace she was still sporting a few bruises and scratches, including a left black eye and a large bump over her right, where she must have been whacked with something very solid. The scratches from the grey cat were starting to scab over, but there was still a bit of puss leaking down her cheek. She dabbed at it, wincing at the sting, as there came a light tap at her bedroom door.

'Phæ'enor, dear, it's time to go. I promised Captain Alba we would be on time. It is not good to keep a military man waiting,' came the voice of Mrs Doven, her footsteps growing faint as she walked away.

Her mother had not been angry, just upset and extremely concerned when Officer Nathryn and his men had brought Phæ'enor back home. She was more worried about her daughter's mental state than the bruising. Her grandmother, however, was most unimpressed.

'Disgraceful behaviour for a young lady! I won't have it! The shame you bring your mother and father … and ME! You will never get a husband now! You are not allowed out of my house! I absolutely forbid you! You can stay in your room for the rest of your life for all I care!'

Her grandmother's remarks only forced Phæ'enor to retaliate.

'I don't care what you think! Fine, I won't go out, this whole city is a bore! There's nothing here for me anyway. And fine, I'll stay in my rooms; if it means that I don't have to see you! And if I remember correctly, this house belongs to mother and father, not you, which means that when my father and brothers arrive in

Benaghar there won't be enough room for all of us, and since I'm no longer going to get a husband, it must mean that you will have to leave!'

A screaming match ensued until Phæ'enor's mother and the housekeeper, Mrs Hally Bride, had to drag her up into her room. She had remained there ever since, eating all her meals there, having refused to be in the same room, let alone at the same table as her grandmother. Around midday the day before, Phæ'enor had heard voices downstairs in the hallway. Shortly after, her mother who had spoken through her bedroom door, informed her who had been to the house:

'That was Officer Nathryn. He came by to inform us that we are to meet Admiral Gull and Captain Alba in The Grand Tea Rooms tomorrow afternoon. They need to finish their questioning of the passengers from The Scavenger.' Phæ'enor did not respond and after some moments of silence her mother continued, 'I'll get Florin to pick something out for you. Maybe we can hide a few of your bruises too,' she finished, sounding sad as she walked away.

Phæ'enor had felt guilty. She was angry at being in a country and city she didn't ask to be in, surrounded by people she disliked, trying to defend her father from a spiteful idiot and just wanted to have a go at someone; only for it to backfire. Her mother had been very quiet, sad, and more than likely disappointed with her daughter's behaviour. She had not stopped to think that her mother may have also felt the same way; alienated and a stranger to their new surroundings, without the rest of their family. She felt awful about putting her mother in this situation. All she could do now was go along with her wishes, and her father's lasts words to her before they had left:

"Keep your head down, don't attract unwanted attention and do as your mother says."

With that she tied back her long hair into a plait, grabbed her hat and made her way downstairs to join her mother. As she walked past the sitting room she heard disapproving noises from her grandmother, 'Still alive, I see.'

Not stopping to respond, Phæ'enor rolled her eyes and walked straight past her mother and out of the front door only to walk straight into the back of Officer Nathryn.

'Ow!'

'Still in the habit of not looking where you are going, Miss Doven?' he said laughing.

Phæ'enor looked away and wondered why he was so happy. He was not in such a good mood when he had to drag her away from O'tila. She was still angry with him for intervening. Phæ'enor glanced at him, seeing he also had scratches and a few bruises. She suppressed a smile and went to step up into the waiting small town coach.

'Here, let me,' said Officer Nathryn, offering his hand.

'No thank you, I'm more than capable of getting into the box by myself,' replied Phæ'enor, a little too disgruntled with the offer as she jumped in.

'And you, Mrs Doven, will you take my hand to help you into the carriage?' he asked half pleasantly, half exasperated with Phæ'enor.

'I'm sorry you have been made to do this officer,' said Mrs Doven, as she took his hand, 'I know my daughter can be wilful at times. She's just not happy here, or with the people she meets it would seem; including family.' She looked back towards the house. Officer Nathryn grinned.

'I'm sorry to have to hear that. Hopefully your daughter, over time, will settle. I'm quite sure she will find happiness soon. And as for me, whilst Master Rasia is unavailable I am more than happy to accompany you both. Once he has served his penance, he can resume his duties.'

'Thank you,' replied Miss Doven, before climbing into the coach with Officer Nathryn joining them.

Phæ'enor's ears had pricked up at the mention of Master Rasia. She had not seen him since the fight in the marketplace. The gossiping servants in the house however had informed her that Master Rasia was being punished for disobeying orders to look after the Dovens. At that time, she was so angry with her own situation that she did not care. But now she had calmed down, she felt a little guilty, had she also got him into trouble? What Officer Nathryn's comments meant she didn't know but instead, "that handsome young officer", as the maids' referred to Officer Nathryn, was to take over the chaperone duties, at least for a while.

Angry, she deliberately looked away and stared straight out the coach window as Officer Nathryn sat down opposite them. "Accompany" us she thought. More like keeping us under guard; or were they keeping her under watch? It didn't make sense to Phæ'enor. It can't have just been the journey or the explosion that they were concerned about because that was over now. Did her father know that Benaghar was not safe after all, and wanted regular updates as to their safety? The chaperoning duties should have ended by now. But then she thought about what O'tila had said to them in the marketplace, "not just an officer's daughter, the officer's daughter." He had also referred to him as a "bastard." She knew that her father had gone to battle, seen war several times; was he one of the bad ones? Did his family need protecting because of deeds he'd undertaken, crimes he may have committed during war? Was that why O'tila went for her?

She felt sick and hoped that was not why they had a guard. Maybe it was just a courtesy for all the hard work her father had achieved, in helping bring about peace in Vanu. He was not just a high-ranking officer; he was good with people, with the Vanuans. Either way, she could not fathom why Master Rasia or Officer Nathryn still had to keep an Officer's wife and daughter under constant watch. If it was really that bad here, why had her grandmother not been watched whilst they were absent and living in Vanu?

The coach tumbled along Grand Town Promenade towards the place they would be meeting Admiral Gull and Captain Rost G. Alba. Now I must answer some questions about the day The Scavenger blew up, she thought, getting more irritated. Questions, she laughed to herself, her grandmother was right, it was going to be an interrogation of a sixteen-year-old girl by officers of the Benagharian Army. She wondered what her father would think of that, had her mother even written to tell him? Phæ'enor looked at her mother briefly, she had one of her fake smiles on again, hands clasped in her lap, trying to be calm. No, she had not informed her father of the events so far, besides the news would not have reached him yet.

She had known from the concerned look and tiredness that had creeped into her mother's face, that day after the explosion, that there was more to the meeting than a few questions. The look on the Admiral's face and Captain Alba's for that matter, not to mention the silence from Officer Nathryn said it all.

As the coach made its way down the promenade and they passed many large white, officer inhabited buildings, she thought of how uninspiring they all were, so alike and un-individual. Just like this whole place. I have had no fun, just arguments and fights.

After a mile or so the four horses pulled the coach to a stop. Here, Officer Nathryn helped her mother out of the coach. Phæ'enor looked out at him from the darkness of the interior; he looked back at her and offered his hand once more.

Her father's last words to her before they departed Vanu came back to her again: "Keep a low profile, don't attract unwanted attention and do as your mother says". She sighed, slipped on her gloves and took Officer Nathryn's hand, stepping out in front of the large glass building, its chimneys billowing many colours of steam high into the sky. The glass reflected the sky to block the view of anything and anyone inside.

'It is unusual, this building, but very popular with the inhabitants of the city,' said Officer Nathryn, also taking in the unusual beauty of the structure. It did not fit in with the rest of the city surroundings. All the same, Phæ'enor liked it. It was different, and it was colourful.

As they walked in through the entrance Phæ'enor felt like she had walked into a wall of hot air. Her breathing became short and she heard her mother cough beside her.

'Dear, are you okay?'

'Yes, I just can't breathe that well,' replied Phæ'enor.

'Unfortunately, the vents don't always work as they should. More of a work in progress,' said Officer Nathryn. 'Please, it is not that far, keep walking and we shall be out of the worst of it.'

After a short while they emerged from the hot steam.

'Is it the same as the clouds outside the building?' asked Phæ'enor of Officer Nathryn.

'Yes, ah, err, yes,' replied Officer Nathryn, a little surprised to be addressed by an excited and well-mannered Phæ'enor.

'Wow, and it must be for all the plants,' she continued, as emerging from the steam it looked as though they had walked straight into a tropical jungle.

'That's right, Miss Doven. This is the biggest collection of tropical plants, flowers and wildlife in the whole empire,' said Officer Nathryn, grinning at the happy look on Phæ'enor's face, 'of course, you many already recognise some of them from your time in Vanu?'

'Oh, yes. It is so beautiful,' she replied breathlessly. She could not help but grin from ear to ear. All thoughts of an interrogation evaporated from her mind like the steam.

The city outside was white and golden but inside this giant greenhouse were reds and bright pinks and yellows, purples, greens and all shades of a rainbow. Some plants towered into the vaulted ceiling, whilst others bloomed flowers larger than the coach they had arrived in. She could hear frogs grunting, see butterflies meandering across the beds and spotted one or two hummingbirds zipping in and out amongst the flower heads. There were other people in here too; mainly couples linking arms and slowly walking and talking amongst wildlife. She could not help but smile also.

'I take it you are fond of flowers, and the wild?' asked Officer Nathryn.

'Yes,' said Phæ'enor, 'it reminds me of home, of Vanu. I used to run into the jungles with my friends. We would spend hours amongst all the creatures and the plants. Giving all the flowers names of our own.' The smile faded from her face. 'I miss it.'

'Well,' said Officer Nathryn quickly, seeing how sudden her mood had changed. 'I'm not sure if you are aware but as residents of Grand Town you have unrestricted access to The Grand Tea Rooms, including these tropical plants.'

'Really?' said Phæ'enor. 'I can come here whenever I want? For free?'

'Yes, but not after closing hours, obviously.'

Her smile returned, and she set off to explore the different plants, and as she left them to it she heard her mother say:

'Thank you, Officer Nathryn. You have lifted her spirts no end.'

***

After some time, Officer Nathryn insisted they move through to the tea rooms above. Phæ'enor's little exploration of the unexpected urban jungle started to make them late and it would not be good to keep Admiral Gull waiting.

They passed through a long, arched glass passageway and up several flights of glass stairs, which spiralled endlessly into the sky. At the top smaller exotic birds chirped and cooed out. They had arrived on a large glass landing and Phæ'enor, not one to fear heights, was uneasy at what felt like walking through air. They could see straight through to the floor below as they made their way over to a double glass-stained door. It was decorated with a large teapot, tea cups and underneath workers in the field picking tea and staring up towards the tea pot as though in worship. Phæ'enor looked at her mother. They both grinned and she felt more at ease. A place that was built to worship tea couldn't be sillier she thought.

Officer Nathryn pulled open the doors to reveal a wall of noise from the people talking in the vast room beyond. Hundreds of tables were filled with china teapots, cups and saucers and cakes a plenty. As they walked through the isle between the many tables Phæ'enor could hear lots of laughter, women gossiping about friends and family, men talking about money and how much they had won at the tables. Some looked worse for wear, clearly nursing their heads from too much the night before. There were also children running in and out between the tables, some being taught the etiquette of how to sit and eat nicely, while others pretended the table they were at was a tent. And through all the bustle the waiters were all smartly dressed in light blue, to match the glass of the building, with small caps, waistcoats, white cotton gloves and clean black boots.

'AAH! There you are Nathryn! What kept you? You are exactly three minutes and twenty-one seconds late,' said Admiral Gull, standing up with his right hand out in front of him tapping his pocket watch.

'My apologies, Admiral Gull,' said Officer Nathryn. He did not elaborate on why they were late.

'Hmm, very well. Mrs Doven, Miss Phæ'enor Doven, please take a seat. You will of course know Prince Taigor and Captain Rost G. Alba.'

Phæ'enor not paying attention, having been too distracted by the hub of the tea house recognised Captain Rost G. Alba and smiled but was startled by the appearance of the prince. He was no longer adorned with bejewelled clothing, nor was he sporting the hideous white wig seen at the harbour. Today he wore plain black attire. A matching and discreet top hat lay upon the table in front of him, but what was most striking was that he had clearly been wearing make-up of some sort when she had first seen him because today his skin was no longer powdered white but olive skinned. His hair was dark and closely cropped to his head.

They made to courtesy, but he suddenly stood up and shook his head politely but sternly. It was clear he did not want to be seen. He was much taller than she had remembered him and much younger, possibly in his late twenties, guessed Phæ'enor.

'You shall call me Mr Dryhten,' and he winked at both Mrs Doven and Phæ'enor who smiled in knowing return. Maybe this would not be so bad after all thought Phæ'enor, as they all took a seat.

'Well, I gather by your lateness that one of you got side tracked by the tropics outside?' said Admiral Gull, clearly still irritated. Phæ'enor smiled apologetically. 'I might have guessed,' he continued, 'although I am not surprised. They would be familiar to you no doubt, having come from Vanu.' He paused and waited for the prince to take his seat before he followed suit and then continued, 'I took the trouble of ordering the tea and cake without you, it will arrive shortly. Anyhow we are late, and myself, Captain Alba and Pri ... I mean Mr Dryhten, need a few questions answered.'

The Admiral was about to continue but Prince Taigor held up his hand calmly and spoke instead:

'You must understand Miss Doven, that although we do not suspect you, this is a serious matter, and besides you were one of the last people to disembark from the frigate. And from what I hear the gun deck also.'

'And tell me, Mr Dryhten, do you think me capable of handling one of the cannons? Or magic fire out of nowhere and set light to the gun powder barrels?'

'No. Miss Doven…' said Prince Taigor.

'And have all the crew been questioned?' she asked.

'Yes, but…'

'I needn't have to tell you that I wasn't the only one down there on the gun deck that day either.'

'Miss Doven, your manner in speaking to the prince…' said the Admiral.

'Then I suppose you, Admiral Gull, have already asked them then?'

'Who?' said Prince Taigor sharply. 'Who did you see down there?'

'Mr Dryhten, no one else was down there. We have confirmation from all crew, including Master Rasia. The only non-crew member to enter was Miss Doven,' interjected the Admiral.

'Do you really believe my daughter could blow up The Scavenger?' demanded Mrs Doven, looking angrily at both Prince Taigor and the Admiral. 'What motive would she have?'

'Please,' said Prince Taigor, and he returned his gaze to Phæ'enor. 'Who did you see down there that day?'

'You're asking me the wrong question,' replied Phæ'enor.

The prince raised his eyebrows at her, the Admiral spluttered some spit out across the table. Officer Nathryn wiped it away with an unimpressed gaze, whilst Captain Alba covered his laugh with a cough. Mrs Doven had closed her eyes and pinched between the bridge of her nose. There was a moment's silence before Phæ'enor realised she needed to elaborate.

'You need to ask me why I was down there in the first place, obviously.'

Laughing, Admiral Gull replied, 'We all know why you were down there…'

'Admiral!' said the prince, a little too abruptly, and louder than intended. A few people from the surrounding tables looked over then turned back to their own conversations.

'So, you are accusing me?' asked Phæ'enor.

'Your father may be one of the best captains in the army, but it does not mean to say that he may not have a nosey and clumsy daughter,' said the Admiral.

'How dare you,' said Mrs Doven, quietly but menacing. 'I should remind you, Admiral, that my husband, although lower in rank than yourself, will always command much more respect than most of you and your kind ever will. Not to mention how you and many of your men would no longer be here if it wasn't for my husband…' At this, the colour drained from the Admiral's face. '… I have written to him, and I am most certain he will be unimpressed with your antics since we have arrived.'

Phæ'enor went still and quiet. Her mother was generally a quiet and pleasant woman. The only other time she had seen her turn this quickly to anger was when she and her brothers were playing with their father's pistol. They had slipped it off his belt whilst he slept in his armchair. She touched her left leg where the scar remained from her beating. Her father did not escape either, being banned from the house for over a month due to his carelessness. She looked over at Admiral Gull who remained silenced by Mrs Doven. The small party had started to attract a lot of attention.

The waiter appeared with their teas and cakes and carefully placed them in front of each of the party. Phæ'enor looked at him as a distraction, watching the way the waiter carefully placed the cups and saucers. Starting with the highest ranking he first served Mr Dryhten, then her mother and herself. Next, the Admiral and Captain Alba were served, and lastly Officer Nathryn. So he would know that Mr Dryhten was in fact Prince Taigor? Not so subtle a disguise than she thought, unless the waiter was a royal servant. Although he wore the same attire as the rest of the waiters, the only difference was that he had black gloves on instead of white, they also seemed quite stiff; he was taking quite a while to serve without rattling the china.

Curious she looked around the large glass tea room. There were many different characters at the tables. She noticed all of them were of a similar rank, nice clothing and seemingly well mannered. There did not seem to be any other people from the city other than well to do people of Grand Town, Queens and Kings areas. As she returned to the waiter, who was placing the cakes and biscuits out in front of them, she glimpsed a familiar figure through the space under his arms. On the far side of the room she spotted the tall skinny and solemn looking man that was forever in the shadows of the drunk on board The Scavenger and who had recently caused the carriage she and her cousins had been in to stop so abruptly. As before he was alone again, tea cup poised in one hand and engrossed in a newspaper on the table.

'Miss Phæ'enor Doven?'

She slowly took her eyes off the man and faced back to the rest of the table. She looked blankly at them not realising who had addressed her.

'Miss Doven? You said to ask why you had gone down to the gun deck in the first place,' said Prince Taigor.

'Oh. No. I didn't specifically go down beneath with the intention of going to the gun deck,' she replied.

'Oh, for the love of…!'

'Please, enough Admiral. Please continue,' said Prince Taigor, once again holding his hand up to stop the Admiral from talking.

Nearby the waiter had moved over to an adjacent table, clearing it of empty plates and tea cups. Phæ'enor was sure he was listening. He also seemed familiar, but she couldn't put her finger on what it was about him.

'Miss Doven?' prompted Officer Nathryn, 'you were saying why you had gone down below deck?'

'Um … yes,' she reached for her tea cup, a blue and white china. The only one of that colour of the six tea cups on the table. She took a sip and continued, 'Ever since Lady Amia had boarded I had been curious to find out who she was, I was bored. For once she was on her own; she normally had all of her guards with her, so I followed her through the doors, below the bridge of the ship. I just followed her down. She … we had both passed several passengers … along … along the…'

Phæ'enor put her tea cup down. She felt oddly queasy and her eyes began to lose focus.

'My darling, are you okay?' said a concerned Mrs Doven.

'Yes. I think I'm just feeling a bit hot. It's very hot in here,' she replied, reassuring her mother.

She took another sip of her tea. The waiter still seemed to be taking his time at the next table. Officer Nathryn's face started to go in and out of focus.

'Waiter,' shouted Prince Taigor, 'fetch us some water immediately and a cooling pot for the tea. It's too hot.'

The waiter disappeared but not before Phæ'enor glimpsed more of his features. His light-coloured hair.

'Who did you pass down in the lower decks, Miss Doven?'

'Umm … that man over there,' said Phæ'enor, as she pointed towards the far end of the room.

'There's no-one there,' said Officer Nathryn.

'Yes. Yes, there is! That tall skinny man … reading the paper,' said Phæ'enor. She felt too hot. Her brow began to sweat, and she wiped it with the napkin on the table, wiping the powder off her face to reveal the scratches on her cheek.

'And … and … Lady Amia did go through the doors. I saw her with my own eyes. But … but when I got further in, she had vanished. I ended up bumping into Master Rasia who shouted at me. He chased me out. Well at least into Captain Alba's cabin.'

'Miss Phæ'enor Doven,' said Prince Taigor, 'Lady Amia was nowhere near the gun deck. Her guards are under royal command and had her under protection all the time. Her movements on board are completely accounted for and …'

'And there was someone else. It was … it was, you!' She shouted at the waiter as she abruptly stood up looking straight at him. It was O'tila. 'You, yes he was on board the ship. He was down by the gun deck too … it's him, it's him from the marketplace, and The Scavenger!'

They had all got up now trying to calm her down.

'Darling, please sit down, you're not well,' said a concerned Mrs Doven to her daughter. People had stopped taking their tea on the surrounding tables to look.

Phæ'enor, not listening continued to talk out loud, 'There are birds inside here …'

She could see them flying quickly overhead. One flew down and sat on the edge of her tea cup, 'Shoo, shoo,' she cried, 'get off. That's mine!' And then suddenly shouted, 'He's getting away, he's getting away!'

She spun around wildly, struggling to break free from the grip of a very strong hand. She could no longer see the waiter O'tila, it was as though he had just slipped away.

'Aargh!' She screamed.

Out of nowhere an extremely tall man, dark haired and dark eyed appeared before her, looking down upon her; his face also in shock. Phæ'enor backed into several tables. Tea cups and saucers, crockery and cakes spilt over the tables and onto the floor.

'Who are … y-y-you!?' she screamed.

The figure came closer. Slowly he moved one arm down his back, pulling out a large wooden sword, sharp pointed teeth imbedded all over it, and walked determinedly towards her.

'Aaargh! Get away from me!' she screamed in panic.

'Miss Doven,' she could hear someone say near to her. She moved further back. The man with the sword had disappeared.

'Miss Doven there is nothing there!' shouted Captain Alba.

'Let me,' said Officer Nathryn, 'something is obviously not right. Mr Dryhten, Captain Alba, take her and Mrs Doven outside, NOW! Where is that waiter? I think there is something in the tea!'

Prince Taigor looked alarmed, 'Fine, go and look. Report back to me as soon as you can,' he said in a low voice, so that the surrounding onlookers could not hear. And with that, Officer Nathryn disappeared towards the far end of the tea room.

'Mrs Doven?' said Prince Taigor commandingly, 'go to the coach and advise we need to leave immediately. I will bring Phæ'enor down. Admiral Gull, send for a doctor.

Mrs Doven, sick with worry, rushed out of the entrance ahead; Captain Alba in her wake.

As they left, Phæ'enor was still shivering and shaking, talking nonsense to herself. Prince Taigor picked her up in his arms and hurrying as fast as he could, made his way out down the many flights of stairs and into the open air.

Chapter Six

Visitors

The days following the incident in The Grand Tea Rooms saw not only a change in the air; the dusk came down upon the city quicker, and cold nights drew in, but there had also been a change in the mood out on the streets. Phæ'enor, once again confined to No 9 Grand Alboreum Circus, although this time not just to her bedroom, found that less and less people were wandering around the streets. The square just outside of the house was virtually empty. When she wasn't staring out the window, she tried reading the many dull books housed in the library that lined the shelves, or lying down staring at the ceiling, or watching the roof tops for any sign of life.

Although she felt unwell for a few days after and was still struggling to eat a full meal, she was okay. Quiet, but she felt fine. The reason for her further confinement she guessed was due to all the gossiping in the city about her display of madness. Her wild outburst and her insistence that there was a man dressed in next to nothing, brandishing a sword at her, was all that anyone could talk about.

The neighbours of Grand Alboreum Circus were the worst. The word of her madness had spread quickly and being so close they wanted to know first-hand what had happened before the rest of Benaghar. First a neighbour from No 15, under the pretence of bringing over some fruit and flowers proceeded to inform Mrs Doven and Phæ'enor's grandmother about all the excellent work the nurses at Blaindower did, and how it would greatly benefit Phæ'enor. Handing them a brochure, she advised them on how much the rooms there would cost for a year:

'You may as well be prepared dears, after all it is not the first sign of madness to appear in your family.'

At this Mrs Jemin snapped, 'Mr Deke! Show this woman out immediately! She is not to be allowed in here again! The cheek of it!'

The next neighbours to show up were a small group of children from No 1 and No 4; two boys of similar age, a much younger boy who looked terribly frightened, and a very loud and obnoxious young girl.

'Well, where is it then?' She demanded of Mr Deke, as he opened the door.

'Where is what?' he replied in his uninterested tone.

'The man, the man! The naked man with the sword!' chanted the two older boys.

'Yes,' said the girl, 'that boy over there said that Miss Phæ'enor would conjure the naked man with the sword again if we paid him a penny each! We demand to see it done!'

The little boy, now hiding behind the girl's legs peered around at Mr Deke and shook his head, 'I don't want to see, I don't want to see bad man,' he said quietly.

Mrs Hally Bride, the old maid, turned up behind Mr Deke and looked over to the green beyond the children. Another, much older boy, standing amongst some other children was laughing in the middle of it.

'Shoo! Shoo now, there is nothing to see here you horrible little children!' and proceeded to hit them with a tea towel, off the steps and back into the street.

Later when Phæ'enor heard about it from the young maid, she could not help but laugh at the ingenuity of the older boy to make money off smaller, stupid children.

The final straw of letting No 09 be invaded by neighbours came when several of the women from Grand Alboreum Circus turned up together. They were eager to offer their help and brought all manner of contraptions with them; one held a jar full of venomous snake heads that bobbed up and down, another clanged together a large set of brass cymbals, whilst a dumpy looking woman solemnly beat a heavy drum hooked about her neck. One woman opened a small wooden box containing several pungent smelling salts. Whilst the woman who spoke for them brandished a very sharp wooden stake in one hand, in the other a handful of leather straps.

'We are here, you need not fear anymore for your daughter's sanity,' they advised Mrs Doven, 'the Brothers at the Temple informed us of her grave situation and there is no time to lose. We are well versed in the art of luring out those evil spirts that come to rest in the children born out in the far east. Mrs Doven, we are here to exorcise that evil demon from your daughter and rid her of his malice for good!'

With a fury of triumphant determination, they all held up their contraptions, ready to proceed. The door was promptly slammed in their faces. They continued to knock, chanting for the evil spirt to leave until, 'Arrrgh!' their screams could be heard as they disappeared back to their homes.

The old maid Mrs Bride later claimed that she was only dispensing with dirty water used to scrub the floors, 'I didn't mean no 'arm by it? I swear I didn't know they were underneath the window, ma'am.'

None of the neighbours came knocking after that.

***

Phæ'enor had laughed at the sight of the women, drenched from head to toe running away across the green, as she looked out of the landing window. But then it cast her mind back to the man; evil spirit or not, he did appear before her. She remembered the feeling of being dizzy and light headed, unable to focus or to control her vision. Her eyes had become heavy, as though someone was controlling how her body should move for her, and then suddenly the man appeared. Staring at her then walking towards her, tall and browned skinned like her mother, but he was not wearing many clothes. Instead, his body was tattooed. Intricate patterns of dots so close together that they formed black bands, lines and sharp patterns across his chest, arms, legs and even his neck and face. His eyes were as dark as the night, as was his long hair, tied back but shaven close at the sides. She had been shocked by his appearance, and had backed away quickly, but looking back he was just as shocked by her as she was of him. She shook her head, maybe I am going mad she thought, but I don't feel crazy.

And then she thought of how they had reacted when she had accused an invisible man sitting in the corner of The Grand Tea Rooms of having also been on the gun deck of the ship, the day it exploded. But she had; she had seen the tall, slim companion of the portly drunk on the ship. He was outside of the entrance to the gun deck. How could she forget his snooty expression as he waited for her to move out of his way before ascending the stairs to the upper deck? Okay, so he may have not been the culprit for the explosion, but he was definitely there. Or am I imagining that too?

It was the same with O'tila, or so she thought. But Officer Nathryn and Prince Taigor advised her that she was still angry with him for the fight in the marketplace. That yes, O'tila was travelling back from seeing family in Banrein but he would have either been in the passengers' quarters of the lower decks, or above. His movements were all accounted for as well. They had also insisted that O'tila was not at The Grand Tea Rooms; that she had mistaken the waiter to be him in her state of delusion.

And as for accusing Lady Amia of being on the gun deck, well, it was utter nonsense as far as they were concerned. Her guards hadn't left her side, not even once since they had boarded. The only explanation that Admiral Gull and the others could come up with was that Phæ'enor was either unwell or she was lying. But being the daughter of one of the most respected men in the Benagharian

Army they would have to go with the former. There was only one thing for it, she must stick to the house until she was better.

***

But being stuck indoors indefinitely meant she couldn't go anywhere; she couldn't explore or even see her cousin's and find out what was going on. So instead, over a couple of days several visitors came to call on Phæ'enor. However, none of them put her mind at ease; they either made her feel even more foolish, uncomfortable or treated her like an interesting species, waiting to see if she conducted anymore madness in their presence. But they also became more interesting to Phæ'enor for what they were not saying in return.

The first visitor was Lady Amia. She came very unexpectedly and very soon after the incident. Exactly one day after she sent a note advising she would be arriving at 11 o'clock in the morning and would kindly like to enquire on Miss Phæ'enor Doven's health. But Phæ'enor, looking forward to seeing the kind and sweet natured young woman, was met with a slightly cautious and worried looking Lady Amia. Gone was the open and joking manner and instead a concerned and serious one; and she was clearly not interested in Phæ'enor's wellbeing.

'Phæ'enor, you don't mind if I call you by your first name, do you?' by her tone of voice it did not seem like she was asking. 'You do know I wasn't down on the gun deck, don't you?' She continued, looking sad but trying not to be patronising at the same time. Trying a little too hard, thought Phæ'enor. 'You know I did hear from the other passengers on board that The Scavenger is haunted,' she laughed unconvincingly. 'I know, a silly thing, but you never know, some people have the gift to see these things.' Lady Amia searched Phæ'enor with her eyes.

At this Phæ'enor made her excuses, lying and saying she felt unwell again and needed to return to her rooms for rest. In truth she did not like the idea of people being concerned for her or laughing the situation off. She knew what she saw. Maybe the man with the sword appearing from nowhere was a bit mad, but he was there. As she left Lady Amia in the sitting room with her mother and grandmother she heard the continued false concern:

'How long has she been unwell for Mrs Doven?'

'Why, only since the incident in the tea rooms,' came her mother's reply.

'No. What I mean is, how long has she been suffering with this … well, this madness? Imagining people to be somewhere they were not on The Scavenger? The visions in The Grand Tea Rooms, and now the lying?'

'What? Don't be ridiculous. No one in our family is mad! You want to look at the one you're marrying into!'

Phæ'enor was a little surprised to hear the angry voice of her grandmother come to her defence. She made her way up the spiral staircase and glimpsed a haughty and displeased Lady Amia leave quite hastily after.

***

Surprisingly and unexpectedly Master Rasia called in the following day, unannounced. He had not come alone either. Trotting in beside him, without a care in the world, was the large grey cat that had started all the trouble in the marketplace. Phæ'enor was still sporting the scratches on her face.

'I was passing by and thought I would call in,' he said, as he sat down in the sitting room. 'You don't mind, do you,' he asked looking at the cat. 'Family cat, he pretty much follows me everywhere.'

Passing by? thought Phæ'enor, and she stifled her laugh through a cough. You could not just walk by Grand Alboreum Circus, these houses were pretty much tucked away in the far corner of Grand Town, so far out of the way of anyone that you would only come here intentionally. He also did not look dressed for a visit; traces of dirt could be seen on the knees and shins of his trousers. She turned to watch the cat; it was much larger than she remembered. It was more like the size of a small bear than a domestic cat, and its grey mane made it look like a miniature lion too. It wandered into the sitting room, looking under and over the chairs before jumping up onto the window sill, looking out to the street beyond whilst its tail slowly swayed behind it.

Phæ'enor then turned her attention to Master Rasia, waiting for the questions and answers to the gossips on the street but they did not come. Instead Master Rasia only apologised to Mrs Doven and her grandmother for the trouble with the fight in the marketplace. How he had let his guard down and had not done right by Phæ'enor; letting harm come to her. She didn't know how to respond, he was not laughing or joking or smirking when he spoke. Master Rasia seemed genuine in his apology. He turned to Phæ'enor.

'I'm sorry to hear about the incident the other day. If I was there I might have been better placed to advise you about which teas to drink, which to avoid.'

'What do you mean?' asked Mrs Doven.

'I'm saying that The Grand Tea Rooms don't have the best reputation for their teas. They don't always stick to the regulations on imports and mixing. Some of them are not as good as they make out to be, and … well, there are some that are just bad, very bad.'

Phæ'enor smirked, 'I don't think I was dealt a bad batch, or poisoned Master Rasia.'

'No?' said Master Rasia. 'Look, my first posting was out at Palestra, where a lot of the tea comes from in the empire. I've seen it being picked, washed, and shipped. Good leaf mixed with the bad, when it should not have been. Sometimes you just don't know what you are drinking.'

'Bah,' barked Mrs Jemin, 'I think you're referring to the other tea rooms in the city. The Grand Tea Rooms is nothing to the likes of Mrs Kuáng's!'

Both Master Rasia and Phæ'enor's grandmother laughed at this. Phæ'enor had no idea what the joke was about, and it didn't look like either of them would elaborate. Instead she interrupted their joke:

'The problem Master Rasia, is that I'm afraid everyone thinks I am mad, and you have the embarrassing job of looking out for me.'

'Ha. They say on the streets that the reason I stopped helping you wasn't because of the fight in the market. It was because I already knew you were mad.' They smiled at each other, knowing how much they irritated each other.

'But I don't think you're mad Miss Doven. You may not like rules, or even behave like the other young women of Benaghar, but it does not make you mad.' It was as though he needed to elaborate but couldn't. But then she thought about how Master Rasia was on the gun deck and would have seen all crew and passengers that had been there. Which meant that if she had seen Lady Amia, the tall snooty slim man and O'tila, then so had he. They looked at each other knowingly and Phæ'enor tried to see if she could read any more from his expression but he cut the visit short.

'I hope this passes soon. Then you can get out of the house. Let me know if there is anything I can do for you. Anything. I am glad to see you all well, at least now your father will not be completely angry with me.'

He bowed slightly to them, then left the house. The cat instinctively jumped down off the window sill and ran out after him, but not before brushing itself on the skirt of Phæ'enor's dress.

Phæ'enor was now curious as to what information Master Rasia knew about the explosion on The Scavenger and why he wasn't saying anything. It was also obvious that he had needed to get away from wherever he had been. He looked worse for wear, far worse than after the fight in the marketplace. She hoped the punishment Captain Alba gave him was not too harsh, but she doubted it, he looked skinnier, downcast and his voice tired. It was as though he needed to tell Phæ'enor she was not going mad and he believed what she was saying. It was odd coming from a person who had wanted to throttle her for three months of her life.

***

The next visitors were her two cousins, Simi and Mimi. Phæ'enor was not best pleased when Mrs Bride advised her that the two of them had arrived straight from worship at The Brotherhoods Temple in Grand Town. She would either have to listen to them hark on about how important their faith was to them, how the empire's foundations were all that mattered in the world or having to put up with them sulking about being scratched by the cat in the marketplace and how it would no doubt be all their horrible little cousin, Phæ'enor's, fault.

They had not called on her since that day to see how she was, but after the madness in The Grand Tea Rooms she was surprised and a little annoyed that they now wanted to come and confirm the rumours.

'Oh cousin, cousin!' cried Simi excitely, rushing to her as they entered the library, Phæ'enor seated at the small reading desk.

'We have not come to wish you good health. You look fine to us. Nor have we come to complain about our scratches. As you can see we have healed,' she smiled and gave Phæ'enor a hug.

Phæ'enor decided not to point out that she could still see the scratches, made more evident by whatever creams they had decided to use on their faces, and could still see the bruising on their necks.

'No! Instead we have come with nice fruit, and games we can play,' said Mimi, as she took some apples, grapes, oranges, a pack of cards and a small box out of a basket she was carrying.

As much as her two excitable cousins annoyed her, they were harmless. They did not seem to hold any grudges and just wanted to have some fun.

'We thought we would take your mind off things,' said Simi, 'and from staring at these walls.'

'And if you cannot come to the fun, then the fun shall come to you!' screamed Mimi, with joy.

They spent the next couple of hours playing board games and cards. Simi and Mimi squabbled incessantly over who had won more grapes, as substitutes for money. At midday Simi called for tea.

'I'm parched,' she looked at Phæ'enor long and hard. Phæ'enor thought she was being weird at first. Then her staring started to irritate her.

'What? Why are you staring at me, cousin?'

Simi looked at her sister then back at Phæ'enor and asked, 'Has Officer Nathryn called in on you recently?' she continued to stare blankly at Phæ'enor. Who looked back at her cousins, her eyebrows raised, bemused at the question.

'No. Why should he?'

'Oh, cousin, as if you hadn't noticed,' said Mimi, having stuffed half a cake in her mouth, dusting the crumbs off her hands as she spoke. 'What? Everyone knows he has his eyes on you.' Some crumbs shot out of her mouth into the skirt of her dress.

'Where have you heard that?' groaned Phæ'enor. They were back onto her cousins' favourite topic of men and marriage again.

'Well, everyone?' said Mimi. 'They all talk about how he never leaves your side, and from what we've seen, well it's quite true is it not, cousin?' Phæ'enor rolled her eyes in response.

'And you can stop that,' said Simi. 'Come on, what's going on?'

So that's why they have come to see me, thought Phæ'enor. They don't care if I am okay or not. They don't want to have an argument about the fight in the marketplace. They just want to talk about their favourite subject.

Phæ'enor sighed at the desperate look for news on her cousins' faces, 'Officer Nathryn is standing in for Master Rasia whilst he is otherwise engaged. And may I remind you the…'

'The guard of honour?' smirked Simi in question, also now raising her eyebrows and leaning back in her chair nonchalantly.

'Well I have no idea why they are looking out for mother and me?' said Phæ'enor, shrugging her shoulders.

'So, what you're trying to tell us is that you have no idea why you have a personal escort everywhere you go?' asked Simi.

'No! I don't,' said Phæ'enor, half laughing, 'if you're so bothered by it why don't you write to your uncle and ask. Better still, ask Mother, or Officer Nathryn, or Master Rasia. I don't really care.'

She leaned back in her chair looking down in her lap, clicking her nails out of boredom. The two cousins looked at each other.

'Well, it doesn't matter. Officer Nathryn probably wouldn't have called anyway, what with recent events,' said Mimi, with a quick and knowing glance at her sister.

'You mean my sudden case of madness?' said Phæ'enor sarcastically, exasperated by her cousins' pretence.

'Oh, no. No one cares about that. It was obvious you were drugged. No, we mean the recent theft from the garrisons!' said Mimi.

Phæ'enor shook her head in a confused response. Drugged? Theft? What in the world were her two cousins on about? She was quite sure she hadn't been drugged. And theft, of what?

'Oh, for Tekan's sake. You, cooped up in here is ridiculous,' said Simi. 'Are you not even allowed to read the papers?' She sighed, annoyed at having to explain everything.

'Have you not seen the daily paper grandmother gets then?' asked Mimi. 'It's all in there, about the chests going missing?' Phæ'enor was still confused and it showed. 'Ugh! Apparently, Officer Nathryn and his fellow officers' boarded The Scavenger with quite a number of chests.'

'Yes, they did,' said Phæ'enor.

'Well, about two nights ago somebody, and they don't know who or how, broke into the garrisons where they were being stored and managed to take them,' said Mimi.

'Right?' said Phæ'enor.

'Oh, it is like talking to someone from Blaindower!' snapped Simi.

'The chests must have been valuable, or at least holding something valuable. The Scavenger has now been blown to smithereens. They were transported to the garrison for safe keeping. Although, I have heard they have been moved several times. And now the garrisons have been broken into and the chests are nowhere to be seen!' She said it so fast she leant back in her chair and took in a deep breath.

'So?' said Phæ'enor.

'Oh, Phæ'enor!' shouted Mimi. 'There is a lot of talk outside in the city. Officer Nathryn's duties were obviously to guard whatever was in those chests. The city guards, Officer Nathryn and others are now looking to recover them. However, there is also the other obvious detail. The chests were being guarded because they are valuable. Lady Amia had a guard because she will be the next queen and the only other person that had, and still has, a guard is you and aunt Doven. Which Officer Nathryn, all of sudden has now taken responsibility for!'

It dawned on Phæ'enor what her cousins were implying. She closed her eyes and breathed slowly before opening them.

'I do not have any of those chests or what was being stored in them!'

'But who else would have what was inside of them?' asked Simi.

'Who knows? Why do you even care?' asked Phæ'enor.

'Well why do you not care?' asked Mimi.

'Why would I? Why would anyone care what those soldiers get up to or what's in their silly chests'?'

'Well didn't you see them on The Scavenger?' asked Mimi.

'Yes, as did everyone else on board!' said Phæ'enor.

'Were you not curious?' asked Simi.

'I wasn't paying attention to the chests!'

'Are you sure?' asked Mimi.

'Yes, are you sure you are not hiding something from us?' said Simi.

'Don't be ridiculous … how can I hide a load of chests? Where would I hide them? Search the house if you don't believe me!'

BANG!

The door to the library hit the side of one of the bookshelves as it swung open.

'Girls, girls, girls! What is all the commotion for? I can hear your shouts down the hallway and into the front of the house! You two, I think your cousin has had quite enough excitement for today. Come along, I shall get the carriage to take you back home,' barked their grandmother. The two girls left dissatisfied and with a 'humph.' Having not obtained the gossip they thought Phæ'enor would proffer.

***

A week had passed by and the weather had not improved. Rain splashed against Phæ'enor's bedroom window and she now craved company from the outside again. She would even have her cousins back, just for a few hours a day. At least they gave her some information to think about, even if it was pointless. But overall, from what she had heard, her little incident was nothing compared to the theft of the chests. Her grandmother, not one to indulge openly in gossip, now sent Mr Deke out first thing in the morning to fetch the daily paper for more information, then back out again in the evening for the next.

From the snippets Phæ'enor glimpsed there had been several arrests by the city guards, but who then were promptly let go. It seemed her cousins, Simi and Mimi, were right about one thing. Officer Nathryn was busy with the case of the stolen chests and had not come by No 09 Grand Alboreum Circus since the break-in at the garrisons. Master Rasia had now resumed his duties to the Doven's, standing guard outside the front door with the grey cat, occasionally checking around the back of the house, but he only remained until the early hours of the evening before disappearing. He never carried out sentinel duties at night and would often leave the big grey cat behind on the front porch instead.

Phæ'enor had sneaked a peak at what Master Rasia was doing from the top floor landing window several times. Today he was back standing outside their front door, not moving in the freezing rain and watching the street beyond. That was until Phæ'enor spotted three figures striding across the square towards the house. She could make out Officer Nathryn with his mop of pale hair and black clothing, one of the other men was unmistakably Prince Taigor, dressed as Mr Dryhten, but she could not make out the third. She watched them stop. Officer Nathryn and Prince Taigor saluted then shook Master Rasia's hand. The third did not; there seemed to be no recognition between this last man and Master Rasia. The knock came at the front door, sounds of voices and footsteps across the hallway then silence. However, after a while

Phæ'enor heard footsteps, soft and slow. They seemed to be making their way up the stairs.

'Hello?' she called out. Nothing. Then there was the sound of metal scraping on wood. It sounded as though someone was trying to open doors. 'Hello there?' Phæ'enor said more forcefully. The noise came again from the landing below but still there was no response. Phæ'enor moved slowly toward the banister, she stopped and started to carefully lean over to check who was there.

'PHÆ'ENOR!' came the boom of her grandmother's voice. Startled, she held her chest in shock, then placed her hands on the railing to support herself. She looked over, there was no one there.

'Yes, grandmother?' she called out.

'There are two gentlemen waiting on you in the sitting room. Hurry up girl, you'll keep them waiting so long they'll die in their chairs!'

Breathing back to normal, Phæ'enor hurried down the stairs, but when she reached the lower landing she noticed her bedroom door had been left slightly ajar. She had definitely closed it behind her. She surveyed the rest of the landing. No other doors had been touched.

'PHÆ'ENOR!'

'Yes, grandmother, I am coming as fast as I can!' and she ran down the stairs so as not to be further scolded by the tones of her grandmother's voice. But as she came towards the bottom she stopped abruptly. Standing in the hallway, close to the door, stood a tall, pale faced and fair-haired boy. There was no warmth in his countenance, nor in his eyes. It was the unfriendly looking boy whom Master Rasia had hissed at from that day at the harbourside when The Scavenger exploded.

'Hurry along girl, and don't worry about him! He's just a royal footman!' barked her grandmother from the sitting room door.

Phæ'enor looked over her shoulder at him, standing still like he had done at the harbourside. He looked like someone, or something. It unnerved her, and she had a funny feeling the footsteps and trying of doors did not belong to the servants of this house.

Officer Nathryn and Prince Taigor stood up as Phæ'enor and her grandmother walked back into the sitting room. Mrs Doven was already seated, looking quite relaxed. A tray of teas lay in front of her.

'Miss Doven,' said Officer Nathryn, as they all came back up from bowing their heads at each other. 'You are looking quite recovered all ready.'

'I was fine to begin with.' Phæ'enor did not like his happy tone.

'Phæ'enor,' said Mrs Doven, curtly through her teeth. 'These men have come all the way across town to see you today.' She gave Phæ'enor a stern look.

'Ha,' barked her grandmother.

Phæ'enor saw Officer Nathryn glance nervously at Prince Taigor, who wore a faint smirk on his face, before taking his seat.

'I'm sorry we have not called by sooner. Work has been busy of late.'

That's nice for you thought Phæ'enor. And why did you come all this way to tell me this? But she tried to be civil, indulge their efforts for coming. Display the false niceties and say something in return.

'Yes. My cousins tell me you have been looking for some chests that were recently stolen?'

'Argh. Yes. Yes, that's right,' came the reply from Officer Nathryn, who tried his best to not look nervous. There was a long silence.

Phæ'enor realised she was still standing up and made her way over to sit on the small pouffe by the fireplace, picking up a teacup as she passed. Officer Nathryn, having also remained standing, awkwardly made his way over to sit next to Prince Taigor.

'Are you both here to interrogate me again?' asked Phæ'enor.

'Ah, no,' said Officer Nathryn looking worried.

'To arrest me then? Or take me to the madhouse?' asked Phæ'enor.

'No. Why would we do that?' replied Officer Nathryn.

'Well because you seem extremely nervous. Like you're about to do something that you have no choice to but will regret,' she said looking back at the two men.

'Ha,' laughed Prince Taigor, 'you might say that.' He was clearly enjoying Officer Nathryn's uncomfortable address to Phæ'enor.

'No. In fact, about that day, at The Grand Tea Rooms. I just wanted to come by and say how much I could see that you had enjoyed the tropical plants and animals,' said Officer Nathryn, stumbling over his words slightly but still smiling.

At this Phæ'enor, her grandmother and her mother looked over their tea cups at each other, little fingers sticking out and eyebrows raised at Officer Nathryn's strange behaviour. Prince Taigor likewise was rubbing his chin trying to take the smile off his own face. There was silence again. You came here to tell me something I already know, thought Phæ'enor. This man gets stranger and stranger by the minute. Officer Nathryn then continued:

'Then I thought of how you liked the Green Rooms so much, you might also like to see the beauty beyond Benaghar's walls, see the rest of Aebra. Has anybody told you about what is beyond our city walls?'

'No. They haven't!' interjected Mrs Doven, slamming her tea cup and saucer down on the table before Phæ'enor could reply. The politeness had worn off her mother and she did not look pleased. Mrs Jemin had spilt her tea, startled by her daughter-in-law's outburst.

'Hmmm. I thought that you had come from the other side of the wall Mrs Doven? And I believe it was marriage that brought you here?' asked Officer Nathryn.

Mrs Doven picked her tea up again and drank deeply, glaring back at him, not responding. Phæ'enor's grandmother nervously glanced sideways at her daughter-in-law. A chill seemed to fill the room.

'What has that got to do with going to the other side of the city wall?' asked Phæ'enor.

'Because that is one of the only ways you are allowed to,' said Prince Taigor, setting his tea down. 'If you come from the other side of the city walls, then naturally you have access to the rest of the country, unless of course you marry someone within the city walls.' He inclined his head in the direction of Mrs Doven. 'But then you are automatically banned from going back through, unless you are with your husband of course…'

'What about the husband, can he go through without his wife?' asked Phæ'enor smirking.

'Well, yes, of course,' said Prince Taigor.

Phæ'enor snorted, 'What a surprise! And what is the third one?'

'If you are of royal blood you can pretty much go anywhere in Aebra,' said Prince Taigor smiling.

'Well, if that is the case then I can't go to the other side of the wall. I'm certainly not getting married just so I can. Why are you telling me this anyway?' she asked, picking up her tea again.

BANG!

They all jumped. There seemed to be a bit of commotion outside in the hallway. Phæ'enor got up and rushed to the door. On the other side lay a flustered looking Mr Deke and the royal footman who had accompanied Prince Taigor and Officer Nathryn.

'Your Royal Highness, I'm very sorry,' came the reply of the latter as he helped Mr Deke up.

He bowed his head when he saw Phæ'enor and the others emerge from the sitting room.

'What has happened?' asked Prince Taigor.

'Well, your highness,' came the reply of Mr Deke, now back up on his feet, 'I was about to go through that door into the kitchen and I collided with your footman and…'

'It was you upstairs, wasn't it?' demanded Phæ'enor, looking at the boy. 'Your man was trying the doors upstairs,' said Phæ'enor to Prince Taigor.

She got no reply from the royal footman who looked shocked, or was it guilt from being found out?

'Phæ'enor dear, please…' said Mrs Doven, pleading for her daughter to be quiet. Phæ'enor turned to Prince Taigor.

'Why are you getting your footman to look through the house? Trying the doors, snooping around? Whatever it is you think I have, or if you think I'm trying to hide something then why don't you just ask?'

'That's a very strange accusation to make,' said Prince Taigor.

They all looked at Phæ'enor, staring at her like they had back in The Grand Tea Rooms, like she was mad.

'I've had enough. I'm going to my rooms,' she snapped.

Phæ'enor, sick of them judging her and accusing her of lying, turned and stormed up the stairs and slammed her bedroom door behind her; furious at being caged, at being labelled mad, and still angry she was in Benaghar in the first place.

She heard the front door open. Phæ'enor got up, hurriedly moved out of her rooms and to the top floor landing window. She glanced out. But not too far or they might see her. As she watched them walk away she heard the laughter of Prince Taigor.

'Don't worry. You have my blessing. But the girl is mad. You'll need a lot of luck with that one.'

He clapped his hand on Officer Nathryn's shoulder and laughed out even louder.

***

That evening Phæ'enor couldn't eat she was so frustrated. When she went to bed she stayed up late, into the early hours of the next day. She finally fell asleep, restless and dreaming of walking the house bare footed in her nightgown. She kept trying not to make any noise but sounded heavy footed every time she put her feet down. Then she kept trying to open all the doors in the house but none of them would work. She tried one and it just kept rattling no matter which way she turned it. It rattled and rattled … and then she realised she was no longer asleep. The rattle of the door handle was real. But it wasn't coming from outside. The rattling was coming from inside her room. She could hear small steps.

'Shit,' came a muffled voice and a loud clunk on the bedroom floor.

Not wanting to but feeling like she had no choice, Phæ'enor slowly opened her eyes. She was lying in her bed, in the dark. The light had gone out in her room, or had someone put it out? The noise of rattling continued. It was coming from the passageway that led from the main area of her bedroom to the landing. She slowly peered around the corner, praying that her bed would not creak as she leaned gently over. At the end of the passageway was someone tall, their back to her. It must have been the darkness, but they seemed to be dressed in black. Their hand, which was covered, was trying to open the door. Phæ'enor slowly moved off the bed and headed for the tall metal candleholder on the dark wooden table. Creeping up slowly behind the figure, she raised the candleholder high above their head. But suddenly the figure turned. They pushed Phæ'enor to the floor, then slammed into the door finally opening it, and ran. Phæ'enor could hear them running down the stairs; she got up and chased after them screaming!

'There's someone in the house, there's someone in the house!'

She could see other doors open as she flung herself down the stairs after the intruder. But it was too late. There was a clash of glass smashing against the floor. They had thrown the small side table in the hallway through the glass window at the front of the house and escaped down the street.

Phæ'enor, having run down after them stood breathless outside, holding onto the railings of the square. Her mother and the house servants had caught up with her; Mr Deke following in pursuit of the intruder. Phæ'enor watched as she saw them disappear down the cobbled streets. Mr Deke, no longer young enough to continue, had stopped and bent low with his hands on his knees. It was then that she saw them again; silhouettes of shabby looking creatures, or was it people, running across the rooftops of Grand Alboreum Circus in the direction of the visitor in the night? She turned to her mother, breathless, and said:

'I've had quite enough of visitors,' Mother. Quite enough.'

Chapter Seven

Polstor & Polstor

The following day saw No 9 Grand Alboreum Circus swarming with city guards. They came, and they went throughout the whole morning, traipsing through each room, turning everything upside down and never putting anything back. The house staff were frantically trying to pick up after them whilst Phæ'enor's grandmother was furious!

'How did he get in here, and where from? The door was locked!' screamed Mrs Jemin, before shouting at the nearest guard, 'He didn't bloody take anything, so you can stop moving that furniture and you can bloody well put it back! You're worse than him! PUT IT BACK!' The guard looked like he had been told off by his own mother. Phæ'enor's grandmother snatched the ornament in his arms, 'There is no point! No point in taking that for examination, it's my husband's ashes!' she cried. Phæ'enor saw her grandmother's eyes well up and her bottom lip shake as she hugged it to her chest before putting it back on the mantel-piece in the sitting room. She was not taking the intrusion very well at all.

'And you can leave that as well,' she continued, rushing out into the hallway after another city guard. The house was in disarray and it all seemed wrong. The guards did not care if the inhabitants of No 9 Grand Alboreum Circus were okay, if they had been hurt or frightened. It was as though they weren't looking for the clues the intruder may have left but looking for something else instead. They finally gave up when Officer Nathryn appeared, screaming orders at them to leave until he was red in the face.

'I'm very sorry Mrs Jemin,' he said to Phæ'enor's grandmother, 'I hope you are okay? Good. Forgive me but I must get back to the garrisons.' And with that he left leaving Master Rasia, who had returned to the house early in the morning, keeping watch over the house again. The grey cat could be seen playing in the flower beds of the green beyond.

Meanwhile Mrs Doven was to be found in the sitting room at the small writing desk on the far wall. With her back to the room, she had been seated there for over an hour; silent and frantically writing, oblivious to what was going on around her. Phæ'enor thought she was writing to her father, and not for the first time since they had arrived in Benaghar, but this time had been different. She no longer looked concerned, worried even; she was angry. Silently angry and it showed in her stiff, tight lipped and cool eyed countenance. Phæ'enor and her grandmother had hardly had a word out of her this morning. Instead, Phæ'enor had taken over the responsibility of the household staff; making sure things were in place, and breakfast was on the table, that the staff had also eaten. That was until the city guards had shown up. Phæ'enor tried to get her mother's attention a few times:

'Mother? Who are you writing to?' Silence.

'Is it father? Has he written lately?' Silence.

'Would you like some tea, Mother?' Silence.

'Is it okay if I go and trace the intruder's steps across the city by myself? Alone and undefended?' Silence.

Now the guards had gone, nothing had changed. She was still frantically writing away. Phæ'enor turned to leave the room and see if she could assist the household staff instead when she stopped in her tracks, her mother having suddenly called out to her.

'Phæ'enor, dear, please ask Master Rasia to fetch us a carriage. Tell him to meet us back here in approximately one hour.' Phæ'enor looked at her mother who had not turned around and was still writing. 'We are going to Newtown, then the marketplace if he asks, and I suppose he shall have to come with us. Be quick about it Phæ'enor.'

'What about grandmother, is she to stay here on her own?'

Mrs Doven sighed, 'Tell Master Rasia to pick your cousins up on the way and bring them back here. They can keep her company.'

'Simi and Mimi are not really the best people to take care of…'

'Just do as I ask, Phæ'enor, please!' said Mrs Doven. She had stopped writing, and had tilted her head back, rubbing her neck. She sounded tired.

Phæ'enor looked at the back of her mother's head, shook her own and went to find Master Rasia. At first, he refused, also concerned for Mrs Jemin. But Phæ'enor had insisted he fetch the carriage and that Simi and Mimi, and the household staff, would keep an eye on her grandmother.

***

The carriage arrived at No 9 Grand Alboreum Circus just under an hour. It was square fronted and drawn by four black horses. Master Rasia was waiting up in the front with the driver but jumped down to open the carriage door. Simi and Mimi got out, and for once did not ask questions. They kissed their aunt on the cheek, held Phæ'enor tightly, then strolled into the house dramatically, ready to do their duty. Mrs Doven handed Master Rasia a small calling card before joining Phæ'enor in the back. As Master Rasia closed the carriage door shut he checked what was written on the card before putting it into his top pocket. He then lent in.

'I suggest that you stay as hidden as possible. Especially you Miss Doven, what with last night's events, and those of the past. Where we are going will only make the people gossip more.'

'We are only going to the marketplace,' laughed Phæ'enor. He did not need to be so concerned.

Master Rasia looked at Mrs Doven instead, with a less than impressed look on his face before he left to join the driver.

'Mother? What does Master Rasia mean when he said, "where we are going." We're not going to the marketplace, are we?'

A resilient and stubborn look had fallen upon Mrs Doven's face. She sat, straight backed, and refused to meet her daughter's eyes.

'Where to Ma'am?' asked the driver.

'Straight to Newtown, the north-west corner, please,' said Mrs Doven, doing her cloak up and slipping her gloves on. It had turned quite cold. Even Phæ'enor had given into finally wearing long dresses and tall eyelet boots which happily concealed very thick and warm stockings. Her dirty wax travelling cloak buried her and kept her warm.

It took just over an hour to reach Newtown but all that time she and her mother spoke not one word to each other. Phæ'enor could see her mother was lost in her own thoughts, and in her state of anger, it was best not to disturb her.

Instead she looked out of the window frowning and kept to her own thoughts as to why her mother had wanted to come to the marketplace after what had happened last night. There had been an intruder in the house, in her daughter's bedroom, but instead of calming grandmother's nerves, or checking on the staff, she had set to writing letters. Even after they had all come back into the house, Mr Deke having gone to fetch the city guards, her mother had gone straight to her bedroom. When Phæ'enor had passed the door it was ajar, and she could see her mother hastily writing a letter. When Mr Deke had returned, tired and cold, she sent him straight back out again with it.

In the morning as Phæ'enor set about checking on the staff, the young maid Florin, had come up to her.

'Miss, I found this at the bottom of the garden stairs that leads from the kitchen.' She handed her a small black envelope. Gold writing simply said "Mrs Valc'easa Doven". And after handing this over to her mother Phæ'enor and her grandmother had not heard a peep out of her all morning.

Phæ'enor remained hidden in the darkness of the carriage, her father's words rang out in her head again, "keep your head down

… try not to attract unwanted attention…" How disappointed he would be now to know that the exact opposite had occurred, and it had only got worse.

'Thank you,' cried Mrs Doven, 'you can stop here.'

As the carriage came to a halt Phæ'enor realised they were back in the marketplace but not amongst the stalls. They seemed to have pulled up near some small and closely grouped shops. The market stalls were off to the right in the distance, busy with the bustle of people. But these shops were quiet. A few people passed, a few people went in. But not as many as she could see thronging the stalls of the marketplace.

'Wait for us here, please.' Phæ'enor heard her mother say to the driver as they got out.

She stepped out of the carriage but hurried after her mother upon the road and onto the pavement. Master Rasia followed behind, a little distance apart. They passed one shop whose windows were made up of different colours, optics and sizes. It looked like a disorganised jigsaw to Phæ'enor. There seemed to be all sorts of stained pieces of glass, bottles and glasses. The sign above the shop read "The Glass Makers". I suppose that was an obvious one, thought Phæ'enor. There was another shop, "The Hat Maker", with various small and large hats, bonnets and caps displayed in the window. "The Shoemakers", with their windows adorned with a puppet shiner, shining shoes, and a set of shoes dancing on the strings they were attached to. Finally, at the end of the row was a very large double windowed shop. But the windows were so dirty that no-one could possibly see through the grime to tell what it sold, and the sign above gave no clue as to what they stocked either. In very weathered gold and bold writing, against a black-board it read:

"Polstor & Polstor"

'Come along Phæ'enor,' came her mother's voice again.

Phæ'enor was a little surprised to see her mother walk through the little iron gate and up the path to the shop's door. She made after her, still wondering as to what they sold. The pathway of broken paving stones, covered in weeds and unkempt flowerbeds either side, did not put Phæ'enor's guessing to an end. As they approached the door, instead of just walking straight in, Phæ'enor's mother took hold of the door knocker above which consisted of two large bronze faces, adorned with dramatic curly hair squashed down by very tall hats. Mrs Doven did not knock once.

'Tap-tap,' pause. 'Tap-tap-tap-tap,' a longer pause, 'Tap!'

There was silence. Mrs Doven looked around at Phæ'enor and Master Rasia, giving a small but impatient smile. She then scanned the horizon before turning back to face the door. Phæ'enor had a suspicion that they were not supposed to be there, or it was not the place people came to. At least not in the daylight. She, in turn looked at Master Rasia for a clue but he was facing the road, looking left and right. Even the driver looked nervous.

'Mother, are we meant to be here?' Phæ'enor asked over her shoulder, also now watching the street. Mrs Doven did not reply and Phæ'enor started to worry but didn't know why. Suddenly, Phæ'enor heard a chiming sound. It was getting louder, like small bells rattling along. She turned her head in the direction she thought it was coming from and caught Master Rasia performing the same action. But then the noise stopped and out of nowhere appeared the big black bird in the sky. Phæ'enor watched as it flew closer and closer towards them. Master Rasia was also watching it.

Bang! Bang! Crash! Crash!

Came the noises from within the shop. The bird was now closer. Even Mrs Doven watched it fly directly towards the three of them.

BANG!

Silence.

Click!

Click!

Click-click! came the sounds from within, clearer and with haste. The bird seemed to be getting faster, sweeping lower as it flew towards them.

Whoosh!

The air behind them moved like a vacuum as the big black door to the shop swung open.

'Quickly, come quickly!' shouted a small and agitated voice. Master Rasia swung around and pulled Phæ'enor in quickly after Mrs Doven, only turning back to slam the door shut before the bird came into land.

***

Everything was pitch black inside the shop. At least Phæ'enor presumed they were in a shop.

'Bloody birds!' spat the sharp little voice. 'You never know who they belong to, who they report back to! They are only bad luck, I tell you. Only bad luck.' There was shuffling and more clinking ahead. 'Here,' the voice said, but this time a little glow of light appeared. A lamp lit in mid-air but obviously held by someone who had started to move away. 'Come on, follow me.' All three of them moved after the lamp. Bumping into objects and tripping. 'Can't you watch where you are going?' The sharp little voice said again. 'Try not to touch anything! Just a little way ahead there will be a ladder.'

As the light flickered up ahead Phæ'enor glimpsed flashes of shiny objects, metal and glass and several suits of armour lining the walls; large and little wooden crates stocked up high in various piles; mechanical looking objects. The shop seemed to go back a long way but did not look like it sold any of its stock, the vast amounts of it left hardly any space for shoppers to come in and browse. What all the rest of the bits 'n' bobs were Phæ'enor could not clearly make out.

'Right this way.' They had come to a stop; at the back of the shop, or in the middle, they couldn't tell. Whoever was holding the lamp placed it down on the floor and opened a small trap door in the floor. As they did so, light flooded the room and Phæ'enor caught sight of one the most bizarre looking people she had ever seen. He was short, slim and well-dressed, wearing a black tailored tailcoat, black buttons, long white socks over the top of them and smart black ankle boots. But it was his hair and features that struck Phæ'enor the most. He had multi-coloured hair! Like the colours of the rainbow all jumbled up in a mass of curls. His head looked a little too large for his body; pale, almost white, with a big gappy toothed smile, that spread from eye to eye. There was also something different about his eyes. They were very large with two different coloured irises. One was bright blue and piercing, the other a resplendent green.

'What are you looking at girl?' asked the man, seeing Phæ'enor gawping at him. 'Climb down then!'

'Err … er … yes, of course,' she stuttered.

Phæ'enor moved forward, glanced down at the small man and turned around so that her back faced the entrance to the trap door. The small man held out his hand for her to take. Phæ'enor did so with a polite smile before lowering her left leg, then her right onto the first step of a wooden ladder below, withdrawing her grip from the man's once she was sufficiently down enough on the ladder to be able to hold onto the sides of it instead. It was still dark, but she could see a pin prick of light at the bottom. She was moving down a long brick vertical shaft, deep beneath the city streets. Above, Mrs Doven and Master Rasia and finally the small man followed suit. Three or four meters before the end of the descent Phæ'enor could see a well-lit floor, a mixture of wooden boards and stone.

As she stepped off the ladder, Phæ'enor wiped the dirt from it off her dress skirt. Brushing her hands together to be rid of the rest she looked up. They had climbed down into a long and brightly lit room. It was more like a large and endless hallway. There were shelves and rows full of more shiny objects, none of which seemed to have any order to it. Clocks, statues, tiny boxes, jewellery, stuffed animals, rolls of carpet, medals, miniature ships, cooking pans, hats, tables, bathtubs, maps, watches, books and more books. It went on and on everywhere she looked. She turned about in wonder.

'CAN I HELP YOU?'

'Argh!' screamed Phæ'enor. The little, multi-colour haired man was now in front of her? She turned quickly, looking up the ladder. Her mother had nearly reached the bottom and she could see Master Rasia up ahead of her, and the little man, as far as she could tell, was still up ahead of him. She turned back to the little man on the ground in front of her.

'How did you get passed them and down here so quickly?' she asked.

'Because I am Archä, Miss Phæ'enor Doven,' he said, peering up into her face, eyes slightly squinting into hers, his hand clasped but his fingers drumming a tune to each other. Phæ'enor did not know what the little man meant by "Archä" but it did not explain why he had got down the ladder so quickly. Confused she turned back to look at the ladder. Mrs Doven, now having also stepped off, was looking at the little man on the ground and then back up the shaft. Master Rasia however was quite unconfused and calm.

'Archä,' he said, nodding.

'Master Rasia,' replied the little man on the ground.

'So, you must be Mëdez,' said Mrs Doven looking at the other little man who had showed them into the shop.

'Yes, I am Mrs Doven,' replied Mëdez, as he stepped off the ladder. He smiled, bowed his hat to her and then suddenly threw himself at her feet and started kissing her shoes. He then jumped back up and shouted, 'Welcome! Welcome! Welcome to Archä and Mëdez! Us! Our little shop,' he finished, before he scarpered off behind the counter in the near distance. Phæ'enor, wide-eyed at Mëdez's little performance, returned her gaze back to the little man Archä. He was mirroring her every move. As she narrowed her eyes, he narrowed his, as she raised her eyebrows at him for copying her, he did the same in return. She put her hand on her hips annoyed, he followed suit again.

'Eh hem … excuse me,' said Mrs Doven, 'I'm sorry to disrupt this little show but we did not come all this way to muck around, Archä?'

'Yes, yes yeeees,' replied Archä, looking Phæ'enor up and down curiously, 'why don't you all follow me. MËDEZ! hurry up!' he shouted, clapping his hand to prompt his fellow little man to move on.

'It's over here,' replied a muffled voice from behind the counter.

'NO! No, it is not!' said Archä, spinning back around and talking as though he was addressing the room at large. 'You can stop stuffing your face with those tarts and get moving! You,' he said pointing at the three of them, 'follow me.'

He quickly grabbed the lantern off the floor and sped off down the hallway. Phæ'enor thought he moved fast for a small man with such small legs and feet to carry him. They passed door after doors, corridor after corridor, with Archä all the time muttering to himself, his head turning this way and that, both hands in the air moving from side to side as his fingers danced to some invisible soundless tune. It looked like he was calculating his steps.

'Aargh, ha! Here we are!' said Archä knowingly. He raised his eyebrows at them before pulling a large and rustling jumble of keys out of his pocket. He picked a small one and opened the door in front of him. They passed through a short narrow corridor which opened into a high-ceilinged, circular room with books lining the walls and ascending into the dark. It was an underground library and full of far more books than Phæ'enor imagined existed. Archä rushed over to a tall ladder and climbed it before jumping off onto a narrow balcony and hopping onto another ladder into the darkness above.

'Mother,' said Phæ'enor quietly, 'why are we here?'

'I think that you need to gain some more knowledge of Benaghar. Whilst you are here you should receive a broader education. I'm aware that your official education has now come to an end, however that is no excuse to remain in the dark about the practicalities, social and wider subjects.' She did not look at Phæ'enor the whole time she spoke.

Phæ'enor was none the wiser as to what her mother meant. Her clipped tones did not help.

'So, tell me have any of you figured out why Miss Phæ'enor here fainted in The Grand Tea Rooms?' shouted Archä from above, now fingering the books in front of him. All three of them stared up. What a weird question to ask thought Phæ'enor.

'Don't say anything,' said Master Rasia in a whisper.

'Keeping things from us, are you?' said Mëdez. All three jumped to see him standing behind them. Smiling and with a tray full of tea cups, a large pot of tea and an assortment of colourful biscuits.

'What? Did you say they are keeping things from us?' shouted Archä.

'Can you both hear everything?' demanded Phæ'enor.

'No,' said Mëdez, walking between Phæ'enor and Master Rasia, the tea tray rattling as he went, 'just the things you don't want to tell us.' He turned his head and winked at Phæ'enor before setting the tray on a small round wooden table in the centre of the room. Archä had now started to throw books down from the shelves, still talking to himself:

'That's the one … and … yes … I'll have that one to…'

Mëdez looked up at Archä then turned his attention to the teapot, pouring the tea for his guests. Mrs Doven and Master Rasia took their tea and drank, Phæ'enor did not.

'You know it's rude not to drink your host's offerings,' said Mëdez, raising an eyebrow over his teacup and saucer. He rolled his eyes, 'We're not going to poison you. But on that note, why did you faint, see visions, etcetera?'

'I don't know, I didn't realise we were here to talk about that!' barked Phæ'enor back, a little too loudly.

'Tut, tut, tut, Mrs Doven. Did you not inform your daughter here the reason for your visit to our shop?' smiled Mëdez, clearly enjoying Phæ'enor's irritations.

'I'm here to get a wider education! Not to be asked more silly questions,' snapped Phæ'enor.

'And in that you are correct,' said Archä, feet now firmly back on the ground. He slammed a pile of books onto the table making the tea cups spill their contents; using the cuff of his jacket he wiped the drops off the books but did not wipe the table.

Phæ'enor looked at the top of the first book. It read "A Woman's Education: How to be beautiful and still be a good house wife". She read the spines of the others, a growing distaste in her mouth developing.

'How to be a lady, by a Mr Peacock.'

'Etiquette: A lady in waiting.'

'The food of love: what not to cook, and what to cook, to get a husband.'

Phæ'enor looked up at her mother and the two little men.

'Are you seriously expecting me to read this? For my wider education?' she added sarcastically.

'Why, yes. How else are you going to get Officer Nathryn to marry you?' said Archä and Mëdez together. Master Rasia nearly choked on his tea trying not to laugh. Phæ'enor took to glaring at him again.

'Why is everyone so obsessed with marriage? With Officer Nathryn? Mother, please can we just go?' The two little men were giggling to themselves. 'I don't see why you two are so pleased with yourselves!'

'Oh, Phæ'enor!' said Mëdez. 'We are only teasing you, from what we have heard about on the streets.'

'And from our sources,' they said together again.

Archä and Mëdez picked up their tea cups and saucers at the same time, slurped on their tea, and intently watched Phæ'enor pick hers up ready to drink. But she stopped and instead asked, 'You're twins, aren't you? Identical, except for your eyes.'

'Ugh,' they sighed together dramatically, sloshing their tea everywhere as they slumped in their chairs. Archä and Mëdez looked at each other and caught sight of one another's drenched shirts, and replied, 'What ever gave it away?' both succumbing to fits of laughter. They only stopped when they caught sight of the bored and unimpressed look on Master Rasia's face.

'We are brothers. Twins. And yes, our eye colour is swapped around,' said Archä in a bored voice.

'You're bloody Harqs! That's what you are!' said Master Rasia. 'It means they are not to be trusted,' he said at the confused look from Phæ'enor.

'Oh, how rude! How many times have we helped you out Ras-i-aar,' snapped Mëdcz.

'Especially all that business with your brother,' said Archä drawlingly.

'Shut-up!' snapped Master Rasia. He fell silent.

'So, is that what you do?' asked Phæ'enor, looking between Master Rasia and the twins. 'You help people out who are in trouble?' They smiled and nodded in reply. That explains the odd assortments of pilfering they had stocked up, thought Phæ'enor. 'But I'm not in trouble, and hardly think these books would help me out of it if I were,' said Phæ'enor, casting more dirty looks at the books on women's etiquette to get a husband.

'Well, not yet you're not,' said Archä, 'but at some point, you may need our help. So, your mother here, dear Mrs Doven, decided to introduce you to us.'

Master Rasia looked on at Mrs Doven, disbelief written all over his face and sat back shaking his head disapprovingly.

'Against your father's wishes no doubt,' chipped in Mëdez, talking into his tea. 'In the meantime, these books will keep you out of trouble. You have a lot of reading to be getting on with.'

Phæ'enor looked at her mother enquiringly. Had she gone behind her father's back in contacting the twins? Was that the reason why she had the feeling they were not meant to be here? It would explain her frantic letter writing in the early hours of the morning.

'I'd watch what they give you, including those books,' said Master Rasia.

'How do you mean?' asked Phæ'enor.

'Archä and Mëdez here say they will help you out, but ultimately they are Harqs, which only means you'll end up dabbling in something illegal. They are untrustworthy,' said Master Rasia.

'Oh, how dare you. We are so offended by your remarks, Master Rasia,' said Archä and Mëdez, dramatically swooning again. They stopped and smiled their big gapped toothed smiles at Master Rasia and Phæ'enor.

'Great, so we are now keeping company with criminals,' said Phæ'enor, now even more dispirited.

'The very best!' said Archä and Mëdez together.

'I think O'scilla Juur would have something to say about that,' said Master Rasia darkly.

'Ha! That man is an absolute joke,' said Mëdez.

'Yes, he has nothing on us,' smiled Archä menacingly.

'Mother let's go,' said Phæ'enor.

'You can't go yet, you haven't drunk your tea,' said Mëdez. 'Ow!'

Archä had whacked him in the chest. He rubbed it, then the two of them, all smiles again, raised their teacups ready to drink. Phæ'enor was also about to drink, but she had a strange feeling that something was not right. She stared at the two men, their bizarre behaviour and their greedy eyes staring at her over their teacups. She looked down at her own teacup. It was a blue painted china with a gold rim. Exactly the same as the teacup she had used in The Grand Tea Rooms. She slammed it down on the table.

'Why would you do that?' demanded Phæ'enor.

'What?' asked Mrs Doven. 'What have they done?'

'It's a copy of the teacup I drank from at The Grand Tea Rooms.'

'Oh, no. We didn't copy it, Miss Doven. We acquired the exact one. It's the same cup. For our collection of course,' said Archä.

'After we heard what had happened, we just had to have it, we were so curious as to why you reacted to it,' said Mëdez.

'And knowing you would be here today we thought, well, it would bring back some memories,' said Archä. The pair laughed out loud.

'You're both sick in the head,' said Master Rasia. 'Let's go Mrs Doven. You got what you came for. Grab the books, we need to be heading back.'

All three got up and walked out of the circular library, through the narrow passageway and out through the hallway toward the ladder. All the while they could hear the two brothers, cackling with laughter. However, when they reached the dark room and were nearly at the entrance to the shop, Archä suddenly appeared behind them, breathless.

'Wait, wait, you can't just leave!' He scuttled to the door, unlocked the many bolts and unhooked the many chains, before

119

looking out. 'Right, you first Mrs Doven.' She moved out into the light and out of the shop. 'And you can go now too, Master Rasia.'

'I'd rather let Miss ... argh!'

Archä shoved Master Rasia hard in the chest and out through the door, slamming it shut. Phæ'enor was still inside.

'Let me out!' she said alarmed.

'Yes, yes, but not until I give you this.'

There was silence. No banging of doors or Master Rasia to come and get her.

Archä pulled a box from his inside jacket pocket, took Phæ'enor's arm and placed it in her hand, 'Take this and don't tell anyone, including those two,' he said motioning to the door. 'Now you can go. And if they ask, I was telling you about your invitation to the palace tomorrow.'

'What invitation?' asked a confused Phæ'enor.

But before she got an answer Archä opened the door and pushed her out too. There were many turns of keys and sliding of bolts behind her. Phæ'enor adjusted her eyes to the light, slipping the box into the inside pocket of her travelling cloak before returning to the carriage where Master Rasia and her mother waited, looking relieved to see her. She quickly looked about as they got back into the carriage. The bird had disappeared and there was no sound of little bells.

Chapter Eight

An Invitation to the Palace

It appeared Archä and Mëdez knew a lot more about the goings on within Benaghar, and not just the information reported in the papers. Along with going out of their way to acquire the blue and white china tea cup from The Grand Tea Rooms, they wanted to know more by sneakily trying to see if Phæ'enor would have another reaction to it. They also knew about the invitation to the palace before she or her mother did. When Phæ'enor and Mrs Doven arrived back from Polstor & Polstor, in the pouring rain, Mr Deke the footman informed Mrs Doven, 'A very important looking envelope is on the sitting room desk for you, Ma'am.'

It turned out to be an invitation to a small gathering at the palace, held by Lady Quenna Amia the following evening, and the day had now come for Phæ'enor, her mother and grandmother to attend.

Phæ'enor was pushed from dressmaker to dressmaker that very morning and was not allowed to return home until she came away with something.

'You must be wearing silk and it must stand out!' decided her grandmother. 'No grandchild of mine is to look a pauper in front of these crown stealing, money grabbing royals!'

'If you are not keen on them grandmother, then why are we going in the first place?'

'Huh. We are not going because I want to. We are going because that woman, and soon to be queen, has taken a shine to you. It would not do your father any favours if we decided not to go. We have no excuse,' said her grandmother begrudgingly, 'I'd much rather have dinner at home, sit by the fire and read a good book,' she finished.

Hmm – I've never seen you read a book, thought Phæ'enor, only gossip and rumours in the papers. That, and moaning all night long about anyone and anything. However, Phæ'enor agreed with her grandmother; she did not want to go either. Not after Lady Amia's reaction to her episode in The Grand Tea Rooms and her patronising manner; if she had taken a shine to Phæ'enor those feelings were surely no longer there. But on the other hand, it would not only be a nice break from just her grandmother's company; she was curious to see the inside of the palace. It was beautiful and centrally placed, and the turrets could be seen from almost every corner of the city. She was glad that she had been given the opportunity to see inside. If that meant pretending to care in the future queen's company, then she was happy to play the part.

In the end, and after several hours of traipsing around the shops, Phæ'enor came away with a golden, white silk dress. It was plain in pattern, and off the shoulder, but nice and warm for an evening indoors. The weather had turned even colder, with fog rolling in from the sea, and she did not fancy travelling in the carriage at night in a thin dress. This time the dress was down to the ground, and she would borrow one of her cousin's cloaks; Mimi's thick velvet and dusky blue one. She had to wear a ridiculous hair piece with white pearls and flowers but at least she could keep it covered with the hood of the cloak whilst they were outside.

***

Phæ'enor, Mrs Doven and Mrs Jemin, along with Master Rasia still on guard duties, arrived promptly at the palace at six in the evening. They had taken a stately carriage, black in colour with golden leafed patterns embossed on the wood and satin inside, sent for them by Prince Taigor, over the Benraeli Bridge, and then King Vane's Bridge. This took them over the River Nebben to the island in the middle, where the palace turrets dominated the skyline above. They all shone brightly into the night, apart from the south tower. For some strange reason it was in complete darkness.

Phæ'enor stepped down. They had arrived at the bottom of some very wide stone steps that ascended to a large wooden door, adorned with intricate ironmongery, vines and leaves, twisting their way across. Standing in front of them was a lone man, dressed in palace attire. Phæ'enor assumed it to be just one of their footmen waiting to take them inside. However, as they drew near she heard Master Rasia speak under his breath, displeased: 'Great.'

It was not just any palace footman, it was Prince Taigor's footman. The tall pale boy with pale hair. He descended the palace stairs and made his way to the carriage.

'Welcome, Mrs Jemin, Mrs Doven, Miss Phæ'enor Doven, and of course Master Rasia,' he said.

His voice was much deeper and commanding for someone who looked so young. He seemed disinterested in his duty to greet them, displeased at seeing Master Rasia. Although it was clear that the feeling was mutual between them.

As they entered through the large double wooden doors Phæ'enor could not help but stare in wonder. The hallway was sort of round but with square edges to the ceiling. It looked as though they had entered a gigantic tree. Delicate, intricate flowers, which had been carved into the wood, travelled across the walls. Scenes of hunting, wild boars, horses and beautiful birds were carved into the wood. The edges of it cascaded down to meet the ground, elegantly disappearing into the wooden floor.

More scenes of hunting prevailed beneath their feet but the ceiling was a complete contrast. It was an opaque bright green, curved glass dome.

'Phæ'enor,' whispered Mrs Doven, 'come along.'

Still gazing, she followed them through a long hallway, up three flights of stairs, through another long passageway that was decorated in similar style to the entrance hall until they came to a long glass walkway. It was open to the elements, and they could see down into the dark grounds below.

'We are still in the outer defence wall of the palace,' advised Prince Taigor's footman.

'It's a bit daft to be having glass as part of the defence shield isn't it?' asked Mrs Jemin.

'On the contrary, Mrs Jemin,' this is Dihelray glass from the Pink Mountains. It can withstand a lot. Bar intense heat.'

'What about the wood? It looks like it moves, like it's still alive?' asked Phæ'enor.

'That's because it is from the Eckera tree.' Phæ'enor saw her mother and Master Rasia look on in wonder. 'The Eckera, or The Tree of Life as others know it. One king managed to obtain a seed from the tree and planted it in the outer defence. It is strong and ever moving. It protects and heals,' said the footman.

However, the intricate, flowing lines, wooden motifs and story boards disappeared as they walked out of the curved glass walkway. It was clear to Phæ'enor they had entered another layer of the palace defence. This time it was made of bright white stone, not dissimilar to that of the houses of Grand Town, yet this one seemed to sparkle as they moved through. It was a show of battle and defence, for here this stone fortress was lined with armour, golden suits and spears. Phæ'enor moved to touch one but her mother pulled her back onto the red carpet that hugged the middle of the floor.

'Don't touch anything,' she said quietly.

Displays of arrows, guns, bayonets, bows and chainmail all adorned the walls but there also seemed to be another sort of armour on display; armour that did not belong to the Benagharian army. Wooden helmets, wooden spears and tips, masks and dried grass body armour to other worldly designs of thin metalled and triangular shaped chainmail over black cotton garments.

They went up some stone steps only to enter another level. This time the walls and floors matched the rest of the city. Golden stone gleamed back at them from everywhere. But instead of armour, or flowers and hunting scenes made of wood the whole floor seemed to be adorned with the hunts' prey. Step after step, dead and stuffed animals stood snarling; their heads and antlers adorning the walls. But what shocked Phæ'enor most of all was the many stuffed leopards, wildcats and cheetahs. There was even a rare white tiger, surrounded by three white tiger cubs. As they turned another corner she gasped. Adorning the walls of a large wide hallway were wings, sets of them, but they did not look like they belonged to any birds that Phæ'enor had seen or heard about before. These were giant wings. They looked as though they should belong to the Flying Demons of The Night that children, including Phæ'enor, were taught about at school:

"Don't stay out late at night or the winged monsters will get you!" they would say or, "If you don't eat your dinner you'll grow wings that will take you away into the sky, never for you to return to your family. They will take you up so high then turn in on you, suffocate you until your eyes close forever, as your body falls back into the abyss below."

Phæ'enor felt shivers down her spine. Why they told children those stories was beyond her. Evil teachers.

'They are not real, the wings,' said the young footman, 'they are created from many small bird wings. An illusion; I believe it was to scare the royal children centuries ago, to stop them coming onto this floor.'

'Why this floor?' asked Phæ'enor.

'Because this is the floor for adults only,' he smirked, looking back at Phæ'enor over his shoulder. Well then, why are you on this floor? thought Phæ'enor. She did not like the footman, he was too cocky and full of himself. He stopped and then turned to face them fully. 'We are here.' At this he pushed open a large double wooden door to their right.

'Your Royal Highness, Officers, Ladies and Gentlemen I present to you Mrs Jemin, Mrs Doven, Miss Phæ'enor Doven and Master Rasia.'

They walked through into a high ceilinged, amber and gold room. The white stone appeared in flecks but for the most part the walls looked to have been painted in golden leaf, interjected with amber stones. Looking down at their feet another mural of hunting, against a backdrop of blue sky, but in fact it was a large mirrored floor reflecting the ceiling above. Arrows from huntsmen flew across the scene. They were hiding in the clouds, being shot at by winged beings, their fangs barred and the men fleeing. Babies were being eaten and women being hacked to death. Phæ'enor started to think the artist that had decorated the walls and ceilings of the palace was obsessed by death.

Bemused by it all, she averted her eyes only to be distracted by the flames from the many candelabras flickering in the bottom of her vision, drawing her eyes back to where the party was gathered. It was not large. Prince Taigor was there, once again adorning a wig, although this time not so large and not so white as the one he wore before. Officer Nathryn was also in attendance, this time wearing his dress suit. It was a very pale blue and sported a very frilly collar. Phæ'enor suppressed a smile, thinking he looked like a peacock. There were a few more officers in attendance, all in their normal regalia. At least two she thought she had seen with Officer Nathryn on The Scavenger. The host, Lady Amia, who smiled at Phæ'enor in welcome, wore a beautiful white feathered dress. Phæ'enor, still surprised at her change in attitude when she visited No 09, felt even more like she did not want to talk to her.

However, she was relieved of having to talk to her immediately as just then the presence of a man she had spoken to before made his way over to her. It was the portly drunk from The Scavenger.

This time she was quite relieved to see him without his miserable looking companion, and instead was accompanied by one of the officers. A tall and dark-haired man with a large moustache that he looked too young to be sporting.

'Miss Phæ'enor Doven, you look radiant!' said the portly man, this time he was sober, although he still sported a purple nosed face. 'Please, let me introduce you,' he said as he turned to the officer, 'this is Lieutenant Oleston.'

Phæ'enor and the Lieutenant greeted one another with a bow of their heads, 'You may call me Hall, Miss Doven. I have heard a lot about you from Re'av?'

Phæ'enor looked blankly at the lieutenant, 'Re'av?' 'Officer Re'av Nathryn?'

'Oh,' said Phæ'enor, a little surprised. 'No doubt he has told you about my so-called misdemeanours on The Scavenger and the marketplace, not to mention…'

'Oh, no. Quite the contrary. He speaks very highly of you, as does Cort here…' 'Cort…?'

'Oh yes, and if anything, I am the one that has painted a bad picture of myself, not you my dear,' said the portly man. 'You must forgive me for my drunken behaviour on board The Scavenger. I hate travelling by sea and feel that the drink is the only way to keep me calm, stop me thinking about all the nasty things that can happen … like drowning,' he said with a pleasant smile. 'And now I must formally introduce myself. I of course know who you are,' he said winking. 'Mr Cort Rohgah at your service,' he said bowing comedically.

'Mr Rohgah here is an adviser, are you not Sir?' chipped in Officer Nathryn, who had walked over, accompanied by Lady Amia. The two officers nodded at each other in greeting.

Rohgah replied dismissively, 'Well, yes I suppose. I advise the government, court, etcetera, etcetera. Whoever needs me Miss Doven,' he replied, winking at her again.

'Such as myself,' said Lady Amia. 'Rohgah persuaded me, and my family, on what a good match King Rothian would be.'

'Did you? I thought you didn't know who Lady Amia was,' said Phæ'enor, addressing Cort Rohgah.

Lady Amia looked confused at the pair of them, so Phæ'enor elaborated:

'When you boarded at the Port of Iscar Lady Amia, I was intrigued to know who you were but Cort here, apart from saying you looked like you were destined for the King's Court, had no idea who you were.' Lady Amia strained a smile; evidently not pleased with the Court Advisor. Phæ'enor tried her best not to laugh at the now irritated Amia.

'Oh … well … like I said, I had drunk quite a lot to get me through the journey,' said Cort, awkwardly laughing at his drunken mistake and avoiding the wrath in Lady Amia's eyes.

Phæ'enor frowned at Cort Rohgah's excuse for not recalling he had advised Lady Amia to marry King Sol. Match making a young woman with an old king was not something you could forget, surely? By the look on Lady Amia's face it seemed the future queen did not quite believe him either. She looked offended at Cort for not recognising who she was, even if he was drunk.

Phæ'enor, Officer Nathryn and Lieutenant Hall were spared anymore awkwardness between the two when there came a clink of metal upon glass.

Ting, ting, ting!

'Ladies and Gentlemen, please be seated,' said Prince Taigor, who had made his way to the head of the large table in the room.

They all moved to the table, laden with white cloth, silver plates and cutlery. Phæ'enor was seated between Officer Nathryn, Cort Rohgah and opposite from Master Rasia. A nine-course meal of small dishes was served, from a tiny dish of soup that Phæ'enor thought she could drink in two spoonsful to a small fish no bigger than her hand that was half skinned and decorated with fish eyeballs. According to Rohgah, this 'was a beautiful delicacy.'

Phæ'enor wondered if he was drunk again or just pretending to like it so as not to be rude in present company. To her the fish tasted like the dregs of the bottom of the sea, and with a texture like jelly where it shouldn't have been. The best bit was the tiny little desserts of chocolate that they were all encouraged to help themselves to. They all laughed at Phæ'enor who did not hold back on filling her plate. As they ate talk turned to politics and then gradually onto The Scavenger's demise.

'Prince Taigor, I hear they are rebuilding your ship from scratch,' said Cort Rohgah, wiping his mouth of grease with his napkin. Prince Taigor replied:

'Yes Cort. We have been looking at what we can salvage from the explosion first, but works have begun on a new frame in the south-west docks.'

'It was your ship?' asked Phæ'enor.

'Yes,' smiled Prince Taigor. 'My first. My father commissioned it for my sixteenth birthday, and she has served my men and I, as well as our empire, dutifully ever since.'

'I heard from Captain Alba that she was a good hunter. Chasing down the enemies across wide stretches of sea, and never once losing her prey or a battle. Always winning,' said Lady Amia.

'Not so much a scavenger but a huntress!' exclaimed Cort Rohgah. They all laughed. Phæ'enor smiled but Prince Taigor did not look so pleased.

'That is why it is important for me to find out who did set off the explosions on board. That frigate was my pride and joy, a symbol of this empires strength,' he said.

'It was also ill-timed was it not? What with the war being over and a new peaceful era upon us. It should not have bowed out in this way,' said Cort Rohgah.

The sound of Master Rasia's cutlery clanged against his plate as he let it drop. 'Do you really believe that your majesty, that we have entered peaceful times?' asked Master Rasia sceptically. Phæ'enor was surprised to hear bitterness creep into his voice. There was silence at the table. All of them watched Prince Taigor contemplating his answer.

'I hope so. But I cannot help your circumstances Master Rasia. Your brother was caught.'

'He was framed, and because the guards of this city are too scared to go into Old Town after O'scilla, he could be hanged for something he did not do. This empire is not at peace. Outwardly, yes, but from within?' Master Rasia had replied quietly but with anger bubbling below the surface. He was not looking at his plate and not at the Prince. Silence had descended upon the table, and all awkwardly avoided eye contact with the two men.

'What is your brother accused of?' asked Phæ'enor, feeling that someone should at least ask. But again, there was silence, and no one answered her. Master Rasia was now silently eating the remains of the food on his plate.

It was Cort Rohgah who broke the stifled air, clearing his throat, 'Err, well, talking of so many events up and coming I believe we have a birthday girl in the room!' Phæ'enor was quite sure no one mentioned up and coming events. She was still staring at Master Rasia and thought it rather rude of Cort Rohgah to have changed the subject.

'Phæ'enor? Phæ'enor?'

'What?' she replied, rather sharply and unintentionally to the rest of the room at large.

'Darling, it is your birthday that is impending,' her mother reminded her out of her thoughts.

'Oh, yes,' replied Phæ'enor, wondering why they cared as she continued to watch Master Rasia, who was now moving crumbs about his plate and was clearly deep in thought.

'And are you going to be having a party? I mean of course you will be. I hear you are turning seventeen?'

Phæ'enor looked at Cort Rohgah and did not reply returning her gaze back on Master Rasia. Instead her grandmother interjected:

'Well, I suppose we should celebrate Phæ'enor's birthday, but it is such a shame that my son, Captain Doven, could not be here. It won't be traditional without him.'

'I really don't care about my birthday, nor do I care for a party,' said Phæ'enor abruptly.

'Yes, yes, but it marks an age when you become a grown woman. Where you can start to decide for yourself what you want to do. Like marriage,' said Cort Rohgah.

'Does that mean I can also decide to leave this place and head back to Vanu?' said Phæ'enor, who had turned her head sharply back to face him. 'Why are you all so obsessed with marriage?' she demanded.

'I. Well…'

Phæ'enor held her hand up to stop Cort Rohgah from talking, 'Don't tell me, you are going to say marriage is a wonderful thing, that because I am the only daughter of an army Captain I will marry well. No doubt to an off-ice-er,' she said sarcastically. Officer Nathryn put down his fork and knife, the last remnants of his smile disappearing, '…and then it would just be so I could live happily ever after, with a litter of children, and then finally I get to jump over the city walls and explore the woods of Benaghar! I mean … what exactly is the meaning of that?'

Lady Amia had dropped her cutlery on the table. She looked most annoyed. Master Rasia had looked up once Phæ'enor had started to rant to the party. Mrs Doven and Mrs Jemin looked shocked and embarrassed at her outburst. The officers', bar Officer Nathryn, who was now looking at his empty plate, were all suppressing smiles. Prince Taigor, however, sat back still gazing into the space in front of him.

'So, Advisor Rohgah. Advise me. I presume you are married and have a wealth of knowledge on the subject?'

'Eh … well … no, I'm not married…'

'I didn't think so,' said Phæ'enor aloud to the room. She turned around to face one of the servants who had remained behind, 'Show me to the toilette, please.'

Everyone stared at Phæ'enor. Master Rasia suppressed a laugh at how Phæ'enor commanded a royal servant to do as she asked, overriding the command of the royal present. The servant looked alarmed but bowed. She got up and threw her napkin on the table behind her, following the servant out of the room, and did not turn around. As she did, she heard the party begin to talk in whispers. She knew she had been rude, churlish even, but she had had enough of all their silly talk about marriage as a diversion to get away from talking about Master Raisa's brother. They were the ones being rude. She thought that was more important than trivial matters of birthday parties and husbands to be.

The footman led her down the opposite way they had come, through a stone corridor. Animal heads continued to decorate the walls and the carpet runners were made up of animal skins.

'The toilette, Miss,' said the footman, who had come to a halt outside a small wooden door.

'Thank you. I can make my own way back from here, it's not far,' she said a little too gruffly.

The footman reluctantly left and walked back towards the dining room. Phæ'enor watched, but instead of going through the door she carried on down the hallway. All she wanted was a break from the party, a little exploring of the palace would help and after all that was the real reason why she wanted to come in the first place. She would make it quick.

***

As she moved around a curved wall in the building, she lost sight of the footman, stopped, turned and quickly picked up speed. After a minute or two she seemed to be coming back around to where she started. They must be in one of the turrets, she thought. She moved back around the corner and spied the entrance to the dining room and the stone staircase opposite. The footman had disappeared and there did not seem to be anyone else about.

Quickly and quietly she made for the stairs. If this was one of the turrets then there would be more floors like this one further up, she may even be able to look out upon the whole of the city if she could get to the top, she thought.

As she ascended to the next floor she passed a deep recessed window, big enough to sit in. Through it the many moons of the world and stars could be seen shinning down upon Benaghar. It was beautiful to see. But her gazing upon the landscape was interrupted, for Phæ'enor could now hear a faint sound of metal upon metal; the jingling of little bells. She stood still, her heart in her mouth, listening as to whether the noise was coming from behind her or from the floor above.

Ting, ting-ting! Ting, ting-ting!

The sound was getting louder, and it was coming from behind her, making its way up the stairs. Not wanting to make a noise, she quickly slipped her shoes off and ran. Running as fast as she could, finally making it to the next floor.

Ting, ting-ting! Ting, ting-ting!

Panicking, Phæ'enor looked about. She did not want to get caught or find out what was following her. That noise was familiar. She, and she was sure Master Rasia as well, had heard it the day before, when they were standing outside Polstor & Polstor.

Ting, ting-ting! Ting, ting-ting!

The floor matched the one below, nearly like for like, but it was much darker, the decoration less extravagant. The walls were less decorated with only a few swords mounted between the doors; of those there were even less. Phæ'enor could see two doors to her left, one to her right.

Ting, ting-ting! Ting-ting, ting. Ta-ta ting, ta-ta ting!

She ran to the one on her right and tried it. It was locked. She turned back to look at the top of the stairs, horrified that the noise was getting louder and closer, but still nothing had appeared.

Ta-ta ting, ting ta-ta, ting, ting, ting-ting!

Phæ'enor ran across to the other two doors. The first was also locked. Then she ran to the second. This time it was open, but she could hear voices inside. The door was slightly ajar, but she could not see inside from where she was; it was opened in the opposite direction.

Ting ting-ting, ting ting-ting. Ting!

She flattened herself against the stone arch of the door way. The noise of jingling bells had ceased. Whoever they belonged to had now reached the top of the turret stairs to the floor and had stopped.

Ting-ting, ting-ting!

The noise had started again. Frozen to the spot in fear, Phæ'enor hoped that whoever was making the noise was not coming her way.

Ting-ting, Ting-ting.

Ting.

Ting.

Ting-ting.

Phæ'enor breathed out slowly. They were moving away in the other direction. Curious she peered around the edge of the stone wall and back down the corridor. What she saw did not settle her nerves. What could only be described as a giant, gangly, multi-coloured and bell topped three eared frog, was bouncing along by its equally gangly legs. It was a jester, but not like the ones Phæ'enor had seen in illustrated storybooks. Phæ'enor watched it as it continued to bounce off and disappear around the curve in the turret, its bells jingling along. Disturbed, Phæ'enor turned back.

This was a silly idea, she thought, I am only going to get caught. She bent over to slip her shoes back on, ready to move off, when her attention was brought back to the voices on the other side of the door. She knew she shouldn't, she needed to get back to the party, but intrigued, Phæ'enor positioned herself in front of the door so she could look through the gap.

On the other side was a large and well-lit room, the walls were lined with mirrors, so that all Phæ'enor could see were reflections upon reflections of the same thing: strange black spinning tops, on top of short marble columns and two men. The first was unmistakably the king, this time dressed in white silk; his fur cloak and ring of white gold crowned his head. But he did not look well. Gone was his joyful countenance. Instead here was a king with a face full of concern, tired eyes and skin drained of colour.

'You should not have come back here. Everything is under control, there really was no need for you to have travelled so far.'

'Your Majesty, I believe otherwise,' said the second man. He was tall, like the king, but wore only black from head to toe. His travelling cloak was thick and waxy, but dusty and worn. It had seen better days, thought Phæ'enor, but the man wearing it was still young. His hair was dark, short and neat, and swept back off his face, which was weathered slightly by the sun. With anger in his voice he said, 'You believe that the empire is at peace, but they are using it against you. You have become blinded by these false friendships, and while you sit here in the palace, they begin to rebuild their forces against you.'

'Stop!,' the king interrupted. 'Your imagination has always run away with you. I know you mean well but you are not a well man … you should have stayed in Achcidium, where you can still be looked after.'

'No. I am quite well your Majesty. I don't believe I was ever unwell. But my time in exile has helped me to understand my real purpose in life. It is to help Benaghar! While I have been far away from her all I hear are reports of more forces building against her. Even here, within her walls the wolves and the rats fight amongst one another! Right in front of you! How long will it be before they join together and take down Benaghar from within? Benaghar will be no more, your Majesty!'

'ENOUGH! That is quite enough!' spat the king. Still strong, he pushed the other man away from him. 'You are deluded! Soon I will marry Lady Amia, the marriage between I and Amia, Benaghar and Achcidium will be joined together, and this empire will be STRONGER THAN EVER!

'But your Majesty…'

'I SAID ENOUGH!'

The king turned his back to the man and started to walk towards the door, and toward Phæ'enor, but then he stopped. She breathed out slowly.

'We had hoped for so much from you … but still, you have not changed. You may stay for the wedding, but after that you must leave. And this time, I never want you to return.' The king turned and made straight for the door without stopping.

Phæ'enor, backed away, clumsily turning on her heels and ran for the stairs. She ran and ran without stopping, until she reached the floor below and made to head for the dining room when the door started to open. Panting heavily, it would be obvious to the party that she would have been up to no good. Behind her she could hear heavy footsteps descending the stone stairs. The king would also know. With no other option left to her, Phæ'enor picked up the hem of her dress to move more quickly and headed for the steps that descended away from the floor.

Running past the displays of wings and wild cats, Phæ'enor made her way down the stone steps and onto the floor full of armour. But dazzled by all the light reflecting off them she took the wrong turn. Instead of having made her way back to the glass domed bridge, Phæ'enor had managed to take another set of steps, out of the turret and onto a very wide landing. She stopped, out of breath. She could no longer hear voices, no one was following her. She just needed to catch her breath here, then slowly make her way back. She would say she got lost if they asked where she had been, after all that was not entirely untrue.

Looking around she spied a large chandelier in front of her. It was hanging high up, centred above a large hallway below. Still breathing heavily Phæ'enor moved across to another set of stairs in front of her. Placing her feet back in her shoes she casually walked down the first set, it curved away down to the floor below, carpeted with a deep blue. A series of small wooden doors appeared on her right as she passed. She could make out smaller turrets of the palace joining here by the long curves in the walls.

Phæ'enor looked down over the bannister, several flights of stairs weaved in and out of each other to the floor laid in marble, a large mosaic motif of Tekan, gold-leaf painted skin and robed in white from his head down, was prominently placed in the middle.

Her breathing had nearly gone back to normal when Phæ'enor heard a door shut below, then the sound of two people talking. She looked over the banister to the steps joining the ones she was on only to see two footmen ascending the stairs towards her.

Phæ'enor looked for the nearest doorway on the stairs, if she didn't get to one quick they would discover her and march her back up to the dining room sooner than she had hoped for. She ran back up the stairs as quickly as she could to the last wooden door she had walked past and tried it. It did not open. She tried the next door up. That also did not open. Then the next. This time it opened, but with a loud creak. Gritting her teeth, she closed the door behind her.

However, the door did not lead off into another hallway, or even into another room. Phæ'enor was standing in a gloomy stairwell. She froze as the footmen walked passed her on the other side of the door. Holding her breath until she could no longer hear them, Phæ'enor then moved swiftly down the spiral staircase. She had started to count the steps but stopped when she reached the four hundreds, having found the counting slowed her down. After about ten minutes, Phæ'enor came to a stop. Out of breath and excited, in front of her was another door, but this time it was less ornamental. Plain black wood with just a small iron knocking handle. A sign in the middle read 'Kitchens.' She slowly pushed it open, just enough so she could peep around the side.

In front of her was a small, narrow corridor, badly lit at one end but full of light at the other where Phæ'enor could clearly see the kitchen staff busy at their work. The smell of some sort of meat stew wafted down towards her. It smelled better than the food served upstairs. She walked cautiously but curiously towards the kitchens, hoping the kitchen staff would not shoo her away. But as she got nearer, she noticed a familiar silhouette leaning against a cupboard door. His large weathered hat covering his eyes, Phæ'enor knew from having met him before that they were ice cold. It was O'tila, lazily cutting up a pear with a small knife. Phæ'enor was just about to say something to him as she emerged out of the shadows when someone else walked out in front of her, their back to her. She retreated swiftly back into the shadows.

'Cousin, what are you doing here so late,' said Prince Taigor's footman. 'We are very busy. There are several parties going on across the palace tonight. I don't have time for your games.'

'O'sea,' said O'tila, 'I'm well aware. You barely have time for anyone these days, so tied up with your new master,' he said half smiling, half joking. 'I hear Miss Phæ'enor Doven is upstairs at one of those exclusive parties,' O'tila smirked.

O'sea looked at O'tila scornfully, 'Why are you still interested in her? She made a fool out of you, and you evidently got your own back. Although publicly drugging someone is not the way I would have gone about it. I'm still mad at you for giving me that batch of tea. Do you know what could have happened if I had given that to Prince Taigor by mistake?'

Phæ'enor breathed deeply, trying hard to control her rage at this news. So it was O'sea at the tea room, serving them tea. The two looked so alike it was no wonder she mistook him to be O'tila.

O'tila shrugged his shoulders, 'Do you reckon she knows they only invited her so see if she'll give away whatever it is she is hiding?'

'Sssh!' said O'sea, carefully looking around them to make sure no one was listening. 'That girl wouldn't need whatever it is that Officer Nathryn and his men were guarding on The Scavenger. Nor would she need the gold. The Doven family is well known to have money and the only way they would get more would be through marriage. They wouldn't stoop as low as you or me, besides, the chest nor its contents were in that house.'

'Yeah, well, girls do like pretty, shiny things.'

'Humph. Not this one, she seems more interested in poking her nose in where it does not belong. Or hitting the likes of you.'

'Yeah, well you had a close call in her rooms making sure of that didn't you O'sea. Entering their house through the loft hatch in the girl's room was madness! Not to mention nearly getting caught on the rooftops by those scumbags. I told you, I should have gone to the house instead, not you. You're out of practice cousin,' he laughed. Some of the kitchen maids shot them filthy looks as they walked past. Phæ'enor drew nearer, wide-eyed and intrigued to hear what else these two cousins got up to.

'You are in enough trouble as it is with the authorities; I had no choice but to do it. If O'scilla wants whatever it is then we'll get it but without causing further scenes.'

'Hey! You know The Scavenger wasn't me.'

'Well it's lucky for you that idiot friend of Rohgah's lied about not seeing you on the gun deck then, isn't it?' said O'sea.

'That's because if he had admitted the truth, they would have known he was on the gun deck too. Snooping git. And anyway, it's not just O'scilla after the treasure. Rasia needs it too, for his brother.'

'Yeah, so I've heard. If we bring it to O'scilla he will stay out of my way. For a while at least, and hopefully stops interfering with things below ground. If Rasia gets it first then, who knows, maybe he will sell to O'scilla for information. O'scilla wins either way then. And anyway, what's this about we?' O'sea spat at his cousin, 'you're meant to be gathering information on that old Harq, not getting into trouble with petty crime and drawing the wrong attention. DON'T, cousin, draw me back out to sort out your mess.'

A bell started ringing from another part of the kitchen.

'Shit!' said O'sea, 'I have to go back upstairs. You need to leave.'

O'sea and O'tila hugged each other, then both disappeared. Phæ'enor peered slightly around the corner. The bell that was ringing lead up to the dining room.

She turned and hurried back down the hallway, through the door and up the stairs, her breathing getting heavier with every step. Finally, and after some time she came to the door that would lead her back to the dining room and the party. She pushed it open, and without looking out first, closed it and started to move up the stairs when she heard a now familiar voice speak behind her:

'Well, well, if it isn't Miss Phæ'enor Doven The Explorer.'

Phæ'enor turned, her stomach churning, to face Prince Taigor's footman, O'sea. He was looking at her. Not cross, but bemused, his arms folded and his eyes searching for an explanation.

'Ugh … um …'

O'sea smiled and said threateningly, 'I won't tell them that you went for a wander, if you don't mention what you clearly must have heard down in the kitchens.'

Phæ'enor, realising she had no other choice, nodded in agreement. O'sea made her uncomfortable. He looked pleasant enough, but his eyes told a different story. They were not smiling back at her. He was much taller, stronger looking than his cousin O'tila; and with family and connections like that, Phæ'enor didn't want anything to do with him.

'I'll show you the way back to the party,' said O'sea.

But as O'sea grabbed her arm and steered her up the staircase Mrs Doven came into view.

'Phæ'enor, there you are,' she said crossly. The others from the party appeared behind her.

'Please, if I may, Miss Doven was lost and quite distressed when I found her at the bottom of the stairs.'

He pinched her, prompting her to agree with his story. 'Ugh … yes. I'm sorry. I went in the completely wrong direction and ended up, I don't know where.' she said quickly, glancing at O'sea to check he was okay with the lie. He made no indication to the contrary. Phæ'enor looked up at the gathered party. By the look on Lady Amia's face she was not so convinced.

'Never mind,' said Prince Taigor. 'I'm glad you were found and did not end up wandering into the underground tunnels.'

The officers' laughed. Phæ'enor caught Master Rasia rolling his eyes at them. Prince Taigor continued, 'However, I'm afraid you were lost a while and now the evening has ended. But I do hope we shall see you again soon. Master Rasia you may take your leave and show Mrs Doven, Mrs Jemin and Miss Phæ'enor Doven here, home.'

***

They made their way down the entrance stairs; Phæ'enor glancing back to see that Lady Amia had disappeared, but O'sea was still watching her, making sure she did not leave unattended. As they walked out into the cold air and down the cobbled path a little, Phæ'enor took another last look at the palace. The night had been more interesting then she anticipated but why of all people was Prince Taigor's footman in No 9 Grand Alboreum Circus, and why did they think she may have the chests? He said he was doing his cousin a favour for O'scilla, the droopy faced man she had seen on the "Wanted" posters about town, but he also worked for Prince Taigor? Was Prince Taigor unaware or did he have something to do with it as well? She had not been interested in these chests; she knew nothing about them and as far as she was aware not in possession of them and could only wonder why everyone wanted to get their hands on them. Phæ'enor still felt eyes upon her, as though the whole palace was watching.

'Miss Doven,' prompted Master Rasia.

'Yes, I'm coming,' she replied. But as she turned, out of the corner of her eye she saw that the top window of the south tower was no longer in darkness. The curtain flickered light as it moved back into place. So, they are all watching me she thought, before turning to get back into the carriage.

Chapter Nine

The Little Black Book

The sky over Benaghar continued to be grey and dull and the fog from the sea had rolled in thick. The newspapers had reported that it was a large storm coming in off the east coast of The Dourbrande Sea and bringing with it a cold chill in the air. As such, it was not a time for anyone to be wandering the streets. It was gone breakfast, but not quite lunch, when Phæ'enor was to be found slumped in her grandmother's sitting room armchair, the table to the left piled high with books from No 9's library, and the small pile that Archä and Mëdez had given her on the arms of the chair.

Mrs Jemin, instead of being sat moaning in her usual chair, had disappeared quite abruptly after breakfast. She had been mulling over a letter at the breakfast table, chewing on some toast, when she suddenly jumped up and declared she must leave at once.

'Such awful news! Deke, come quick and fetch my cloak and hat. Quick man!'

'Whatever is the matter Odora,' asked an alarmed Mrs Doven.

'It is Mrs Lili Oleston's son, Lieutenant Hall Oleston,' she replied, flapping the letter about in mid-air. 'She has written to me, informing me that he has disappeared!'

'Isn't that one of Officer Nathryn's men, from the palace last night?' asked Mrs Doven.

'Yes, yes. The very one.'

'Seems like I am not the only one getting lost,' sniggered Phæ'enor.

'This is not a laughing matter dear!'

'Sorry, I…'

'I must go at once and give her my support … and eat up dears, I can't have this food go to waste!'

Phæ'enor and her mother watched Mrs Jemin flapping for another five minutes until she left with Mr Deke to a neighbouring Grand Circus, Bilgana. Phæ'enor did not think her grandmother would be much use to Mrs Oleston, not in that state of panic. However, it had given her the opportunity to make use of the big armchair, at least for a little while.

Meanwhile Mrs Doven was once again sat at the writing desk compiling her letters to family and friends.

'You know we may be invited to the palace again,' said Mrs Doven, as she continued to write. 'It would be good next time if you didn't go off on one of your explorations, and actually stick with the party, my dear.'

'I got lost,' replied Phæ'enor, half mumbling whilst turning the pages of a large blue leather bound book: Benaghar: The Heart of an Empire.

'We both know that's not true. The footman, whatever his reasons, decided to be a gentleman and lie for you.'

Phæ'enor half looked up at her mother, back still facing the room and huddled over her letters. Gentleman? He is more like a thief than a footman thought Phæ'enor, and he definitely had reasons to cover for me. For both of us.

Phæ'enor returned to her book and fell upon a page and section titled, Crime and Punishment in the City. Beneath this was a black and white illustration of a starry night, below which a ragged man with mad eyes was being pushed over the side of a bridge; a heavy weight tied to his feet. And underneath this the waterline of the river displayed many fins and teeth of sharks. The paragraph below it read:

> *For serious crimes: those who commit the most heinous of crimes are sentenced to death at the hands of our Holy River Nebben. First, their hands and feet are tied together. Then a heavy*

weight, measured to exactly three times that of the person being committed, is tied to them so that they have less chance of escape.

Once in the water, if they do not escape they drown. But if they can breathe, they are subjected to the Blue-tip sharks, who sleep by day but come alive and hunt by night.

If the criminal manages to escape both drowning and the teeth of the Blue-tips they are cleared of all crimes, as only the innocent live.

What rubbish thought Phæ'enor, as if anyone is going to escape the weights in the first place. And sharks in the river? She flipped through the pages, and in a bored voice she asked her mother:

'Who is it that you are writing to?'

'My family, your family in the north.'

'Which ones exactly?'

'Just some distant cousins,' said Mrs Doven, continuing to write.

Phæ'enor did not press further. She knew she had family in Aebra's Northern Territories, but her mother never really liked to talk about them. Her father had said there had been a family feud, back before she had been born. All he said was that her mother was no longer speaking to her siblings. She only kept in touch with some cousins.

'They may visit soon,' said Mrs Doven, from the corner of the room.

'Oh,' replied Phæ'enor, not quite sure what to say to that. She didn't know the cousins and if they were anything like Simi and Mimi she really couldn't care less. She pulled down another book from the armchair onto her lap but managed to knock several flying at once. She grimaced, waiting for her mother to tell her to stop making a noise, but it never came. Bending down to where the books had fallen at her feet she spotted her grandmother's newspaper. It had been folded open onto a page where the face of Wolf Canis stared back up at her; the same photo of him on all the posters on the streets of Newtown. Phæ'enor picked it up and read the article underneath:

Turf war between the Wolves and Rats of Old Town

It would seem that even after the demise of His Majesty's Ship The Scavenger, the accused, a Mr Wolf Canis of Old Town, is still able to continue his influence over his wolves and events in this city; even from his cell. The leader of the wolves, not content with his firework display in the harbour has managed to mastermind the recent break in at the garrisons and the theft of some of the Crown's rarest jewels.

Brought back by Prince Taigor's men as a peace offering from The Kingdom of Illraea, it was believed the chests contained rare emeralds and diamonds, Lapis stone and pure Emaz.

Only empty chests, strewn across the city, have been found. However, in a statement released by the palace late yesterday afternoon the city guards now believe more people are involved:

"It would seem, after a lengthy investigation that it was not just the wolves involved in the attack of the garrisons and theft of the chests. As most people of Benaghar are aware there is another group of criminals, the rats, which are suspected of also being involved. This complicates matters, not just because the wolves

*and rats are sworn enemies (because of their daily
fight over the area of Old Town) but if they have
also taken some of the jewels then it will make it
much harder to retrieve what was lost to the
crown."*

*What the city guards were referring to became
clear in the early hours of this morning. The head
of the city guards, Garron Alesand, confirmed
that late last night, several city guards and
officers of the Benagharian Army entered the
notoriously dangerous area of Old Town, seeking
to reclaim the crown jewels. Twenty-four of them
entered the area, only nineteen have returned.*

Phæ'enor read on but the article did not mention which guards and
officers had not returned; she had a feeling that one of them may be
Mrs Oleston's son, Hall. It went on to complain that the city guards
were inadequate and that only the army should have entered Old
Town, and complained that after decades of infighting the situation
had not been resolved. Old Town should be locked down and its
inhabitants locked up or shipped out of Benaghar to some distant
land.

Phæ'enor closed the paper and put it back on the pile of books
and was about to reach for the book underneath when she looked
up, remembering the small box Archä had given to her before he
had let her leave their shop. She got up and went through to the
hallway directly to the cloak stand and rummaged through her
travelling cloak. In the left inside pocket, she found what she was
looking for. It was a smallish brown box, lightly wrapped. She
undid the ribbon it was bound in, to reveal a yellow, leather-bound
book, small enough to fit into the palm of her hand, and beneath it a
thicker, black leather-bound volume.

She walked back to the sitting room looking at the two books in the box. On the front cover of the yellow book it showed several symbols filling the border, jagged and uneven. In the centre there was a much larger symbol. At first glance thick lines and a triangular shape grouped together, but up close it was made up from small dots:

She opened the book and flicked through the pages. The symbols inside were like those on the cover, also made of fine lines of tiny dots, joining together to make triangular shapes, lines, blocks and crosses. The symbol on the front was in the top right-hand corner of every page. It varied ever so slightly but judging by the less then eloquent lines and dots of the symbols Phæ'enor dismissed it as down to poor drawing skills by the author. Unable to decipher the symbols, she closed the little yellow book and flung it onto the pile she had already casually flicked through.

As she sat back down in her grandmother's armchair, she put the box to one side and went to open the little black book, but her mother interrupted:

'Your father and brothers are well.'

Phæ'enor glanced over at her mother who was still writing with her back turned to the room. She clearly hadn't heard Phæ'enor leave and return and wondered if her mother had been talking to her when she wasn't there.

'I didn't know they had written. What do they say?' replied Phæ'enor.

'Your father has written a few times since we have arrived. Nothing of importance, just that he and your brothers are doing well. They have moved the camp further south and are hoping to be on the next ship, and to join us within the next three to four months.'

Phæ'enor lit up at this. Finally, she thought, I can have some real fun and exploration with my brothers, unlike my silly cousins. Mrs Doven reverted into silence again and carried on writing her letters.

'You're writing an awful lot lately, Mother,' said Phæ'enor.

'Mmm … yes, I suppose there is a lot to catch up with.'

What kind of answer is that? thought Phæ'enor. She didn't have the energy to continue a bitty conversation with her mother and instead slouched back in her grandmother's armchair, returning to the book. It was slightly bigger than the yellow book of symbols; thick and black, tatty and ripped in places. On the front it read: The Namorian Curse. A disfigured animal skull with sharp fangs and what looked like shredded feathers poked out of the top, along with torn butterfly and bird feathers creating a silver border surrounding it. Thinking it was some silly children's book Phæ'enor went to put it on the pile of read books when it slipped from her hand, landing face up. She picked it up leaving her thumb in the page it landed open on, and casually checked the other pages by flicking through it with her fingers.

Unlike the cover of the book, the pages were immaculately cared for. Black ink depicted more animal skulls and feathers as borders for each page but interwoven with those images was the symbol she had seen on the cover of the little yellow book of symbols. She picked this one back up to double check. Sure enough the same lines and dots appeared, but smaller. She could make out symbols from the yellow book in The Namorian Curse borders as well.

That's odd she thought as she could clearly read the writing, though it was very joined up and in italics; an old style of writing probably written by a quill, thought Phæ'enor. It did not seem like a children's story either, at least it was not in the style of one; the page that it had fallen open on read:

> At the battle of Benaghar, the last between Tekan and The Namorian King, knowing that his reign was near its end, and unable to bear the sight of the rightful heirs of the Benagharian throne celebrating in victory, the Namorian King offered Tekan back his and his people's power.
>
> But it was a trick. For this treasure was everything. The Namorians after all had stolen it from Tekan and they knew Tekan's people wanted it back in order to rebuild the foundations of their world.
>
> But as King Tekan took The Namorian King's last breath from him, his life spent, the curse was sealed. As King Tekan came upon it, the treasure vanished before his eyes.
>
> He and his army, his people had nothing. The Namorians, what was left of their army took their chance and killed all they could, before they also died.
>
> King Tekan's people began to perish and either died or separated from each other to seek new worlds. King Tekan, although eventually able to rebuild his Kingdom, never saw the treasure again. It took many generations later, when King Barr of the Indzini fell upon it and in doing so met with The Namorian curse, through the poison of the Atro Hibdaluca flower."

Below this an intricate illustration of ten chests, some closed but others open, all overflowing with diamonds, jewels, rings, vibrant stones and what looked like to be gold and silver coins, sat on top of a pile of bones and human skulls. Beneath the illustration was a caption:

The Namorian Treasure

Phæ'enor stared at the page and thought of the chests that Officer Nathryn and his fellow Officers' had brought on board The Scavenger. Surely they were not the same ones?

She looked through to the opening pages of the book, her thumb still placed on the page she had just read and tried to find the date the book was published, but there was nothing. She then flicked forward to see if there was an index for the chapters, again there wasn't one. It must be old, thought Phæ'enor, some sort of ancient text, why else would there be no date?

But as she looked over it again, only the cover looked old with its torn and tatty black leather. The pages within were pristine.

She turned to the first chapter, titled: The Namorian Downfall; then to the next: The Namorian Challenge; then the next: The Battle of Benaghar. Phæ'enor flicked through several more chapters. They all seemed to be about various battles and nothing to do with the title of the book, until she came back to the page, bookmarked by her thumb, returning to the snippet about The Namorian Treasure.

She thumbed through a few pages falling onto the start of a separate book within. This time titled: The Curse of The Namorian Treasure Through the Ages.' She closed the book on her thumb mark and looked at the depth of the book. The curses of the treasure seemed to cover more than three quarters of the volume. Reopening it, Phæ'enor turned to the first chapter in the section: The First Recorded Case of the Namorian Curse. It may not seem like a children's story, but at least it's as simple as one to read she thought, and read on:

The Year Six Hundred and Sixty-Six and The Coming of The Fourth Purple Moon, Hindwin, was a promising one. The sun's gentle rays had risen early from its dark sleep, the flowers bloomed, and new-borns came into this world. Yet as the year moved on the sun's rays grew from warm to hot and the bud of the Atro Hibdaluca, appeared; its pinks were beautiful to the eye and King Ettan of the House of Asarbrian, so enamoured with them, demanded that they all be picked just for him and his royal gardens. His guards set off with the task of retrieving all the pink shades for his collection. But one day they stumbled across more than they had expected. Beneath the pink shade flower beds lay twelve intricately, beautifully decorated chests. Twelve chests for the twelve places the flowers were found. Excited with their find the guards rushed back to the palace, chests and flowers in hand. King Ettan was delighted but there was one problem. They could not get into the chests. No keys were found with the twelve.

The guards were sent to all the blacksmiths across the land. Keys were made and when they did not fit, axes, swords and all manner of tool and weapon were made to help open them. But it was not to be. Weeks and months passed as King Ettan, so obsessed with his treasure, slowly retired from his duties. It is said that he went mad, talking to himself, wandering the palace at night, talking to the chests, caressing them and caring for them as if they were his own children. Queen Mercia, seeing how the king she married had all but disappeared had them removed from the palace. Yet instead of making the king well again he grew further into despair. He took his life by throwing himself off the top of the highest tower of his palace.

Queen Mercia in anger called on all the guards that had found the chests. In secret they were all ordered to take the chests to the furthest reaches of the Kingdom and bury them deep and unmarked. On their return, Queen Mercia had all the guards executed. It was said she did it herself; all of them, disarmed and locked in the Grand Palace Hall, were slaughtered with the king's sword.

Now Queen Mercia could rest in peace at the knowledge that all those who knew the whereabouts of the chests could not tell another soul where to find them. The Kingdom was also in peace.

Along the edges of the boarded illustrations depicted the mad king caressing a chest, soldiers in search of keys, the queen in distress, the king plummeting to his death and the slaughter of the King's Guard. Phæ'enor, bemused turned the page to the next story:

The Year Seven Hundred and Eighty-Eight and The Reign of the Mad Moon Ancless'star. Decades after the death of King Ettan a letter was found, written by one of King Ettan's twenty-six guards. Evidence within and a map of where all the chests lay was found. Greedy for more jewels, treasure, and power, the current King Edus of the House Dorach, ordered their retrieval.

King Edus with his army, after months of searching finally came upon them. But once again The Namorian Curse struck. King Edus and his army were plagued by fire all the way back to their homeland, and only by the skin of their teeth did they make it back. But when they returned the Kingdom was under attack and ablaze. King Edus and his men took back their Kingdom from the attackers. Thereafter the Dorachs were known as the House of Fire.

However, for some it was too late, Queen Ode, the woman who gave him his throne through marriage, burnt to death in his absence trying to save their children; only the daughter survived.

The King, disgusted by his greed for The Namorian Treasure and what it had done to his Kingdom, his queen and family, vowed to forget the chests and help rebuild his Kingdom and Empire for his daughter.

But by then it was too late, The Fire King's Kingdom came under attack and was once again ravaged by fire. The twelve chests were taken. But they did not remain with the attackers; for some were killed and their chests taken, whilst others mysteriously disappeared along with the chests on their travels back to their homelands. The Fire King chose never to seek them again.

But the legend of the chests and the treasure that they hold was too ingrained in the minds of all the monarchs, their allies and enemies. All have since actively pursued the whereabouts of the chests.

Phæ'enor raised her eyebrows, another likely story she thought. What else will this book tell me that I can't already guess? She flicked through a few more pages only stopping when she landed about halfway through:

The Year Nine Hundred and Seventy-Three
and The Blue Dying Moon, Hicca.

This time a Queen, Bairana of the House Dorach, had found the treasure, or at least a ship of explorers had at the bottom of the Tyrrschan Sea. Instead of twelve chests they had found but two. One which was open, but with nothing inside. The other was locked. Yet this one was strange. It kept catching fire on its own accord. The only way to stop it was to permanently enclose it in a glass display box full of water. It wasn't just any water, but the water from the Tyrrschan Sea that it was found in; the only water that could keep the flames at bay:

The Queen Bairana curious as to whether the treasure from the other chests was still in the sea bed sent the expedition back to where they found it. They, nor their ships, ever returned home, believed to have been destroyed, the men having met their end at the bottom of the sea.

Meanwhile Queen Bairana waited for signs of their return. She would take one look in the morning and one last look at night at the chest in the glass display as a reminder.

Yet this sovereign did not come to a sticky end, she lived a full life, longer than most would naturally and passed away in her sleep at the grand old age of 159 years old.

Again, there were more illustrations in the border of the pages; an empty chest, a chest on fire, a ship sinking in the sea, its men drowning, the skeletons of their bodies lying at the bottom of the sea, and an old lady resting in her bed. Well at least she did not meet a violent end thought Phæ'enor. She flicked on through the book, more blue moons, some red, some pink. Some finders of the chest died unnaturally, some did not, living out their lives in peace. Some of the chests disappeared altogether and most that were found had been opened, apart from two. Yet all the time the book never really explained how the chests were come across by whoever had found them; why some people died, others did not. And not once did it say how they were opened and what was found inside each one. Phæ'enor, although entertained at first was about to give up when she flicked through to the last couple of pages. It seemed the curse of the chest was not over; the last chapter was titled:

> *The exploration of the chests continues…*

> *It is believed that over the centuries and millennia that all but two chests lay undiscovered. Who will seek and find them, no one knows. If they find them shall they live, or shall they die?*

Below this information was a more detailed illustration of the chests, spanning two pages; six on one page, six on the other. Each chest was more detailed than the one before. The locks were different shapes as were the ironmongery patterns and each chest was made from similar wood. On ten of the chests arrows pointed to different sections, writing beside it describing the patterns of the knots in the wood. And underneath each of these a date and description of who they were found by; under what circumstances, and what curse had been laid upon the founder. The last two were blank, only outlines of the chests were drawn, and underneath them question marks appeared instead of a description.

'What are you reading my dear?' asked Mrs Doven, from the sitting room desk.

'Err- um…,' Phæ'enor quickly grabbed another book and placed it over the top of the little black one; remembering Archä's departing words to her not to show the contents of the box he had given her to anyone.

'…It's a book on … on… housewives and how to keep your husband happy.' She looked at the book she had picked up in disgust.

'That sounds interesting, I wondered why you were so quiet…' said Mrs Doven, trailing off.

Phæ'enor made to put the book back where she had found it when she knocked the newspaper she had read from earlier from underneath it onto the floor. She leaned forward to pick it up and put it back when she noticed the front cover:

> *"The chests were found, all twelve of them. We*
> *believe they were not containing any valuables*
> *but the break in at the harbour garrisons was a*
> *serious offence and we ask that if anybody has*
> *seen anything to come forward to the city guards*
> *without delay,' stated Admiral Gull."*

The picture showed the large moustached Admiral on the front, next to this a picture of the twelve chests. Phæ'enor pulled the newspaper right up to her face to study it in detail. Twelve? She thought. That's just a coincidence, and anyway the little black book says two have never been found so they can't be the same ones.

Yet it was bizarre, thought Phæ'enor. Ever since those chests, twelve of them, came on board The Scavenger, there had been nothing but trouble in her life. She had got into trouble with nearly everyone on the ship, then The Scavenger exploded in the waters of Benaghar's harbour, there was the fight with O'tila in the marketplace, her episode in The Grand Tea Rooms, the intruder, O'sea, at No 09 Grand Alboreum Circus and not to mention nearly getting caught listening in to the king's conversation in the palace.

And now she was sat with two books relating to the mystery of the cursed chests. What if all this time the chests had been there, on the ship, in the city, in the papers? What if the other two chests had been found and now all twelve have been brought to Benaghar?

She looked back at the illustrations in the little black book. This time her stomach summersaulted. Above the lock on each chest was a symbol, like the symbols from the yellow book, made-up of many dots, but one of them, the last fully completed chest, was different. She turned back to the newspaper. Sure enough, on the chest that was in the foreground, the symbol matched the last illustration; a circle!

'Mother!' asked Phæ'enor.

'Yes dear, whatever is the matter?' asked Mrs Doven, who had now turned around at the excitement in her daughter's voice.

'Oh, nothing … I … err … I've been sat in doors far too long today and…'

'It is raining outside…'

'Yes … I know … but I would really like to see … to see Simi and Mimi,' said Phæ'enor, the words spilling out of her mouth. She didn't know why she thought of those two of all people, but she would need to have a legitimate reason for wanting to leave the house in this awful weather.

'Oh. Well, do you have to go now? Can you not wait for the rain to pass over?'

'YES! I must … I mean I would really like to go and see them now … if … if that's okay, Mother?'

'Are you sure you're okay, dear? I can come with you if you li…'

'No. No thank you. You carry on with your letters. I'll get Master Rasia to fetch a carriage. It won't be long either, and I will be back in time for dinner.'

With that Phæ'enor picked up the two books, and the newspaper and hurried out the door to find Master Rasia.

Chapter Ten

The Unwitting Promise

Phæ'enor knew she would now have to call on her cousins whether she liked it or not. She did not think Master Rasia would lie for her, and she needed an alibi just in case either her mother or grandmother asked where she had been. If she was with her cousins everyone was likely to suspect they were heading for the clothes shops or the market, not somewhere out of the ordinary. She definitely didn't think they would approve or let her go if any of them actually knew where they were headed. Phæ'enor had only sneakily informed the driver of the carriage, the same square fronted one they had taken before, when Master Rasia had gone inside to check with Mrs Doven if she needed any errands run in town whilst there. The driver, about to protest, was easily convinced when Phæ'enor handed him some more money.

And so it was that the carriage arrived at No 24 Queens High to the excitement of her two cousins. It took longer than Phæ'enor had hoped to get them ready and out the door.

'So, cousin, where is it you are taking us? Is it a surprise?' asked Simi.

'Um … yes, I suppose it is,' said Phæ'enor, trying not to catch the eye of her cousin in case her look gave it away.

'Oooh, are we going shopping in Newtown?' asked Mimi.

'Ugh … yes. Well, we are going that way.'

When eventually they had dressed and clambered into the carriage, much to the annoyance of Master Rasia, they set off again. So far Master Rasia hadn't questioned Phæ'enor on where they were going. She supposed that he was probably just glad for the change, to not be standing on the doorstep of No 9 Grand Alboreum Circus.

***

As they drew in through the gate from Queens High to Newtown, Simi and Mimi were still arguing over which shops to visit first.

'No sister. There is no need for more hats, besides the last one you bought was hideous. I mean honestly cousin, you'd think she was an old woman wearing it!' said Simi.

'Hmph. If I say I need a new hat, then I need a new hat! Besides, I don't need new shoes, it's only papa that says he wants us to get new shoes. But I already have some to go with my outfit,' said Mimi.

Phæ'enor looked at her cousins and interrupted them, realising she had not thought to ask the question before, 'Your mother and father, I've not met them?'

'Oh,' said Simi, a little softly with surprise, 'did grandma and auntie not tell you?'

Phæ'enor shrugged, 'Tell me what?'

'Mother is … is not with us, as such. Father works in politics, so he is hardly at home,' said Simi.

'Yes, we pretty much take care of ourselves. He gives us a lot space. You know, shopping and stuff,' said Mimi, a little awkwardly. Phæ'enor looked at her cousin's lap. Mimi's fingers where nervously entwined and twiddling with each other. That explained why they were always over in Grand Town, whether that be at worship or at the house in Grand Alboreum Circus. They needed something to fill their day, and sought company, besides each other.

The carriage started to draw to a stop. Simi was looking out of the carriage curiously.

'When you say that your mother is … not with you … what do you mean by that exactly?' asked Phæ'enor, tentatively.

Simi, still looking out of the carriage and now wide eyed replied, 'Never mind that! Why in the world has the carriage pulled up here? And in broad daylight!'

They all looked outside to see that the carriage had pulled up right outside Polstor & Polstor. Phæ'enor sheepishly looked at her two cousins.

'Ah, yes. I just need to make a short visit.'

Her cousins glared at her, mouths open, as she moved to get out of the carriage, but was momentarily stopped by Master Rasia who hissed at her. He had jumped down from besides the driver and was now standing in front of the carriage door.

'Miss Doven, why have you brought us back here?' he demanded.

'What? Brought you back here?' asked Mimi.

'Look, I need some answers to some of the questions, information even, that Archä and Mëdez gave me … for my lessons, my homework. They are giving me lessons remember?'

'I hardly think these two will give you the lessons that are actually suitable for you,' said Master Rasia.

'Lessons?' exclaimed Simi.

'Wha … wha … well, why did you not think to write to them instead? It would have saved you, any of us coming here?' said a distressed sounding Mimi. Phæ'enor realised she had not thought to do this. But shrugged her shoulders and made to get out of the carriage.

'Move out my way,' demanded Phæ'enor. She shoved the carriage door so hard that it swung open and into Master Rasia's chest.

'Huh!' he groaned, winded.

'I'm sorry, but I have to see them!' said a haughty Phæ'enor, who climbed out and strode up the unkept path to the front door of Archä and Mëdez's shop. She banged hard on the door and turned around.

'Are you coming or not?' she asked her cousins and Master Rasia.

The two cousins looked utterly bewildered at what Phæ'enor was doing. Master Rasia was still clutching his chest. The door still hadn't opened and Phæ'enor could feel invisible eyes watching her. She tried to remember the sequence of knocks her mother used last time they were here, and rapped on the door again:

'Tap-tap,' pause. 'Tap-tap-tap-tap,' a longer pause, 'Tap!'

This time they did not have to wait as long for the door to open and as they waited there was no bird or the strange sound of bells. Small and rapid footsteps came soon after the knocks. A small crack in the door opened where there appeared a bright green eye, looking this way and that, then up and down at Phæ'enor.

'What are you doing here?'

'I need to see you both. About the books you gave me and ...'

'What? Now? You could have written a letter!'

'I told you so,' sulked Mimi.

'Yes, I know but...'

'Quick get inside. Before anyone sees you! Are you coming too?' demanded the little man of the other three.

With a look of horror on both Simi and Mimi's faces they jumped from the carriage and hurried up the path, looking around them to make sure they had not been seen. Master Rasia turned to the driver.

'Go around the block a few times. It's not good to be seen once here. Twice is inviting trouble.'

The driver nodded and moved the carriage on. Master Rasia then followed the girls up the path looking one more time at the street beyond. Phæ'enor caught him pausing for a second, like he was looking at someone. She peered over his shoulder; sure enough there was someone standing still and facing them, but far away. She could not make out who it was, and so it seemed Master Rasia couldn't either for he walked backwards inside the shop and closed the door. The series of bolts and locks rapidly went on against the glow of a lamp nearby.

'Come, come, come,' said one of the brothers impatiently. Phæ'enor guessed that it may be Mëdez but did not like to say. They followed the light of the lamp to the trap door at the far end of the darkened room and made their way, albeit clumsily, down the long ladder into the brightly lit chambers below.

'Ouch,' said Simi.

'What? You're moving too slow,' said Mimi.

'No, I'm not!'

'Yes, you are!'

'PLEASE! Be quiet,' shouted the little man.

The two girls became quiet as they finally descended the ladder.

'Now. Miss Phæ'enor Doven,' he said, 'why in the world did you come back here without an invitation?'

'We didn't have an invitation the first time as I recall.'

'As I recall I gave your mother the invitation.'

'Oh.'

'Oh,' he replied annoyed.

'We won't be here long, will we Miss Doven? She just needs to ask you something and we will be on our way,' said Master Rasia, more irritable than usual. Phæ'enor could detect a note of nervousness in his voice. Mëdez certainly was not as welcoming as the first time.

'Hmmm. Come with me.'

Mëdez lead the three girls and Master Rasia along the corridor. Phæ'enor heard the muted gasps of her two cousins. They were no doubt looking at all the crooked, ill and suspicious objects that lined the walls. Mëdez sped up and they all hurried up to keep pace. But instead of turning down the narrow corridor that lead to the circular library as before, he carried on until they reached the end, where from a distance the floor looked flat. Close up it revealed the beginning of a staircase that seemed to descend further underground.

'Oh, no, not more steps,' groaned Simi.

Phæ'enor ignored her protests and followed him down, the others following reluctantly. The steps were made of the same golden coloured stone as the corridor and very clean like everything else in Polstor & Polstor. Phæ'enor had noticed how everything inside Archä and Mëdez's shop was meticulously placed, even if they had not been touched for years.

They made their way down the ziz-zag staircase. After about fifteen minutes they came to a small hallway. Mëdez took a bunch of keys off the hook on his trouser belt and moved forwards towards a small wooden door, unlocking it in a most unusual way. At first Phæ'enor thought he was being idiotic, clumsy even, but after a while it looked as though Mëdez was deliberately turning the key in opposite directions. The door clicked every so often, left-left-right then left again. Phæ'enor looked at Master Rasia who shrugged back, seemingly in the same confusion.

The door clicked one last time which the little man opened up onto a long narrow corridor. It looked like an exact replica of the one leading to the circular library. However, as they moved through the room, although it opened in to a corridor, it was much larger. It made Phæ'enor feel extremely small. The room was wide, and the ceiling seemed to never come to a stop. But instead of books, although Phæ'enor spotted a few, the shelves were lined with more objects. Thousands, upon thousands of them. She moved over to one of the walls. A stained pillow sat limp on a low shelf. Attached to it was a brown label that read:

Used in the Death of a Mr Harland Howl; his
wife Mrs Liriene Howl, so sick of his endless talk,
used this pillow to suffocate him. The stain is
from Mr Howl having bitten his tongue and lips

in the process of trying not to be suffocated by his wife.

Phæ'enor grimaced as she turned the tag over. It read:

For killing her husband Mrs Liriene Howl was sentenced to a course of punishment befitting her crime: to spend the rest of her life in Blaindower, where she was played the sound of nails being dragged down a blackboard via a gramophone, day and night.

Note: Mrs Liriene Howl died after only two weeks into her sentence, having gone insane and thrown herself through the window of a top floor room at Blaindower.

'What is all this stuff?' asked Phæ'enor, repulsed. She felt the need to wash her hands.

'IT IS OUR COLLECTION!' came a shout from somewhere above. There was a loud click up ahead then a whoosh! That grew louder and louder. The other little man came sliding down a very tall brass ladder, jumping off as he got nearer the ground.

'Brother,' he said, inclining his head at the other little man.

'Archä,' said Mëdez.

'Miss Phæ'enor Doven, this is our collection of all the objects, instruments and pieces of every crime committed in the kingdom! And the empire of course,' said Archä proudly.

'What? All the crimes? You can't be serious?'

'Why not? What could be more fascinating than say … a silver rattle that was used to strike a blow and kill a man in an instant!' He grabbed a silver rattle, tag attached, and waved it around in Phæ'enor's face.

'Or … what about this …' Archä took a small bottle out of his inside jacket pocket. It was fat bottomed with a long neck and inside was a dark and oily looking liquid. 'Do you know what this is?' he asked the room at large.

'Oh, my,' said Mimi, 'that's, that's Purple Death from the Atro Hibdaluca plant.'

'What?' said Phæ'enor, surprised at her cousin's knowledge of such a thing.

'You know you're very good at pretending to not know anything dear,' cried Archä, 'I mean, that is why you're here isn't it?' he smiled mischievously at her from a side glance; still caressing the small glass bottle in his hands.

'What? What are you talking about?' asked Phæ'enor, confused by what had just happened.

'You come here uninvited, without very willing … what? family?' The twins nodded folding their arms and looking disapprovingly at Phæ'enor. 'And of course, with this one,' Archä said, flicking a finger at Master Rasia, 'all because you want to discuss the object, or objects from the biggest crime ever committed, don't you?'

'You've completely lost me there,' said Phæ'enor, getting irritated.

'Is it true then?' said Mimi, returning to the question of the bottle.

'Well of course my dear, if it wasn't do you think we would have the bottle?' Phæ'enor looked to her cousins then to Master Rasia for some sort of explanation as to the strangeness of the conversation. Master Rasia rolled his eyes, clearly, he did not think that what Archä and Mimi were talking of was serious enough to warrant caring about. He looked bored. Mimi continued:

'So, the poison of Atro Hibdaluca was used to kill King Barr?' asked Mimi.

'Yes, and the poison was made with the flowers found on the ground in the grass where the chests laid buried,' advised Mëdez.

'Wha … what … ? This is crazy. You're talking about that book? Those stories from The Namorian Curse?' asked Phæ'enor of Mimi, who nodded back, 'and … and … Officer Nathryn said one of his officers had carried that plant, the Atro Hibdaluca, on board The Scavenger…'

'Whoa, hold on there! No, no, no! I know you dragged us here for a reason but I'm not going to discuss this here, least of all with these two, who of all people we shouldn't even be seen with!' snapped Master Rasia. He had gone from being bored to highly agitated. Archä and Mëdez smiled and started to giggle. 'This isn't funny. We need to go!' shouted Master Rasia. He grabbed Phæ'enor by her wrist and made to pull her, shouting at the twins, 'MOVE! We need to head back above, onto the streets!'

'No!' shouted Phæ'enor, her thoughts still on the plant the officer had carried on board the frigate. 'These two owe me some answers!' She yanked her wrist free of Master Rasia's grip and pointing at Archä she snapped, 'You need to tell me why you gave me that small yellow book! I can't even read it because I can't read the symbols…'

'Symbols, what kind of symbols?' asked Simi, worried.

'Ssssh!' said Phæ'enor, holding her hand up to her cousin to be quiet before carrying on, 'and then there is that little black book about the Namorian Curse. It is full of these strange stories about hidden treasure in chests that are cursed. They kill whoever finds them, including King Barr. Then suddenly, in the newspaper, there's a picture of these chests that look exactly like the ones in the book you gave me, with symbols on the locks. And now you're telling me you collected the poison that killed King Barr in the first story of the book?' Phæ'enor stopped, breathless. Simi, Mimi, Master Rasia, Archä and Mëdez were all quiet but looking at her. Mëdez moved closer to her and took her right hand in his gently.

'My dear, not everything you read, in fact most things you read, never tell the whole story. History likes to leave out the most important facts. The, shall we say, bits that are more incriminating to those that committed the crime. They like to weave stories, or in other words lies, so ridiculously elaborate that only stupid people would believe them,' he cast a quick glance at Simi and Mimi as he said this.

'Then why did you give me those books if they are full of lies?'

'This is your first lesson, Miss Doven, to not believe everything you read, or what people tell you,' said Archa.

'I still don't understand?' said Phæ'enor. 'Are the cursed chests not real then?'

'Oh, they are quite real,' said Archä and Mëdez together, staring up into Phæ'enor's face in a matter of fact manner.

'Right, well this is why I came back here. Those books seemed to coincidently be linked to the recent theft of the twelve chests from The Scavenger. I was reading about them alongside the newspaper articles.'

Archä and Mëdez nodded at her to continue.

'So according to the little black book, all of the chests are cursed and bring bad luck, just like all the trouble that has been caused since the arrival of those chests in Benaghar, including the deaths of some of The Scavenger's crew.'

They bowed their heads and nodded. Master Rasia shook his in dismay whilst the twins stood gawping, ready for more.

'The difficulty I am having is that there were twelve chests on The Scavenger, I even counted them I was so bored, but the little black book says that ten of these have already been discovered and two are unaccounted for. So, if the chests on The Scavenger are the same ones from the little black book, then Officer Nathryn's men have found them all … or …'

'Or … ?' said Archä and Mëdez nodding, smiles on their faces.

'Or only some of them are real. I mean ten of them must be decoys and the other two are real?'

They nodded in agreement again.

'So, you think they are real?'

They nodded again.

'What, all of them are real?' said Phæ'enor excited.

They shook their heads.

'Wait, wait, wait,' snapped Master Rasia. 'Slow down. If these chests, or some of them are real, and they were on board The Scavenger, are you saying because they are cursed that they caused The Scavenger to blow up?'

Archä and Mëdez shook their heads with knowing smiles.

'No,' said Phæ'enor, 'others, besides Officer Nathryn and his men, must have known they were the cursed chests; or at least presumed they were. It was those others in pursuit of them that caused the ship to explode, and the theft of them at the garrisons. Which means there are people out there who believe in these stories? They believe they hold treasure. And they have linked the chests from The Scavenger to the story?'

'But according to that book not all of the chests have ever been found together again. There is no evidence of what has ever been found inside them.' This time it was Simi who had spoken. They all looked at her surprised. 'What? We've all read these stupid stories,' she said defensively.

'What do you two know?' demanded Master Rasia.

'Us?' said Simi and Mimi shocked.

'No! You two!' he pointed at Archä a Mëdez. Archä smiled up at Master Rasia slyly, Mëdez looked between the two of them, wary. 'You know what I mean. You've deliberately given Miss Doven here a strange book on symbols, that contain the very same symbols found on the cursed chests and then the book on the cursed chests themselves. It then so happens that Officer Nathryn and his fellow men bring said chests on board The Scavenger, which then proceeds to blow-up in the harbour. These chests then get moved to the garrisons. They then also get broken into and the chests are strewn all over the city. It's a bit of a coincidence isn't it? I mean for all we know they aren't the real ones and…' Archä, though small, managed to reach up high enough with one hand placing it over Master Rasia's mouth, his head and body facing the other way.

'There, my boy, you have hit the nail into the chest…'

'Mmm?' replied Master Rasia in a muffled response.

'Come with us,' said Mëdez.

They all reluctantly followed Archä and Mëdez over to the other side of the room to a small door concealed by all the objects surrounding it. Mëdez pushed it open. There was nothing but darkness beyond. He motioned all of them to follow him inside. They walked in, Mëdez closing the door behind them. It was cramped. They were all banging into each other.

'Ouch!' shouted Master Rasia.

Suddenly light filled the room. Mëdez and Archä were both holding lamps, illuminating the others. Behind the brothers hung a dark curtain. Master Rasia was rubbing his head and had lowered it so that he wouldn't hit it against the ceiling of the tiny room for a second time.

'Well?' said Archä and Mëdez.

They motioned for all to look behind them. Where the walls should have been there were instead deep rectangular recesses surrounding the entrance. Placed inside them were chests. Nine chests in total and they were all open. Phæ'enor moved closer to them, looking back at Archä and Mëdez to check it was okay to move forward. They nodded their approval.

She came to the first chest. The wood was rotten and full of holes. She looked inside. Nothing. She pulled the top of the chest down. The iron catch and lock had come away from the wood ever so slightly. Above the keyhole was a symbol imprinted into the iron, she put her fingers to it and traced the outline, slowly moving down to the keyhole.

Strangely, this was also an outline etched into the iron; maybe the hole only appeared when pressed into with a key? Phæ'enor carried the check out on all the chests. All nine carried the same symbol and were all made of the same rotting wood. They were all empty.

Phæ'enor retrieved the book from her travelling cloak and flicked through to the page of illustrations. The symbol on the chests in the room were the exact same as the symbols that appeared on the first nine chests in the book.

'I don't understand,' she said, turning back to Archä and Mëdez.

'What don't you understand, Miss Doven?' asked Archä, 'surely you can see before your eyes what is in front of you?'

'So … the chests do exist … and … and you have them here. How did you find them?'

'Ha,' barked Master Rasia, 'I think we all know they didn't "find them". Here you have the two most famous thieves and collectors of crime memorabilia. Whether it be true crime or ones they have created themselves.' At this Archä and Mëdez feigned a look of shock. 'When did you steal … how did you steal these chests from the garrisons?' demanded Master Rasia.

'No, I don't think you understand,' interrupted Phæ'enor, 'these chests are old, really old. They are falling apart.'

'They still stole them!'

'No, they didn't. Well at least not from amongst the chests found at the garrisons or from The Scavenger. Check the photograph of the chests in the paper, they are not as old as these ones, not by several hundred years, probably more,' said Phæ'enor.

'Besides, the ones that were stolen have all been recovered,' said Mimi quietly.

'Hmm … ,' said Archä. He delved into his jacket pocket and pulled out a pair of black gloves. They looked stiff, and Archä seemed to be having trouble putting his hands into them.

'Wait,' said Phæ'enor suddenly, 'O'sea was wearing a pair like those at The Grand Tea Rooms.'

'Quite,' said Archä and Mëdez in reply. Mëdez moved away from the nine chests and turned to face the back of the small room, pulling back the dark curtain against the wall. There in another deep recess of the wall, lay a tenth chest made of dark wood. Archä moved forward and undid the catch of the lock. There was a sharp intake of breath from Simi and Mimi.

'This is why I have gloves on,' said Archä. 'They are lined with oro stone so whatever the chest is coated, or soaked in, cannot harm me.'

'Oro stone protects you?' asked Phæ'enor.

'Yes,' said Master Rasia, 'it stops all manner of poison, not least of all emaz gold, from killing you. Why do you think the walls of the city are made of the stuff?'

Phæ'enor shrugged her shoulders.

'The enemies, more notably the Namorians used emaz gold in their weapons. It was quite ingenious, as they were the only ones who could touch it without dying,' said Mëdez.

'Anyway,' continued Archä, as he opened the chest up to reveal another empty shell, 'as you can see the lock on this one also has the same symbol as the one in the newspaper and is made of the same wood. However, my point is that Master Rasia here was right to some extent. We did take the chests from the garrisons.'

'I knew it!' said Master Rasia.

'Yes, yes, however Miss Mimi Doven here is also quite right in her thinking that the chests have all been recovered. This one is not a fake, however, it travelled independently of the ones brought over on The Scavenger.'

'So, what are you saying?' said Master Rasia.

'The chests on The Scavenger, in the garrisons, we believe they are all fake, bar one which I am sad to say we never got hold of,' said Archä.

'What you see are ten of the chests that your book tells a story of,' said Mëdez, who held his hand up to stop them from talking over him. Master Rasia looked as though he was about to. 'And you are correct, Miss Doven, they are extremely old. I'd say thousands of years old.'

'But how have they survived so long?' said Simi and Mimi.

Archä explained: 'We have, as we have done with all of our collection, and over the years and years of travel and research, quite possibly with a little help, acquired some knowledge regarding them. Then once acquired we have gone further; checking the type of wood they are made from, who may have made them, how they are preserved, etcetera.' He moved over to the display of chests and started to touch each one as he carried on explaining, 'We believe they were all made by the same person, or people, from the same tree or types of tree. But ultimately, there are two things that we can fathom of their long life and how they have lasted so long. It is due to what they are made of and what they were all inevitably carrying at some point or another. All of them looked at Mëdez and Archä, waiting for them to continue, 'There is only one tree in the world that could produce a wood like this, and of which would have a natural long-life span regardless. The Eckera tree which can only be found in certain parts of the world, indeed I don't think they even exist within our empire, maybe not even in our time.'

Phæ'enor thought back to when she was at the palace, when they had entered through the south gate and O'sea had shown them through the wooden hallway and the moving tree. It was grown from the Eckera. She looked over at Master Rasia, but his mood had darkened, and he held his hands over his face.

'The Eckera Tree is unusual because it only grows in the light of the moons,' said Simi in awe.

'And can be preserved by being kept in dark places,' said Mimi.

'The bark of an Eckera tree cannot be broken by brute force either,' said Simi.

'And even when you cut it down, it continues to live,' said Mimi in awe.

'It also takes on the elements in its surroundings, even when it has been cut; absorbs anything it can use to defend itself, and as it does so it makes the wood stronger, more durable, so it lasts longer than it's natural life span,' added Master Rasia.

'That explains the story about the chest that was constantly aflame and then could only be put out by the sea it was found in,' said Phæ'enor.

'Exactly, but they do eventually disintegrate and turn back into dust and disappear back into the ground like everything else,' said Mëdez.

'So, what could preserve the wood even longer then?' Master Rasia looked on at Archä but this time his face was serious and his eyes eager, 'it's emaz gold, isn't it?' He said it in an unnatural manner, eager, possessed even. Phæ'enor looked at Master Rasia and his sudden change in mood. She knew he was a soldier, that they were trained to kill but she had always seen him as a boy and an irritation. Yet with that look on his face, his demeanour changed, for the first time she sensed that he could be dangerous.

'Pre-cise-ly,' said Archä. He smiled his sly smile and stared straight back at Master Rasia.

Simi and Mimi looked worried.

'The emaz gold is rare, and very dangerous,' said Simi.

'Why?' asked Phæ'enor.

'Well … to you or me it can kill instantly. Just by touching it,' said Mimi.

'That's ridiculous,' laughed Phæ'enor. 'A gold that can kill a person?'

'You may laugh Miss Doven,' said Mëdez, 'but you have come in direct contact with this gold. You made quite a display of yourself at The Grand Tea Rooms because of it. Master Rasia here even said not to trust what they give you in there.'

'Yes, the tea, not a block of gold.'

'No. No, Miss Doven,' continued Mëdez, 'we don't think it was the tea that affected you.' He turned away and walked back out of the small room.

Phæ'enor and the others stood in silence, listening for Mëdez's footsteps. Archä who was playing with his fingernails gave her a quizzical look.

Mëdez returned a couple of minutes later and, wearing a pair of black gloves to match those of Archä's, he carried a teacup and saucer, cupped like it was precious. It was the blue china with a gold-plated rim around the top, the teacup they tried to make her drink from the last time she was there, and the exact teacup she drank from in The Grand Tea Rooms. Mëdez must have known what she was thinking.

'This teacup is the reason for your … shall we say … episode?'

'The gold on the rim is emaz gold. It should have killed you,' said Archä, still searching Phæ'enor with his eyes.

'Oh my,' said Simi and Mimi, together. Master Rasia no longer looked dangerous. He looked worried.

'This is madness! What are you trying to say? That O'tila and O'sea tried to kill me? With a … with a teacup?'

'Oh no, they're not that clever,' said Archä.

'Or that resourceful,' said Mëdez. The two little men laughed, then sighed. Phæ'enor raised her eyebrows at them unamused,

'Well?'

Mëdez shrugged his shoulders, 'After your little episode we tracked down O'tila for the gossip on what had happened, and he told us everything.'

'Yes, it seems he was still angry with how you showed him up in the marketplace, with Master Rasia here and that cat of his. Word got around that he was looking to get revenge and of course our favourite person O'scilla Juur turned up and gave him what he needed. A pair of black gloves, lined with oro stone, a teacup so say laced with poison and a waiter's uniform for O'tila to wear in The Grand Tea Rooms; but evidently he gave these to his cousin instead.'

They all looked at Archä and Mëdez, stunned.

'All that trouble just because Phæ'enor had hit him?' said Mimi astonished.

'Well, like we said, O'tila is not a clever boy, and neither is that idiot O'scilla Juur,' said Archä.

'So where did O'scilla Juur get the emaz gold rimmed cup from and the gloves and the waiter's uniform?' asked Master Rasia.

'Hmm … that I'm afraid we don't know, but whoever did give it to him knew what they were handling and told them a different story. You see there was never any poison in or on the tea cup, we checked. Whoever originally gave the teacup to O'scilla knew the emaz would cause an effect, albeit not the one they were expecting.'

'You mean death?' asked Master Rasia.

'Well, yes,' replied Archä and Mëdez

'But … but O'tila, O'sea and this O'scilla could have died?' said Phæ'enor.

'Oh, don't worry about them, it's hardly a loss to the world if they died!' said Mëdez. 'It would be quite fun to watch actually.' Archä nodded in agreement.

Exasperated, Phæ'enor continued, 'So, if O'scilla Juur, O'tila and O'sea, also had a set of those gloves … then whoever gave them to them knows about the chests?'

'Not necessarily, those gloves are quite common to find in the Isles of Cairdax and Banrein. There are a lot of gold mines there and unfortunately the miners come across emaz gold now and again. So you understand they need to be quite careful. However, that does not mean that you are wrong Miss Phæ'enor Doven. Mëdez and I are still looking into the source. And don't worry, those idiots don't have a clue that the cup and the chests are connected.'

They all nodded, trying to take in all the information Archä and Mëdez had given them. Phæ'enor touched her lips realising she was lucky not to come off worse after sipping from the cup, thinking of how it may have got O'sea and O'tila too, ignorant to what they held in their hands. And then it occurred to her, Archä and Mëdez had said that the only rumoured people to be able to handle the emaz gold were the Namorians, who were now extinct from this world.

'If the story is true, then the Namorians knew to make the chests from the Eckera wood so they would last longer,' said Phæ'enor to the room at large, 'and it would be hard for their enemies to penetrate the wood because it's so strong. But placing an object made from emaz gold within each chest would protect and preserve the chests even more. Like you said, Master Rasia, the Eckera wood absorbs anything it can use to defend itself, so if their enemy opened one of the chests they would die from touching the emaz gold.'

The room remained silent, but Phæ'enor thought about those who had come into contact with emaz gold, how they would die, unless they had some sort of protection made from oro stone, like the gloves. So how come she was still here?

Just then Master Rasia interrupted the silence, 'So, those nine chests over there are made from this Eckera wood, the same as the tenth chest, but they have started to disintegrate. Does that mean that those nine chests never contained the emaz gold, or it was removed from them way before the tenth one?'

Mëdez giggled, 'Very good, you are getting there Master Rasia.'

'Okay, so when do you think the emaz gold was removed from them?'

'The gold from these nine were removed hundreds of years ago,' said Archä.

'So they started to wilt away as soon as the gold was removed,' said Mëdez.

'Which means the tenth one,' said Master Rasia, 'is in better condition, because it had its gold removed much later. Maybe not that long ago?'

'Well, nearly,' said Mëdez. 'This one definitely had the emaz gold in it. There are traces of it, not to mention whatever was made from that gold was strapped down. Look inside.'

They all moved over and peered inside the tenth chest, careful not to touch it. Attached to the base of the chest were two leather straps, unbuckled and lying haphazardly.

'The rest have no traces of the gold, not anymore anyway,' said Mëdez. 'The reason for their disintegration is just age.'

Archä looked at all of them in turn and spoke, 'Whatever you may say, or others do, about The Namorian Curse, the chests do exist as does the treasure that was once within them. Kingdoms have fallen because of it.'

'All the same,' said Mëdez, 'we would like to acquire the eleventh chest for our collection here, along with its contents. And eventually from the others. You see we can't just have part of a crime in our collection, we want the whole lot.'

'However, our problem is that although we want it, we can't touch it, for naturally it would probably kill us,' said Archä.

'But surely the gloves lined with emaz will protect you?' said Phæ'enor.

'Ah, yes, well they don't always work ...' said Mëdez, 'not on emaz gold anyway.'

'That's great,' said Master Rasia, 'so not only could you have died just now, both of you, but the walls of our city are rendered useless if someone wants to attack us with weapons made from emaz gold.'

'There's no need to be so dramatic Master Rasia,' said Archä, now taking the gloves off and putting them back in his pocket.

Phæ'enor became irritated with the brothers, 'That's why you made me read the books, because you knew after examining the tea cup that the emaz gold may not affect me in the same way. You knew I would come back and ask you about it as well. My question is, if I do come into contact with the gold again how can you be sure I won't just die?'

'But it doesn't affect you Miss Doven, well, apart from The Grand Tea Rooms incident. We deliberately wanted to test you drinking from the tea cup again to make sure, but even holding the cup and saucer without protection would have killed you. You have just demonstrated that again by touching the last chest without any side effects. The poison of the gold effects everything it touches, apart from you it would seem, plus some china, stone and the Eckera wood.

I have had to replace the table in the library already and lined the tea tray with oro stone to stop it from burning through. Even The Grand Tea Rooms had to get rid of the table you were sat at, the tea cup scorched a whopping great big hole in it! So, you see, you will be absolutely fine; just don't put your lips to it the next time. We don't want any more attention being brought to you, not whilst we need your help.

You see, you were given those books on purpose Miss Doven, so you would come to understand a little about what we are after and how you can help us. You are going to get the eleventh chest and whatever it contains to go with our wonderful collection here. We tried our best, but it didn't quite work out for us at the garrisons did it, Mëdez?'

'What, that's absurd! Why can't you just be happy with the last chest that you "acquired" … surely you got the emaz gold from that one already?'

'Alas, we did not,' said Mëdez sadly. 'Believe me, we have tried and even though we tracked down the person who had come across it … but that trail has led to a dead end.'

'I'm sorry, but I'm not just going to help you after reading a few books!' snapped Phæ'enor.

'Well no, I suppose that's true. However, we thought you might be otherwise persuaded. You see Master Rasia here is in a sticky situation. Whilst he was away his older brother got into a spot of bother and was found guilty of a crime, he says he did not commit.' said Archä.

'You know he didn't!' shouted Master Rasia.

'Hmmm … well, yes, we do know actually,' said Archä, 'but more importantly we can give this information over to you. So you can speak to the city guards, who will then arrest the real culprit and your brother will then be set free. At least this is how we hope the scenario plays out.'

'Why can't you just give that information to him now?' demanded Phæ'enor.

'I'm afraid that is not the way we work Miss Doven, nor is it the Benagharian way,' said Mëdez, 'if you want something, then you must give something in return and vice versa.'

'I think it's an awful thing to do, and an appalling idea. You're both disgusting!' she snapped.

'No, it's not,' said Master Rasia. 'She'll acquire the chest and whatever gold is in it for you,' he said, addressing Archä and Mëdez.

'What?' exclaimed Simi, Mimi and Phæ'enor altogether.

'This is not the worst offer I have heard, in fact it's much better than what I would have thought of, and if it helps my brother…'

Archä and Mëdez nodded at him.

'You know who the real culprit is, you're sure?' asked Master Rasia.

'Yes,' the two brothers replied.

'And if we do this then you will give me the information to free my brother?'

'Of course,' replied Mëdez. 'But only if you get us what we want,' said Archä, 'that is the deal.'

'Fine. I don't see that I have any other options. Miss Doven, you must help me, help these two, no matter how devious they are. And they're right, this is the way of Benaghar, the sooner you learn that Miss Doven the better.'

Phæ'enor looked at Master Rasia, resolute and unmoving. She turned to her two cousins, who discreetly shook their heads in protest.

'Let me think about it first,' she replied.

'I hope you don't think about it for too long,' said Archä, who with a glint in his eyes stared straight into Phæ'enor's.

'We don't have the luxury of time Miss Doven,' said Master Rasia, before addressing the two brothers again. 'Do you have any idea where the chest might be?'

Archa and Medez shook their heads, 'It could be anywhere, but your best bet would be with those officers. You best be quick too, they seem to be dwindling in numbers and we hear your brother does not have long.'

Master Rasia nodded at them and turned to leave, 'Come on, the sooner we leave the sooner we can find this chest,' said Master Rasia. He grabbed Phæ'enor by her wrist and pushed the two cousins through into the narrow passageway and out the door, making their way hastily up the stairs, through the long corridor, up the ladder into the darkened shop floor above, finally stumbling toward the exit.

'Don't come back unless you have what we want!' shouted Archä and Mëdez behind them. There was the noise of tiny feet striding across the floor. The four of them had just stepped out into the street beyond when the door was swiftly slammed shut, the noise of bolts and locks sliding into place behind them. Another charming goodbye from the Polstors thought Phæ'enor to herself.

She followed the others, trying to keep up with Master Rasia, 'Why did you make us leave so quickly?'

'Like I said, we don't have time to linger. Plus, we stayed too long with them and you can never trust those two,' snapped Master Rasia.

'But, you heard what they said, they can prove your brother innocent if we get the chest and whatever is in it,' said Phæ'enor. Master Rasia was striding off down the path back to the carriage. The three girls ran after him. 'Well, are we going to then?' asked Phæ'enor.

'Of course we are!' he growled back. 'But how can I help my brother when I don't know where to start!'

'I don't know either, but I'm sure we'll find a way,' said Phæ'enor. The groans of disapproval came from her cousins' direction.

'Who is your brother anyway?' she asked, trying to keep Master Rasia from moving so fast, and her cousins moaning at her.

He paused, and then reluctantly turned around to face the three girls. 'Do you promise to help me?'

The three girls looked at each other uncertainly.

'DO YOU PROMISE?'

'YES, yes of course!' replied Phæ'enor, hoping that agreeing with him would keep Master Rasia from raising his voice again. 'Well then?' she prodded, 'who is your brother?'

'Wolf Canis,' he replied blankly, before turning back and marching off down the path. Phæ'enor, as well as Simi and Mimi, froze on the spot. She had just agreed to help the man who was accused of stealing from the crown, blowing The Scavenger up and, although wrongly, of stealing the chests from the garrisons. Master Rasia had now stopped in front of the carriage and shook his head, angry and confused, 'Just get inside, all of you. I'm taking you all home. NOW!'

Chapter Eleven

The Elusive Miss Phæ'enor Doven

The freezing weather had not abated from the streets of Benaghar and with it being too miserable to be outside, the inhabitants of the city had chosen to remain at home for another day. No 09 Grand Alboreum Circus was no exception. Master Rasia stood sentinel outside the front door but huddled in his cloak had kept to the shelter of the porch, out of the wind. Inside Mrs Jemin snored gently, having fallen asleep in the sitting room armchair. Mrs Doven was once again sat at the writing desk in the corner of the room, sipping her tea and reading through letters from friends. Phæ'enor was nowhere to be seen.

After the events of the day before, Phæ'enor had taken to avoiding everybody. Her grandmother and mother had asked her too many questions about whether she and her cousins had had a wonderful time or not and after exhausting the lies of the different shops they had visited did not want to get caught out. But all she could do was get angry thinking about how she and her two cousins had screamed, shouted and sulked all the way back home:

'I can't believe you dragged us both in there!' cried Simi.

'I hardly dragged you, as far I can remember you walked in of your own accord,' replied Phæ'enor.

'Huh, we hardly had a choice did we sister,' continued Simi. Mimi nodded sulkily back at her sister.

'You know we shouldn't even be outside the shop, nowhere near it in fact, let alone inside and entertaining the likes of Archä and Mëdez!' Mimi practically spat their names out she was so disgusted.

'What is so wrong with them?' snapped Phæ'enor back. 'Yes, they look slightly odd, but they can't be too bad. Not that bad anyway, they are trying to help Master Rasia's brother!'

'Who may I remind you is a crim-in-al!' said Mimi, emphasising the last word.

'Yes or lure you in!' snapped Simi. 'And at a pretty stupid price too I might add!'

'They always want something in return and I'm quite sure they don't just want that chest in return for Wolf Canis' freedom!' snapped Mimi.

'What's that supposed to mean?' shouted Phæ'enor back.

BANG! BANG! BANG!

The noise had come from above them. Their shouting at each other had been so loud that both the driver and Master Rasia had banged on the roof of the carriage for them to keep their voices down. Phæ'enor had looked out of the carriage window only to see concerned and shocked faces on the side of street as the carriage passed. Their arguing had attracted quite a lot of attention.

'Ouch!' screamed Phæ'enor. Simi had yanked her back inside the carriage by her hair, and then slammed her into the seat. Pressing her by the shoulders, Simi looked Phæ'enor in the eyes.

'When Archä and Mëdez ask for something it is usually like for like. If they ask you for a chest you get a chest in return, if they ask you for gold you get gold in return, and if they say they will free your brother or another's life, then they'll want your life or someone else's in return.' Phæ'enor fell silent. It was Mimi who spoke next.

'Archä and Mëdez don't just collect objects of crime; valuables that have either been used or found at a crime scene. It's also rumoured that they sometimes make these things happen. Owning criminal souvenirs is not always enough for them.'

'Rumours, that's all that is. You have no proof,' replied Phæ'enor, staring back at her cousins.

'Yes, we do,' said the twins together. They were no longer shouting and spoke softly, unhappiness creeping into their voices.

'We mentioned to you earlier that our mother … that she is not really with us anymore?' Phæ'enor sat silent and still, dread filled her bones and she thought she knew what they were about to tell her.

'Mother got into some trouble with The Grand Temple. She also believed in these chests and their treasure and asked Archä and Mëdez to seek more information. On her return she had gone quite mad. We don't know what happened to her in there. Really, we only have little to go on. Father never likes to talk about it. But she has never been the same person since.' Simi stopped talking and looked out of the carriage window, silent.

Phæ'enor looked at Mimi who stared back at her and said, 'Mother is in Blaindower. It's a sort of jail, but for sick people. All we are saying is just think, long and hard, before getting involved with those two. They go too far. You'll go too far, and you won't come back.'

'And don't forget, as much as they dislike O'scilla, they are all Harqs, and Harqs always stick together, they are like one big family,' concluded Simi.

Just then the carriage had stopped. Master Rasia had jumped down and opened the door to let the two cousins out. They did not look back at Phæ'enor, nor did they say their goodbyes. Master Rasia had slammed the carriage door, glaring at Phæ'enor unimpressed, before hopping back onto the carriage and pulling away.

It had not been a good day, she had lied to her mother, grandmother and her cousins. Now they were mad with her and as Mimi had pointed out she had agreed to help a convicted criminal!

It had made Phæ'enor think twice about helping out Master Rasia and his brother, so much so that when he came to the house in the early hours of the next morning she had taken to keeping out of his way altogether. Phæ'enor had made sure she was busy with chores even though she didn't have any. The young maid Florin had told her she was being silly and marched her back downstairs into the sitting room. But Master Rasia had called out to her from the front door:

'Miss Doven ... psstt ... Miss Doven.'

'Yes ... yes ... hang on a minute ... I'm just coming,' she replied, before checking no one was looking and slammed the front door shut on Master Rasia, locking it, before returning to her bedroom. But it was no good. Master Rasia, throwing stones at her window, was still able to shout for her attention from the cobbled streets below:

Tap!

'Psst ... Miss Doven!'

Tap!

'Why are you avoiding me?'

Irritated Phæ'enor opened her bedroom window a little way and hissed back down to him, 'Who said I was avoiding you ... I'm just busy.'

'Oh, yeah, what with? Making sure your hair looks pretty?'

At this remark there were sniggers from the rooftop across the way, but Phæ'enor could not make out anyone there.

'I'll have you know I am ... I am researching on how to help your brother. Now leave me in peace and I shall come to you when I have found something!' She slammed and locked her window before moving back downstairs to the back of the house into the library. But still Master Rasia persisted, this time knocking on the windows.

Knock, knock!

'Miss ... hey Miss Doven. What have you found out?' Phæ'enor had thrown herself on the floor, crawled over to the window and sat underneath it at this latest disturbance, with a book called The

Many Moons of Ëbe clutched to her chest. Master Rasia peered in through the windows.

'Look … I know you're avoiding me, but it was your idea to take me and your cousins to see Archä and Mëdez. You promised you would help me, help them … looks like you can't keep your promises!'

Furious at the accusation Phæ'enor had violently pulled all the curtains in the library shut, plummeting herself into darkness. But Master Rasia was right. She had not looked at the little black book, The Namorian Curse, to see if it revealed any information that would help them either find or unlock the chests, or if anything else in their pages would set Master Rasia's brother free. Instead, Phæ'enor had left them in the pocket of her travelling cloak, which was still hanging in the hallway from the day before.

***

It was late afternoon and the Dovens and Mrs Jemin, having taken a light and early dinner of sandwiches, were settling in for the evening.

But unlike her grandmother and mother in the sitting room, Phæ'enor was in the only room in the house where Master Rasia could not disturb her.

Sat in a dusty armchair and huddled over the large blue volume on Benaghar: The Heart of an Empire, and the book The Many Moons of Ëbe, Phæ'enor had been warming her feet by the cook's open fire in the basement kitchen; at the same time the cook, Mrs Tior Tibba, Mr Deke, Mrs Bride and Florin all ate their dinner at a small but very sturdy wooden table in the middle of the room, gossiping about the news and events in the paper in front of them:

'Oh … looks like the king has come down with another illness,' said Mrs Tibba, as she scanned the front page.'

'Really, what with?' asked Mr Deke.

'Some sort of tropical illness?' replied Mrs Tibba, shrugging her shoulders.

'Mmm … that's odd, he's not been near the tropics recently,' said Florin.

'Hmm … I doubt he ever did,' said Mr Deke.

'Oh, Farris!' exclaimed Mrs Bride at the cheek of Mr Deke. They all laughed.

'It does say that his treatment is going well, though, and he will still be able to make the Festival of Heramar.'

Phæ'enor looked up at the mention of this, 'What is the Festival of Heramar?'

'Oh, well I suppose it is like the Moon Festival that you would have celebrated in Vanu,' said the cook, 'to celebrate the reign of King Sol and the moon that watches over him. It's also an excuse to celebrate the ending of the last wars in the east.'

'Except here we get to re-enact the battles that we have won in the various parts of the empire. We all dress up and wear masks, so no one knows who's who. There is street entertainment from morning 'til night; fireworks, dancers, foods stalls … there is just so much fun and…'

'Yes, yes, yes Florin … I think she gets the idea,' said Mrs Tibba.

'I bet you don't re-enact the battles the empire lost,' mumbled Phæ'enor.

'What was that?' said Mr Deke.

'Oh, nothing … I was just wondering when it takes place.'

'Why, it's tomorrow Miss Phæ'enor. But I'm afraid you won't be taking part, dear,' said Mrs Bride.

'Why not?'

'Why it's your birthday silly.'

They all laughed and carried on chatting. Phæ'enor not overjoyed by the prospect of her birthday returned to her books.

She had turned a page opening onto a section about the laws of marriage. This did not lighten her mood. After having to endure being lectured on the subject by Archä and Mëdez, and it being the favourite subject of her cousins, Phæ'enor did not linger too long on these pages, skimming her way through sections that only made her wrinkle her nose as she read through:

> *"…after a woman is married she is then allowed to attend social gatherings in the city, walk about town without a chaperone, and not before then or under any other circumstances…"*

> *"…after the marriage vows the woman must show that she is married, not just through the type of dress she wears (skirt must now be below the calves, shoulders and arms covered at all times, no matter the weather), must wear a hat in public and shorten ones hair (this must be done within seven days of the vows having been made)…"*

> *"…she may now be allowed to venture beyond the northern city walls, accompanied only by her husband, and no other. Depending on the purpose of the venture will depend on the licence both she and her husband have been given…"*

It went on like this, page after page, until the section ended on a footnote:

> **For Laws on Royal Marriages and Celebrations see p. 713*

Let's see if a queen has to abide by her king, thought Phæ'enor sarcastically, before turning to page 713 in the book. She read through the section, everything was nearly the same for a princess or potential queen, except their chaperones had weapons and they were under constant guard, with or without a king. Maybe they are just used to it, thought Phæ'enor, thinking how lucky she was that she had much more freedom to roam the city. But what did stand out was how many wives a king could have compared to an ordinary man:

> "…Whereas a male subject of the king may marry only one woman, unless he be widowed then marry again, a king may be entitled to take as many wives as he so wishes. However, this is subject to debate amongst royal councillors. Some say that the king may have multiple wives either for sanctioned pleasure or so that they may produce as many royal heirs as possible. An example of the latter was recorded in 612 whereby Queen Rohmora was unable to conceive any children for King Dronic of the House Asabrian. So in love with her that he could not execute her for being barren, he married for the second time to Queen Ena. Again, infertility struck with her so King Dronic married again. Unfortunately, none of the eighteen queens to King Dronic were able to fall pregnant. It was clear that there was something wrong with the king and in the end the royal council had no choice but to have him sentenced to death; not just on the account of his inability to produce heirs, but on the account of how much money his eighteen marriages had cost the court. The eighteen queens were also executed, reducing the expenses of the court dramatically. His nephew

*Ettan, succeeded him as King, taking only one
wife in his lifetime and producing eight male
heirs and one female."*

Phæ'enor smiled to herself at the turn of events for King Dronic and
the royals, serves him right for being so greedy, she thought, as she
turned the page, landing on a section about royal celebrations. It
covered all sorts from birthdays to coronations. Phæ'enor thought
them all rather strange, some unfair and others just slightly sadistic.
On royal birthday celebrations, it noted the following:

*"…a royal birthday parade is held whereby the
royal in question is paraded in a gold box carried
by those of the inhabitants of the city; who were
fortunate enough to have won the
competition…"*

Phæ'enor looked at the illustration below to see a fat king, robed in
furs and wearing a large crown, squashed into a gilded box and
several, hunched and sweating men, women and children, at either
end grimacing with the weight they held on their shoulders.

*"…on the royal birthday all inhabitants are
exempt from paying tax for the day…"*

Well at least that is a bonus, thought Phæ'enor. They should have
more birthdays, she thought, before she read on:

*"…instead they have the pleasure of bringing to
the box gifts for the royal's birthday…"*

Below this were items and gifts listed as acceptable to give to a
royal; from food offerings, a live cow or lamb, silk garments and

jewellery, a day's wages and even a daughter or two for the court's pleasure. Disgusted, Phæ'enor turned the page over onto royal weddings and coronations. Here an illustration of a king and queen laughing on their thrones headed the page; their court entertainers dancing about them. Along with more illustrations it listed the many days leading up to, and after a wedding or coronation, and of more offerings to the royals; along with festivities in the streets, balls and parades.

As well as the proceedings of the ceremonies, the rituals and vows included a funny image of a naked king, albeit adorning his crown, wrestling a shark that had managed to lock its jaws across his midriff. It read:

> *"…a king, in order to show his strength and power to his future queen and her family may choose to wrestle a bear, a wild cat, a heard of Giant Long Haired Bos or even a Blue-tip shark from the River Nebben…"*

Phæ'enor had scoffed aloud at this latest bit.

'What's so amusing?' asked Mrs Tibba.

Phæ'enor looked over trying to keep the mirth off her face. The cook, maids and Mr Deke were still sat at the table reading through their own books and papers, now eating the left-over sandwiches.

'Oh, nothing, just some funny pictures,' replied Phæ'enor. Mrs Tibba shrugged her shoulder at the others before they returned to their own conversation. Phæ'enor turned her attention back to her book and the section on royal marriage rituals. These included the likes of a game called "Eksymirya," whereby the new king or queen, under supervision of The Grand Temple priests would spiritually cleanse the decay from the old sovereign's reign by the execution of the masses. Phæ'enor read the description of what was meant by the "masses:"

Those to be executed include but is not limited to the following: the population of the gaols in the city or the empire at large; where it has been deemed by the guards to be overpopulated. Enemies of the empire; including heirs to the throne the new sovereign may wish to be rid of, such as courtiers, generals and commanders the new sovereign no longer needs the services of, as well as the undesirables and members of the population in general.

Phæ'enor, bemused read on to the rules of the game:

This game is performed by the new sovereign, who must announce the name or names of those to be executed so that under law the priests and all those present may bear witness. The only exception to the rule is if the new sovereign is unsure who to pick. He may choose a member of the court to carry out the naming for him. This can include, princes, musicians, dancers, and courtier's etc. However, throughout history the baton is generally passed onto the lead entertainer as a way in which to make more light of the game.

Execution can hardly be made a light matter of, thought Phæ'enor, before carrying on reading the footnotes below it:

*It is highly advised that a new sovereign must appoint their own courtiers and entertainers before Eksymirya is performed. If they carry it

*out with the courtiers or entertainers chosen
under the old sovereign then they no longer have
a choice in how the game proceeds, forfeiting the
choice of those to be killed. An example of this
happened in the year 1298 when the new King
Cail II of the House Eborath declared the game to
begin the celebration of his coronation only for
the lead entertainer, a lute player by the name of
O'hals who had been appointed under King Cail I
of the House Eborath, to take over proceedings.
He sung for nine days and nine nights, killing
his fellow entertainers right in front of the king
and his guests at the dinner table; due to some
private dispute over who was the best musician.
Naturally King Cail II was not impressed
especially since he himself was not allowed to
execute O'hals (under the rules of the game, the
one named to carry out the executions are
themselves exempt from death by Eksymirya).*

'Kuh!' scoffed Phæ'enor aloud again.

'Now what is it Miss?' asked the young maid Florin.

'Nothing,' replied Phæ'enor dismissively, before turning the pages of the book again searching for the index and hoping to find something a bit more pleasant to read about. But it seemed the book was not intended for light entertainment, having come across yet another unpleasant topic about The Undesirables in the City, under the section called Crime and Punishment in the City. Phæ'enor, intrigued, turned straight to the section on p. 999.

Having opened the book it revealed images of various people and writing next to each one, detailing what type of Undesirable they were; why to stay clear of them and laws both they and other inhabitants of the city should abide by concerning each one.

Phæ'enor, taking her time, turned the pages of this section, coming to a stop on an image of a woman, who looked quite normal, with her lace dress and a nice floral hat. She looked above and read the words Undesirable No 19: The webbed variety. Phæ'enor looked at the image again to see the lady had indeed very large webbed fingers and very large webbed feet sticking out the bottom of her dress. She scoffed at the idea of a frog like woman wandering the streets of Benaghar and turned over a few more pages, this time stopping on an image of two people: small, smartly dressed in large top hats covering unruly hair, one peering around the side of the other. It was no mistaking who these two were meant to be. Above the image it read Undesirable 29: The Collectors. Underneath the image of Archä and Mëdez all it stated was the following:

> *Under no circumstances are The Collectors to be approached! Believed to be the masterminds behind a series of crimes in the empire, all in pursuit of criminal souvenirs. Many a crime has thought to be unsolved due to their meddling, and many criminals still on the loose due to their actions.*

> *All inhabitants of Benaghar, indeed any member of the empire, should not make any contact with The Collectors. If approached unwillingly by The Collectors inform the city guard immediately.*

> *Punishment: If a Collector you will be sentenced to death. If you work with or come in contact with The Collectors, you will be sentenced to death.*

Phæ'enor scoffed again. It made sense now why her cousins were so twitchy about their visit the day before. But her mother had not seemed to care, and Master Rasia had clearly been in contact with the Polstors before. It was also a bit strange and funny that according to the book they had a sentence of death over their heads, yet they were still alive, going about their business with that shop of theirs for all to see. If the authorities wanted them that bad then surely, they would have done it by now.

'Kuh!' huffed Phæ'enor again, before slamming the book shut and throwing it on the floor by the fire.

'You have been huffing and puffing all evening Miss, what are you reading that causes you so much trouble?' asked the young maid Florin.

'I was reading the book on Benaghar: The Heart of an Empire, she replied.

'Ha!' laughed Mr Deke, 'you want to stop reading such nonsense.'

'It's not nonsense, it was given to me by Ar … by my tutor, to help me learn the ways of Benaghar.'

'That book won't teach you nothen' about the ways of Benaghar, girl,' laughed Mrs Tibba.

'Yeah, all the laws and punishments in there are so old now no one uses them anymore. They probably can't remember most of them!' said Mr Deke.

They all laughed at Phæ'enor. She frowned back.

'It's all a load of bollocks,' said Mrs Tibba.

'Mrs Tibba!' exclaimed Florin. They all laughed at this, including Phæ'enor.

'Anyway, you want to be more careful of what they haven't put in that book,' said Mrs Bride.

'Have you read it?' asked Phæ'enor.

Mrs Bride nodded, 'Yes, we all have at some stage. When we went to school. Can't remember most of it of course but I know for a fact that it doesn't include a lot of things.'

'Like what?' asked Phæ'enor.

'Well like what we have been talking about all evening Miss Doven,' said Mr Deke

Phæ'enor looked at them blankly.

'Whilst you have had your head in that book Miss, we have been talking about the latest news and the recent war of course,' said Florin, looking at her like she was daft.

'War?' said Phæ'enor, alarmed.

'Yes, you dafty,' said Mrs Tibba, 'the latest one between the wolves and the rats in the city.'

Phæ'enor frowned. She had been out in the city quite a few times now, and the only fight she was aware of was the one between her and O'tila in the marketplace. The only other major disturbances were the destruction of The Scavenger and the break in at the garrisons. She could not recollect any war between the wolves and rats out on the streets, she hadn't even seen any of them and if she had she wouldn't know who they were.

'Are you quite sure about that Mrs Tibba? I couldn't see any fighting out on the streets.'

'Well of course you wouldn't have, Miss. It all happens at night, so you wouldn't have seen any of it anyway,' replied Mrs Tibba knowingly.

Phæ'enor was still unconvinced and it showed.

'Here, take a look at this,' said Mr Deke, throwing the newspaper in Phæ'enor's direction.

She caught it and looked down at the front page. The headline and article below read:

The Wolves V The Rats: Battle for the   Streets of Benaghar

After the recent disturbances in the city, including the break in at the garrisons and the destruction of HMS The Scavenger, there is speculation amongst the city guards and politicians that both the wolves and the rats in their attempts to gain more ground and power amongst the undesirables of the city, have escalated their criminal activities. More recently, there have been burglaries and break-ins at homes amongst the elite of society; unexplained disappearances of soldiers and city guards and an escalation in reports from people being followed home at night, held at gun point and mugged.

One politician, who did not want to be named advised, "It is my opinion, and that of others, that the disappearances in the city are down to the rat gang. Home owners have reported sudden appearances of them coming up from the sewers and grabbing unsuspecting passers-by. It is also believed that to match their antics, like for like, members of the wolf gang have been behind the recent burglaries, accessing homes via the chimneys and staff entrances."

When questioned on how the wolves could be doing this under the direction of their leader, who is currently in gaol, the politician failed to answer the question. Many home owners are also questioning their members of staff, some of whom have direct links to both gangs, as to whether they have been giving them access. As yet, no one

has reported whether they had dismissed a
member of their household staff.

The city guards are also still refusing to confirm
if there is evidence to suggest there is a direct link
between the two gangs and the wanted criminal
O'scilla Juur, with the possibility that there are
further links to the infamous Polstor twins. For
more background information on these criminals
please turn to page 6.

Phæ'enor finished reading the article, knowing that the involvement of the two gangs in the garrison break-in and The Scavengers demise was not true. But she remembered her grandmother had visited Mrs Oleston the other day; her son Lieutenant Hall Oleston had disappeared, plus there was the matter of those boys on the roof opposite her bedroom window.

'Do you think it's all true?' she asked the others in the room.

'Who knows?' said Mr Deke.

'I must admit, that lately there has been much more pandemonium in the city, well since you arrived actually,' said Mrs Bride.

Florin nodded in agreement and said, 'You were also broken into, they got straight into your bedroom, Miss.' Yes, but that wasn't a wolf or a rat, thought Phæ'enor, it was another servant and a royal one at that. Then she remembered what the article had said about the burglaries across the city and staff links to the two gangs.

'Do any of you have friends or family in either of the two gangs?'

There was uproar from Mrs Tibba, Mrs Bride, and Mr Deke at the suggestion.

'No, I bloody do not!' snapped Mrs Tibba.

'I wouldn't associate with them if you paid me more than my wages!' roared Mr Deke.

'I can't believe you would think of such a thing!' gasped Mrs Bride.

'Okay, okay. I'm sorry. I was just curious whether you knew anything about them. I didn't mean to offend you.'

They all simmered down, looking out of sorts and ruffled. Florin was silent, looking down at her hands. After a few minutes of awkward silence, the cook spoke up:

'Right, well, I think it's time we all went to bed. It will be another early start.'

'Hmm,' said a disgruntled Mr Deke, as they all started to get up from the table and made their way over to the stairs.

'Make sure you don't stay up too late, Miss Phæ'enor,' said Mrs Bride, as she locked the kitchen door to the garden, 'you have a big day ahead of you tomorrow, what with your birthday celebrations.'

'I won't,' said Phæ'enor.

'And make sure you lock your windows, Miss,' said Florin, with a shy smile and followed the others up the stairs.

***

Phæ'enor leant back in her chair by the fire, blowing hot air out of her cheeks. She thought about the article in the newspaper, information on the undesirables in the city and the reaction of the staff of No 09, when asked about the wolves and the rats. It only reminded her of what she had agreed to help Master Rasia with. His brother was not only a member of one of these gangs, he was the leader of the wolves and currently locked up in the city gaol. From what she had read about the Polstors she should also be locked up, awaiting her sentence of death, just for associating with them.

It was dark and quiet outside, but the fire was still going and still restless from all the information swimming around in her head,

Phæ'enor stayed in the kitchen a little longer. She bent down, and as to avoid more horror stories, picked up the book The Many Moons of Ëbe. It was beautifully illustrated with many detailed drawings of the moons that Phæ'enor had gazed upon for many years, from Hallumera to Ephynus. The pages were boarded by gold leaf and brightly coloured inks. Moons, and stars twinkled back at her; like they had come alive on the page.

As she casually flicked through her eyelids began to droop, words passed her vision; *"Only one moon, the moon of Ëbe existed … thousands of years ago a great collision caused Ëbe to separate into many moons. Some believed it nearly destroyed the world … over the years many of these moons have died or collided with one another … new ones have been created …"*

'Miss Doven…'

Phæ'enor felt herself shake from her shoulders down.

'Miss Doven, wake up!' She rocked even more, slowly opening her eyes. She was still in the basement kitchen, having fallen asleep by the now dying embers of the fire. The Many Moons of Ëbe was on the stone flagged floor and the grey cat gently purred as it pawed at her feet. Something shook her again.

'Oi, Miss Doven, over here.'

Stiff necked, Phæ'enor turned her head only to be faced with someone she did not expect.

'Master Rasia!'

'Sssh! Keep it down.'

Master Rasia's cat intertwined itself through Phæ'enor's legs.

'Why are you here, you never come into the house? Hang on … how did you get in? The doors are all locked.'

'Sssh … that doesn't matter. I'm here because I need to show you something…'

'What? now?'

'Yes now!'

'But … it's still the middle of the night!'

'Actually, it's early in the morning, very early. Happy birthday by the way.'

'What? This is silly … can't it wait until later?'

'NO! No, it can't. You have been avoiding me for too long … don't think I don't know why. You're wishing you hadn't agreed to help my brother out, right?'

Phæ'enor looked at Master Rasia and didn't answer. The cat stopped what it was doing and looked at her, casually flicking its tail.

'I know you don't want to … I know you think it's a bad idea. It's written all over your face. Criminal or not, I know he didn't commit these crimes. He needs help, our help Miss Doven. And if you can't be persuaded by me then I have no choice. Get up!'

'Ow!' grimaced Phæ'enor, as Master Rasia pulled her out of her chair, 'what choice don't you have?'

'Sssh … just put this on and be quick about it.' Master Rasia handed Phæ'enor her dirty and worn travelling cloak.

'How did you get this? It was upstairs in the hallway…'

'Does it really matter? Come on, let's just go!'

'I'm not going anywhere…'

Master Rasia faced Phæ'enor, inches from her face, 'You are coming with me whether you like it or not. If you don't help me, it won't just be me that you'll have to deal with. Archä and Mëdez will come after you too. You made a promise to them as well as to me, remember?'

They stared at each other in silence. Phæ'enor remembered what her cousins had said about their mother being in Blaindower after her dealings with Archä and Mëdez, how the law stated that she herself would be a criminal if she associated with them, and how Archä and Mëdez always got what they wanted.

'Put your cloak on. Florin already took the books out of your pockets. They are safe in your room.'

'Did she let you in? Did Florin let you into the house?'

Master Rasia unlocked the back door of the Kitchen, 'Yes, or course she did. Now get moving.'

Phæ'enor stood still gawping at him and at the audacity of the young maid.

'Move!' hissed Master Rasia, before he walked over and pulled Phæ'enor out the back door, locking it behind him and pocketing the key. 'Come one!'

Phæ'enor was pulled up the basement stairs and onto the lawn of the back garden, Master Rasia forced her cloak onto her and then grabbing her wrist continued to pull her behind him, walking faster and faster.

'Why would Florin do that? She could lose her job! Did you force her to?' said Phæ'enor, in angry whispers.

'Why would I need to force Florin to help me? She's my sister!' replied Master Rasia, yanking Phæ'enor through the garden gate into the street beyond, leaving it to creak closed behind them.

Chapter Twelve

The Wolf King

'Will you please let go of me! My wrist is starting to burn!'

Phæ'enor kept tugging and twisting, trying to break free of Master Rasia's grip. He had been moving fast and pulling the weight of Phæ'enor behind him; yanking her when she tried to dig her heels into the cobbles. It had worked a few times but in the end Master Rasia would spin her violently, and then shove her hard from behind until she gave up.

'Just keep moving!' he would snap, never looking back, only moving ahead.

Phæ'enor looked about her. They were not heading down Grand Town Promenade to one of the other areas of the city. When they had left the garden of No 09 Grand Alboreum Circus Master Rasia had instead led them across the green squares of similar looking Grand Circus buildings, in and out of the different cobbled streets that connected them all together. The street lamps had started to reduce in number as they got further from the house. Now it was only darkness that surrounded them.

Phæ'enor became more aware of both her footsteps and Master Rasia's, only the cat was silent as it easily kept pace. But there were others. Swinging her body around, left and right Phæ'enor tried to see who was following them.

'Ow!' shouted Phæ'enor, crossly.

'Pay attention and keep moving! The less you struggle the easier this will be and the sooner it will be over and done with!'

'If you stopped yanking me then I wouldn't be slowing you down!'

Master Rasia stopped suddenly. Phæ'enor slammed into him. He glared down at her, she glared back.

'You have got to be the most irritating person I have ever had to deal with in my whole career!'

'Well why don't you just quit then? You can take me back to the house and bugger off!'

'It's not that simple, Miss Doven! You are coming with me and…'

'With you and who else? It's not just us out here is it? I may have promised to help you, but you promised my father to watch over me and my family, yet you have dragged me out in the middle of the night! I don't know where we are going and who else is following us!'

Barring his teeth in frustration, Master Rasia whistled out loud. Then taking Phæ'enor by her shoulders roughly turned her around and waited.

'What? I don't see anything. Is this some sort of stupid game? You know you can be such a … such a…'

Phæ'enor stopped talking. In the darkness that they had left behind, strange little reflections of light drifted in mid-air towards them. She tilted her head wondering what they were. They looked like bright fireflies, hundreds of them surrounding the pair. She looked up at the backs of the houses from the last Grand Circus they had passed; their roofs were lit up with the same lights, only this time she could see the silhouettes of the bodies they belonged to.

'What are they?'

'Wolves. They are keeping watch for both of us, none of them will harm you whilst I am around,' said Master Rasia. 'Now come on, we haven't much time.'

He turned Phæ'enor back around, this time letting go of her, and walked off towards the shadow of some tall trees, before disappearing between the trunks of two of them. Phæ'enor turned to look at the light from the many eyes behind her. They had all vanished. She backed up before turning and moved swiftly after

Master Rasia, the grey cat following as they disappeared beneath the cloak of branches and leaves.

***

Phæ'enor tried to keep pace with Master Rasia, his long strides forced her to jog to keep up. Sometimes this caused her to trip and fall over amongst the roots of the trees and the dry soil. The cat took everything in its stride, pausing every now and again with a bored expression, waiting on them.

They had been walking up a steep incline of a wooded area on the edge of Grand Town and for every step Phæ'enor took she felt her throat get drier, her lungs constrict as the air became warm and closed in on them.

'Master Rasia, how much further until we scan stop? I can hardly catch my breath in here!'

He carried on walking, ignoring her questions. He had started to slow down and was nearly bent to a crawl as the incline became rapidly steeper.

'I said, how long until we...'

'Not long!' he shouted back. 'We are nearly at the entrance, just keep up and watch where you step.'

Phæ'enor grappled with the dirty forest floor, using the roots to pull her up the steep bank. Up ahead Master Rasia had finally stopped. He had stooped over with his hands on his thighs to catch his breath.

'Come on Miss Doven, you can do better than that … I thought all that running around in the jungles of Vanu would have kept you fit!'

'Shut up! I didn't do that in the dark you idiot, and not in a dress!'

'Ha!' laughed Master Rasia. He straightened up and turned his back to Phæ'enor. As she finally reached the top she sat on the ground to catch her breath and saw what he was looking at. Through the branches and weeds that had crawled up the side of it, glimpses of the oro stone glittering between, stood the city wall. But unlike the walls that divided the different areas of the city this one reached further into the sky above, looming over her and Master Rasia. He was gazing up at it.

'What? Are you expecting us to climb that? I don't need to remind you that I am not exactly dressed for climbing walls … or trees if you think that is how we are going to get over it.'

'No. No we are not going to climb the wall,' replied Master Rasia. 'We are going through it.'

Phæ'enor looked at him bemused, 'Good luck with that one. It looks pretty solid to me unless you're going to tell me you have some sort of magical power that lets you walk through solid walls.'

'Ha, if only that was the case, it would make my life much easier.'

Master Rasia walked over to the wall. From behind, Phæ'enor watched as he reached into his clothing and leaned into it, making small but quick movements, shifting about from left to right. It reminded her of Mëdez with his set of keys in Polstor & Polstor, turning the key in a series of movements and clicks.

'Right, get up,' said Master Rasia, as he moved over to Phæ'enor and pulled her up. She looked over his shoulder to see that an opening in the wall had appeared.

'How did you know that was there?'

'I grew up in this city remember, I know a lot more about its secrets than you do Miss Doven,' he said with a smile, but this soon disappeared.

Phæ'enor looked at him, her eyes wondering over his clothes; dirty knees and shins, 'You have been here before, the day you came to visit me, after I was taken ill at The Grand Tea Rooms. This is where you had come from, wasn't it?' Rasia looked at her and nodded in reply. So, he had just been passing by after all, thought Phæ'enor.

Above them flashes of the light from the moon of Hallumera shone down upon them, and the rustle of the trees at the bottom of the hill caused Master Rasia to look in their direction. They were silent for some moments until someone spoke:

'Rasia, you need to get going. There are less city guards in there now, but not for long, the patrols will only be short this evening.'

'Fine. Thank you, Cana,' he replied and then looked back at Phæ'enor, 'let us go.' Without a struggle this time, he took Phæ'enor by the hand and led her to the opening in the city wall, 'Stay close to me, at all times, and make as little noise as possible.' He turned back to the cat, 'Rama, stay here with Cana and the others.' The cat looked up from the middle of its groom, licked its lips, and then carried on as though it had never been addressed. 'Right, are you ready?' he asked Phæ'enor.

She nodded in agreement and together they entered the dark passage of the wall, the doorway closing gently behind them, gradually blocking out the light of Hallumera.

***

It was surprisingly warm inside the city walls and it was not long before both Phæ'enor and Master Rasia had started to work up a sweat. It did not help that after entering and taking a turn, they continued to ascend a steep stone floor that had no grip to it. Phæ'enor did as Master Rasia had asked, sticking close behind but also to the wall so that she could help feel her way through.

After some time, an orange glow appeared up ahead, but instead of picking up speed Master Rasia slowed down, creeping slowly towards it and speaking over his shoulder to Phæ'enor.

'The passage we are in joins onto a large walkway… no, it's more like a street but hidden by the city walls. Usually it is teeming with city guards and other officials from the city. They have patrols both out in the city streets and within the city walls. Luckily for us the timings of their patrols never change.'

'Isn't that a bit pointless then, having a guard that keep to the same watch? If an enemy of the city were to find out then it would be easier to take them unawares and take the city by force.'

'Exactly,' said Master Rasia. Phæ'enor could hear a faint hint of joy when he spoke.

'Idiots!'

'Yes, they are. But our purpose is not to take the city by force.'

'Really, I would never have guessed? What is our purpose then; I mean why exactly are we inside the city walls in the first place? Can we not get to where we need to be by taking the normal routes?'

'Not unless you want to get caught. Besides where we are going we wouldn't be allowed in through the normal entrance, so this is the only option,' he replied, 'wait here, I'll check that the coast is clear before we can move on.'

Phæ'enor watched as Master Rasia disappeared around the corner towards the orange glow of light. She glanced behind into the dark, it was still and not even the smallest sound could be heard. She adjusted the collar of her dress, it was sticking to her from the heat of the place. She wondered if the way they had come was known only to Master Rasia and his friends or if others held its secret.

'It's clear.' Master Rasia appeared around the corner and beckoned Phæ'enor to follow him again.

Phæ'enor, still using the walls as a guide moved towards the orange glow, turned the corner and stepped out in wonder at where she was. The walls towered high above them and were decorated with simple stone arches as though they were in some sort of temple. It was indeed like being on one of the city promenades, except here they were enclosed. Everywhere she looked oro stone twinkled back, even in the cobbles beneath her feet. Was it the stone that made everything light up, she thought? Openings in the wall lead off into smaller passageways, or to the top of a set of stairs.

'Psstt!'

'Hmm?' replied Phæ'enor, still in awe at what she saw.

'Hurry up, stay close, we need to get to a passageway just a little way up ahead.'

'Oh, right, yes of course.'

Phæ'enor now paying attention, followed Master Rasia quickly. They kept close to the side of the wall they had come out at, until after several hundred metres they stopped abruptly across from an unassuming entrance. Phæ'enor could see the top of some stairs.

'That is the way we need to take. It's a long way down and we don't have a lot of time, so we need to move fast. Right now, no one is about but that will change. As soon as we get to the stairs you need to run like the wind, don't question me just do as I do.'

'Okay, whatever you say,' replied Phæ'enor.

'Ready?'

'Ready.'

'Let's go!'

Faster than she had expected, Master Rasia ran across to the opening of the passageway and descended the stairs. She followed, struggling to keep up and hoping she would not trip over the hem of her dress. It was so impractical, and it angered her that she had to wear such a ridiculous garment in the first place. I bet if Master Rasia had a dress on he wouldn't be able to run as fast as he does. She smiled at the thought of Master Rasia wearing a dress.

'Do you have to run that fast?'

'Yes, and if you think this is bad we have to come back this way to get out. This is the easiest part! Just keep your voice down.'

Great, thought Phæ'enor, I'll be sure to fall on my face going up. The stairs were narrow, uneven and dimly lit, unlike the covered street they had just come from. And as for trying to keep her voice down there was no reason to, the noise of their boots upon the steps would surely attract more attention.

After some time, her legs tired and as she began to wobble, Master Rasia slowed down. The light in the stairs had diminished, but there were smaller flickers of light travelling up to them. Instead of the noise of their boots, Phæ'enor could hear indistinct groans, rattling, and what sounded like screams. She froze. Slowly, she looked down at Master Rasia. She could see the top of his head, his shoulders and back moving rapidly from the run, but he looked to be regaining his composure.

'Where have you taken me?' Phæ'enor asked him quietly. But he did not answer her.

'Remember what I said? Stay close to me and do exactly what I say?'

'Yes,' she replied, now anxious and concerned. The screams and the cries reverberated up the stairs again.

'Keep your eyes on me, follow my every step and stay close, keep away from the sides and don't speak to anyone unless I say so.'

Still watching Master Rasia from above, Phæ'enor did not reply. He seemed to be saying the words more for his own reassurance, than hers.

'Did you hear what I just said?'

'Yes, I did, let us just do whatever it is we came here to do.'

Master Rasia looked up at her briefly, nodded once and moved off the last step. Rattling of metal on metal echoed out as she thought to herself that it was complete madness what they were doing here and as she stepped off the stairs after him, the wall surprised her again.

Expecting some sort of horror to explain the screams, cries and rattling, Phæ'enor was surprised to step into some sort of underground chamber, but it was not made of the bright oro stone. The golden bricks of the city wall had been left behind in the stairwell. In its place a yellow, red and brownish structure that was translucent in some areas, solid in others. It gave off a burnt golden hew, the source of the orange light, she thought.

'What is this stuff?' asked Phæ'enor.

'It's amber,' replied Master Rasia, 'from the Eckera tree.'

'Amber?'

Phæ'enor in silent wonder followed Master Rasia. Chambers and passageways appeared to their left and right, stairs made of amber led up and down through amber archways. It was a labyrinth, and all the while screams, shouts and rattling came from beneath them. Phæ'enor looked down as she walked across a part of the amber flooring that was translucent.

'Oh my…'

'Move,' said Master Rasia, as he grabbed her by her wrist again and pulled her away.

'Where are we? That man … he looks so ill?'

Master Rasia did not answer and pulled her on further until they came to a set of stairs in the middle of the amber corridor and still gripping onto Phæ'enor's wrist, they descended.

She couldn't understand what he was so worried about, apart from that man she had just seen laying beneath them, no one else was here. The chambers they passed were empty and they hadn't even come across any city guards.

Yet as they made their way down the set of stairs, the noises became louder, echoing out until it started to hurt Phæ'enor's ears. As they stepped off into another warren of chambers and walkways it was apparent where all the noise was coming from.

'Remember, try not to attract their attention, stay close to me and away from the walls of the cells.'

Phæ'enor nodded again, with her fingers in her ears, she stayed as close as she possibly could to Master Rasia without bumping into him. She didn't need to ask again where she was either, that was obvious now. The screams and the shouts, mumbling of men and women talking to themselves, arguing with each other from one cell to the next; they were in the city gaol.

They walked on quickly, Master Rasia turning up one corridor, over a walkway and down another set of steps, through an archway and around another corner. It continued like this for some time and the further they descended into the warren of amber cells, the hotter it got and the louder the noises became.

As they passed one cell a woman suddenly reached out through the bronze bars, which were planted in the solid amber surrounding them, nearly forcing Phæ'enor to fall back into another across the way. Master Rasia grabbed her.

'Little girl, such a beautiful girl … have you come, finally to save me?'

Phæ'enor shook her head at the woman. She was dressed in dark red and ragged clothes; her hair was wild and her eyes white with blindness. She looked like she had not been fed in years.

'No, I'm sorry.'

The woman started to sob, 'Please, pleeeeaaase, lit-tle girl, please!'

'Come, we can't do anything for these people,' said Master Rasia in her ear and this time gently pulled Phæ'enor away, the screams of the woman echoing after them.

'Pleeeeeaaase … pleeeeease lit-tle girl, don't leave me here … aggghhhh …'

The noise she made encouraged other prisoners to chip in as they walked passed the cells.

'Help me too …' shouted a scrawny man in dirty rags and next to no hair, a large wisp of it jiggled from side to side as he jumped about his cell.

'And me … and me,' chirped another man. His crossed eyes bulged as he licked his hands like a cat.

The requests for help, or food and questions as to who they were, continued. But as they rounded one corner, Phæ'enor, struck by what she had just seen came to a stop; a small boy was sat in the middle of a large cell. He must have been about eight or nine years old, she thought. Both of his hands and feet were chained to the floor, but unlike the other prisoners he was calm and looked almost bored.

'That one is Alva Klyn, the Mantas Child.'

'The what child?' asked Phæ'enor, as she turned to look at Master Rasia in question. When she looked back at the boy he was no longer in the middle but pressed right up against the bars of his cell, his mouth drooling and his sharp teeth bared. Suddenly he started to howl like a dog.

'AAArrrrggh Wooooooo! Argh Wo-wo-wo-wooooooo!'

Phæ'enor felt a chill spread down her spine.

'He has killed hundreds in this city,' answered Master Rasia, as he pulled Phæ'enor away again. 'He always had a taste for raw meat, but it got worse, moving from dead animals to live ones, then eventually…'

'Ugh, yuk…'

'In the end, his father had no choice but to turn him in.'

'Why? I mean that's obvious but…'

'He ate his own mother, brother and sisters.'

Phæ'enor felt sick as they descended another set of stairs, the noise from the floor above fading. The prisoners seemed much tamer here.

'Why are some of those prisoners not in Blaindower, that mad house my cousins told me about?'

'They are not deemed mad enough?' shrugged Master Rasia in reply. 'Who knows how Benagharian law works. But you're right, some people just don't belong here.'

Phæ'enor detected more bitterness in his voice as they rounded another corner; it led to a dead end.

'This is why I have brought you here,' said Master Rasia, as they slowed and walked towards the wall.

Phæ'enor looked at Master Rasia as though he was the one that should be behind the mad house bars, 'To what? Look at a wall?'

'NO! And enough with the sarcasm!' he snapped back, before pushing her forward to the dead end.

'Ow! What is wrong with you!' shouted Phæ'enor back, rubbing the top of her arm.

Master Rasia had walked towards her and pointed into the far corner behind her. Phæ'enor reluctantly turned to see a very tall but narrow gap in the amber. There were only two bars to this cell; it was about the size of the kitchen pantry at No 09 Grand Alboreum Circus thought Phæ'enor.

Beyond them sat the man she had seen in those wanted posters across the marketplace, who she had heard about, but never seen herself, and who now she had promised to help. It was Wolf Canis.

'Brother…' 'Rasia,' said Wolf Canis, his deep voice cut through the silence as he rose from a small wooden stool that barely looked to carry his weight. 'Who is she?!' he said sharply. He had looked Phæ'enor up and down at first but now, looking away, he addressed only his brother.

Phæ'enor did not feel at ease in his presence. For a man whose photo had made him looked frightened and which had described him a thief and a tea addict, forced into crime against his will, a victim of O'scilla Juur's games, he certainly looked like he could take care of himself. He may have lost the muscle but the man standing behind the bars was far from frail, there was still a grace and power to him as he towered above both his brother and Phæ'enor.

'This is the girl I have told you about, Miss Phæ'enor Doven, the one that will help us.'

Still looking intently at his brother, Wolf Canis replied, 'The one who is reluctant to help us you mean? Don't tell me, you had to force her to come tonight. She doesn't have the air of someone who cares to be here in my presence.' Master Rasia did not reply at first.

'HA! I thought so. No one wants to help a wolf, and the brother is no use at all to me!' He looked up at the amber ceiling smiling, his teeth half missing, the others browned or chipped. Master Rasia looked away from his brother, trying to find the words to say.

'You disappear, train as a solider, yet when you come back to us you are still as pathetic as that little boy you were all those years ago. How did I think you could do anything to help me and our family? Oh, the letters to send for your immediate return, your promises to fight for us, FOR ME! AND ALL YOU BRING ME IS THIS GIRL! A GIRL? HA!' Phæ'enor watched the two brothers, worried for one and wary of the other.

'What would you have me do Brother? Huh? WHAT? I have tried everything!'

'EVERYTHING?'

'EVERYTHING! I have spoken to the guards, to Alba, to O'scilla! I HAVE EVEN TRIED PRINCE TAIGOR!' spat Master Rasia at his brother. 'And the only ones that are willing to help you are Archä and Mëdez and this girl! I came back to help you as you asked, I risk losing my job and imprisoning myself to help you! I am trying!' At this, Master Rasia's voice broke, but he steadied his breathing. Phæ'enor watched as his body shook under the weight of seeing his brother behind bars.

'No, no, don't cry, don't cry little brother. You have nothing to cry about. You have your freedom. It is I who is stuck behind these walls; I have been here for weeks! THIS STUPID LITTLE GIRL CANNOT HELP ME! SHE CANNOT HELP YOU TO HELP ME! You are meant to be my brother, my family! And what have you done to help me? I am set to rot here!'

'What have I done?' Master Rasia looked at his brother, angry tears falling down his face. He shook his head in disbelief. 'What-have-I-done? I have done terrible things brother, much more than you and much more than you can imagine. And not once did I want to do it, but I had no choice. I HAD NO CHOICE, BROTHER!

Always under threat of being killed if I did not do as they asked. But I thought if I did it at least I would stay alive, just that bit longer, hoping that ONE DAY! One day my big brother would come and get me … huh? But where were you when I needed you? In some dingy tea house, taking your fill? WHERE WERE YOU, BROTHER?'

Wolf Canis had stepped back from the bars of his cell slightly, not sure how to react to his brother's outburst. They were both crying now.

'Where was I, little brother?' Wolf Canis was looking at his feet, bare and scarred and dirty, 'where was I? Ah, yes, I was here. Father had been killed, Mother also, you had disappeared, and I was left to look after everyone else. To keep them alive and make sure no one else amongst us disappeared or was taken away by the city guards to rot as I do now. So forgive me if I didn't come looking for you. But you're back now and it's about time you made the effort to get me out of here, not through your little diplomats or some officer's daughter! I need to get out of here Rasia! I have a duty to our people and I cannot be stuck behind these walls!'

'But it's your fault you're in here in the first place, not your brother's,' said Phæ'enor.

'Don't Miss Do…' said Master Rasia, failing to curb Phæ'enor's anger.

'No! All I have heard is this so-called leader whinge and complain about you not helping him, how it's your duty to help him, but look at him! Look at you,' she said, now addressing Wolf Canis. 'A leader? How were you ever a leader?'

'How dare she speak to…'

'You let yourself be taken in by O'scilla Juur…'

'That is not true…'

'Used you as his puppet so that you could get your fix…'

'No, I…'

'Abuse and then abandon your position…'

'I…

'You are no leader and in no position to command the help of others, let alone your own brother after what you have done!'

'Miss Doven, plea…'

'You are exactly what they say you are, a liar, thief, addict and a murderer!'

'No, noooo …' Wolf Canis let out a silent scream as he slowly slumped to the floor of his cell. 'Arggghhh-ha-haaaaaa,' he sobbed.

Phæ'enor watched him without sympathy, as he crumpled into a heap, rocking backwards and forwards.

'How do you let him get away with speaking to you like that? You're only trying to help him and then look what he goes and does when he hears the truth. It's pathetic!'

Master Rasia watched his brother a while before bending down and putting his hand through the gap in the cell. He touched his brother's hand then shook his head.

'Can't you see that he is ill? He doesn't mean what he says. He is scared and desperate. I should never have spoken to him like that. He's right, I need to do more to help him.'

'But he is a criminal, whether or not he has committed these crimes he has committed many others before. The city guards are not going to let him go. He is a wanted man just by the fact he is the leader of the wolves.' There was silence between them, bar the low sobs coming from Wolf Canis. It dawned on Phæ'enor, and she could tell Master Rasia too, that this was going to be an impossible task no matter what they did, chests or not.

'I have to take over from my brother, at least whilst he is in here. I know you are not happy to do this, but you promised Archä and Mëdez, and …'

'That's before I knew who your brother was, what he is…'

'Your father knew that, and he still let me have leave to come back here.'

'What?' said Phæ'enor, her train of thought derailed by the mention of her father.

'That was the deal.'

'What deal?'

'Other members of the wolves wrote to me, to get help for Canis but at the time I was based in Palestra and I was refused leave. The commander in charge there, Major Jest Benson, he knew what I was, what I really was.'

'Which was what?' asked Phæ'enor not thinking straight; she wanted to know what her father had agreed to.

'I am a wolf, just like my brother here. Surely you know that by now?'

Phæ'enor looked at him and nodded. When her cousins had informed her of who Master Rasia's brother was it had not taken her long to figure out he was also one of them. But he was also a soldier of the Benagharian Army; that was all she had thought of him as.

'I still don't really understand why that matters,' said Phæ'enor.

'We are outcasts, like the harqs and the rats and all the other undesirables in the empire. We are not wanted anywhere. Why do you think they try and hide us behind the walls of Old Town? It's so we don't mix with the rest of the city, with the likes of people like you. Our ancestors were the puppets and the machines for this empire and when it had finished using them and the generations of us after, it didn't know where to put us or how to feed us. The empire had millions of us killed, those that were left were scattered across the empire. Old Town is where Benaghar's remnants are. The only problem was that we still had to fend for ourselves; find our own water, food, jobs. The laws of Benaghar state no Benagharian is to help an inhabitant of Old Town unless they want to see the inside of a prison cell.'

Phæ'enor looked at Wolf Canis' amber, narrow barred cell, and thought how she would not want to be in his place.

'Fighting broke out between the wolves and the Harqs, there has always been bad blood between the two and housing both in the same place was never a clever idea. In the end the city guards called in the Army. Boys and girls were taken out of Old Town. Many disappeared, others were killed or sent aboard as servants to military families, some stayed here.'

Phæ'enor wondered if Florin, the young maid and more notably Master Rasia's little sister was one of them.

'I was one of many young boys that got taken aboard the ships and trained to be a soldier. I had just turned seven.'

Wolf Canis raised his head, kind eyes looked at his brother who smiled back.

'I can remember that little wooden sling shot Mother had given me.'

'You ran around picking up all the stones and rotten food left out in the streets, shooting the bits at passers-by,' laughed his brother. 'Until you hit O'scilla Juur in the face with some large rotten tomatoes!' The two brothers laughed through their tears.

'Yeah, and for a small price he handed me straight over to Captain Jest Benson. I was put on a ship with some other children the very next day, bound for the east.' Their laughter stopped.

Phæ'enor felt nothing but sadness for them both. They had been forced apart from each other at an early age, growing up amongst the dirt, the fighting and being segregated from the rest of the world. Nothing had changed.

'Anyway, when the wolves wrote for help and I asked for leave, my commander knew there had been more fighting in Benaghar. He refused to let me go and instead I was sent further away from my family; to the far eastern waters of The Raanian Seas and Vanu, where I thankfully came under the command of your father. It was too late anyway but your father could see how upset and distracted I was. I think he wondered why I had not approached him as well.'

'Why didn't you just ask him to leave, despite what some of you think I know my father to be a fair man,' said Phæ'enor. Wolf Canis sniggered at this and Master Rasia, with a smile, lifted the back of his shirt to reveal long and raised scars across his back.

It was not just a shock to Phæ'enor; his brother had gone rigid unable to move at what he had just seen.

'I thought I would just be whipped again, like had been been by Captain Benson in Palestra, so I didn't ask. But your father is an odd man Miss Doven.'

'Phæ'enor … just call me Phæ'enor, please.'

He nodded in agreement, 'Captain Doven approached after a Company's dinner one evening. It was just small talk to begin with, "How are you finding Vanu?", "What was my opinion on the war?" Then he spoke about the decampment and how he needed to stay behind longer, with his sons, that they still had work in the north of Vanu to complete but he wanted the rest of his family back in Benaghar as soon as possible. Being two women, they would need a chaperone to escort them back, and that the chaperone would need to stay with them in Benaghar until he or his sons arrived, "I am your commanding officer Rasia, and I command you to be my wife and daughter's escort. I believe this would also be agreeable to you for you have not seen your family in many years, have you not?"

'That's a command, not a deal,' scoffed Phæ'enor.

'Yes, but this is still your father we are talking about. If I agreed to do this, to look out for you and your mother until they arrived, he would sign the licence for me to enter back into Benaghar as a soldier and not a wolf, allowing not only the freedom to wander the city at my leisure but to afford me the opportunities to help my brother.'

'You need a licence to roam the city?' asked Phæ'enor.

The two brothers nodded. They all went silent.

'But you're right, Phæ'enor,' said Master Rasia. 'After all that and even if we did get that information out of Archä and Mëdez, they are never going to let you go, Canis.'

'What about the rats, Rasia. Have you tried them?' asked his brother. He was still slumped on the floor, but his tears were dried on his cheek and he had a steely look in his eyes.

'Ha! The rats? Really? What can they do, brother, to help us? They hate us as we hate them, they would never…'

'Yes! But they hate O'scilla Juur more, after what he did to them.'

'Brother, think about what you are saying, it does not mean that they…'

'No, it does. The Rat King hates him, even more than I do. They would take any opportunity they could to get to him…'

'It's not a good id…'

'Ssshh!' whispered Phæ'enor, 'there is someone coming!'

They all froze as they heard the faint sounds of several footsteps above them, the clanking of armour and the sudden hush of noise from the prisoners. Wolf Canis jumped to his feet and spoke quickly to them:

'Go, go now, but think about what I just said.'

'I don't know, it's not a good…'

'Please, brother, we have to find a way.'

The sound of footsteps and clanking armour had moved closer.

'We have to go!' urged Phæ'enor, this time it was her turn to tug and pull at Master Rasia's clothing. She did not want to get caught down in the amber cells, especially with present company.

'I love you brother, I love you. And I am truly sorry for what I have done. I have let you down. But if you can get me out of here, I promise! I promise I will not let this happen again, I will look after you, I will look after all of us.'

The two brothers embraced as much as they could through the bars of the cell, and then in hurried silence Master Rasia once again grabbed Phæ'enor by the arm and fled.

They ran up some stairs and around several corners, but they could not follow the same path they came down on. A few times they had to stop after a city guard, or gaoler doing the rounds, came into view. Quickly, Master Rasia would pull Phæ'enor back and they would head back, down more flights of steps and back up another set. It was a maze of amber and felt to Phæ'enor as though they would never get out.

At one point they had made it back to the level just above Wolf Canis' cell. They watched as a city guard, his back to them, slowly walked past the cells before disappearing around a corner. Master Rasia, with Phæ'enor behind him, followed in the guard's wake trying to make as little noise as possible and without attracting attention. But suddenly Phæ'enor was yanked back and let out a loud scream:

'ARRRGGGHHH!'

She felt herself being drawn back by the hem of her cloak. She struggled and tried to turn and pull her cloak back but couldn't. Horrified and panicked by who was pulling her back she had stopped, only making it easier for him to pull her towards him. It was the Mantas Child; drooling and with menace in his eyes, he let out a howl:

'Arggghh WOOOooooooo!'

With his filthy and greedy hands nearly upon her, Master Rasia grabbed Phæ'enor by the waist. His feet dug in and pressed against the edge of the Mantas Child's cell. Nearly horizontal he managed to turn Phæ'enor around pulling her out of the cloak. They fell to the amber floor as she was released. Both out of breath, they watched as the boy tore at her cloak with his teeth but realising he had not got her flesh started to howl again:

'Arrrgh WOOOOOOOOOOO!'

Hurried footsteps sounded, and a gaoler appeared around the corner.

'HEY!'

'RUN!' shouted Master Rasia.

The two of them quickly scrambled to their feet and as fast as they could they pelted straight for the gaoler. Master Rasia bowled through him knocking him sideways. They ran up more flights of stairs, then back down again where they came across three city guards who gave chase. Rounding another corner, the pair finally found the long set of stairs and they ran as fast as they could all the way up.

This time Master Rasia did not wait to check if the coast of the hidden street was clear. They ran straight across, with the guards coming up behind them and attracting more as they went.

'DON'T STOP! JUST KEEP RUNNING!' he shouted back to Phæ'enor, who had no intention of stopping and was just going as fast as she could.

They ran and ran but they were not losing sight of the city guards, even as they ran into the narrow and dark tunnel that led back to the woodland on the edge of Grand Town. They had slowed to feel their way through, but they were still moving quickly.

'What are we going to do? They are coming after us!'

'Just keep going!'

Phæ'enor could feel as well as hear her heart pound in her chest. The city guards were talking in a panic behind them.

'Where are they going?' demanded one.

'Is this how they got in?' asked another.

'YOU CAN'T ESCAPE SO GIVE YOURSELF UP!' shouted another.

But Master Rasia and Phæ'enor did not give up and did not stop until they reached the end of the tunnel. Master Rasia turned to help Phæ'enor out. As she stepped back into the woodland and the steep slope of the ground she was met with hundreds of eyes reflecting back at her.

'You stayed too long Rasia!' said one.

'I know, and they are coming up the tunnel,' he replied, his back to them and fiddling with something in his hand. Phæ'enor heard a lock click.

'What? They found the secret passage?'

'No … we sort of led them to it …' said Phæ'enor, out of breath.

Hissing reverberated around them.

'IT IS NOT HER FAULT!' shouted Master Rasia. They all fell silent. 'We had some unexpected trouble with one of the prisoners.' No one said anything. Phæ'enor and Master Rasia looked at each other. They both knew it could have been a lot worse. Then suddenly they all looked at the wall as they heard dull thudding and faint muffled sounds. Phæ'enor could no longer see an entrance into the wall, there wasn't even a trace of an outline of a door. Whatever Master Rasia had just done they were sealed out, the city guards sealed in.

'Cana?'

'Yes Rasia?'

'Take Phæ'enor here back home. Choose at least five others to go with you. Make sure Florin sees her back into the house and cleans her up.' Phæ'enor looked at her hands and her dress. She had not realised how filthy she had become. She was covered in soil and twigs from the woodland and dust and dirt and scratches from being inside the wall. 'Continue to watch over the house until I return in the morning.'

'Yes, Rasia,' replied Cana, before he started to shout commands to his fellow wolves. Phæ'enor could now see that the reflective eyes were not their own but the eyes of the wolf heads they each wore on top of their heads.

'Everyone else go back to your stations.'

They all started to move off, apart from the five which Cana had chosen who started to slide down the steep slope, stopping at the end and waiting for Phæ'enor and Cana to follow. Phæ'enor did not particularly see that this was a great idea, but it was quicker, and probably safer than walking down, trying not to catch her feet in one of the tree roots. As she sat down on the twig ridden ground, Master Rasia called to her:

'Phæ'enor.' 'Yes?' she replied, turning her head to look at him. The grey cat had reappeared, purring loudly at his feet.

'You can also call me Rasia; Master is wearing a bit thin now. Besides I'm not currently assigned to any ship.'

She smiled and nodded back at him before Cana came up behind her and with a sharp shove sent her flying down the side of the wooded crater.

Chapter Thirteen

Celebrations

Back in Grand Alboreum Circus, Phæ'enor and the rest of the inhabitants of Grand Town were swamped with the preparations for celebrations; The Festival of Heramar and in No 09 Phæ'enor's birthday. Normally Phæ'enor would have been looking forward to her birthday but after the dejection of seeing Wolf Canis and the despair from Rasia she was not in the mood. Even as she stood at the window in the library, watching the neighbours decorate the square with flowers and bunting for the festival, with people on stands selling sweets and hot food to the last of the children taking part in their fun before it got dark, and before the adults came out for carnival, Phæ'enor could not take any joy in the celebrations. She did not feel up to it after seeing Wolf Canis, lonely, mad and wasting away in a tiny cell whilst facing the prospect of execution. He didn't even know his fate; his brother Wolf Rasia could not bear to tell him.

Besides, her birthday was never going to be as fun this year, not without her father and brothers present. But unaware of how Phæ'enor was feeling, and of events the night before, apart from Florin, the household staff had been up since the early hours of the morning preparing for the day's events. They were being bossed about by Mrs Jemin whilst Mrs Doven was fretting about the food around them. Curtains, cushions and ornaments were being taken down and replaced with new silk, heavy drapes, or large vases full of flowers. In places, No. 09 looked to have been turned into an indoor garden.

Still tired from the lack of sleep and exasperated by the noise and the chaos, Phæ'enor had retreated to the one room that had not been fussed over; the library. Sitting with the little black and yellow books on her lap, she had taken to looking through them again, checking to see if they made any more sense, or if they would provide her with clues on how to find the chests. Maybe if she stared at the symbols long enough she would start to understand it?

CRASH!

The sound came from outside in the hallway, then her grandmother's shouting: 'NOW, LOOK WHAT YOU'VE DONE, THAT VASE SHOULD HAVE BEEN IN THE DINING ROOM!'

Phæ'enor sighed. It was just her birthday, she had never been made a fuss over before, this wasn't even a big birthday. She was turning eighteen next year, I wonder if they have forgotten that she thought. She shook her head. If that was the case, then she would be having two like this in a row. Nevertheless, her family insisted on throwing a small party; it would be a gathering of friends she had made so far since they had arrived. There would be several guests attending for dinner including Prince Taigor, Officer Nathryn and some of his men, Admiral Gull, and her two cousins and uncle.

***

It would not be a comfortable reunion between her and her cousins this evening. She might have to avoid conversation with them during the night, just in case it blew up into another argument. However, it would be good to finally meet their father. After what her cousins had told her about their mother and Blaindower it did not look like Phæ'enor would be meeting her anytime soon, but she had yet to be introduced to her father's brother and knew next to nothing about him.

Apart from her uncle she knew most of the guests attending. The only one to decline the invitation was Rasia. After their little midnight excursion, Rasia, having reminded Phæ'enor of the party, had advised he could no longer attend; he had urgent business to attend to and sent his apologies to her family. Urgent business? I bet

I know what that is, thought Phæ'enor. He was going to look for the chests without her. I'll find more information about them myself she thought and had been sat in the library trying to see if anything would spring out of the books, but no clues had materialised. The symbols on the locks of the chest, although they matched those of the chests Archä and Mëdez had in their collection, still looked like lines of dots, joined to make funny shapes or circles, nothing jumped out from the pages to tell her what it all meant.

Phæ'enor huffed out loud and looked out the window to her left, it was getting dark outside and she could hear the muffled sounds of footsteps and laughing. She went back to her books only to be interrupted again by the noise from outside.

Splat, splat, splat!

She turned her head fast back to towards the window. It was covered in some sort of slime. Pinks, greens and blues smeared down the window and the liquid slowed down and dripped onto the ground below. It looked like it was the start of the main festivities of The Festival of Heramar and as the cook Mrs Tibba had explained the night before, was a celebration of King Sol, The Moon of Heramar and end to the war in the east. Phæ'enor was not accustomed to how they celebrated this in Benaghar. Back in Vanu, they celebrated all the moons, and was a feast with friends and family, a time to cherish those close and remember those that had been lost in the Illraean Wars, for both sides. In Benaghar, however her grandmother had advised her, just as Florin had, that the celebrations were less restrained. Instead each area of the city, in turn, would re-enact parts of the battles. Instead of guns and swords, paint was used, mainly for some of the younger children to be able to join in. Masks and costumes were adorned so no one could tell who-was-who, you could pretty much get away with anything and go anywhere you wanted, although the palace and its bridges were off limits and the entrance to Old Town was heavily guarded.

Apparently, the fun did not apply to the inhabitants of Old Town. No doubt, that would include Rasia and his sister Florin, whose wistful account of the festivities was probably more of a longing to take part. Maybe that was another reason for Rasia to not attend the dinner that evening, not just the chests after all thought Phæ'enor. She got up and looked out of the window. There were a few lanterns bobbing around, dusk falling on the street. She wiped the condensation from inside the window to see better. A handful of girls and boys dressed in colourful costumed silks and masks looked to be playing a game of some sort; they were running around after each other and throwing the paint. A few girls screamed whilst the boys roared with laughter.

'Phæ'enor?' called her mother from the doorway; She had not heard her approach. 'It is time for you to get ready. The guests will be here in the next hour.

**

'I don't like my hair in curls,' said Phæ'enor, irritated with Florin. The young maid had quietly gone about her duties, getting Phæ'enor ready for the evening ahead. Neither of them had said anything about the early hours of the morning, where Florin had to quietly help Phæ'enor back into the house and get her washed and into bed without disturbing anyone else. It would cost Florin her job and no doubt endless arguments between Phæ'enor and her grandmother, not to mention she would have to tell more lies about where she had been. Instead, a silent agreement had fallen between them; nothing needed to be said. They knew what had happened and no one else needed to know.

Florin continued to curl her hair, 'Nonsense Miss. This is your birthday, so you must have curls. All the girls here have them.'

'I don't see why? They make me look like a child.'

'They make you look beautiful, Miss Phæ'enor.'

Phæ'enor, looked in the mirror, her black curls looked ridiculous, like a mop on her head she thought. Her hand was placed on her left shoulder, nursing the spot where Florin had burnt her with the hot irons having accidentally rested them there. The guests had already started to arrive and Phæ'enor felt more and more as the minutes went by that she didn't want to be there, wishing she was outside with the other girls and boys enjoying the Festival of Heramar. She wondered, hoped even, that she would come down with a temperature and make her excuses. The maid Florin seemed to have read her mind.

'Look, you must be the only girl in the town I know, who doesn't like dresses, doesn't like to be made pretty, and hates the attention of young men.'

'Do you know all the girls in this town?' she replied rhetorically.

'Miss, it's your birthday and it's one evening. You will have fun and it will all be over soon.'

'I hope so,' said Phæ'enor.

There were loud bangs outside, more screaming. Phæ'enor jumped up and rushed over to the window, knocking Florin as she went, 'Arrgh, Miss!'

'Beautiful,' said Phæ'enor. She looked out to see sparkles of light fanned out in the sky above. 'I've not seen fireworks since before the night we left Vanu to come here.' As she thought about Vanu, she thought about her two brothers and father, and her heart sank a little. They would not be here to join her for her birthday. The maid had got up and dusted herself down.

'Come away from the window, Miss. I still need to put the flowers in your hair.'

Sulkily, Phæ'enor sat back down. It was cramped inside her bedroom with the two of them. She looked at herself in the mirror again and looked to watch Florin add the small yellow and white flowers to her crown and remembered the rather strange conversation she had with her grandmother a couple of days before:

'So, what's your favourite colour, child?'

'Why?' asked Phæ'enor.

'I was just wondering,' she said, trying to sound uninterested. Phæ'enor ignored her.

'Well then, what is it?'

'What is what?' asked Phæ'enor.

'Your favourite colour child, honestly it's a simple question. Though it seems I have a simple grandchild.'

'It's yellow!' cried Phæ'enor, and so a dress of yellow was brought in for her to wear that evening. Phæ'enor looked at herself again. The flowers in her hair to match.

'I look like a giant lemon,' she said aloud.

'An expensive yellow lemon as well,' said Florin. They both laughed hysterically until they were interrupted by Mrs Doven peering around the door. She smiled at Phæ'enor.

'You look beautiful.' Phæ'enor and Florin smirked at each other. 'And not at all like a lemon.' Florin looked away and Phæ'enor looked down at her hands.

'I think you are ready to meet your guests now.' She followed her mother down the stairs. 'You must be on your best behaviour tonight, Phæ'enor.'

'I will be,' said Phæ'enor, slightly in protest at the implication in her mother's voice.

'I know but I want there to be no sulking, or arguing with your guests, or your grandmother!'

'Mother I…'

Mrs Doven turned on the stairs to look her daughter in the eye. 'It may be your birthday, but you are still a young woman and must behave like one. Your guests have given up their evenings to be here tonight so make sure they enjoy it. I should also remind you that your Uncle Eron is joining us this evening.' She turned back and continued down the stairs into the entrance hall. Phæ'enor sighed, breathed in, and forced a smile on her face before joining her mother. She walked down the corridor.

'I suppose I better do this for Mother. Maybe the evening will go quicker. I might even enjoy myself,' she said aloud to herself.

'I hope you will, Miss Phæ'enor Doven.'

Phæ'enor, who had grabbed at her chest with a start, turned around. In front of her stood Officer Nathryn.

'Oh … it's you,' she said catching her breath, 'I did not expect you to be there. Behind me.'

'Ha. No. of course not, I'm sorry if I startled you. I was just coming out of the sitting room. Your grandmother has quite a view of the festivities on the street from that window. I was just watching the fireworks. They are quite good I suppose, but not as exceptional as the ones in Vanu!'

'You've been to Vanu?' asked Phæ'enor, surprised, 'I never saw you at any of the gatherings there.'

'Yes, I served there, with your brothers' and father.'

'Really? I thought you served in Maiorban?' Phæ'enor realised then that no one, including Officer Nathryn had told her this. She had just assumed that he had because he had boarded The Scavenger at the Port of Kiriso in Maiorban.

'Yes, well I was there, on official duties but I have served alongside Captain Doven's Company in Vanu prior to Maiorban.' He smiled at her, 'You must miss your brothers and father.'

'Um, yes. It's odd not having them around. Even when we were out in Vanu and they were still on duty, mother and I would still see them most evenings,' she looked at Officer Nathryn curious, thinking about Wolf Canis, the chest and all the reading she had been doing earlier, and the appearance of him and his men with the chests on The Scavenger. 'You found the chests then?'

'What? Oh, yes. I suppose you saw that in the papers. A bit embarrassing really.'

'Is that because you were in charge of guarding them then?'

'Ugh, yes,' he replied awkwardly. He looked uncomfortable. 'Maybe we should move into the dining room, I expect they are all waiting for us.' he said hastily.

Phæ'enor did not move out of his way. 'They're decoys, aren't they?' she said.

Officer Nathryn looked back at her expressionless but Phæ'enor could tell he was wondering how or where she came by this information.

Knowing she had thrown him she continued, 'What was inside that chest? The one with the strange symbol above the lock?' Still Officer Nathryn looked at her and said nothing. He looked very unnerved but was spared any more questions from Phæ'enor when another man appeared in the hallway, and grabbing the excuse to change the subject, Officer Nathryn quickly addressed him:

'Mr Eron Doven! How wonderful it is to see you. I have been meaning to call but your daughters always inform me you are at work.'

Phæ'enor was slightly taken back at their greeting. Instead of a handshake the two men embraced in a warm hug.

'Yes, it's just work, work, work Re'av. But you Sir, are looking very well. I see the heat of the tropics has not completely drained you.'

The two men laughed. Phæ'enor looked at her Uncle Eron. He was slightly shorter than her father, less fit but he was slim and had less grey hairs amongst the black swept back from his face. He had a kind face, but he looked tired.

He turned to face Phæ'enor then, addressing her warmly, 'My dear niece, I am so sorry I have not come to the house sooner, work has kept me far away from all family this year and I will endeavour to make amends to you and your mother. However, I gather from your cousins you are settling in well, that you have made some friends, or shall I say acquaintances?' he winked at her as he said this, and Phæ'enor knew he was referring to O'tila, but hoped her cousins had not mentioned Archä and Mëdez.

'Yes Uncle, I suppose I have.'

'And although this is our first meeting, I feel like I know you already … and every bit my brother's daughter, especially with the fists.'

Phæ'enor and her Uncle laughed. She liked him. Officer Nathryn looked uncomfortable at the idea he was okay with his niece getting up to no good.

'You three!' barked Phæ'enor's grandmother, 'come along, dinner is about to be served. You can carry on with your conversation over food!' She walked over to Phæ'enor and turned her around to usher her into the room. Officer Nathryn, still silent, followed. As Mrs Jemin opened the double doors into the dining room all inside cheered, 'Happy Birthday!'

Phæ'enor had not really taken much notice or been a part of the preparations and was surprised to see the table laden with so much food. Fish, potatoes, beef, sauces, a large bowl of soup in the middle, fruit cakes, jelly and vegetables. It was laid out like a banquet.

'I argued with your grandmother for this. It's your birthday so I thought we should have it in the style of Vanu. None of this three-course meal nonsense,' said Mrs Doven quietly into Phæ'enor's ear smiling. Phæ'enor smiled back and kissed her mother on the cheek.

'Thank you, Mother, it's wonderful.'

As was tradition, Phæ'enor was ushered into the seat at the top of the table. To her right sat one of Officer Nathryn's men, to her left Officer Nathryn who slowly took his seat. He did not seem as cheerful as he had been before their conversation in the hallway, but at the same time he did not look displeased, instead he was deep in thought. Everyone took their places, with Prince Taigor at the end of the table facing Phæ'enor. There was a moment's silence and confusion from the guests as what to eat first. Did they start with the fish or did they go for the jelly desserts in the middle? Mrs Doven smiled at Phæ'enor then spoke:

'In Vanu you just get stuck in, so help yourself!'

They all smiled and laughed, and the noise of chatter broke out again. Phæ'enor looked around, her mother and grandmother were eagerly chatting to her Uncle Doven, and her cousin, Simi was sat next to Prince Taigor chatting away, however he only looked half interested in the conversation and kept looking away to glance at Phæ'enor. She turned her gaze away from his. He had looked too often, and it had started to make her feel uncomfortable. It was as though he knew something, and hoped he hadn't guessed where she, her cousins and Rasia had been over the last couple of days. Instead, she directed her eye to Mimi who was wildly flirting with one of the other officers. He laughed back at her jokes uncomfortably; it was clear he was not interested. A gold band on his left hand told her why. She smiled as she drank a glass of wine. As she put it back down she noticed Officer Nathryn staring at her from the corner of her eye.

'You look truly beautiful this evening Miss Doven.'

Phæ'enor looked at him as though he had gone out of his mind, 'Um … thank you?'

He smiled, 'You really don't know how to take a compliment do you?'

'And if she can't recognise or take a compliment, she will be hard to please,' laughed the officer on her right side. Both men smiled.

'What do you mean by that?' asked Phæ'enor frowning.

'I meant that you are a very strong-willed young woman, unlike your two cousins,' he nodded in the direction of Simi and Mimi, still making fools out of themselves without realising.

Phæ'enor turned back to the officer to her right, genuinely puzzled as to who this man was. She did not recognise him, 'I'm sorry, I don't think we have met?'

This man was unlike Officer Nathryn, although not unattractive, his hair was dark, with slight greying around one ear and his eyes were almost black. They looked like they had seen a lot for his life time. Just then Phæ'enor jolted in her seat, she had a flashback of the tattooed man in The Grand Tea Rooms.

'Are you okay?' asked Officer Nathryn, concerned.

'Oh, yes,' said Phæ'enor, 'I just had … a moment of the shivers then. I'm sorry what did you say your name was again?' Asked Phæ'enor, turning back to the officer on her right.

'I didn't,' he said, then smiled. 'My name is Farren, Kaimi Farren. I'm an officer of the Benagharian army, under Officer Nathryn here. I also served alongside your father and brothers in Vanu.'

'Kaimi Farren … Officer Farren …. You're the officer who brought the Atro Hibdaluca plant with you on The Scavenger?'

'Err, yes,' said Officer Farren. He looked at Officer Nathryn curiously. Phæ'enor knew it was because she had been told this by his fellow officer and he was wondering why.

With a blush, Officer Nathryn diverted the conversation, 'Err, quite a few of the men that came back on The Scavenger with me served with your father,' advised Officer Nathryn. 'I think most have already met yourself and your brothers over the years. Prince Taigor obviously knows most of the serving officers, as does the officer having his ears chewed off by your cousin Mimi.'

'And he is…?'

'Captain Letho Oldus.'

She nodded and smiled at the two officers but was not distracted from her curiosity, 'So, you all helped take care of the chests then?' Phæ'enor said this a little more loudly than she had intended. The hub of chatter had died down and everyone, bar her two cousins who were looking anywhere else but, were now staring at Phæ'enor. Her mother looked nervous whilst her grandmother who didn't seem to care said:

'What chests?'

Clearly you don't read the paper you get delivered then thought Phæ'enor before she said, 'I … I was just curious, it's in all the papers. And there's not much else to talk about around here.'

'All? All the papers, I thought there was only one,' said Prince Taigor.

Phæ'enor could feel herself grip her knife and fork tightly. He knows I'm making stuff up. 'Well, yes, and what people are saying about there being treasure, or no treasure in the chests.'

'Hmm, I suppose the newspaper,' said Prince Taigor emphasising the word, 'doesn't always tell the truth. Isn't that right Captain Oldus? If it's true what they say about your wife, then we're all in trouble.' All the men in the room broke out in laughter. Mimi looked at Captain Oldus confused. He looked uncomfortable. 'It's not a clever idea Miss Doven to take stories as fact, or listen to the unsavoury types in this city,' finished Prince Taigor, without breaking eye contact.

At this Simi and Mimi both stiffened and glanced at Phæ'enor with a 'he knows we've been to see Archä and Mëdez' look. Phæ'enor had a sneaking suspicion that it was Prince Taigor, in his guise as Mr Dryhten, who Rasia and herself had seen lurking in the distance outside Polstor & Polstor but couldn't fathom why.

She breathed in slowly' 'Well, if that is the case, then maybe yourself and your men here should not carry chests that attract unwanted attention, onto a serving naval frigate, that then suspiciously blows up, then take them to the garrisons where someone tries to steal them. Surely it is you who are giving these so-called unsavoury people and the newspaper something to talk about? … anyone for dessert?' She finished with a smile.

Everyone went silent bar Phæ'enor's grandmother who barked a laugh. This time Mrs Doven shot Phæ'enor an angry look. They were all silent until more sounds came from outside.

Splat, splat, splat, BANG!

Someone had thrown more paint at the window, they couldn't see for the curtains had been drawn and the fireworks had been set off outside again.

'Auntie, why don't we move into some of the other rooms, we've still yet to give Phæ'enor her presents,' said Simi, smiling a fake smile at Phæ'enor, daggers swimming around in her eyes. Phæ'enor glared back at her.

'Yes, that's a wonderful idea,' said Mrs Doven. 'Florin, Mr Deke? Please, take the desserts through.' Everyone else followed. Phæ'enor waited behind before catching up to Simi and Mimi at the back as they went through into the drawing room.

'Why did you have to interrupt and change the subject,' hissed Phæ'enor.

'Why were you even talking about it?' hissed Simi back.

'Prince Taigor, he clearly already knew we'd been to Archä and Mëdez!' said Mimi panicked.

'Shush, be quiet,' said Simi as they moved into the room to join the others. All three put on their sweetest smiles and pretended they had not been arguing with each other seconds earlier.

'Phæ'enor, come along girl, and sit here,' said her grandmother gruffly.

Phæ'enor made her way over to her grandmother, sitting down on a large mustard coloured pouffe. They rarely came in here, it was bright, light and spacious, unlike the dark and cramped sitting room her grandmother favoured festering in, thought Phæ'enor as she sat down. No one made a move but Phæ'enor could see a small pile of presents on one of the side tables.

'Eh, hem,' said Simi and Mimi's father, clearing his throat. 'I suppose I should go first,' he said rather awkwardly. He moved over to the table and picked up a small squared present from the pile. He smiled at his two girls then made his way over to Phæ'enor, 'When my wife Hariah, Simi and Mimi's mother, became ill she made me promise to give this to you when the time came. That so happens to be now, that you have turned the good old age of seventeen! Ha, ha, ha – ha.' No one else laughed. 'Um yes. Well anyway, when your two cousins here were born they were also given one of these each, a little token of Hariah's love. Of course, you being her only niece she wanted for you to have one also. So …' he moved a little closer to Phæ'enor and held out his hand to her. Phæ'enor reached out and took the present. She felt a little embarrassed and didn't want to be ungrateful, but she hoped it wasn't some childish rattle that would have been of use to her about sixteen years ago. 'You don't have to open it now. If you don't want to,' said her Uncle Eron, seeing how reluctant she was to open it.

'Don't be silly Eron, of course she will open it, that's half the fun!' barked Phæ'enor's grandmother. 'Go on girl, we're all getting impatient here.'

Phæ'enor smiled at her uncle and started to unwrap the present. It was a small wooden box and carved into it were little flowers and circles. It opened easily to reveal a necklace. It looked almost like copper.

'Is that what I think it is?' asked Prince Taigor, sounding alarmed and moving a step too hastily towards Phæ'enor.

'Oh, oh no. No, your Majesty,' said Uncle Eron. 'It's made to look like that. The chain is made from a more delicate type of oro stone and mixed with bronze. So that it looks older than it is.'

During this exchange Phæ'enor glanced over at Simi and Mimi who looked as intrigued as she did at Prince Taigor's sudden change in behaviour. She looked back down at the necklace. A key shaped pendant was attached, it was made of amber. It reminded her of the city gaol, and her heart sank at the thought of Rasia and his brother.

'Your aunt's favourite stone is amber, Phæ'enor. Hariah said for you to wear it always, to open up possibilities for you throughout your life, a token of good luck.'

Phæ'enor thought he was barmy but took it out of the box anyway, and fastened it around her neck, the amber key hanging below her collar bone, after all it was a present and she did not want to be rude, 'Thank you, uncle, cousins, it is very beautiful.' Simi and Mimi had both wiped away tears.

'I also have a key, of sorts,' said Prince Taigor, having composed himself from his bizarre outburst. He handed to Phæ'enor a long dark blue envelope, sealed with golden wax. Mrs Doven passed her a silver letter opener. Once she broke the seal Phæ'enor pulled out a thick piece of parchment. It had the seal of the crown in one corner, Taigor's signature at the bottom, in the middle. Phæ'enor read aloud:

> "By order of the Crown this here licence permits
> Miss Phæ'enor Doven free access to the palace
> grounds and gardens for one year only."

'Oh, wonderful,' said Mrs Jemin.

'That is truly fantastic,' said Mrs Doven.

'Oooh,' said Simi and Mimi together.

Phæ'enor looked at them all mildly bemused. Prince Taigor explained:

'You may not be aware, for when you came to the palace it was dark outside, but the grounds and gardens of the palace are very beautiful and very rarely is anyone granted access to them. However, I thought after your little detour in the palace…'

Phæ'enor blushed a little at this and threw her mother a guilty look.

'…plus, it was obvious how much you enjoyed the exotic plants and flowers at The Grand Tea Rooms. I thought giving you access to the gardens would be a fitting gift. Not to mention would give you good exercise away from the bustle of the streets and get you out of the house.'

Phæ'enor and Prince Taigor smiled at each other. Phæ'enor's grandmother did not look so pleased. The other officers gave Phæ'enor a shawl. Farren gave her an odd present of a travelling bag, but it was not made of leather, instead it was woven together by the leaves of a coconut tree. Admiral Gull had bought her a small pocket watch. Her grandmother, yet another dress of white lace and her mother a set of writing papers and pens, insisting it was a nudge for her to write more to her family, and friends from Vanu. Officer Nathryn was the last to give his present. The jolliness of the present giving had died down and the room suddenly became hushed when he started to speak.

'I was not quite sure what to get you, at first. You're a difficult person to please I think?' She smiled whilst the others laughed at this. 'So, I realised I should buy you something special, but which would also come in handy…' He picked the largest parcel off the side table and handed it to her. Well, thankfully being this big it can't be a wedding ring, that Simi and Mimi keep harking on about she thought. The two cousins looked disappointed. The parcel was soft. She carefully opened it to reveal a bright yellow material.

'Ooh,' gushed Simi and Mimi.

Phæ'enor touched it and felt the thick soft material beneath her fingers; lifting it up out of the package to reveal a warm, bright yellow and hooded travelling cloak. It was beautiful, inside it was thickly lined to keep the cold out and finished with a silk pattern. She put it on to try. It was certainly warm and the copper glinting lining inside felt smooth to the touch. She turned to Officer Nathryn, 'Thank you, thank you so much!' said Phæ'enor.

'I thought it was about time that you replaced that sea battered cloak with a much more suitable one for this climate, especially our winter months.'

Phæ'enor smiled, no one knew, apart from Rasia and Florin, that she no longer had that cloak.

She was not normally one for taking care of her appearance but was eager to see what the cloak looked like on, 'Excuse me, I shall be back in a moment,' and she rushed out of the room and into the hallway to take a look at herself in the long mirror. She twirled around, and tried the hood on, it covered her face from the view of others, and then turned the hem out to look at the silk pattern. It shimmered a copper, but it was not just a pattern, there were flowers, and birds, people, and scenes sewn into it. After she had looked at it long enough, she went into the library and quickly retrieved the little yellow and black books, stowing them away in one of the large inside pockets of her new cloak. I will keep them about me this time, hopefully this cloak will not go missing, she thought. She bowled back into the room, only to be met with just her mother and Officer Nathryn, the others had left.

'Oh, where has everybody gone?' She had not wanted the party to begin with, but she had now been enjoying herself and wanted it to continue.

'They are just in the next room dear.'

'Shall we join them then?' asked Phæ'enor, but as she moved towards the other linking door her mother touched her on her shoulder.

'Not just yet. Officer Nathryn has another present to give you.' And before Phæ'enor could ask what, Mrs Doven made her way to the linking door and closed it behind her. Phæ'enor stood there perplexed by Officer Nathryn. He started to pace the small area of carpet he was standing on, twiddling his fingers. It did not look like he had another present, or at least there wasn't another visible to Phæ'enor on the small side table. Finally, Officer Nathryn spoke:

'I don't have another present to offer you, as such. At least not a birthday present.'

Okay, thought Phæ'enor, waiting for him to continue.

'Please, take a seat,' he said, gently placing his hand on her shoulders and moving her to sit down. 'I'm not quite sure how to do this. I've never done this before.' He looked at her and smiled. Still standing and pacing, he continued with his strange talk, 'You see, we have all been talking, your mother and father, Prince Taigor and I. The Prince especially said that you would be a handful,' he laughed a little awkwardly here, Phæ'enor looked at him raising her eyebrows intrigued what he meant by that. He no longer looked like the aloof soldier she had known before, he was nervous and unsure of himself. 'Right, well, I suppose I should just get on with this.'

He put his hand in his left jacket pocket fumbling, then tried his right. Phæ'enor's stomach lurched, as she watched him she felt suddenly sick, and not with butterflies. Officer Nathryn pulled out his closed hand, moved towards Phæ'enor and got down on one knee. He grabbed her left hand, but Phæ'enor did not let him have it. He looked at her a little confused. Officer Nathryn opened his right hand to reveal a small gold band, and paused, looking at Phæ'enor who had now gone as stiff as a board in her seat and was looking over his head.

'We have to do this Miss Doven,' said Officer Nathryn. 'I have to, you have to, it's part of our duty. Besides, your parents have agreed, and we have the blessing of the crown, before it's even announced.' Phæ'enor still sat and said nothing. He grabbed her hand more forcefully then and pushed the ring onto her finger before closing it firm. His hand still clasped on hers he said, 'Miss Phæ'enor Doven, you will be my wife, and I your husband, it's the only way.' Officer Nathryn returned to his feet, 'I shall let the others know you have accepted.' He walked over to the dining room and opened it. There was a roar of congratulations, 'We are to be married!' he shouted happily. He was showered with hugs and kisses and laughter, but the cheer soon disappeared when Phæ'enor's grandmother spoke:

'Well, where is this new wife of yours to be then? Have you misplaced her already?'

They all turned to look. Phæ'enor was no longer in the room. The gold band was spinning on the floor and the door into the hallway was opened.

BANG!

The sound of the front door slammed shut, vibrating through the floor beneath them.

Chapter Fourteen

A Way into Old Town

The night sky was black, stars intermittent between thin clouds blowing rapidly across, but the streets were full of colour. Masks sparkled, dresses and costumes twinkled and glowed, cloaks flashed by and the colourful paint and powders made the cobbled streets, buildings, and everything they touched light up. Some colours merged together so much so that no one could recognise one from another and so it was that Phæ'enor Doven, in her bright yellow cloak managed to disappear into the night, lost to Officer Nathryn, her mother and the rest of the birthday party gathered at No. 09 Grand Alboreum Circus.

Phæ'enor ran through the cobbled streets of Grand Town, weaving in and out of the masks and cloaks, but slowed down once she had left the tall white buildings behind her. The crowds were not as dense, and she did not want to be recognised. A group of female and male revellers were screaming and coughing, trying not get hit by the powder and paint just up ahead of her. There was a scream from one girl as she was hit in the head with a plume of powder. Her mask slipped, but too busy having fun she ran after the masked men, leaving a brightly feathered mask lying on the ground. Phæ'enor sped up, checking about her to make sure no one saw. She picked the mask up off the cobbles and carried on walking, as though nothing had happened, slipped the mask over her head and onto her face. Just to be careful she pulled her cloak hood over her head and merged back into the festivities.

***

It took her just over an hour to get to Grand Town gate and into Queens High by foot, the revellers had made the journey much slower to navigate. Her feet felt sore. She had left the house in such a hurry she did not think to put on her walking boots. Instead, she had worn the silk heels she had been wearing indoors. She knew that her feet had started to blister.

Phæ'enor stopped outside one of the shops, a shoe shop; it was still open. If only she had grabbed the purse of money off the side table in the hall, she could have at least paid for a comfy pair of slippers or boots to walk around in. Her heart was pounding, and she was out of breath, yet she knew it wasn't just because she had run and then walked there so quickly. Her heart was racing with anger. She looked around. No one had followed her. The last she saw of the party were the backs of Officer Nathryn and her mother before she left the house.

As she reached the other side of the cobbled circus she heard a man shout her name a few times but that was it, she had not waited to hear more. All she wanted was to be on her own. How dare he ask me … tell me … to marry him! Marry? Ridiculous!

Yet it had not just been Officer Nathryn. She replayed his words in her head.

"You see, we have all been talking, your mother…"

How dare she, thought Phæ'enor. My own mother trying to get rid of me and those books from Archä and Mëdez about female etiquette, marriage and pleasing your husband! Phæ'enor felt sick realising that she should have known what was going on earlier. The hints to her on how to behave around a potential new husband.

"…Father."

Phæ'enor breathed in hard, her nostrils flared, "… your mother and father…" They had planned this from the start then! Maybe her father had written to advise of the match? But wait, no, it was Mother! She had made the final decision, hence why she was taken to see Archä and Mëdez, for a woman's education! Tears of anger spilled down beneath the feathered mask as wild thoughts went through Phæ'enor's mind. Is that why we came to live here? I've grown up. The war is over. My brothers have left home and are serving abroad. My mother and father now believe it's time for me to go too? Her bottom lip trembled. She breathed in deeper trying to control her tears but could not stop thinking. "…Prince Taigor and I…" rang the words of Officer Nathryn.

Prince bloody Taigor. How dare he! Whether I marry or not is nothing to do with him. A Prince and a busy body. Spying on me and my cousins and Wolf Rasia. If he can't trust me then why agree to let one of his officers marry me? Or is it another way to keep an eye on me instead? Phæ'enor wiped the tears from under her mask and tried to control her breathing. She felt angry and alone. But she wasn't alone. As she wiped the last tear from her eye, she spied someone watching her.

A silhouette of a gangly and three eared man, was stood leaning against the city wall. It was the jester from the palace the other night. He crooked his head, moving it back and forth, with an unnatural jerky movement.

'Hello?' asked Phæ'enor, but it continued to cock its head in silence.

'Hello there, who are you?' she asked for the second time. Still cocking its head, it slowly went down into a crouch, like some animal waiting to pounce on its prey.

Phæ'enor started to slowly back away when she heard a man speak loudly behind her.

'Guards have you seen a young woman, about this high? I believe she may be wearing a yellow cloak…'

Phæ'enor held her breath startled and looked back to see Officer Nathryn on horseback speaking to the guards at Grand and Queens Gate. She looked around, the jester had disappeared. Panicking that she might be seen by Officer Nathryn and disturbed by the presence of the jester, Phæ'enor spotted a carriage starting to move off up the road towards Newtown Gate. She hurried over to it.

Crouching down low amongst the crowds, she trotted along by its side and out of sight, but she could just make out the hooves of the horse Officer Nathryn was riding, and the jingle of bells following close behind. The carriage moved faster, Phæ'enor began to run. It was starting to outpace her, and she did not want to be caught out in the open. The last thing she needed was Officer Nathryn to spot her, or that creepy jester. All she wanted was to be as far away from him and everyone else she had seen tonight. They are all against me she thought angrily.

She looked to her left, and then to her right, spying a narrow street that looked to run parallel to the one she was on and linked by a large alleyway. She turned to check behind her. The jingle of bells had gone quiet and there was no sign of the jester.

Quickly she checked back under the carriage and managed to make out more of the horse, it was still at the gate; Officer Nathryn's feet on the stirrups. She dived off into the large alleyway taking her directly to the other. It was well lit, lanterns lined the street and there were still plenty of crowds laughing, joking, running and dancing up and down it. Phæ'enor made sure her mask was firmly fixed, her hood on over her long dark hair and picked up speed. She didn't care that her feet had started to bleed, she just needed to get to Newtown Gate and then roughly she would know where to go. The narrower street rose and then curved back around towards the direction of Newtown.

Phæ'enor pushed through the pain in her feet but they still slowed her down and it took her longer than she anticipated. She was just grateful that her feet and the blood were hidden by her heavy hemmed dress. When she reached the top more costumed women and men, girls and boys laughed and screamed as they went by. Phæ'enor eyed the Newtown Gate; there did not seem to be any guards on duty tonight. She checked to her right, then to her left. There was no sign of Officer Nathryn, but she paused and listened hard. The sounds of bells could be heard in the distance, intermittently jingling to the beat of something jumping.

Walking fast over to the gate, Phæ'enor reached it and went under the arch, trying to lose her follower, but had to suddenly run to her right and hide in the shadow of the city's walls. She had spotted the guards, their backs to her, talking to Prince Taigor and what must have been Officer Nathryn trotting up ahead of them. He looked to be going in the direction of Archä and Mëdez and the ringing of little bells was getting louder the nearer, her follower got closer to the gate of Newtown.

Phæ'enor, wide eyed looked about her. Where do I go? She thought. I can't go back, I'll run straight into that thing and I can't go to Polstor & Polstor now, they'll see me and take me back home! She stepped back further into the shadows as one of the guards turned and started to make his way back to the gate, but in doing so he revealed someone else who had also been standing there. Suddenly the jingle of bells stopped. Phæ'enor looked but no one else had entered Newtown.

In front, Wolf Rasia, and his shabby grey cat weaving in and out of his feet, stood talking to Prince Taigor, up on his horse. Phæ'enor could not make out any of what they were saying; although quieter here there were still people in costume running amuck in the streets. Phæ'enor watched them for a while not knowing what else to do. It seemed that Prince Taigor was giving instructions, pointing this way or shaking his head when Rasia looked to be suggesting something, his hands pointing back towards the gate or shrugging his shoulder in reply. Eventually he bowed his head to Prince Taigor, turned and walked away.

He did not head towards Phæ'enor and the gate as she had expected, instead he had turned to his right and walked off in the direction of the marketplace, across towards the city wall that boarded Old Town; the cat trotting beside him. Phæ'enor, although still some distance away, made her decision. She couldn't go to Archä and Mëdez or turn back through the gate. They would definitely see her. So, she took the risk and sticking to the shadows she followed Rasia across Newtown, glimpsing him every so often through the end of a lit street. But still in pain, keeping up with him was getting harder, yet luckily for her Rasia seemed to be going in one direction, parallel to her, not up, or down. She thought this strange for she knew the gate to Old Town, where Rasia was from, was up ahead and to the right of the Highland Gate.

Her heart sank then for she had remembered what her cousins had said:

"…that gate is always guarded to make sure the only people who go in there are the ones that live there…"

Yet if Rasia was going into Old Town, why was he not heading north, towards it? Deep in thought Phæ'enor had nearly lost sight of Rasia. She ran to catch up, it felt like an age before he finally stopped. Phæ'enor had to keep from falling out of the shadows and revealing her whereabouts in her hurry to keep up. He had come to the end of a street and stepped out onto the road that ran around the edge of Newtown, as it did in all other areas of the city.

The lanterns hanging from the high city walls illuminated Rasia's face as he walked across and stood directly beneath one of them. He looked to be listening for something, then the cat turned around facing where Phæ'enor was hidden.

'Meow. Mee-ooow,' swishing its tail it moved slowly towards her then broke into a fast trot. Phæ'enor gritted her teeth and started to back away against the city wall.

'Oi! Rama, get back here!' snarled Rasia.

It stopped, turning to look at its master, then turned back to Phæ'enor and licked its lips, before finally heading back to Rasia. He looked out of the corner of his eyes in each direction, then stepped forward and disappeared into the shadow of the wall, the cat took one last look at Phæ'enor before following its master.

***

Phæ'enor held her breath, did Rasia realise where she was and was now making his way towards her? She waited. A minute went by, two then three, until she had been there a while and still Rasia had not discovered her. It would have taken him seconds if he had known. The street had gone quite quiet, no bells to be heard. Phæ'enor could no longer see anyone about, let alone Wolf Rasia. There were only the sounds of singing and laughing in the distance.

Still in shadow, Phæ'enor slowly moved towards the lantern that marked the spot where Rasia had disappeared. She could feel her heartbeat race as she got closer and closer. She didn't know why she was so scared; it wasn't Rasia she was running from, but she knew she shouldn't have been there. Not just because she was a young woman out at night in the streets, alone and unchaperoned, breaking the city rules, but she was just on the other side of Old Town, a place she knew she should not be anywhere near and certainly not at night.

Phæ'enor took a few last steps and reached the place where Wolf Rasia had last been seen. There was nothing. Even more confused, Phæ'enor looked around her. Nothing again, no one was in the street behind her, no one was making any noise. Not on this side of the wall and from what she could tell, there was no sound from the other side either. She looked back at it. Where was Rasia? Frustrated and with her feet bleeding more steadily she pressed her back to the wall and lowered herself down onto the ground.

Phæ'enor leaned forward and slowly took her shoes off. There was blood and pus from the blisters everywhere. I should have worn my boots, she thought. The white satin heels were soaked, pink and patchy red in places. Fed up, hungry and tired she sighed and went to put the back of her head against the wall. It was cold. She moved her head slightly to get more comfortable. The wall had changed temperature. Bemused, Phæ'enor moved her head back to the spot where she had rested it before. It was cold again. She moved it away, warm again and moved it back again, still cold. She leaned forward then looked behind her. Where Phæ'enor had been resting her head on the cold spot a darker shadow appeared on the wall. She moved around and felt with her hand, tracing the outline of the cold shadow. It was metal and there was no mistaking that it was a keyhole. She turned around fully to face it and crouched down trying to balance on her bad feet. She felt the keyhole again. This is madness. Is this where he has disappeared? She thought.

She looked around thinking again, and then it came to her, cousin Simi had also jokingly mentioned about a secret way into Old Town:

"…there are stories that you can still get in, but by a secret passageway that only the inhabitants of Old Town know about…"

Maybe it's not a passageway then, thought Phæ'enor, maybe it's a door in the wall? But it doesn't matter, I can't get through. I don't have a key. Disheartened and getting cold she wrapped her cloak around her pulling it in at her neck, letting the necklace her uncle had given her that night, accidentally get caught in the fastening. Trying to get it out she looked at it, then at the pendant. A KEY! No, that's silly, why should a pendant my uncle gave me fit this keyhole? She fiddled with it in her fingers, then looked at the keyhole again, shrugged her shoulders and tried it.

As she did, thoughts went through her mind: this is not going to work, this is not going to fit, and then … it fit! Perfectly! Her heart raced again as she turned it, the pendant glowed, and the wall in front of her clicked. Her heart raced as she turned it to the right. Nothing. The wall had not revealed its opening and there were no more clicks. She stepped back in confusion looking at the wall, and then it came to her. The series of clicks Rasia had made to open the secret passageway into the city wall so they could get into the gaol and Mëdez with his sequence of clicks when unlocking the entrance to another corridor in their shop.

Phæ'enor looked at the wall again and took hold of the key. It would not turn any further right, so she slowly turned it left until, yes! It clicked and glowed. She tried left again. No click or glow. Right, it clicked and glowed again, brighter every time. Left again, right-right until the key shone so brightly she could hardly see. The wall made a low noise. Phæ'enor pushed harder and this time it moved. There was a low whooshing noise as the air was pushed out of the entrance towards her, but then she heard another sound. She turned around, not only could she hear the bells getting louder and louder but the silhouette of the jester, jumping like a frog on the cobbles towards her, was moving faster and faster.

Wide eyed, Phæ'enor quickly turned back to the hole in the wall. Inside was a low-lit passageway, short in distance, with a gate on the other side. She placed the pendant back under her cloak, it had stopped glowing. Hearing the jingling of the bells become more frequent and louder she looked behind her onto the streets of Newtown, the Jester was only metres away. Well, I have nothing to lose she thought. She turned, walked into the wall and closed the door behind her. Her blood-soaked shoes remained in the shadows of Newtown.

**

Phæ'enor had waited quietly, staring at the way she had come in. The sound of bells had stopped when she had closed the entrance, the Jester had not followed in after her. She walked carefully through the dimly lit tunnel in the wall, it was cold beneath her feet, but she was grateful, for it soothed the pain. She reached the other side quickly. There was no door here, just a tall iron gate, with a metal latch for a lock. She pushed the lever open and pulled it, stepping out onto a dark, dirty, wet and muddy street. She could hear trickling water, but when she looked down she couldn't see anything.

Then she looked in front of her. Just a few feet away was another wall standing parallel to and as tall as the one she had come through. Lights and distant noise flickered between gaps and holes. She moved towards it and tiptoed through over to one of them. Colours danced before her eyes, many people were bustling around the place, she couldn't quite make out but there seemed to be an assortment of buildings behind them, lights on in nearly every window. She did not expect to see so much activity.

She pressed her ear to the hole instead. There were definite sounds of music, laughing, and drunken cheers. Looking back through the gaps in the wall, she watched the people of Old Town; one looked to be showing his fellow friends how to dance, but he slipped, his beer flew through the air, while he landed on his backside in a splash of whatever was on the ground. His beer jug soon landed on top of his stomach, with his friends roaring with laughter.

She looked to the left. A plump woman who was spilling out of a very decorative red corseted dress laughed out loud at the man, whilst a small boy dressed in rags brushed past her. Moments later he smiled to himself as he slipped a silk bag from his sleeve and emptied the gold and silver coins into the palm of his hands. To the left a girl was skipping with a rope directly above a puddle, her pale dress being soaked pink. Phæ'enor did not have time to figure out what kind of liquids the little girl was hopping in because at that moment Wolf Rasia appeared in view. He was walking fast; he turned and went up and away out of sight, down the side of one of the buildings and its brightly lit alleyway.

Phæ'enor stood up and looked at the wall. If she was going to follow him she needed to find a way through. She couldn't see another keyhole. Looking quickly around the wall in front she decided there was nowhere through at this point and turned to her right; walking but with her left hand on the wall, still feeling her way for any more keyholes.

She moved along, getting faster and faster until she broke out into a run, aware that she would soon lose sight of Rasia altogether if she was not quick enough. Dirt splashed up onto the hem of her dress and cloak. Suddenly her hand fell away from the wall and in shock she stumbled and nearly fell. She looked in front of her at the wall. It was still there, or at least she thought it was. Phæ'enor put her hand forward to touch it but did not make contact. She tilted her head and realised then that there was more than a wall in front of her. She stepped forward. It had turned into some kind of small maze that she could not quite make out with her eyes alone, so she pushed forward using her hands to feel her way through. It seemed to her like she was zig zagging her way forward until eventually she came out on the other side.

The noise of music, people having fun, kids playing on the street, and those at work hit her senses immediately. It was vibrant madness. People were everywhere but the buildings, they were nothing like she had seen so far in Benaghar. Wonky and crowded, the alleyways were framed by buildings of all different shapes and sizes that leaned in on each other from the top down. Some were extremely narrow, others short or tall. There were round windows, long windows, crooked doors, no doors, thatched roofs, multi-coloured tiled roofs. There was even an assortment of bridges linking them together; stepped, planked, bricked and roped. Ladders led in from one building to another. It went on and on.

Although they were all jumbled together somehow, and without room for more, they had an abundance of life to them, certainly more than the grand tall white and plain buildings of Grand Alboreum Circus. Phæ'enor, lost in colour, checked herself. She needed to get moving if she wanted to find Rasia. It may not have been a clever idea to follow him, after all she had not heard from him since their visit to see his brother and after seeing him with

Officer Nathryn and Prince Taigor this evening he would surely know that she had run away with the intention of heading to Archä and Mëdez. There was also the matter of his duty to her father, to look after her. Rasia may even decide to take her back home, something she was not willing to do right now, maybe never again!

She moved quickly, towards the first building in front of her, it was made of every coloured brick she could imagine possible: reds, blues, yellows and greens. She then turned left and hurried along as fast as her sore bare feet could take her, heading in the direction of the alleyway that she had seen Rasia go down. Luckily, all she had to do was keep an eye out for the girl skipping in the puddle and the drunken man who had slipped and fallen on his back. They were just up ahead of her; and not as far as she thought they would be. As she hurried past the little girl and looked at the puddle, it was red and had a stale smell about it. The girl giggled at her as she screwed her face up in disgust. Behind the girl was a narrow stream of blood gently making its way down from a row of hanging skinned animals to the girl's feet. The butchers behind, in strange symmetry, chopped and hacked away at more skinned animals on their workbenches.

Phæ'enor walked on and around the drunk man passed out on the ground and headed down the alleyway. If it was crowded out on the main street it was even more so down here. People barged into and knocked her as they passed. Food stalls filled the air with steam and the smells of hot meat and drink. Light from open doorways lit the cobbled streets, as well as mismatched and misarranged lanterns hanging from the various buildings above her. She looked up ahead to see jagged edges of buildings leaning in against one another where their beams and floors had obviously failed to hold together. Stairwells interlinked and washing lines intertwined.

Phæ'enor had no idea where she was or where Rasia had headed to, so she kept going straight. After a while she gave in and turned down a side street, narrower but less crowded. Then turned down another street, then another, until it became so quiet no one else was around.

I'm lost, I'm completely lost she thought. Annoyed with herself she headed back to the street she came from, but she must have taken another wrong turn for the street was completely quiet, still and dark. She walked down a little further just to see if there was another way out; everywhere she turned there seemed to be an exit and a way back, yet none of them took her anywhere. She looked up above, only to see more crooked buildings and stairs. Maybe if I climb up them I will be able to make out where I am, thought Phæ'enor.

She ran over to some wooden stairs, carefully making her way up several flights. She still had a way to go to get to open sky so went to take another set of stairs opposite when she glimpsed Rasia through some dirty windows. Quickly she crouched down beside it at the bottom of the stairs. Above her, swinging and creaking gently, a sign read The Raed Wolf Inn. A large black wolf, teeth barred and blood dripping out its mouth stared back at her menacingly. Still looking at it she moved closer to the window, the better to see Wolf Rasia, but as she did so something dripped on top of her, it was scarlet red.

'Urgh!'

'What was that?' shouted a voice from inside.

Panicked, Phæ'enor moved further up the stairs, away from the window. As she did so she heard more noises and then movement.

'Check outside,' came another voice. But instead of someone coming through the door of the inn, Phæ'enor slowly realised that the eyes of the big black wolf on the sign of the Inn started to move. Scanning the stairs outside, around, below, then above. It was looking for her! She jumped into the shadows of the building behind, the eyes continued staring in her direction. Then suddenly the door of the inn swung open and a furry headed boy peered out.

Looking in her direction Phæ'enor could make out that it was Wolf Cana, the boy who helped keep watch when Phæ'enor and Rasia ventured into the city gaols and escorted her home afterwards.

'Do you see anyone?' came a shout again.

Wolf Cana shrugged his shoulders, 'Nah. Thought I saw something move through the Wolf's eyes, but no, nothing there.' He moved back into the inn and shut the door behind him.

Phæ'enor breathed a sigh of relief, waited a moment then slowly made her way back down the stairs to the window, wiping the blood from the sign off her face as she went.

Remaining out of sight, she looked and listened through the slight crack in the window glass at Rasia talking to a group of men and women, and some boys and girls:

'Look, I said I think I know where it is, but I'm not certain so I need all of you to help me.'

'You really think this is a good idea?' said one of the men.

'Yes, how else am I going to get my brother back? This is your leader!' he shouted. There was a murmur of agreement amongst those gathered.

'So, we can trust Archä and Mëdez to deliver then?' said another man.

'We can never trust those two, but they seem to like the girl. I don't think they will do anything with her around.'

'What makes you say that?' asked one of the women.

'They seem to think she is the key to getting the chest, or at least opening it. Something to do with some symbols.'

Phæ'enor sneaked a peek at them. Rasia was pacing the room. Some were standing, others sat contemplating around a table. For a moment, Phæ'enor thought she was seeing a giant pack of wolves. Squinting, it became clear that most of the men and women gathered were wearing hats made from wolf heads, the fur falling onto their shoulders. The girls and boys gathered wore plane, tatty clothes, the same as Rasia.

'Well let's hope they don't do anything to the girl. We have your brother to think about, we don't need someone else to rescue either.' They all murmured in agreement again. The one who spoke did not look much older than Phæ'enor, but she was surly and had an unfriendly look about her.

'So how are we going to get the help of this girl then?' asked another, 'we can't exactly get her to help us out with Officer Nathryn sniffing around.'

'Ha!' barked Rasia. 'Well I think Officer Nathryn has already helped us with that one. Miss Phæ'enor Doven is not exactly his biggest fan right now.'

'Oh yeah? Why's that then, did he give her some flowers, maybe even a kiss?' asked one of the younger boys, pouting his lips and mimicked kissing the air. The room at large laughed.

'Something like that,' said Rasia. 'Although it might be harder to get hold of her than I planned.' There was grumbling in the room then.

'You guard the Doven's house, don't you? She pretty much talks to you all the time and from what you've told us so far has a habit of coming and going when she wants anyway.'

'Mmm…' said Master Rasia rubbing his chin in thought.

'Well, what's the problem?'

Master Rasia stopped pacing the room, 'She seems to have disappeared into the night.'

'What? So, what are we going to do without her?' snapped the surly girl again.

'Look, first we need to get to the chest, then we'll think about Miss Phæ'enor Doven.'

'Right, so what's the plan of action then?' said another.

But Phæ'enor did not hear what their plan of action was, just then she felt a vice grip over her mouth and was held tightly across her chest from behind. She tried to make a noise, to alert Rasia, but no sound came out.

'You're not very hard to find Miss Doven. The cloak and the …
err … the colourfulness of it kind of makes you stand out.' She tried
to kick the person, but with no shoes on she groaned as the pain
from her bleeding feet shot up through her legs. 'I know you
wanted to hear Rasia's plans here, but you see, it seems you are
needed by quite a few people to get into those chests, and I
personally don't want to hear what plans they have, nor does my
boss. Because we need you for ours.'

Roughly her hood was pulled back and the mask she had been
wearing was ripped from her face, she was pulled around, and
before a large piece of cloth was rammed into her mouth and a large
sack pulled over her head, she glimpsed O'tila. She felt herself being
lifted off the ground and carried away. She screamed and screamed
but no sound came out.

Chapter Fifteen

Mrs Kuáng's Tea House

'Ow!'

'Arrgh!'

'SHUT UP!'

'We can't, she keeps kicking us!'

'Mmmmm … MMMMMmmmmm!'

Muffles, scraping and scratching emitted all around Phæ'enor, she was still being carried but it seemed O'tila and his accomplices were trying to get her inside somewhere. She could feel the heat of a fire hit her as they moved over an invisible threshold.

'Mmmmm..!' she tried to shout, as her side hit something hard and cold. Whatever it was it was pretty solid, and her left hip felt very sore.

'Chirp, chirp. Chirp, chirp.'

Phæ'enor turned her head trying to listen, she was sure she just heard the noise of tiny birds. Then it came again.

'Chirp, chirp. Chirp, chirp.'

'ShaaaaaAAAA-TUP!' came a roar of a voice.

The noise of chatter died, and she heard more staggered footsteps, something being dragged across a floor, then moments later she was turned upright and forced down onto something hard; it wobbled unstable beneath her.

'A gift, Sir!' announced a breathless O'tila. There was no response. Instead more scuffles of boots, more dragging noises, then silence.

'Thsssk.'

Phæ'enor could not make out what had just made that noise. Then she heard wheezing and a loud cough before someone cleared their throat.

'Haa – Hum!'

She tried to breathe through her nose but the sack over her head was being sucked in towards her. Instead, she started to panic, trying to breathe properly. Then suddenly, light flooded her senses. The sack had been lifted by O'tila who was standing beside her, sack in one hand dangling by his side. He sniffed at her and looked as though she was some rare species he hadn't seen before. She screwed her eyebrows back at him, unable to speak; she still had the cloth in her mouth and over her nose. He smiled and walked over to the other side of the room. Phæ'enor's eyes followed him and then moved onto the room at large. Besides O'tila there were three other boys, two not much older than herself, and scrawny. The third looked slightly younger and had obviously eaten the other two's fair share of rewards by the size of him. The room itself wasn't very wide, but it was long and light, with yellow and green tinges to it; many candles flickered from around the room. Crooked wooden floors led to a dirty bar.

'My regular please Ma'am.'

Phæ'enor looked to see who O'tila was speaking to but couldn't see anyone. All she could make out was the sound of scuffing and clinking; steam rose up from behind the bar. Then up popped a small and bedraggled woman. What Phæ'enor took to be black matted hair was a hat made of some sort of hide wrapped around two large horns, and a dirty red cloth plaited about a woman's forehead holding it in place. Her face was so aged with wrinkles that she looked like a dried prune. She had small dark eyes but a very big mouth.

'Here you go O'tila, one ho' wa'er,' as she spoke she revealed a mouth sparse of teeth and what remained were either black or replaced by small wooden pegs. Water? Thought Phæ'enor, I would have thought O'tila would drink something stronger.

'Chirp, chirp.'

Phæ'enor's eyes were diverted by the noise, from the bar to the ceiling. It sounded like a bird, but instead of one there were hundreds. The ceiling was full of various sized cages, all home to budgies, canaries, little tits, parrots and what looked like to be an albino bird of some sort in the corner next to a tiny owl in a tiny cage. As she looked they all broke out into conversation.

'Grrr... BE QUIET!' came a loud shout.

BANG, BANG, BANG!

The table in front of Phæ'enor vibrated with two large fists slamming down onto it. At this Phæ'enor looked across and gulped. When she was first taken outside The Raed Wolf Inn she was not scared, only angry with O'tila for grabbing her unawares. What she saw opposite made her rethink. It was hideously big and hideously ugly. She was sure it was a man and she was sure she knew who from the pictures she had seen, but he looked a lot worse in person. Obviously, he was much more photogenic than she thought possible.

He looked to be about seven foot tall and the same wide. The whites of his eyes were bloodshot; one bright green, one bright blue, surrounded by a painted green face. Phæ'enor stared at his skin, I hope it is painted she thought, that or his skin is melting. It seemed to fold in blobs by his cheeks, and little blobs of green trickled down his forehead. He had not yet looked back at her, instead he was preoccupied with a rather unhealthy-looking chicken, at least it must have been unhealthy before it was cooked, for it was slimy and green just like his face. The man pulled the skin off the breast, dangled it into his mouth, slurping as it went down and wiped the grease from his mouth across his cheek. Then he looked across at her, still eating the chicken, and cleaning his teeth with his tongue.

'Want some?' His voice was deep and gravelly, mocking.

Phæ'enor shook her head disgusted. The man looked at O'tila, whilst motioning with his head and his grease coated hands towards her. O'tila walked over to Phæ'enor and pulled the cloth from her mouth. She coughed profusely and wanted to grab her throat and control it somehow, but her hands were still tied. The birds up above started to make small and infrequent noises again.

Finally gaining control of her senses, Phæ'enor had begun to wish that the cloth had remained in place. Her senses now unblocked, she was hit with the heat of the steam and vapour coming from the bar and the smell of the place. It was a pungent mix of wood and fire, herbs and spices, flowers and plants, animals and bird shit; she tried not to gag.

'HA. Ha, ha-ha,' came the booming laugh of the man sat in front of her. 'Welcome, to Mrs Kuáng's Tea House.' He looked at her obviously finding some amusement in her situation for he smiled and asked, 'Would you like to try some teas?'

'NO!' It wasn't Phæ'enor who spoke but O'tila and firmly. 'She's not here for the bloody tea, you know that!'

'I could always make Miss 'ere som' fing ... som' fing like yours?' said the tiny and horned woman to O'tila.

'Fine. Would you like Mrs Kuáng here to boil some hot water for you?' Phæ'enor did not say anything so Mrs Kuáng busied herself with making her a cup of "som' fing".

'Hmm,' breathed the man out through his nose. 'You know O'tila here, maybe not some of his friends,' he said gesturing to the other three boys sitting, leaning and standing around. But, do you know who I am?'

Phæ'enor looked at him, 'You are O'scilla Juur.'

'I'm famous! Ha, ha, ha!' he looked at her, laughter in his eyes. 'Very clever. Rumour is it that you're quite a bright girl ... or ... maybe just too nosy.' It wasn't a question, more of a statement. O'scilla turned his attention back to his ill looking meal; stripping the chicken from the bones with his hands, one gloved the other bare. His nails were dirty, but he did not seem too bothered as he slurped the bits of grease covered chicken into his mouth and proceeded to lick his fingers, the gloved hand soaked with grease.

Phæ'enor watched him with a grimace. He wiped the rest of the grease on the front of his battered and hole ridden jacket. Balancing his elbows on the table and clasping his hands together he asked:

'So … what brings you to Old Town Miss Doven? We thought we would have to venture out and come and find you but it would seem that you have found us first.'

Phæ'enor, still grimacing, backed away in her chair, his hot breath had reached her from the other side of the table. It was not pleasant, rotten teeth and gums mixed with rotten chicken and there was definitely a smell of fish lingering there too.

'Well? Answer the man!' said O'tila, who was casually leaning against the bar whilst sat on a rickety looking stool. The candle flames casted yellow and green shadows across the room. Phæ'enor looked back at O'scilla. She thought before answering.

'I got lost.'

'HA!' came O'scilla's booming laugh again. 'Funny, I thought you were following young Wolf Rasia into Old Town. A detour, I believe, after running away from home?' Phæ'enor scowled as chuckles reverberated around the room. 'Not as clever as we thought then…'

'Well, if you already knew why I was here then why waste your time asking me,' she snapped back.

'Thsssk,' came the sound that Phæ'enor had heard when she first entered the tea house. She realised now it was O'scilla kissing his teeth in disapproval. He licked his lips.

'What I want to know is why I am here?' asked Phæ'enor getting angrier. O'scilla smiled and licked his lips again.

'Well, you didn't lie about her being mouthy,' said O'scilla to O'tila. He did not look happy and turned back to Phæ'enor. 'Like I said, rumour is it that you're a very clever girl.' Phæ'enor said nothing whilst he continued to talk, 'but how useful I'm not so sure.' O'scilla shifted in his seat and started to eat again. Phæ'enor turned and glared at O'tila.

'Well then?' she demanded.

'WELL THEN WHAT?!' spat O'scilla across the table. His halitosis nearly made Phæ'enor sick this time. She closed her eyes and tried to compose her senses and her stomach. When she could finally breathe she shouted back:

'WELL THEN! WHAT – DO – YOU – NEED – ME – FOR? I think I have better things to do than sit here watching you eat!'

O'tila swiftly walked over to Phæ'enor and whacked his hand across her head.

'OUCH!' she screamed.

He pulled her chair around to face him.

'STOP!' shouted O'scilla.

He got up and walked over, shoving O'tila out the way. He was massive. Towering above Phæ'enor, in her little wooden rickety chair, his shadow swallowed her. He bent down close to her and spoke in a low voice:

'You want to learn some manners Miss Phæ'enor Doven. You're not in Grand Town now, so you can't command or tell anybody else what to do. Old Town is mine...'

'It's odd that you should say Old Town is yours, I was told it was and has always belonged to the wolves.'

'GGgggrrr!'

O'scilla grabbed Phæ'enor by the neck of her cloak, knocking the chair out from underneath her. She dangled in the air, her hands still tied behind her back unable to stop the choke. Face-to-face he snarled at her, but still choking, Phæ'enor tried to speak:

'Old ... Town ... belongs ... to ... them. People ... they ... know ... I ... am ... missing...'

O'scilla sneered and leaned in closer, Phæ'enor could feel her throat constrict and tighten, her face swell up, but still she continued: 'They ... they will ... find me ... and you ... you will ... be ... ripped ... limb ... from limb...'

'AAAaaahh, ha, ha, ha, ha, ha!'

O'scilla laughed uncontrollably. Phæ'enor felt like she was going to pass out, and not just from the strangulation, his breath was toxic. Suddenly he slammed her back down into the chair.

Wheezing, Phæ'enor tried desperately to breathe. Dizzily she looked around. They were all laughing at her. When O'scilla finally composed himself, he stared back down at her, then grabbed her again out of the chair, this time by the cloth of her cloak below the neck. He breathed out his hot and rotten breath into Phæ'enor's face. Again, she tried not to gag.

'They won't be able to rip me limb by limb … and d'ya know why?' he said, in a deadly whisper. Phæ'enor shook her head. 'It's because I don't have any, unless you count the one I'm holding you with.'

There were sniggers all around from the boys gathered. Phæ'enor saw O'scilla's eyes divert to them with a look of displeasure. The hub of noise died down again. O'scilla looked at her, then slammed her onto her feet, grabbing Phæ'enor by her left wrist.

'Ow.'

'Feel this Miss Doven.'

O'scilla yanked her hand onto to the top of his right thigh, and slowly dragged it down his leg. Phæ'enor could feel the vast muscle beneath her hands and then suddenly nothing. She looked down in wonder then back up into the face of O'scilla Juur confused. He grinned, grabbing her right hand and as with the other dragged it down his left leg. This time instead of muscle to nothing, Phæ'enor felt the hardness of metal, the coldness of it through his clothes, along with strange whirring and ticking noises.

O'scilla slapped her hands away from his legs, bent down and pulled up his right trouser. It was a wooden stump, carved into a leg, albeit one too skinny to support someone of O'scilla's size.

He then pulled up his left trouser leg. This time, Phæ'enor looked on in wonder. It wasn't just some leg made from metal it was a mixture of mechanics and weapons. It all seemed to be made of a bright yellow gold. The strange whirring and ticking noise came from several sets of brass teeth gears, engaged with an assortment of little and large wheels, and inside every nook lay golden knifes and pistols. Phæ'enor could not fail to notice a large wooden baton clipped to the side of the metal cage of O'scilla's leg.

He smiled at her and pleased with himself rolled back the sleeves of his jacket. As he crossed them Phæ'enor noticed his left arm was also made of the same golden metal cage, but this time it housed many knifes, before it disappeared under his right arm. The glove hid the metal of this hand.

'These people of yours. They can come and rip my limbs off, but they'll have a very hard time trying.' Nobody was laughing now. 'So, whilst you are in my company, we play by my rules. If you decide to start with all the chatter and abuse, or think about escaping, then you may not leave this place for a long time. Maybe not at all.' Phæ'enor had been holding her breath and had stopped breathing in so that she wouldn't have to smell his stench. 'Do you understand?' sneered O'scilla.

'Mmm…hmmm,' said Phæ'enor, nodding frantically hoping that O'scilla would move away from her face.

'Good.'

As he let go and moved back to his seat and away from her, Phæ'enor let out her breath and a sigh of relief. She knew he would think it was because she feared him but Phæ'enor was just glad to not have to smell him so close.

'How did you find me and what do you want from me?' asked Phæ'enor.

The birds above were chirping more quietly now. One or two of the ragged looking ones started to hoot whilst the tiny owl in the tiny cage tried to fly without success, banging into the bars.

'Mrs Kuáng, please shut those bloody birds up!' he snapped.

'Yes, yes … I doin' it, I doin' it,' said the little old woman, who came bustling out from behind the bar with a small rickety stool. Phæ'enor watched as she climbed up it towards a low hanging cage, reached in and clasped her small hands around an equally small exotic looking bird. Then the woman made her way back down the stool, bird still in her hands and over to a window at the far end of the building. With one hand, she seemed to fiddle with her apron, then with the bird's feet. It sounded as though the woman was talking to the little bird, before she opened the window and let it fly out.

The woman made her way back muttering, 'Stupid little bird.' before disappearing behind the bar again.

Phæ'enor's attention was drawn back to O'scilla after he started to click his fingers at her.

'Pay attention girl!' he growled. He looked at O'tila and spoke again. 'It so happens that O'tila here saw you in Newtown trying to get away from some of the city guards…' he rolled his tongue out over his bottom lip, '…whilst on another of my errands, but had spotted you instead, following that useless idiot Rasia.' He spat the name and leaned back in his chair with his left arm leaning on the table, his hand holding the emaciated chicken bone. 'I'm after the same thing that Rasia, Prince Taigor, his puppet Nathryn, and your new friends Archä and Mëdez…'

'They are not my friends. None of them are!' said Phæ'enor, stony faced.

'That's not what I've heard. As far as I can see your father has friends in very high places. The Prince. Nathryn. He's even got poor boys like little Rasia running jobs for him.'

'What?'

'Sssh!' said O'scilla holding his finger up to Phæ'enor. 'They all seem to be trying to protect these silly little chests and whatever is in them. And I don't particularly know what they are and whether there's gold, or treasure or fucking keys to the whole of Benaghar stowed away in them! All I know is that they are extremely valuable, they will soon be mine, and word is you can help.' He picked up the chicken bone and wagged it at Phæ'enor. 'The problem is if all these other fuckers get hold of it before me!' O'scilla ripped another chunk of rotten chicken out with his teeth.

'And what if they do?' asked Phæ'enor, 'so, what?'

'So, what? So what Miss Doven? These chests have already caused me a headache. It's torture trying to get anything out of those officers of Nathryn's, believe me!'

'HA! HA! HA!' laughed the three boys, O'tila just smirked. Mrs Kuáng, apparently not finding it funny slammed a glass she was cleaning down on the bar and stared at O'scilla.

He stopped laughing and silently stared back before turning back to face Phæ'enor.

'They are holding something that will become very valuable to me.'

'HA … I've heard a lot about you, but nothing is more valuable to you than how much money you can make. You will only sell it if you do get your hands on it.'

O'scilla nodded his head, 'Well exactly, but this time for a much more substantial amount than I'm used to, Miss Doven.' He leaned back in on the table, Phæ'enor leaned back away from it and O'scilla. 'But I hear they are also valuable to you and your little friend you were following this evening. He means to trade the contents of the missing chest for information on his brother. Or his brother dies, right?' He grinned at her again. Phæ'enor tried to keep calm. This man had no morals and clearly didn't care about whether Rasia's brother died or not so long as he got his price. 'But I have a better deal to offer Rasia, and you Miss Doven, better than those two cheating rats, Archä and Mëdez. You see, I also have friends in high places … and I mean very high … who not only can offer me more money but will help Wolf Canis out of that amber lair of his … plus help you Miss Doven so that you don't have to marry that pretty boy Nathryn. Not only do we all get what we want, I win either way.'

'I wouldn't trust you with Wolf Canis' life and I don't need money to stop Officer Nathryn from marrying me!'

'Well suit yourself, but I could give you enough, so you could set up on your own. He won't find you.'

'Humph … thank you, but I'm not that desperate. I'll find another way to not marry him. It has just been a mistake! And you can't bribe me with more money, or information you say you have to set Rasia's brother free. Where's your information?'

'Where's Archä and Mëdez's evidence?'

'I … I … well…' Phæ'enor was careful not let slip about their collection of chests.

'Hmm … so it seems you're willing to do whatever Archä and Mëdez have asked of you and Rasia … but they've not given you any proof of Wolf Canis' innocence in return, have they?'

They all laughed at Phæ'enor. She hadn't thought much further than what Archä and Mëdez had advised her and Rasia. She just assumed they were telling the truth from what information they had given her so far and from having viewed the chests. Yet there was no physical evidence of the emaz gold from the chests, just their word. Phæ'enor went quiet. The others continued to laugh. There was also the matter of whether the stories behind the chests were true. O'scilla may know a lot about her, her footprints across the city, but did he know about what Archä and Mëdez held in their collection? Besides, as far as she was aware, Rasia had no clue where the emaz gold from the last chest was now hidden.

'I can read your mind girl,' hissed O'scilla. 'You're thinking you don't know where the chests are…'

'Um … yes. I mean no, you're right. I don't know where the chests are,' said Phæ'enor, realising that O'scilla couldn't actually read her thoughts.

'Well, you're in luck. Because I do. Or at least I know a man who does.'

'What?' said Phæ'enor, confused and slightly alarmed that O'scilla may get to the emaz before her or Rasia did.

'Like I said, I also have friends in high places, and I know the only place in this city where those chests will be kept now.'

Phæ'enor couldn't think where, bedsides Archä and Mëdez's stash, and looked at O'tila to see if it was a trick. O'tila smiled back at her and drank his now luke warm water.

'Think, girl,' said O'scilla, 'you of all people should know. I must admit that the way your house has been guarded, the thought that you may have the chests crossed my mind. And even if you didn't they may be stashed somewhere in your house. Yet even O'tila with his attempts, couldn't find it.'

Phæ'enor looked back at O'tila sharply. He nearly choked on his water for they both knew it wasn't him that had broken into her home. She didn't know how much O'sea had told him, whether O'tila knew that O'sea's search had not extended beyond her bedroom. Phæ'enor quickly turned back to O'scilla who was now filling his face with more chicken whilst trying to talk.

'So, if they're not at your house, it's no longer in the garrisons or The Scavenger … or what's left of it. It's certainly not on any of the other ships … I made sure of that … then with all the guards and interest from up high, I conclude, it's in the palace.' He smiled at Phæ'enor, bits of chicken still stuck in his teeth. 'Thsssthk,' he kissed and sucked his teeth clean, at least of the bits that were visible.

'Huh! And how are you supposed to get in there without being detected? It's not like they won't miss you,' asked Phæ'enor sarcastically, 'and even then, if you do, how will you ever find them?' Her heart was racing trying to divert O'scilla's attention. Hoping that he hadn't noticed the brief exchange with O'tila.

'I don't' need to go in there myself, Miss Doven. I'm well aware that my presence will not go unnoticed.' He gestured to O'tila, who was looking into his now empty glass. 'O'tila here and his cousin know their way around the palace. It won't be long before he finds it and when he does he'll bring it back here for you to decipher the locks and open!'

'Excuse me?' said Phæ'enor.

'You – missy – are – going – to – open – those – chests!'

'And how, exactly am I going to do that?' she asked.

'HOW?' said O'scilla indignant. 'Word is that Archä and Mëdez think you are the key to opening the chests. Normally they are not wrong about these things!'

'I know they think that, but they didn't explain it to me, they just said something about some symbols … I've got no idea how to open the chests, or where the keys are!'

'Well then, Miss Doven. I suggest you start to think about how to; if you don't…'

'If I don't? Why can't you just break it open? They are only made of wood!'

'It's not just wood! It's Eckera wood. It cannot be broken by force. The lock is the only way to get inside them except there is no keyhole to unlock!'

Phæ'enor already knew about the wood of the Eckera tree being too strong to break by force from what her cousin had mentioned about it in Polstor & Polstor, but she was taken aback by the lock, no keyhole?'

This was news to Phæ'enor; she thought all the chests had keyholes. But now she came to think of it her mind turned back to when she was in Archä and Mëdez's shop. Surrounded by the chests she had felt the outline of the symbols and below them the keyholes. They were no more than etchings outlining the shape of one. O'scilla leaned across the table and growled at her.

'You need to think harder than that Doven. You're not as stupid as you make out to be. So when the chests arrive you better know how to open them.' He leaned back and got up, moving over to her. 'In the meantime, you'll stay here with Mrs Kuáng. She may look harmless but she's a nasty little woman, especially if you try to escape. And just so that you are not as easy to recognise if you do manage to get away, I think I'll be taking some of this from you as well.'

Phæ'enor froze on the spot and held her breath again as O'scilla's large body leaned into her; his face resting on the side of hers, he moved his right hand to her head and slowly, carefully, started to pull the little yellow flowers and pins out of her hair, letting it fall around her shoulders.

O'tila and the other boys looked on nervously. Forcefully, O'scilla grabbed hold of the back of Phæ'enor's head, pulled it to the side and slammed her face down onto the table. Still able to see O'scilla, she watched as he pulled her hair loose, moved it to the side and grabbed a handful of it then took a meat cleaver out of his left arm with his teeth, and then with a quick swap of his hands he grabbed the knife in mid-air and chopped it clean off.

Dangling it out in front of her, he then walked over to the fire and tossed it into the flames. But instead of sizzling the fire glowed bright, omitting a powerful flame and heat back out into the shack of a room. Everyone backed away, then stared back at the fire as it returned to crackling. They all looked at Phæ'enor, eyeing her with suspicion. O'scilla had looked down at the hand he had grabbed her hair with; he looked to be watching it to see if it would also go up in flames.

Phæ'enor instinctively went to touch her hair. It was still there but short, very short, slanting at an angle down to her right shoulder, which fell slightly in front of her right eye, straight and black.

'Mrs Kuáng! Get her changed out of that dress. Find something that doesn't make her stand out! The rest of you, move! We've been here long enough!'

One by one they left the shack of a tea room. O'scilla was last but turned before leaving to say, 'Don't even think of trying anything. I'll know exactly where you are!' He turned and slammed the door. As the room shook, the birds began to chirp; they seemed happier now that O'scilla and his men had left.

Phæ'enor looked at the bar only to see Mrs Kuáng sharpening a set of knifes whilst a kettle next to her hissed on the boil and she thought to herself, I hope one of those is not for me!

'Come, girl, come,' said Mrs Kuáng, 'you nee' ta get changed. No goo' what ya wear, no good.' Phæ'enor felt a sharp and strong pull and was dragged into the next room.

Chapter Sixteen

Dumplings

Phæ'enor woke in the light of the dawn having slept uncomfortably. She lay on a dirty mattress, surrounded by too much heat from the steam emitting from the floors below; it made breathing unbearable. Phæ'enor stared at the floorboards where little vapours, and strands of light, appeared in the gaps. She rolled over and felt the hardness against her left leg and realised she had rolled onto the books Archä and Mëdez had given her.

When she was dragged off by Mrs Kuáng to get dressed she had retrieved the books from the inside of her cloak, stuffing them down her dress as quick as she could before Mrs Kuáng took the cloak away from her.

The little woman had looked at her funnily before taking the present from Officer Nathryn out of her hands, handing Phæ'enor some other clothes to get changed into. The books were now placed in the thick brown and baggy trousers that she had been given to wear instead; one in the right pocket, the other in the left. They were itchy, and her skin was red from the constant scratching in the night.

Alongside these she had put on long socks with ankle boots; her feet were still sore but at least they had stopped bleeding. And she wore a thick overly large cotton shirt, covered with a thick brown waistcoat, that was so small it kept riding up at the front. To finish the look, she had been given a matching flat cap. If anybody came by she was told that this was for her to tuck the remaining strands of hair into so that she could not be recognised, well at least not immediately, thought Phæ'enor.

She ran her hand through her hair. It felt strange, her head was a lot lighter. She was not too sad about losing it though as it had always got in her way; getting caught in doors, taking ages to comb at night, easy to tangle and easy to catch her food in at the dinner table. As much as she disliked O'scilla he had done her a small favour.

Phæ'enor moved and rolled over again, swung her legs out from beneath her, off the mattress and onto the floorboards. They creaked as she got up and walked through the mists of vapour to the small window. She had slept in a small attic at the top of the building, just above the tea rooms. From the tea room below all she could see were a few other buildings, stairways and windows, but through the window in the attic she could make out most of the old town rooftops, the many multi-coloured shapes and sizes of the buildings; they looked just as crooked from above as they did from below.

It was a beautiful dusky morning, Phæ'enor could still see two or three of Benaghar's moons fading in the distance whilst the sun rose in the east. Nothing, bar a few gleams of red sparks shooting up in the distance disturbed this. Phæ'enor assumed it was Old Town not yet gone to sleep.

'You wake up dah?' came a shout from below. It was the unmistakable voice of Mrs Kuáng. 'Come don girl, I've mae tea! Come don, come don!'

Phæ'enor moved quickly to the door, checking the books were still in her pocket before opening it; more to stop Mrs Kuáng shouting at her than the yearning for pungent tea. She walked across the crooked floor towards an even more crooked wooden staircase and started to cough badly. Her eyes began to water from the smell coming from a small room opposite. The door was ajar and Phæ'enor could just make out boxes and tins and sacks of all colours and sizes on the floor. Loose tea spilled out from all of them.

Phæ'enor moved hastily towards the stairs then down them to get away from the smells and vapours of the attic. As she descended she could hear Mrs Kuáng's small footsteps scarpering backwards and forwards in the main tea room. The birds were silent. Phæ'enor pushed open the door from the stairs into the room, it creaked badly, but as far as Phæ'enor could tell Mrs Kuáng had not heard her enter. The birds were all perched, eyes shut in their cages, hanging from the ceiling above as they swayed slightly from the rising heat. Phæ'enor felt she was sweating already.

'Come, come girl!'

'Argh!' screamed Phæ'enor. Mrs Kuáng had appeared from nowhere in front of her holding a tray. Small and metal, it was crammed to the edges with a teapot, tea cup and saucer and a stack of little baskets with a lid; and like everything else in there, expelling steam.

'You startled me, Mrs Kuáng,' said Phæ'enor, as she caught her breath and her lungs slid from her throat back into their rightful place. Mrs Kuáng smiled her rotten wooden toothed smile.

'You Miss, need hot drink and hot food. Come,' and she turned and headed over to a small table in the middle of the room. Phæ'enor slowly followed Mrs Kuáng over, watching her unloading the trays contents.

'Sit don, girl,' said Mrs Kuáng, gesturing for Phæ'enor to sit in a rickety bamboo chair she had just pulled out from underneath the table. Phæ'enor smiled, gingerly sitting down and was about to drag the chair forward when, with much more force than she had expected from such a small woman, Mrs Kuáng pushed the rickety chair so hard that Phæ'enor thought she may crack her ribs on the table.

'Here, move, ya chin,' said Mrs Kuáng. But before Phæ'enor could move Mrs Kuáng grabbed her chin in one hand and tucked in a rather large napkin into the top of Phæ'enor's shirt.

Mrs Kuáng smiled at Phæ'enor again, 'You dress like a boy. You make a good boy. No one recognise you if day see you.' She winked at Phæ'enor then reached over the top of the stack of baskets. Close up, Phæ'enor recognised them as bamboo steamer baskets. Having

281

been to the tea houses in Vanu with her family she knew, or hoped she knew, what these ones would be filled with.

Her doubts about whether to trust the cuisine of a tea house that stank of very strange teas, that not even O'tila would drink, with its dirty and dank feel to it, the ragged looking birds and the wooden toothed hostess, were soon quashed when Mrs Kuáng opened the first of the three stacked baskets. Three, small glazed buns stared back at her. She didn't need to be told and grabbed straight for one of them out of the steam, stuffing it into her mouth. She closed her eyes and smiled as she ate. It brought back memories of family breakfasts at the local tea houses in Vanu, where she, her parents and brothers, would spend hours drinking tea, eating dumplings and other steamed goodies. Exotic and beautiful coloured birds would sing songs in harmony and they would laugh and joke as they played games.

Phæ'enor gulped down the last bit of her pork filled bun and opened her eyes. Mrs Kuáng was staring straight at her agog.

'You, you have tried dese before?'

'Yes,' said Phæ'enor nodding, 'I used to live in …'

'Vanu?' said an excited Mrs Kuáng.

'Um, yes,' said Phæ'enor, astounded that this little woman knew of Vanu.

'I am from Vanu too!' said Mrs Kuáng, gleefully clapping her hands together. She stared a little longer at Phæ'enor then reached for the baskets again.

'Now you try this too…' she said, opening the next layer to reveal several tiny dumplings filled with shrimp. Phæ'enor looked up at Mrs Kuáng, and smiled even more before tucking in, nodding in approval as her mouth was too full to speak. She demolished that layer before finishing the third; egg custard tarts. Phæ'enor laid back in her rickety chair, her hand over her satisfied stomach. She hadn't realised how hungry she had been. Mrs Kuáng busied herself with clearing the bamboo baskets away before turning to the tea.

'You can own-ee have basic gree' tea. O'tila say no ta you havin' any ov'er. Very bad he says, very bad! And he be right!' She cackled out loud and then tutted to herself as she passed Phæ'enor a small cup.

'Could I possibly have more of those dumplings, especially the shrimp ones, they were....'

'NO!' snapped Mrs Kuáng. 'No! no! no!'

'Oh,' said Phæ'enor alarmed, 'I didn't mean to...'

'No! You nee' ta pay, or he does,' said Mrs Kuáng, pointing sharply into the corner of the room. There, his large brimmed hat pulled down over his face, snoozed O'tila, his legs up on the table in front of him.

'It is true you know, no one take piss out of me. You want more, you pay more, or he does!' She said before turning hastily and walking through a pair of small double doors with the bamboo baskets. Phæ'enor's belly rumbled out aloud. She felt even hungrier now that she had eaten Mrs Kuáng's food. She glared at O'tila in annoyance and patted her pockets to see if by some chance money was in them, left by the previous owner. Disappointed, she huffed and slumped in her chair.

The illusion of being back in Vanu with the eating of dumplings, pork buns and egg tarts, had disappeared only to be replaced with a hollowness and realisation that she was still in Benaghar, and worse, stuck somewhere in Old Town.

BANG!

FLASH!

BANG!

The loud noises and flashes of light came through the windows, reflecting off the buildings surrounding the tea house.

'What the...?' said O'tila, as he fell out of his sleep onto the floor. He picked himself up as the dust from the floorboards and cages above floated down. The birds started to wake up and chirp as their cages swayed from the vibrations, bits of dirt and everything else tipped out of their cages onto the table below whilst the many candles flickered.

'What? What, what, what?' shouted Mrs Kuáng, as she came rushing through the double doors with a large pan nearly as big as her and raised above her head ready for a fight.

'It's okay Mrs Kuáng, well at least I think so,' said O'tila. Rising to his feet he looked out of the window but realised he couldn't see what was going on and rushed up the stairs. He appeared back several minutes later a lot calmer.

'What? Wha' it is then?' demanded Mrs Kuáng.

'Oh, it's nothing. Just the city guards bombarding the place. Probably after her,' he advised, nodding in Phæ'enor's direction before walking over to one of the bar stools and slinking down onto one of them. 'So, can I have some breakfast then?'

'Oh, okay,' said Mrs Kuáng lowering her pan, 'she wan' more food too, you gunner pay?' and held out her other hand to O'tila.

'No, I told you woman O'scilla can pay for the food. Not … OW!' Mrs Kuáng hit him over the head with the pan.

'You naugh'y man! Pay first then get food or fuck off!' before storming through the double doors, steam billowing out in her wake. Phæ'enor sat staring at O'tila, her arms folded on her chest and smiling in amusement.

'What are you looking at?' said O'tila.

She shrugged her shoulders nonplussed, 'So they are looking for me then?'

'Obviously,' said O'tila rolling his eyes, 'so, what?'

'Well they'll find me soon enough then your boss won't get the information he thinks I have to help him.'

'Ha, they won't find you, stupid girl, or boy as the case may be. They try and get into Old Town all the time, and every time they give up and walk back through that gate with their tails between their legs. It's too difficult for them, they don't know the terrain and no one on this side of the wall is ever gonna help them. They won't find you, trust me. And as for that information you need to give O'scilla, well you need to come up with something pretty quick because if you don't he's not just going to hand you back. You'll just disappear.'

'So, you know I don't have the information he's after then?' said Phæ'enor, ignoring his threats and wide eyed with surprise. 'But why does he think I have it then?'

'Because I told him you did.'

'WHY?' demanded Phæ'enor.

'To knock him off the scent of course.'

'But, he's your boss, isn't he? Why would you do that?'

'Ha, ha, ha,' laughed O'tila out loud. 'He isn't my boss, I don't have a boss. I have something better than that.'

'Which is?'

'Family, Miss Doven. Family.'

'O'sea?' O'tila nodded with a smile. Mrs Kuáng returned with a small glass of hot water, went behind the bar and jumped up onto the hidden platform so she was the same height as O'tila, handing him his glass.

'So, O'sea has told you to give O'scilla the incorrect information … I've been kidnapped by O'scilla on O'sea's orders, but O'scilla doesn't know that … so … O'sea knows where the chest is … or he works for someone that does?' Phæ'enor had been talking to O'tila but also to herself. She looked at him, he smiled back and raised his glass at her in congratulations.

'So, the chests are in the palace? Which means that O'sea knew that all along, because he works for Prince Taigor and it would seem that so do you?'

'Eh, I help O'sea out. He is my cousin after all.'

'Then O'scilla … he said he had a better reward coming to him if he delivered the information to … to … Prince Taigor, that doesn't make any sense?'

'Trust me it's not Prince Taigor – he's the one trying to keep the chests from everyone. He would never entertain the idea of working with O'scilla, and technically O'scilla doesn't really work for anybody Miss Doven. He just goes to the highest bidder at the time.'

'What do you mean by that?' asked Phæ'enor.

O'tila shrugged his shoulders thinking, 'Say tea for instance. A shipment of rare tea leaf comes in from Palestra. This particular tea leaf has interesting properties. O'scilla already knows this because he has his little spies everywhere, so he puts word out amongst Old Town, Newtown, Queens High and Queens Low, you get the idea. He gets a substantial amount of interested parties, offering various prices. The one that offers the most gets the deal, although it doesn't always mean that they are getting what they paid for, if you know what I mean.' Phæ'enor looked at Mrs Kuáng and then at the shelves of tea and remembered the heavy-laden store cupboard upstairs.

'So, he mixes some of the goods with lower class leaf and gets a higher profit from it?'

'Exactly, but the point is…'

'He goes for the highest bidder,' finished Phæ'enor. 'So, who is the highest bidder this time and why? The stock on offer is of more value than tea leaf this time.'

'Some people may disagree with you there,' said O'tila, smiling at Mrs Kuáng, who smiled back. Phæ'enor screwed her face up at him.

'Look, I don't have a clue who his highest bidder is, I'm just keeping him off the scent of what he's really after this time. O'scilla tends to let only a few of his most trusted little minions in on the details of his dodgy deals.'

'Like who?'

'Like his dumb son.'

'What, O'scilla has a child?'

'Yeah, he was the fat one that helped me bring you here.'

'Does he have a wife too?' asked Phæ'enor, horrified at the idea that something as hideous as O'scilla could breed. O'tila shrugged his shoulders.

'If he has, I've never seen her, probably killed her. Or she died giving birth to that ugly sod.'

Phæ'enor shook her head in wonder, 'So, do you have any idea who the bidder might be, any at all?'

'Why don't you have a think about who you already know is interested in getting their hands on those chests, or who is already linked to them.'

Phæ'enor looked away from O'tila and tried to think who she knew was after the missing chests. Archä and Mëdez wanted them to complete their little collection, 'Archä and Mëdez,' she said aloud, counting on her fingers. Officer Nathryn didn't want them but seemed to be in charge of protecting them and he works directly for Prince Taigor, 'Prince Taigor,' she counted a second finger on her hand.

O'tila shook his head and said, 'Like I said before, Prince Taigor knows where they are. After all they are his and he is in charge of looking after them, he is just protecting what is already his.'

'So, your cousin, O'sea, he is not after them either then?'

'O'sea wouldn't have an interest in emaz gold even if you paid him with it,' said O'tila.

Phæ'enor frowned. This was odd. O'sea was a servant with little to his name, as far as she could tell. The same as his cousin, O'tila here. If she were in his position she might be tempted to get the gold or at least some of it, and it would be easier to when the person you worked for knew where it was.

'So, if O'sea is not interested in the chests, and what's in them …
but, you are still clearly working for him and O'scilla…' Phæ'enor
trailed off as she remembered the conversation between the cousins
down in the palace kitchens. It seemed like on the one hand the pair
of them were working together to get information out of O'scilla,
possibly for Prince Taigor; on the other it seemed more personal:
"…if we bring it to O'scilla he will stay out of my way…"

'O'sea is asking you to keep information from O'scilla, mislead
him … but why?'

O'tila returned to his drink and then replied, 'He does it for a
friend. O'sea and O'scilla used to be on good terms, but not
anymore. Let's just say that O'sea has his reasons.'

'Yes, but what I don't understand is that you are all clearly alike,
I mean…'

'Ha! What? So, you're saying that because O'sea and myself look
like O'scilla, and I won't take that as a compliment, we're all meant
to just get along and…'

'No, no that's not what I meant. Yes, you have the same eyes,
complexion, whatever but it's what some people have told me.'
Phæ'enor had remembered what Simi had said to her the day they
had visited Polstor & Polstor. "… Harqs always stick together; they
are like one big family."

'Hmm, one big family?' said O'tila, contemplating this to himself
as he got off his stool and walked back over to the window, peering
up. The ceiling and the birds hanging from it started to shake and
sway gently; flashes of light appeared randomly but more regularly
through the window. 'We used to be one big family. Against the
rest of the city, but things changed. You don't always get on with
everyone. Some people's opinions stay the same, others don't and
then you end up clashing. People become more interested in money,
their reputation and thinking their opinions matter the most and
they always want more than they got the last time…' said O'tila
quietly.

Phæ'enor looked down at her fingers. Only one remained up, it was for O'scilla, 'Wolf Rasia is after the chest, but he is trying to get it so he can trade it for information with Archä and Mëdez, so he can't be working for O'scilla.'

'Yes, he wants to exchange it for information, not for money like O'scilla.'

Phæ'enor was at a loss as to whom O'scilla was hoping to trade the chests with. As far as she could work out no one liked him, even his own kin were against him. She looked out of the window behind O'tila. The sun was nearly fully up, but the light was still coming from more and more flashes, and Mrs Kuáng's Tea House was now steadily and continuously shaking. I need to get out of here, she thought.

'O'tila, I can't help you, or your cousin. I doubt I can even help Wolf Rasia and his brother. You need to let me go before those guards get here.'

'You're not going anywhere,' said O'tila, as he also turned to look outside. The birds up above were slowly vibrating across one side of their perches to the other as the shaking got worse.

BANG!

BANG!

There were more flashes of light.

'Besides, I don't think it's just the city guards causing all the noise and flashes … and anyway there's a reason why O'scilla has you, why Archä and Mëdez and even that Wolf need you…'

'Yeah, mistakenly…' muttered Phæ'enor to herself.

'What?' asked O'tila.

'Nothing,' muttered Phæ'enor again, which annoyed O'tila even more.

'Look, Miss D…'

'You can call me Phæ'enor you know.'

'Phay-en-noor!' said O'tila, sarcastically, 'Officer Nathryn wants you found, albeit it's your own fault for following that snitch Rasia in here in the first place. He may want you for another reason but Rasia, O'scilla, Archä and Mëdez for some unknown reason think you can open the chests…'

'Chest! A chest,' said Phæ'enor sternly at O'tila, 'there is only one chest in the city, the rest are decoys which I think you already knew.' She thought O'tila stupid, but O'sea would surely know about the decoys and no doubt would have informed his cousin.

O'tila narrowed his eyes, 'Whatever. The point is, whoever has you gets access to the gold inside and they can do whatever they want with you after.'

'Umm, I don't have access, or know where to find it or how to open the chest even if O'scilla has it, or if Rasia gets it first. There's also another obvious point, O-Till-aaar, from what I've been told and heard so far even if I can get into the chest whatever is inside it is bound to be cursed. So, good luck to anyone who has it. They'll be dead soon enough.'

'Dats no' wha' I 'ave heard, Miss Phæ'enor.' Mrs Kuáng had reappeared in the doorway to the kitchen rubbing her hands dry on her pinafore. 'I'm eve'n more surprised tha' comin' from Vanu, and with a mother 'ike yours, you ave no' heard story of chests before, or another story abou' dem?'

Phæ'enor looked at O'tila enquiringly, 'Ah, don't bore the girl with your stupid stories Kuáng. Phæ'enor, it's just a load of …'

'IT'S MRS KUÁNG TO YOU, STUPID BOY!' shouted Mrs Kuáng, as she picked up an empty glass off the bar and threw it at O'tila. It missed by an inch and smashed off the wall behind him instead.

'FOR FU...'

'SSSHHHH!' Snapped Mrs Kuáng at O'tila, 'I tell my story because day are t'ue!'

'Well you better be quick 'cause it doesn't look like we'll be here much longer if those guards keep at it,' said O'tila to Mrs Kuáng, as the dust from the floor above shook further into the room. Scowling at him, Mrs Kuáng made her way over to Phæ'enor and sat down. She removed her hat made of horns and hair and placed it on the table. Then held her hand out to Phæ'enor.

'You book. Han me you books.'

Phæ'enor looked at Mrs Kuáng in surprise and replied, 'What books?' She hoped she had not left them hanging around and tried discretely to rummage in her pockets and see if they were still there. As she located them Mrs Kuáng raised her left eyebrow at her.

'Da one in your righ' pock-et, Miss.'

Phæ'enor looked at O'tila who was now picking his teeth with a toothpick and sat back on a stool at the bar. She was sure he and even Mrs Kuáng, in fact no one was meant to see this book.

'Give me da dam book, girl!'

'...but … I'm not sup...'

'Of course, you're not suppose' to. No one is meant to hav' dose books. They banned!'

O'tila's ears pricked up, 'What books? Which banned books?'

'Not the kind you are after!' snapped Mrs Kuáng over her shoulder and wagged her hand at Phæ'enor to hand it over. 'If it makes you feel betta I already have one. Most banned things can be found in Old Town. No one here gives a shit!' Phæ'enor reluctantly removed the little black book from her pocket and passed it to Mrs Kuáng over the table.

'Is that what I think it is?' said O'tila smirking.

'Sssh, you,' said Mrs Kuáng, growing impatient with his interruptions.

'Bloody stupid curses,' muttered O'tila, still smiling to himself.

'Hey!'

'WHAT?'

'Be quiet!'

He rolled his eyes and turned to face the bar. Mrs Kuáng started to rifle through the pages of The Namorian Curse and only stopped when she came to the pages with the chest illustrations, laying it flat on the table. She squinted and moved her face closer to the page, intently studying the drawings. She chuckled to herself and rotated the book to face Phæ'enor.

'What do you see?'

Phæ'enor leaned forward and looked down, 'Err... chests?'

'Yes, and what else?'

'Well ... there are obviously twelve ... the first ten illustrations of the chests have all been completed.'

'And why is dat?'

'Because they have been found?'

'Yes, and what do you notice about dose ten chests?'

'Well, they all look the same, apart from the tenth one, that is shaded darker.' Like the one Archä and Mëdez have, she thought to herself. 'They are all made from the same wood and they all have the same lock and symbol, apart from the tenth one,' said Phæ'enor, thinking again of the matching chests in Archä and Mëdez 's possession.

'And, go on...'

'I don't know ... they all give their owners some sort of curse ... it says so in the description under each one,' finished Phæ'enor, a little impatient and feeling like she was being patronised.

'No. No, dey don't,' said Mrs Kuáng, and pointed to the last three of the twelve chests, 'What do you see?'

Phæ'enor looked at them again. The last two illustrations were just outlines of chests, unlike the other ten that were all completed. But as she looked closer Phæ'enor could just make out a small symbol above the lock in the eleventh chest. She looked up at Mrs Kuáng in surprise, 'The eleventh chest, it has the same symbol as the one drawn on the tenth chest! I didn't see that before.'

Mrs Kuáng nodded as Phæ'enor studied the symbols on the chests further, trying to make out what they were. And then it came to her. She thought back to the book The Many Moons of Ëbe, and the book of symbols, 'They are moons ... different moons ... the first nine chests have half-moons on their locks … the tenth and eleventh have full moons on theirs,' she muttered to herself.

Mrs Kuáng nodded at her again and continued, 'The symbol on dee eleventh chest means dat it was also found, but no one knows any' ting about it except for one ting. They knew which country and century it was found in.'

'What?' asked both Phæ'enor and O'tila together.

Mrs Kuáng smiled, 'Dere are rumours dat dee chest was found in the 1100s.'

'Yes, but there are rumours about all the chests,' said O'tila.

'So, you know all about these too?' asked Phæ'enor. Her cousins, Rasia and now him?

'Its standard folk law here, surprised you weren't told by your parents either.'

'Anyway, Illraea used ta be a poor and desolate land. It was full of noth'in but sand and dying people. But is has grown ta be one of the richest countries outside day empire with a mighty king in charge.'

'So? Countries grow, prosper,' said Phæ'enor.

'Not when this empire is still around,' chuckled O'tila.

Mrs Kuáng continued, 'Yes, but not with an army of two million soldiers and gold so rare and beautiful and plenty.'

'The Illraean soldiers?' asked O'tila in awe.

'Yes,' nodded Mrs Kuáng. 'They say their black armour is lined with emaz gold.'

'But isn't emaz gold poisonous?' asked Phæ'enor.

'Oh, that is just nonsense. Silly story to ward men off from looking for it. To stop men being greedy!'

'What? That's crazy. Don't listen to her. Old woman doesn't know anything. She may not die from the stuff but the rest of us can!' said O'tila.

Phæ'enor thought back to when Archä and Mëdez showed her, Simi, Mimi and Rasia the ten chests that had carried emaz gold in their possession, as well as the blue china teacup's emaz gold rim. The brothers were adamant that emaz could kill anyone who touched it, hence the protective gloves they wore. Except for Phæ'enor, who so far was very much alive. O'tila was probably right then, so she chose to ignore Mrs Kuáng's little rant and stuck to the facts. But she was still puzzled, 'I still don't understand what your story means?'

'I hav' not finished yet, impatient girwl,' said Mrs Kuáng. Phæ'enor caught O'tila from the corner of her eyes tapping the side of his head, rolling his eyes and sticking his tongue out in gesture that Mrs Kuáng was mad.

'In dese stories dare are twelve chests, and throughout hist'ry day 'ave been recorded as 'avin' been found and lost, found and lost an' so on. Day also hurt many pe'ple. How'eva, one of dese chests is linked to da prosperous nation of Illraea,' as she said this she pointed to the tenth and completed illustration of the chests. 'But this one,' she said tapping on the drawing of the eleventh one, 'is linked to da sudden wealth and prosperity of another nation, Ar - inth - scar! But what about this twelfth and last chest?' Mrs Kuáng tapped the outline of the last, uncompleted chest. 'Who is to say that it has not also been found, it may even be here in Benaghar.'

Phæ'enor thought about the twelfth illustration and the chest that Archä and Mëdez were trying to seek out in the city. She looked the little woman straight in the eyes. Mrs Kuáng winked back at her.

'Who knows about the symbols, and how the tenth and eleventh chest, and possibly the twelfth, are different from the rest?' asked Phæ'enor quietly of Mrs Kuáng, so that O'tila could not hear.

'About the symbols?' Many, but many also don't understand,' said Mrs Kuáng. 'Dee other book you have,' she continued also quietly, 'day show you many symbols, no?'

'How do you know about that?' asked Phæ'enor.

Mrs Kuáng smiled, 'cause it used ta be mine!' Phæ'enor looked back at her astounded. Mrs Kuáng put her finger to her lips and left the room. She came back shortly after and sat down again with the bangs and shaking of the building getting worse. She pulled out another little book, but in depth it was very thick.

'Da symbols from your uver book dat also appear on dese chests, they are very ancient writing, be'fore words were ever conceived or 'ritten don.' Phæ'enor opened her mouth to speak but Mrs Kuáng shook her head at her to be quiet. 'Day go as far back as dis book and are very much related with other story.'

Mrs Kuáng handed Phæ'enor the other book and pushed the little black one back towards her. Phæ'enor turned the new book over. There were no words, just a large symbol embossed on brown leather matching that of her little yellow book.

'You should prob'ably speak to your two cousins, maybe even...'

BANG!

BANG!

Mrs Kuáng stopped talking as the tea house shook violently. There were screams and shouts from outside. Blasts and further flashes of light. The birds in their cages above began to screech and hop and fly around aimlessly. O'tila had reached into his torn and dirty coat, retrieving a rusty looking pistol, and stared at the door bracing himself.

'Who is it?' he demanded. There was no response. He moved closer to the door as Mrs Kuáng whispered to Phæ'enor:

'Put dese away girwl, you will be needing them.'

Phæ'enor did as she was told and placed them down her shirt. The waistcoat was so small and tight that there would be no risk of them falling through. Suddenly the door blew open with a loud bang, the tea house shook violently and clouds of smoke billowed in. She could not make out who had come through the door but heard a very angry voice.

'Put down your weapon O'tila!' they said, as Phæ'enor watched O'tila slowly draw his hand from his coat, but too late. Something flew across the door to O'tila's head knocking him out cold.

'Where is she?' came the voice again. Phæ'enor startled, realised it was a woman's voice. But not anyone she recognised, at least not someone with that much anger.

'She's okay, she's over here,' said Mrs Kuáng.

'What?' said Phæ'enor, indignant that Mrs Kuáng could hand her over so quickly, but at the same time not surprised. There were firm and loud footsteps across the room before Phæ'enor felt herself being dragged by tiptoe across the floor and into the smoke.

'Thank you Mrs Kuáng!' … sorry about the tea house,' said the woman, as she directed Phæ'enor towards the door.

'Quickly, we have to go…'

'S-Simi?' said Phæ'enor, 'what are you … I mean what the...'

'Well someone had to come and get you cousin,' said Simi, but realising how it must look she replied, 'look, I'll explain later, but now we need to move. O'scilla is on his way back and the guards are a lot more persistent than they usually are, not to mention the almighty fight between the wolves and the rats outside.' She made to move off but turned when Phæ'enor did not make to follow her. Simi pulled her gun out of her pocket and aimed it at Phæ'enor.

'Oh, not you as well,' groaned Phæ'enor.

'Just move!' snapped Simi.

Phæ'enor and Simi ran down the stairwell and away from the tea house disappearing into the smog and fumes of the streets below. Mrs Kuáng watching them as they went.

Chapter Seventeen

The Rat King

Phæ'enor hurried after Simi through the narrow and low alleyways of Old Town, through smoke and shouting and people rushing past them. Small fires burned across the streets as miniature missiles flew through the air and landed on the ground. Some just missed Phæ'enor by a few inches. She held one hand over her mouth and nose and used the other to feel her way through and past people.

'Keep close, and hurry up,' shouted Simi over her shoulder to Phæ'enor.

'I'm trying,' she shouted back through her muffled mouth, 'where are we going anyway?' She was not sure how to get back to the secret entrance into Old Town where she had followed Rasia through.

'Just keep up, we will be out of here soon and ... STOP!'

Phæ'enor slammed into the back of Simi who had her hand held back using it to push Phæ'enor against the wall, before grabbing the back of a small boy's collar who had run by; stopping him from running out into a kind of small plaza up ahead. Simi put her hands over his mouth to stop him from making a sound. Phæ'enor peered up ahead. There in the middle was O'scilla and some more of his people, including the two boys and his son that had accompanied him back at Mrs Kuáng's Tea House the day before. He was stood in front of several mounted city guards but there was an exceptionally large horse right in front. Jet black and menacing.

On top of the horse sat a man dressed head to toe in black. But instead of the thick and waxy travelling cloak that Phæ'enor had seen him wear the first time, he wore what looked like it was made of velvet. His face no longer looked so weathered from the sun, but his hair was still neat and swept back.

'I've seen that man before,' she whispered to Simi.

'What? Where, where have you seen him?' asked Simi in alarm.

'At the palace dinner.' Phæ'enor did not want to elaborate and tell Simi that she had been listening in to the king's private conversation.

'Was he there at the dinner?' asked Simi, desperate for more information.

Phæ'enor shook her head, concerned at the panic in her cousin's voice, 'No, no he wasn't...'

And as though Simi had guessed what her cousin had been up to in the palace she asked, 'Did he speak to you, see you at all?'

'No, cousin, no he didn't.'

'Good,' said Simi.

'What is so bad about him?'

Simi put a finger to her lips, gesturing to Phæ'enor to stop asking questions and shook her head. She turned back around and bent low, whispering to the boy, 'We don't want to be here. That is no guard. It's the king's eldest son, Prince Heolbus. You boy, turn back and get away from here, now.' Wide eyed he nodded. Simi took her hand off his mouth and he retreated quietly backwards before turning and running off.

'This doesn't look good,' said Simi. They both glanced another look out onto the plaza. They couldn't hear anything but O'scilla did not look like he was being reprimanded by the prince or being arrested. They looked to be on good terms. O'scilla haphazardly moved his hand in Simi and Phæ'enor's direction.

'This definitely isn't good,' said Simi, 'let's move, I know another way.'

They backed off then turned and started running again. Left, right, right again, up some stairs, across a walkway, then Simi stopped before jumping a small gap quite high above the streets, to a platform on the other side.

'Come on Phæ'enor, we need to move. Just Jump!'

'Are you insane, I could fall through and…'

'Sssh! Sssh!' said Simi panicked, and pointed down below. Phæ'enor looked then flung herself flat against the building. The mounted city guards from the plaza and O'scilla's men had clearly fanned out, slowly making their way down the alleyways. Phæ'enor thought she knew where they were heading. She didn't like the boy but hoped O'tila had left the teahouse. She also hoped that Mrs Kuáng would be okay, that she was able to disappear for a while. The woman was crazy but Phæ'enor had quite liked her company.

As they disappeared down the alleyway Phæ'enor did not need to be told twice and took her chance to jump. She stumbled on the landing but soon got her balance, nodded at Simi that she was okay, and they carried on their way out of Old Town. After about an hour of trying to navigate their way out of the labyrinth of buildings, stairs and streets, Simi lead them back to the hidden entrance. Phæ'enor breathed a sigh of relief.

'Don't think we are out of this yet cousin. We still need to get out of here and back home without being seen; and that isn't helping us either,' said Simi, pointing up at the sun.

She slowed and Phæ'enor made to copy her cousin, moving quietly through the zig-zag hidden wall. They stopped at the end of it and sticking to the wall made their way to the secret passageway. Simi gestured for Phæ'enor to stay back whilst she checked the empty cobbled alley, then strode across and pushed open the gate through to the tunnel in the wall ahead. But Simi had not checked the wall itself. Up above, prowling the edge, was the large grey, pointy eared and amber eyed cat. It stopped and looked at Phæ'enor before disappearing again.

'Psstt … cousin. What are you doing?' said Simi. 'Stop stalling and hurry up.'

Phæ'enor, her attention drawn back to the cobbled street, ran across to the other wall and into the narrow tunnel. She watched as

Simi closed the gates behind them, placing a necklace back over her head; it matched the one she wore herself.

But it made Phæ'enor wonder how her cousin knew she was in Old Town in the first place, 'Simi?'

'What?' snapped Simi, as they made their way to the other end of the passage, and the walled door into Newtown.

'How did you know where to find me? I mean, clearly by the necklace, you knew I could get in through this entrance, but how did you know I would be here and at Mrs Kuáng's?'

'Well, Mrs Kuáng of course. She sent one of her birds with a message to father. He told me where to find you.' Oh, thought Phæ'enor, recalling Mrs Kuáng taking her time when letting that little bird out of the window back at the tea house. 'She's a crazy old woman but she is not unkind, and definitely no fan of O'scilla's.'

Simi returned her attention to the walled door, breathed in and opened it a crack to peer out. She couldn't see anything so gestured for both to proceed, 'As a rule, people only use this entrance at night. The shadows of the walls help conceal the comings and goings.'

They moved out swiftly, but the sun blinkered their view as they stepped out. It happened so quickly, that before Phæ'enor knew it she had been picked up from behind, kicking and shouting, Simi was screaming, and the last thing she saw before they were pulled down into the darkness was the grey cat.

***

Phæ'enor tried not to be sick as the smells coming for the blackness overwhelmed her.

'Oh, no … ugh, yuk!' she heard Simi say, against the noise of running water. 'Ugh!'

Phæ'enor had the same reaction as she was put onto her feet, landing in ice cold water up to her ankles, she gagged again.

'Don't worry, you'll get used to it,' came a voice up ahead.

'Only rats get used to it!' came another voice out of the darkness. This time from behind them.

'Rasia?' said Phæ'enor, surprised.

'Yeah, it's me,' his reply came bitterly.

'I was looking for you … well, I followed you and…'

'That's why you find yourself with me,' said the first voice again. Phæ'enor was not quite sure who was talking. She still couldn't put a finger on who the voice belonged to.

'She's here because I found her and then you dishonestly kidnapped both of us,' snapped Simi. 'Into … into this … awful place! Yuk, I can't believe I am here. I thought all this stuff about sewers…'

Phæ'enor's heart sank, realising the worst. The combination of the darkness, water and that pungent smell.

'It will get better,' said the first voice, 'and for your information Rasia here and myself saved you from being caught.'

'One of our younger members had seen somebody in a yellow cloak being taken away from the Inn by O'tila and some of O'scilla's boys. He also found your mask and informed me of what they saw and after my little conversation with Prince Taigor in Newtown I guessed it might have been Phæ'enor here,' said Rasia. 'And even if you did make it out of Old Town there were more guards waiting for you at Newtown Gate.'

'I still got her out,' said Simi, sounding even more offended.

'Well I think we can all say we are safe down here, for a while at least. But if it wasn't for Phæ'enor here we probably wouldn't be in this situation,' said Rasia.

'You know that's not true!' said the first voice sharply.

Phæ'enor had been cautiously making her way through the water, sloshing its way around her feet in the darkness but after a while her eyes had started to adjust, and she could make out the figures in front. Simi and a boy were in front of her, and she could hear the splashing of Rasia's feet in the water behind. After several more minutes the sound of water rushing past could be heard, getting louder and louder. She glimpsed a slight light up ahead.

'Oh, please tell me when this going to end,' groaned Simi, as Phæ'enor realised through the ever-increasing light that the water rushing past their feet was not exactly clean. Flotsam and jetsam of the human kind floated by. She tried not to look too much and resorted to staring at the back of Simi's head.

'We need to veer to the left in a minute, so make sure you all grab onto the person in front of you,' came the first voice again, echoing off the tunnel walls.

They all did as they were told. Simi put her left hand on the shoulders of the boy in front of her, Phæ'enor grabbed a handful of Simi's cloak and Rasia rested a hand on her right shoulder.

They trudged through the murky water, not talking until they reached a void in the tunnel. Here it spanned out and light flooded in revealing a large abyss of water where several bricked tunnels met up; all the water and sewage flowing into one. Although Phæ'enor could clearly make out all her companions now, she still didn't recognise the leader.

One by one they followed him through another tunnel that lead off from the void. Here, there was hardly any water, nothing more than puddles, and the tunnel became wider and taller, so they no longer had to hunch or touch the wet walls on either side. Voices could be heard in the distance, echoing down towards them.

'Who's that?' she whispered to Rasia.

Over her shoulder, he replied, 'You'll see … unfortunately.'

'We are nearly there,' said the leader again.

'That hardly matters,' grumbled Simi over her shoulder to Phæ'enor, 'we will still be in the sewers!'

Phæ'enor could see flickers of golden light up ahead as she peered past Simi's shoulder, but they soon turned into a glow of light as they walked into a large cavernous tunnel. Phæ'enor looked up, it was like the underground library and rooms found in Archä and Mëdez's shop, except this was darker and wet.

'Welcome to the centre of Benaghar's sewers!' said their leader. He turned around.

'No wonder I didn't recognise you,' gasped Phæ'enor.

'Well I suppose it's not every day you see...'

'The Rat King?' said Rasia sarcastically.

Phæ'enor looked at their leader; he wore a tan and dirty brown leather travelling coat and matching hat. It was made of fur with teeth and little feet sticking out at the edge, which rested over the top of his eyes. Before them stood O'sea, no longer garbed in the red of the palace servants but instead dressed like a giant rat.

'What are you supposed to be then,' said Simi, laughing at Rasia in turn. Phæ'enor had also stopped to stare in Rasia's direction. Instead of his navy uniform he was clothed in grey cotton trousers and shirt. In place of his navy hat his head was cloaked in the head and skin of a grey wolf. Four Amber eyes staring down on them all, just like the other men and woman Phæ'enor had seen at The Raed Wolf Inn adorn.

'Why has your wolf skin got four eyes?' asked Phæ'enor.

'Argh!' screamed Simi. The second pair of eyes moved, revealing the large grey cat. It slinked down off the top of the grey wolf skin and laid across the back of Rasia's shoulder; head on one side, tail on the other.

O'sea laughed out loud as did several dozen others around them, 'I am the Rat King and Rasia the Wolf!'

'WHAT?' said Simi concerned.

'You have taken your brother's place?' asked Phæ'enor.

'For now, until he is better and until we can set him free, I am in charge of the wolves.'

'YOU KNEW ABOUT HIM?' screamed Simi at Phæ'enor.

'Surely you did too, after seeing Archä and Mëdez?'

'I knew he was a wolf but not *the* wolf!'

'Well neither did I until now!' snapped Phæ'enor.

'And him?' demanded Simi of Phæ'enor, 'did you know about him?'

O'sea looked bemused back at a pointed finger from Simi. The boys in the cavern were still laughing.

'No! No, I didn't!' shouted Phæ'enor.

'Good, but this day just gets worse … you … you two are the ones they talk about as the king who controls the underground, and the king who controls the streets of Benaghar? Prowling the rooftops at night or springing up in the dark from nowhere to take souls below?' asked Simi.

Phæ'enor laughed, 'Those stories are just told to children to scare them.' No one else laughed.

'They are boys that have been to war …'

'And seen death …'

'Masters of your city…' The voices rang out from around the tunnel. Phæ'enor turned to see silhouettes and faces lit up by small fires. They were sat on steps, staggered in pyramids. The cavern tunnel was a giant step well.

'I thought that your two gangs hated each other?' asked Simi.

'We do,' said Rasia and O'sea at once.

'Things change though, we need each other's help,' said Rasia.

'Like what?' asked Phæ'enor, she continued to look around their surroundings. Many faces and eyes followed hers. 'I thought you weren't going to take your brother's advice.'

'I changed my mind; last night's events forced my hand. After I realised O'scilla may have you the only other person I knew who could help was O'sea. If he knew where his cousin was then we would be able to find you. O'sea and I hatched a plan, between the wolves and the rats to cause a diversion; a fight to keep the city guards away from Kuáng's for as long as possible. We didn't want them to find you first. Besides…'

'Besides what?' snapped an increasingly hysterical Simi.

'Besides … we have a lot in common,' said O'sea, moving to sit down on the lower step.

'You mean you're both gang leaders, running criminal activities across the city. You're probably even working for O'scilla for all we know. You're all wanted for the same things too!' said Simi, looking about her frantically.

Phæ'enor had been staring at their surroundings. They weren't just in a step well. Besides the fires, and the other boys around them, hammocks hung from the walls with piles of bedding, clothes, food and tools.

'Do you live down here?' asked Phæ'enor.

'The boys do, most of the time; so do I, but I am needed elsewhere as well,' replied O'sea.

'With Prince Taigor?' asked Simi.

There was silence then O'sea replied, 'Yes.'

'How can you serve a king that opposes you?' asked Phæ'enor.

'I don't serve the king!' snapped O'sea, 'it's a job.'

Phæ'enor looked at him, 'O'tila said that you work against O'scilla as a favour to a friend. He meant Prince Taigor didn't he? Some sort of debt you owe him? He said it was one of the reasons you no longer speak to O'scilla.'

'And the reason you're known as the rat!' sneered Rasia.

O'sea looked straight at her and smiled, not answering her questions, 'How is my cousin? Did he manage to get away from Mrs Kuáng's?'

Simi and Phæ'enor looked at each other, 'He … was unconscious when we left him…'

O'sea looked worried, turned and nodded in the direction of some of the other boys. They jumped to their feet and disappeared down another of the tunnels that led off from the step well. Phæ'enor continued as she watched the boys disappear:

'He said that O'scilla and you were family?'

'By blood, yes, but no longer by choice! O'scilla and I don't see eye to eye … that's where Rasia and I have something in common.'

He nodded in the direction of Rasia who was stood still like a sentinel. Phæ'enor thought he would always look like that, uptight and ready for duty.

'My brother,' said Rasia, 'the reason why my brother is set to stand trial, why he may be sentenced to death is all because of O'scilla.'

'He knows nothing but greed,' continued O'sea, 'all he wants is power, control and he'll do anything and everything to get it. You're right about Rasia and I. We don't like each other. The harqs and the wolves of this city have always been divided. However, that changed a little, when several years ago O'scilla did something myself and others couldn't forgive. My sister O'urra; he disapproved of her choice in man, as did the man's family of her when they learnt of his choice. But where the man's family banned him from seeing O'urra, and was sent abroad, O'scilla … O'scilla killed my sister.'

Simi and Phæ'enor stared in horror at O'sea.

'O'scilla and his dealings are everywhere. So, when O'sea here says he will do anything to retain power he literally will do anything,' said Rasia.

'The tea?' asked Phæ'enor.

'No one smart enough touches it in Old Town,' said O'sea. 'It's dangerous. It makes you addicted, changes your personality. At its best its hallucinogenic, at its worst it can kill you.'

'O'scilla had heard about my brother's, inability, to keep away from it. So, he used it to lure him in. Make him steal, and cheat and commit crimes he shouldn't … and couldn't remember doing,' said Rasia.

'So, your brother is guilty of these crimes...?'

'He didn't know what he was doing … but yes, he did them. Thanks to O'scilla and his scheming,' said Rasia bitterly.

'Looks like his scheming continues,' said Simi.

'What do you mean by that?' asked O'sea.

'We saw him, Phæ'enor and I, as we were making our way out of Old Town. He was in that plaza, I think it's called Smugglers Square, with Prince Heolbus.'

Hissing rang out around them at the mention of Prince Heolbus.

'Prince Heolbus?' said Rasia, 'but he's meant to be abroad?'

'It doesn't look like it anymore,' said Simi.

'I don't understand,' said Phæ'enor, 'Simi, you panicked when you saw Prince Heolbus, and now you lot are all hissing … is Prince Heolbus to be feared?'

'Feared?' said Simi, 'the Prince … well, he is worse than O'scilla, much worse than his father and…'

'He's mad! Completely mad!' said O'sea, 'and to top it all off, he did and still does hold favour with the city guards; he was their captain until he was banished by King Sol. The guards are more than likely to side with the prince and therefore the laws of this city are controlled by him, regardless of the king's authority. So, if Rasia's brother wants a light sentence let's hope Prince Heolbus has another ship waiting for him.'

'Why, will he make things worse?'

'More than likely,' said Simi. 'Prince Heolbus has a reputation for the sadistic and is a firm believer in capital punishment. His father is more lenient since the wars have ended but Prince Heolbus still believes in it all and takes his duty as a Brother of The Grand Temple to the extreme. If he can't influence the guards, then you can be sure he will use The Brotherhood to get his way.'

'But Prince Taigor, he's…'

'Nothing like his brother?' said Rasia, 'what a future king should be.'

'And that's the way it should remain. Prince Taigor is set to be king if his brother continues as a Brother of The Grand Temple,' said O'sea. 'Let's just hope that Prince Heolbus in the meantime is only visiting Benaghar for a short while…'

'Did you hear any of what O'scilla and Prince Heolbus were saying to each other?' asked Rasia.

'No,' said Simi, 'it did look as though O'scilla was helping the Prince … and …'

'And what?' asked O'sea.

Simi looked at Phæ'enor, 'I think they were after her.'

Phæ'enor interrupted, ignoring Simi's comment, 'O'scilla is working for Prince Heolbus. That's what you tasked O'tila with finding out wasn't it? To see who O'scilla was getting his highest bid from for the chest?'

'So, you have Prince Taigor and you have Prince Heolbus set against each other,' said Rasia. 'Both brothers want the same thing.'

'Is it really because of what lays inside? I mean why does one prince want to keep it from everyone, hidden away, and the other, a Brother of The Grand Temple want to claim it for himself? We know Archä and Mëdez just want it for their collection, O'scilla just wants payment,' said Phæ'enor.

O'sea looked at Phæ'enor, 'What have you found out about opening the chest?'

Phæ'enor looked at them all and spoke, 'I don't know anything, not really. Mrs Kuáng mentioned another way of looking at the chests. The symbols. And O'scilla mentioned something else about keys … or the lack of no keyholes. Anyway, I have a hunch, but I don't think it's for me or another person to open it.'

They all looked at Phæ'enor confused, then Simi spoke, 'Look, I came to get my cousin back on my father's orders. Her mother also wants her safe, along with a few other people.' Phæ'enor thought she knew who Simi was referring to. Her cousin continued, 'You need to forget about these chests, Phæ'enor is not here to get involved in whatever silly games you're playing against each other.

She needs to come home, there are other things to think about.' She finished, glaring at Phæ'enor.

'I'm afraid we can't let either of you go until we get what we need,' said O'sea, 'Rasia and I need to stop O'scilla from getting hold of the chest and its contents. If he gets it before us, then we can't trade it with Archä and Mëdez who in return will be able to get Raisa's brother out of trouble.'

'What, even if that means defying Prince Taigor, stealing them from him? The chests belong to him after all,' said Simi.

'I work for him, I may owe him a debt, but he owes me many,' said O'sea. 'I hate O'scilla more than anyone in this world for what he did to my sister, what he did to our family. He will not get his hands on that chest just so he can keep his power.'

'So, you're just going to keep us here, in this, ugh, disgusting place?' asked Simi. More laughter rang out.

'We'll take you where you need to go to figure how to get into that chest, but you stay with us until then,' said Rasia.

'Oh, don't tell me you already have it,' said Simi sarcastically.

'No,' it was Phæ'enor who spoke. 'But I think that we all know by now they have it at the palace. At least Prince Taigor and possibly Officer Nathryn know the exact location. But we will have to tail them, or work on them, they will never tell us directly where it is.'

O'sea and Rasia nodded in silent agreement at the task they had ahead of them. Simi huffed in disapproval.

'Fine, we'll figure out a way to get hold of them soon enough, but do you know how to open it?' asked O'sea, giving Phæ'enor a very curious look.

She nodded, 'I think I do, but I'm not sure.'

'Okay, but do you know what to do? asked Rasia. Phæ'enor nodded her head, still unsure. 'What will make you sure?' asked Rasia.

Phæ'enor looked at the three of them, 'I think I need to talk to an astronomer,' said Phæ'enor.

They all looked even more puzzled. The boys around the stepwell were all turning to look at each other, shrugging their shoulders or shaking their heads.

'An astronomer? You're sure?' asked Rasia.

'Yes.'

'This better not be a joke,' he said. Phæ'enor glared at him.

'Fine, you two,' said O'sea pointing to two small children in the corner of the well, 'go up ahead and check the coast is clear.' He turned and then spoke to the others, 'Follow me, I know who will help you.'

Chapter Eighteen

The Astronomer

Simi, Phæ'enor and Rasia, with the large grey cat, Rama, balanced on his shoulders, followed O'sea through tunnel after tunnel. Sometimes it would lead into areas full of water that came up to their knees, others their waste, but now the water was running just below their feet. Every time they entered a new tunnel it felt as though they became longer, veering left, or right, having to steady themselves against the tunnel wall as they descended or sometimes having to climb ladders into other underground chambers. It was not easy work. All of them had built up a sweat trying to keep up with O'sea, but at least it had made them forget about the smell.

After what seemed like a couple of hours they came to a halt just in front of another tunnel that sloped towards them.

'Right, after we head up this tunnel we will enter a small chamber. A bit like some of the others we have passed through. It forms part of the foundations for the city observatory,' advised O'sea. Simi and Phæ'enor raised their eyebrows in surprise then looked at each other, sweaty, dirty, wet and covered in all manner of things. O'sea seeing their reactions continued, 'Obviously, looking and smelling beautiful as we all do, we will need to be careful where we tread.'

'Then what?' asked Rasia.

'Then, Wolf, we need to find Mr Consta.'

'Who?' asked Rasia and Phæ'enor.

'He's the Court Astronomer,' said Simi.

'Amongst other things,' said O'sea, not sounding too pleased about whatever else Mr Consta got up to. But none of them enquired.

'I may be some time, but I'll try to be quick. You can't always guarantee someone will be at home. Consta is one of the more elusive astronomers. You three, stay here. Try not to make too much noise either, it travels through the vents,' he pointed above them where a couple of small metal grates were built into the top of the brick walls. With that he trudged up the wet stairs and through a slimy wooden door, closing it tight shut behind him. All three looked at each other not knowing what to do. Rasia, with the cat now on top of the wolfskin head, walked over to the bottom tier of some bricked steps that lead to nowhere and sat down. He looked at Phæ'enor.

'Why are you dressed liked a boy?' he asked her. Simi looked at her too.

'Mrs Kuáng. O'scilla ordered her to dress me in something so that I would not be immediately recognisable.'

'I suppose that's a smart move coming from that oaf O'scilla. The hat suits you cousin; covers all that long dark hair of yours too,' said Simi, smiling.

'Yeah, what's left of it, but actually he...'

'What do you mean what's left of it?' Simi asked half joking, half concerned. Rasia looked at Phæ'enor, puzzled by her comment too. 'Take your hat off!'

'No,' said Phæ'enor, feeling self-conscious.

Simi looked at Rasia then suddenly stormed over to Phæ'enor and ripped it off her head. Phæ'enor's hair, or what was left of it, fell out at an angle just past her shoulders.

'Oh, my!' said Simi.

'HA, HA, HA! Officer Nathryn is not going to be happy about that!' laughed Rasia, rolling about.

'What. It's not that bad!' said Phæ'enor, feeling annoyed and embarrassed. 'Stop laughing at me!'

'Yes, stop laughing Rasia. This isn't funny!' snapped Simi.

'Yes, it is,' he gasped, through breaths of laughter, 'Officer Nathryn is not going to be happy when he thinks that his wife to be has been tainted by another man's touch, and O'scilla's at that! HA!' When he finally got his breath back from laughing, he answered the fuming looks coming from both Phæ'enor and Simi. 'In Benaghar a woman is meant to have long hair and can only cut it off, get it shortened when she is married? It sort of shows that she is taken.'

'What? So, a ring isn't enough to state that, or are Benagharian men so dim that they need more of a visual reference to remind them who their wife is?' snapped Phæ'enor.

'Ha,' snorted Simi at Phæ'enor's remark.

'No. But it also means that if a woman hasn't been married she's been tainted by another man, so she shouldn't be touched.'

'Ha!' replied Phæ'enor, now it was her turn to laugh, 'well, surely that's a good thing in my case. It means Officer Nathryn will no longer want to marry me-eeeee! OW!' Phæ'enor had been forced back up against the wall behind her. Simi's red angry face was glaring at her.

'THIS – IS – NOT – A – JOKE – PHÆ'ENOR! YOU - WILL – MARRY – THAT - MAN – WHETHER – YOU- LIKE – IT – OR – NOT!'

'Well, that is if you can find a very long dark wig,' came a drawling voice to their right.

Phæ'enor turned reluctantly away from her cousin's anger, still pinned to the wall but able to move her head. Through the door, with O'sea behind him in wonder at what was going on between the two women, was the thin, sallow faced and unjoyful travelling companion of Cort Rohgah. He wore tight trousers, with a fitted waistcoat of bright blue silk and a crisp shirt. His short black hair seemed to be longer in the front where it merged together into one big curl.

He stood there looking as still and unamused by his situation as all the other times Phæ'enor had come across him. He twirled his long, thin and black goatee at the end of his long, thin face. The only thing that Phæ'enor had seen now what she hadn't noticed before was his eyes. They were big but made swollen by his large and purple hooded eyelids that seemed to droop over them, yet they were most definitely like O'sea, O'tila and O'scilla's. One bright green, one bright blue.

'You know, if you told me I would have to deal with two squabbling girls I would have come a lot quicker,' he drawled at O'sea, 'as it is…'

'You had nothing to do anyway. Move out the way,' said O'sea, pushing past the man, clearly irrigated with him, even though he hadn't actually done anything wrong.

'This is Mr O'Starr Consta. The Court…'

'Your Astronomer,' he continued, lazily disregarding O'sea's introduction of himself to the others. 'Mind, I think you can stop worrying about your hair. Officer Nathryn will be more offended by your smell.' He chuckled softly to himself. 'What happened? Did you all go for a midnight stroll, miss your footing and fall into this never-ending pit of shit and scum?'

'Shut your face!' shouted O'sea. 'No one is here to listen to your bullshit.'

'I'm most offended O'sea. If you didn't want to listen to my so called "bullshit" then why am I here? You did ask for my opinion did you not brother?'

'Brother?' asked Phæ'enor, Simi and Rasia all at once.

'YOU – ARE – NOT – MY - BROTHER!' snapped O'sea turning and poking Consta in the chest.

'I think we are, you see…'

'We know, you're both Harqs and therefore practically family,' stated Phæ'enor.

'Clever. Someone has been reading her history books,' said Consta.

'And talking to O'scillia, and O'tila,' said Phæ'enor.

'The little cousin,' he said more to himself, still twirling his goatee in his fingertips.

And Phæ'enor was reminded of what O'tila and O'sea had talked about in the kitchen that evening at the palace. The astronomer had lied about seeing O'tila on the gun deck for he also did not want to be placed at the scene of the crime. Was he also looking for the chests as well as O'tila, who had been on the watch for both his cousin and O'scilla?

The astronomer looked Phæ'enor up and down slowly, 'You know, I didn't think much of you the first time I clocked eyes on you on that bloody ship. You still haven't improved, why they all talk about you in such amore is beyond me, and I like to think I am the best judge of character.' Phæ'enor did not feel offended at what he had just said to her. She smiled in amusement at his ridiculous get up and in her opinion ridiculous face. He smiled back at her. 'I can see you don't care for other's opinions of you.'

'Will you just please get on with it,' said O'sea.

'Fine then, follow me. And be careful not to leave traces of your shit all over the place.'

***

The four of them followed O'Starr Consta through a narrow passageway, and up several flights of even narrower stairs, all made from the same bricks as the sewers below, but clean. When they reached the top, he opened a small wooden door that led off through another narrow-bricked corridor, so cramped that all of them were brushing their arms on the walls as they walked through it. Finally, Consta came to a stop outside another door. He took out some keys and unlocked it.

'Wait here. I need to fetch a towel, or several … something for you all to walk on and which I can burn later. I can't have the place smelling like you do.'

He pushed the door and slid through, leaving it slightly ajar so light from the room appeared in the gap, and a feint drone of a noise could be heard. O'sea rolled his eyes and leant against the wall of the passageway. They waited for several more minutes before the astronomer returned, pulling the door wide open.

'You may enter. But don't veer off the towels!'

One by one they left the narrow passageway and stepped into a long and dark panelled room. At their feet were towels for them to step on, so as not to soil the dark wooden floors and the beautiful indigo patterned rug than lay in the middle of the room. Several spinning globes of the planet, telescopes, and books lined two shelves that stood either side of the rug in the middle, stretching the full length of the room. A large panelled door stood central at the opposite end. But what struck Phæ'enor the most was how the room seemed to be suspended in the middle of a giant solar system. Moons and planets swooped gently underneath the floor then back overhead to the ceiling casting light shadows onto the room; omitting a drone as it continued to move. They were in the middle of a large planetarium.

Phæ'enor turned to the others and the door they had come through. It had been concealed by the panelled wall, a secret passageway. Rasia, O'sea and Simi had gathered around a large desk which the cat, Rama, had already jumped onto; Consta had sat down in the chair behind it looking up at them all.

'Well then, fire away with your questions. I do have better things to be doing with my time than spending it with silly children.'

Rasia, Phæ'enor and Simi all glanced at each other, their faces querying if Consta was being serious. He seemed to be play acting to Phæ'enor. Behaviour put on to try and intimidate and impress. All Phæ'enor could think of was what a complete idiot he was, but apparently this idiot was the court astronomer.

'I hardly think you have anything to do,' sneered O'sea.

'The king is in need of my services.'

'Your services? He needs a Physician not an astronomer!'

'Why? Is the king not well?' asked Rasia. They all looked at O'sea.

'He's come down with a cold again … he's old.'

'Hmmm…' drawled Consta, looking at O'sea disdainfully.

'Phæ'enor,' said O'sea, taking his attention away from the astronomer, 'ask what you need to ask.'

Phæ'enor looked at O'Starr Consta. She was no longer sure she was right in her thinking but at the same time needed to know. The astronomer, however, did not put her at ease. She felt she should not be asking this man anything. Phæ'enor had not liked him after their first encounter and he, in her opinion, had also not improved since. She felt uneasy in his presence. His laziness and drawling mannerisms felt false to her.

'Phæ'enor?' prompted Rasia, from the corner of the room, pulling her out of her reverie.

'Uh, yes. I need. I mean it would be helpful to know if you had some sort of chart, or calendar for the cycle of the moons,' she said.

Consta narrowed his eyes at her and asked with suspicion in his voice, 'How far back?'

'Um … about a few, or five thousand years ago … if that's possible. Maybe even more? As far as they go, please.'

The astronomer's eyes were now so narrowed that they were barely even slits, 'Why in the world would you want to go back that far?' They all looked at her now.

'I … I just need to make sure my theory is correct. Or wrong.'

'Hmmm … I may not have all the information. It may not have been recorded that far back.'

'If you're an astronomer, why wouldn't you have that information? The history of the moons, and the stars, has been recorded for centuries, Mr Consta. I think you need to look amongst all your books here. Take your time. I'm sure you'll find it,' snapped Rasia.

'Hmm … of course you would know, wouldn't you wolf, about the stars and the moons. The night and her lights are your mistress after all.'

Phæ'enor shook her head and rolled her eyes at Simi who rolled her eyes in return. They were both growing tired of this skinny, sullen man's performance.

'Fine,' said Consta, lazily getting up and slowly walking over to the largest bookcase, stretching across the full length of the room. It was made of dark wood and not a single space wasn't filled with some large leather-bound volume. After taking some considerable time, deliberately thought Phæ'enor, he picked out a large dark blue leather book, the size of a tombstone and carried it over to the others who had gathered around his desk. He dropped it on the table, so it made an almighty bang. The thin sallow man was stronger than he looked thought Phæ'enor. He slowly pulled open a drawer in the desk to his right, reaching inside to pull out a small pair of thin gilded spectacles and popped them onto the hook of his nose. He leaned back and looked at Phæ'enor.

'Well then?'

'Well then what?'

Consta sighed, 'There is a lot of astronomy to go through. You must have a starting point, do you not? There's no need to be rude girl.'

They all looked at her. Phæ'enor was not so sure this was a good idea. This man did not seem the type to trust in any case, but to give him, maybe any of the others information if she could find it, was also questionable. She and Rasia had not got off to a good start and he wanted the chest in exchange for his brother's freedom, even though he had clearly committed a crime. Yet her father had entrusted Rasia to look after her and her mother. Although, even then he had not completely stuck to the books. Simi was a different sort altogether. You should trust your family no matter what, even if you didn't really like them. Yet she had only known Simi a few weeks and she had turned out to be a completely different person in the last several hours from the one she had met before. As for O'sea, well he was related to O'scilla but had apparently severed ties and was now working for Prince Taigor, whilst maintaining control over the streets of Benaghar. He had more than one agenda; they all seemed to.

She didn't know why she was getting so protective over the information that may never come to light or why she cared about the chests so much; they all wanted them, not her. After all it was Archä and Mëdez who had got her involved. If she could just solve it, then she would no longer have to deal with it.

'Yes?' prompted Consta.

'I remember reading a book that said just over three thousand years ago there was a huge astronomical disaster … or collision of some sort?'

'Right,' he said and leaned in towards her, eyes narrowed.

'Was there?' she asked.

'Well, yes. It happened in the year 3200 if you take our year as 5024, yet of course by today's methods we know it as the year zero, the reign of King Tekan and the creation of all life. Ah ha - HA!' He laughed hysterically and only stopped when he caught the look on Phæ'enor's face. She had raised her eyebrows puzzled by all the bizarre dates he just reeled off, and his amusement at it all. 'Anyway,' he continued, seeing how bored and indifferent the others looked, 'this planet only used to have one moon. A very large moon at that.' They all laughed at him bar Phæ'enor.

'Really? Just one moon? That seems a little odd,' said O'sea, flashing a smirk at the others.

'Why?' he said glaring back at him. 'Many planets in this solar system have just one, while ours and some others have several.'

They all stopped laughing. It was clear to Phæ'enor that O'Starr Consta was a serious man and did not find anything amusing least of all his profession as an astronomer.

'You are referring to the Many Moons of Ëbe, aren't you?' Phæ'enor asked, encouraging him to continue.

He nodded in response, 'In the year 3200 the moon Ëbe exploded, separating into 37. No one knows quite what happened but there are several theories, such as a large comet collided with it, or another planet in the solar system, maybe it was once active and imploded from within. Who can tell?' he said rhetorically. 'But, the fact is there was an almighty explosion. So, what of it?'

'So … the many moons that we have now …'

'Yes?'

'I also read that every so many years, two or three collide to create one moon or…'

'Or they die out and fall out of orbit. Again, what of it?'

'I wanted to know how many collisions and dying moons there have been, and the dates they happened. If possible?'

He stared long and hard at her before delving back into the large volume in front of him. He ran his index finger from top to bottom, flicking through several pages, taking his time. He looked up at her again, with curious eyes, before lifting the book up onto its spine. He then opened it just over halfway and turned back a few pages, coming to a halt at a double page that revealed some sort of map. They all leaned in over it.

'This is a map charting the history of the 37 moons,' said Consta. 'There,' he said pointing at the middle, 'that is Hallumera, or the shadow moon as some call it, the first and largest moon created by a collision and these are the moons created by further collisions.' Here he moved his finger across the page and around the diagram of Ëbe, pointing at all the other moons. Phæ'enor leaned in staring at them all. Thuos, small and shaded a pale blue, Iken larger, pink with giant craters and Usaras, grey with half of its surface looming in the shadows.

'After the astronomical disaster of our first moon Ëbe, thirty-seven smaller moons appeared in the world's orbit. Some like Hindwin were so small they did not influence the sea tides, or peoples' moods as some lunatics claim. Others died out, like Hicca and Steyk.' Consta pointed to two miniscule circles to the middle of the left page, 'These two were so far away from us that they were bound to just slow and stop orbiting. They are no longer part of the system and are now just classed as debris.'

'And these?' asked Simi, clearly enraptured with the beautifully illustrated diagram of all the moons, having pointed to several that had been connected by lines and a number next to each one.

'These moons have all collided to form one, which would be the one you see now in the middle of each diagram, or to the side of it.' He turned over the page where each number was given a name and the name of the moons that had been created by the collisions so far. Phæ'enor looked down, the name beside the eleventh was, Ephynos. Beneath this were the numbers twelve and thirteen, blank spaces beside them.

'Hmm,' she said, more to herself than the room at large.

'Hmmm?' said Consta, now looking at her, interested again.

'So, according to this book, the last collision, or fallout of a moon resulted in our eleventh moon, Ephynos, being formed?'

'Yes, I suppose,' Consta said, drawling again, he twiddled with the curls on his head.

'And, on this page, it says there will be further fallouts or collisions?' She was getting excited now and they were all looking at her. She felt she was on the edge of a breakthrough, 'Flip back to the map, please.' The astronomer did so, still looking at her, 'The eleventh,' she said muttering to herself, 'that was formed seventy years ago …' she started rapping her fingers on her bottom lip thinking, 'Mr Consta?'

'Yes?'

'Is there a pattern to the creation of the new moons?'

'How do you mean?'

'Well, clearly from the history they don't have the same pattern of how many collide, or how many disappear. What I mean by it is do they have a time pattern, and does it always stay the same?'

He looked genuinely surprised and leaned in at the chart next to each of the moons three or four-digit numbers that appeared just below. They all looked now. After some time, it was clear there were no patterns to when the new moons were created.

'Wait!' cried Phæ'enor excited, 'so, since the explosion of the first moon Ëbe, there has been the creation of eleven new moons from further collisions,' she pointed at the page, 'so, there does not appear to be a specific time period between the creation of each new moon and another … however … what month were they created?'

'I'm sorry?' he said.

'For instance, the first new moon of Hallumera, that was created in 260, but which month of that year?'

'Look girl, I don't really see what you are getting at here, and quite honestly I am beginning to get fed up with the smell too!'

'Just do as she asks!' snapped O'sea, 'we need this information no matter how obscure it seems to you.'

'For what?' Consta said irritably.

'That's none of your business, Harq!' snapped Rasia.

'Hey,' said Simi, 'let's not get angry, we are trailing off the point. The sooner we get the information Phæ'enor needs, the sooner we will be gone from here. Mr Consta, we will be out of your way.'

He fell silent, appeased at the idea he may soon be rid of them. He sighed and flipped over a few more pages to further information about the moon Hallumera. There was another diagram; bigger, pale, and with craters drawn all over it. The date listed below was 260. The circumstances of its creation being a collision of three smaller moons, Akor, Torathia and Maron, into a larger moon. The month was the first of the year, Faolterra. It then trailed off in more detail recalling the cycle of the other moons at the time, the colour of the moon seen from the observatory and so on. He turned the next page. The second moon Thuos, created in the year 377. Coalesced from moon Eson moving too fast in orbit and colliding with the moon Atu. Created the second month of the year, Gearrmon.

They went through each one like this, but each time it moved to the next month of the year. From Faolterra to the eleventh month Naimtol, where in the year 1755 the moon Ephynos had been created.

'Okay, I am starting to follow your thinking Miss Doven,' drawled Consta.

'I don't follow,' said O'sea.'

'Well, its lucky Miss Doven here and I do,' said Consta. 'You see there is a pattern when the moons have been created, albeit if you discount Hicca, Steyk, and Asphall who have died or fallen out of orbit. The ones that are left, one by one have all been created in the months of the year, from one through to eleven and in the correct order.'

'But we have thirteen months,' said Rasia.

'Smart, aren't you?' said the astronomer, disdainfully.

'And they all have been created under similar circumstances,' said Phæ'enor, ignoring the contempt between Rasia and Mr Consta. 'Nine have been created during all other moons at half-moon, the only two that differ are the moons of Illraea and Feldstar. These were created whilst all other moons where at full moon cycle.'

O'sea stood there rubbing his temples, Simi was pulling a confused face, and Rasia with one hand leaning on the table just looked fed up.

'Miss Doven, why do you care?' asked Consta, and he started to close the book.

'Because it's the key to opening the last chest!' she said irritated, but then realised she may have said too much.

The astronomer stopped dead at what he was doing, 'Go on…'

'There are twelve chests, well at least throughout history.' She took out the little black book on the cursed chests from her shirt, opening at the page of illustrations; ten completed, the last two not. Pointing at the first nine she explained, 'These nine are all the same wood and have the same symbols above their locks. Yet the tenth is different, darker in colour, and has a different symbol above its keyhole…'

'What?' asked all four of them.

'Wait … let me finish. The tenth has a different symbol above it from the first nine, however if you look closely the eleventh illustration, although incomplete has exactly the same symbol as the tenth.'

As she pointed out the symbols the other four lent in for a better look. Above the first nine were symbols that looked like half-moons, but above the tenth and eleventh chest appeared a symbol of a circle, just like a full moon.

'I still don't get it,' said O'sea.

Phæ'enor sighed, 'They all match up! The stories from The Namorian Curse, the illustrations and creations of all these new moons! Nine moons have all been created when all other moons are at half-moon cycle. The illustrations of nine of the chests even show the symbol of a half-moon above their locks. The stories, curses about the chests all match up to the dates when the new moons were created. It could all just be a coincidence…' They all nodded in agreement, still unsure of what Phæ'enor was trying to explain, '…but then there are two moons which were created when all other moons were at full-moon cycle. The tenth and eleventh chest illustrations in the little black book; they both have a symbol of a circle, or full moon, above their locks. But this time the stories surrounding them are vague. When I was at Mrs Kuáng's she mentioned two countries to me who from nothing have become as, if not more, prosperous and powerful than our own empire.'

'Illraea,' said Simi.

'And Arinthscar,' said Consta.

Phæ'enor nodded in agreement, 'Illraea even named itself after one of the new moons, and instead of being cursed it seems that these two nations have been blessed, if indeed they did come across two of chests.'

'I still don't get it,' said O'sea.

'Don't you see? Nine chests opened when all other moons where at half-moon cycle, the other two at full-moon cycle. We know from Archä and Mëdez that there is a twelfth chest, the one that was in the newspaper, and it also has the symbol of a full-moon above its lock.'

'So?' said Simi.

'So, if the theory is correct, then once we find the chest that is in possession of the crown, all we have to do is wait with it until the twelfth month of the year when all moons are at full cycle. O'scilla was right, there is no actual physical key to open the chests. When I touched them back at Polstor & Polstor it was just an outline of a keyhole, just like the stories in the little black book, no key made can open them. These chests will only open when the moon cycles match the symbol above the lock and the month they are meant to open, in order of sequence. All we need to do now is try and find out what year the twelfth new moon will appear and then open the last chest.' She stood there smiling. All four of them looked at her in silence.

'That is a crazy idea!' said O'sea.

'No. It's not,' said Consta. 'Miss Doven is correct in her theory. The creating of the new moons add up to the dates when the chests that have been discovered so far were recorded. The tenth and eleventh in the book are a little harder to pinpoint. However, if your theory is correct about the chests only opening at their set cycle then you may be disappointed.'

'Why?' asked Phæ'enor, looking at O'Starr Consta like he was the one that had now turned mad.

'Because since the creation of the eleventh new moon, Ephynos, in the year 1755, another new moon has been created.' To the left of him sat a pile of notes, parchment, maps and drawings. He ruffled through them to produce a rough sketch of a moon with some writing beneath it. It read:

> *Moon: Heramar*
> *Created: By the collision of three moons, Lyxa, Bek and Nuris*
> *Year: 1807*
> *Moon Cycles: All others at full-moon*
> *Month: Dlacherramon*

'After all, there are twelve new moons in our skies, not eleven Miss Phæ'enor Doven. You see? If what you say is correct, then this twelfth chest has already been opened for some time now and its treasure more than likely taken.'

Chapter Nineteen

Archä and Mëdez's Information

O'sea, Rasia, Simi and Phæ'enor all looked at each other, crestfallen. No words were said but they all knew that if what O'Starr Consta said was true then they had no chance of retrieving what the chest held. They would not be able to exchange it for information with Archä and Mëdez. Rasia's brother would not be set free. For O'sea there was still the danger of O'scilla. If he found out, what would he do? Phæ'enor knew that he was not a man to be messed with and worse still he was in cohorts with Prince Heolbus. As for Prince Heolbus, if he was working with O'scilla then surely, he knew his brother, Prince Taigor, was in possession of the chest, so why did he just not ask him for it?

'You all need to leave,' said Consta suddenly and sharply. 'Go, I have things to do and you have taken up much of my time, and my sense of smell. I'm a busy man.'

'I'm sure you are,' said O'sea sarcastically. He nodded at Rasia, who along with Rama now back on his shoulders, turned and opened the door in the panelled wall that lead back through the secret passageway. One by one they slipped out of the planetarium and O'Starr Consta's office.

Phæ'enor looked back to see the astronomer ferreting through his papers on his desk and placing them in the large volume, before hastily moving towards the door at the other end, carrying them in his hand and slamming the door shut behind him. As he did so a small piece of paper slipped out of the book and floated slowly down onto the rug.

'Wait,' said Phæ'enor, as she brushed passed O'sea and gently tiptoed over to the piece of paper, careful not to stain the rug with the sludge from her clothes and shoes. She picked it up. There was no writing, just a sketch. It was the same symbol on the front of the book of symbols and the brown leather-bound book Mrs Kuáng had given her. Phæ'enor frowned.

'What is it?' asked O'sea.

'Nothing, just rubbish.'

O'sea turned around and she slipped the piece of paper in her top pocket before following.

***

'We are going back via Archä and Mëdez,' said Rasia. They had been trudging through the tunnels, up and down brick stairs and metal ladders for over half an hour in silence.

'We need to get back home!' snapped Simi. 'We haven't time to speak to more strange men. You do realise how long we have been missing for don't you? Hmmm?'

'None of us can go anywhere looking and smelling like we do. They will help us,' said O'sea.

Simi and Phæ'enor looked at their clothes again; Phæ'enor still dressed like a boy. They looked down, sludge and debris coated them to their feet.

'Fine,' said Simi, 'as long as we don't have to stay too long.'

'No, but I need to tell them what has happened. There may be another way to help my brother,' said Rasia.

'Good luck with that one,' said O'sea, 'they'll want more from you this time.'

They all fell silent again, too despondent to speak. After about another hour they turned into a short, wide tunnel and at the end stood a circular metal rusted door. Rasia knocked hard. Nothing. He knocked again, hard and impatiently. They waited for minutes and minutes until finally the familiar sound of frequent steps moved closer to them from the other side of the door, and then came shouting:

'WHAT? WHAT? WHAT? WHAT?' I'm busy can't you see …
oh? Oh, it's you lot.'

It was clearly Archä who had answered Rasia's knocks, with his
corner smile and the glint in his eyes. This soon faded when he
caught sight of Phæ'enor.

'What happened to you child? I could have sworn you were a
young woman … but … all I see is a dirty looking boy … you know
I never really saw that in you, but you are quite boyish, aren't you?'

'Shut up,' said O'sea, 'can we just come in?'

But without waiting he pushed past the small body of Archä,
and they all followed him in. They walked into a bricked chamber
lit up by many lamps. Either side were four cubicles. Phæ'enor
walked up to them and as she passed each one in turn she noticed
that they all had a large metal barrel inside up against the wall,
emitting a gentle stream of steam.

'In you go then,' said Archä, 'and may I suggest you all pick one
from the same side, that way you can't see each other when you
undress.'

'Excuse me?' said Simi.

Archä spun around to face her with his queer little smile, 'Miss,
that is the reason why you have come here is it not? You need a
wash and a good scrub by the looks and smell of you all.' He
scanned the filth and muck on her dress, 'I suggest the cubicles to
the left of the room. Undress near the entrance of whatever cubicle
you pick; fling your clothes or whatever assortment of garments
you all seem to be wearing in the middle. Use the scrubbing brushes
on the left. Hot water is in the barrels and your towels are on your
right. Once you're done go through the door in the right-hand
corner of the room. There you will find some cleaner clothes to
wear. I shall see you when you are all ready.'

With that Archä turned on his heels and disappeared through
the door in the right-hand corner of the room; Rama trotting after
him. Simi, Phæ'enor, Rasia and O'sea all looked at each other

awkwardly then slowly they picked a cubicle each and did as Archä had instructed. They all flung their clothes in the middle as they undressed. The chamber was soon filled with the sound of vigorous scrubbing and splashing of water, more steam rising from the top of each cubicle. Phæ'enor felt all the dirt and smell wash away along with the disappointment, coldness and tiredness of the last couple of days. She wrapped a large towel around her and one on her head, then shouted so they could all hear her, 'I'm ready!'

'So am I.'

'And me!

'And I.'

They all peered gingerly around the corner of their cubicles. Simi did not look impressed at all, but all Phæ'enor could do was smirk.

'Nice head gear, Doven,' sneered O'sea.

'Look, we are all naked, let's just get a move on. We've got things to do,' said Simi impatient.

They tiptoed around the dirty clothes in the middle and headed through the door in the corner. This time the room was more to the liking of Archä and Mëdez's style. It was much smaller, but the bricks were golden yellow and the walls full of artefacts and books on one side. In the middle was a long bench with four piles of clothes.

'TAKE A PILE!' shouted Archä, out of sight. He wasn't in the room. Phæ'enor looked about and saw where the tail end of a pipe was sticking out above one of the shelves, 'I said pick a pile! Then get dressed! I'm afraid there are no cubicles for you to change into here. Once you are done go through the door to the left and all the way up the stairs. Mëdez and I will see you there and you can tell us all about your news!'

Simi, Phæ'enor and·O'sea all looked at Rasia. The happiness of a hot wash had vanished from his face, he had returned to being downcast.

He picked a pile of clothes, 'We should do as he asks then,' and turned around.

O'sea followed suit; Simi and Phæ'enor also. They all started to dress, back to back; the girls on one side, the boys on the other. When they were ready, O'sea and Rasia looked relatively smart in grey and blue tweed, caps and white shirts. Simi and Phæ'enor in white lace dresses, black bows around their waists and eyelet boots that laced up so high they disappeared underneath the skirts of their dresses.

'Come here,' said Simi, 'I shall sort your hair out,' and with that turned it into a loose bun.

'Do we have to use these lace umbrellas as well?' asked Phæ'enor of Simi, but it was Archä who answered:

'YES, YOU DO!' his voiced echoed through the pipe.

Rasia moved to the door and they all followed one by one up the stone steps until they reached the end of another wide corridor.

'Second door to your left,' shouted Archä through another pipe. They opened the small door just off the corridor and ended up in another, familiar narrow corridor. As they entered the large circular library with its endless ceiling Phæ'enor realised they must have come in from the opposite way to the first time she was there. Archä and Mëdez sat, ruffling papers and looking at documents and books on the table in the middle of the room; Rama sat amongst their papers cleaning himself. It was a lot lighter than the previous table, that one having been burnt through by the blue and white china teacup lined with emaz gold. The brothers seemed even smaller compared to everything else.

'Please, sit, now that you are all freshened up,' said Mëdez. 'Biscuits? Sandwiches? Some tea?'

They all looked at each other then nodded back at Mëdez eagerly. They were all starving and took up their seats quickly whilst Archä and Mëdez served them food and drink.

'So,' said Archä as he poured them their tea, 'you have news of the remaining chest?'

Rasia looked at him then Phæ'enor, his mouth still full.

'We do,' said Phæ'enor, 'but I don't think you will like it.'

'Go on, do tell,' said Archä and Mëdez together, staring intently at Phæ'enor whilst still managing to pile up food on the plates and fill the tea cups.

'Well,' said Phæ'enor and she continued to relay the events of the night before and what had happened since. O'scilla was also after the chests and that he is working with Prince Heolbus, although they had no specific proof. What Mrs Kuáng had told her about the chests being linked to two other successful empires. Then Mr Consta the astronomer and how they had worked out how each chest was opened, the matter of the key, or lack thereof and that it was likely that all had been opened and their contents gone. When she had stopped, Archä and Mëdez sat furiously wolfing down pieces of cake too big for their mouths and slurping their teas.

'Well, this is shit!' said Archä. 'Mëdez, we are going to have to find another way to get hold of the evidence!'

'Hmmm!' said Mëdez nodding furiously, crumbs spilling out of his mouth.

'So, I take it you are no longer willing to give me the information that will set my brother free, or at least get a fair trial?' asked Rasia.

Archä shrugged his shoulders, 'I wasn't going to,' he took a large bite of a sandwich, 'you've tried your best, but you still didn't bring us back what we sought. However, I'm sure you are aware that things changed whilst you were gone, so in light of that I don't see the point in keeping the information from you. Not that it will do your cause a lot of good now.'

All four of them were frowning at Archä and Mëdez who were staring back, mouths full and reaching for more food.

'What's changed since we have been gone?' asked O'sea.

'Oh? ... so ... you don't know?' said Mëdez through mouths of food. 'I thought a servant of the palace would have at least heard by now?'

They all just continued to stare at Mëdez.

'The king. He's dead,' said Archä casually, also now stuffing his face with a large iced biscuit and slurping it down with more tea.

Simi, Rasia, Phæ'enor and O'sea, in reply, all began to choke on their food and tea.

'What ... do you ... mean?' asked O'sea, trying to get some air through the crumbs in his throat.

'The king, he's dead,' said Archä and Mëdez in unison, 'you know ...' they looked at each other, drew their fingers across their necks like a fake knife and hung their heads into their chests, their eyes rolling and tongues out. 'Dead, dead, dead!' It sounded like a song. They looked at each other and burst into a fit of laughter.

'Is this a joke?' asked Simi. 'The king can't be dead, he's getting married in a couple of days!'

'Maybe ... that's why ... why he died!' said Mëdez through laughter, 'He couldn't face ... yet another wife in the household! All the demands! Ha, ha, ha!'

Archä and Mëdez continued to laugh until O'sea got up and grabbed both by their collars.

'Oh!'

'Tell me, honestly, is the king dead?'

'Why, Yes! Why would we joke about that?' they both said.

'So, Prince Taigor will take the throne, right?'

'Ah, you see, therein lies the problem,' said Mëdez.

'And why our information about your brother is now rendered useless,' said Archä, pointing at Rasia.

O'sea had not let go of their collars. Archä looked at his brother and continued, 'Prince Heolbus, has decided to take the throne and...'

'Give up his role in The Brotherhood?' said Simi.

'Eh, no. He still remains in his position of the Brotherhood, albeit in a much more elevated position,' said Mëdez.

Phæ'enor thought of Lady Amia and what would now happen to her; would she go back to her home country? 'What about Lady Amia?'

'Oh, well its quite simple really. Prince Heolbus will now take his father's position at the altar ... of course it will also be a joint celebration. He is to have his coronation on the same day,' said Archä.

O'sea dropped them back in their seats. They both readjusted their collars.

'So now, Master Rasia,' Archä said, casting a displeased look at O'sea, 'the information we have on your brother's innocence no longer matters.'

'Why? I don't see how Prince Heolbus becoming king changes that.'

'Because the one implicated, instead of your brother, is soon to be king!'

They all looked aghast.

'Are you saying that Prince Heolbus set my brother up, with the robbery at the teahouse, stealing from the crown and his own family?'

'Yes,' said Archä and Mëdez, as though it was an obvious thing to do.

'Along with more recent events of course,' said Mëdez.

'How do you mean?' asked Phæ'enor, bewildered by it all.

'The Scavenger,' said Archä.

'Your so-called kidnap,' said Mëdez.

'The whole lot,' finished Archä. They both picked up their cups and saucers and drank from them in unison then put them back down on the table before Mëdez continued:

'So, you see, now that the man who set up your brother and plotted to get the chests is to be king, no one will listen to you, or believe you.'

'You'll probably be thrown into the Nebben and eaten by the sharks for accusing the ruler of our empire for a crime that no one will believe he committed, even though we all know what an awful man he is,' said Archä, sipping his tea again and eyeballing Rasia over the top of his teacup.

'I still don't understand. Why frame my brother?'

'Ah well, you see,' said Mëdez, 'Prince Heolbus can't just get anyone to help him in his mindless little quest. Prince Taigor and he do not see eye to eye and the father, now deceased, was so pathetic, that he couldn't control Prince Heolbus if he tried.'

'Prince Heolbus was sent away at a relatively early age because of his mad behaviour and the radical punishments he inflicted on the citizens of Benaghar,' this time it was Simi who spoke. Archä and Mëdez looked at her and nodded for her to continue. 'He was a bit of a wild one; playing in the streets, making friends outside of the palace walls with people he shouldn't have been. When it came to King Sol trying to get Prince Heolbus to take his place in the military, he refused. He just wanted to do what he wanted to do. The king even gave him the command of the city guards, to make him take some sort of responsibility, leaving him in charge whilst away at war. But when King Sol returned Prince Heolbus had taken his position too far. Most of the city was in chaos. Many people starved because their food was taken from them and anyone that had stood up to Heolbus was either imprisoned, tortured or killed. The king could not tame him; but unable to end his son's life he did the only thing he could and sent the prince to live with The Brotherhood, in some hidden monastery abroad, where no one would be able to seek revenge on him.'

'Go on,' said Archä.

'I only know what I have heard from those at The Grand Temple, and the High Priest, Colla Anwir. Prince Heolbus wrote back to the king regularly, saying he still did not want the throne and that it should pass to Prince Taigor instead. He had found his place in life as a priest of The Brotherhood. That's where he wanted to be. It was a bit suspicious, Prince Heolbus was not known to be solemn and quiet. Anyway, the contact stopped for some time. It is well known that Prince Heolbus has been on a pilgrimage for the last decade, but out of nowhere he has returned. He was sighted in the Isles of Cairdax a few months ago.'

'And out of nowhere he has resumed his chaotic behaviour,' said Mëdez.

'What has his pilgrimage and sudden return got to do with O'scilla, Rasia's brother and the chest?' asked Phæ'enor.

'Everything,' said Mëdez, his eyes lit up.

'Did you even bother to read those books we gave you?' asked Archä and Mëdez. Archä rolled his eyes.

'Yes, I'm…'

'Not hard enough it would seem,' said Archä, putting his teacup firmly on the table. 'Prince Heolbus' pilgrimage is exactly those chests!'

'How do you even know this?'

'Because the bloody fool keeps asking us if we have them!'

'Well you do, don't you?'

'Yes, but we didn't tell him that,' said Archä offended.

'He can keep his hands off them!' said Mëdez. They were both getting visibly stressed.

'Okay, okay, so Prince Heolbus, he has been looking for those chests, just like everybody else. Why get O'scilla and Rasia's brother involved?'

'Prince Heolbus does not have many friends outside of The Brotherhood. He did though, as your cousin has stated, have friends in other places; the streets. Although I wouldn't exactly call them friends even if O'scilla and the prince have known each other for years. More like old acquaintances,' said Archä.

'So, Prince Heolbus needed to gain his trust. See what O'scilla could do for him, a test?' asked Phæ'enor.

'Precisely. You show me what you can do and then I will give you a better job with better rewards.'

'But why? Why choose my bother?' demanded Rasia.

Mëdez shrugged his shoulders and replied, 'Why not? When has O'scilla ever been picky about who he chooses to do his dirty work, just as long as he knows how to exploit them for his own gain.'

'Whether you like to admit it or not it is a well-known fact that your brother has a weakness for Miss Delphi tea, plus it's not exactly a secret that the wolves, the rats and O'scilla all hate each other. If he can get rid of the competition at the same time, why not start off at the top. He can't quite get to O'sea here, so why not go for the wolves first. It's a smart move on his part; take out the leader, destroy the pack.' Rasia balled his fists in anger. 'So O'scilla tempts your brother with the leaf, getting him to rob the crown of one of their most valuable imports. It's a win-win, O'scilla proves his worth to Prince Heolbus. Then Prince Heolbus also has a laugh and a dig at his father's expense and your brother gets what his heart desires.'

'How long has this … business relationship been going on for?' asked Simi.

Archä sneered a big smile, 'You don't miss a trick Miss Doven. Quite a few years. O'scilla and the Prince have been doing their little dodgy deals all over the empire, and naturally any money made by Prince Heolbus went to funding…'

'…funding his pilgrimage in search of the chests,' finished Simi.

Rasia now had tears in his eyes; too upset to speak. His cat Rama stopped pruning itself and gently made its way over to him, brushing its head on Rasia's hand before jumping into his lap where it continued to stare up at Rasia.

Mëdez continued, 'Your brother becomes so intoxicated and incapable of thinking for himself without the leaf he will do anything for it. Quite simply they have him hooked and naturally he will do as he is told.'

'He dresses as a shipmate, loading and unloading goods, food and materials from The Scavenger, whilst his brother who is escorting the Dovens', and looking forward to a reunion with said brother, walks straight past him and instead bumps into you Miss Phæ'enor Doven, only for you then trip on that bloody cat and fall down the gangway. The disembarking of a ship is always chaotic. People coming and going, sailors and crew greeting their family and friends. It gives him an opportunity to get on board unnoticed. There he waits for another of Prince Heolbus' acquaintances to give him the go ahead. The gun-powder is already on the ship, he just needs to know which section to light, but only when the coast is clear,' said Archä.

'But why if the chests are no longer on the ship? Officer Nathryn and the other officers had already taken them off by then. They disembarked before us,' said Phæ'enor.

'Another sly dig at his family, this time his younger brother Prince Taigor, I suppose? The favourite son and heir to the kingdom. He and his ship, the jewel in the empire's crown, loved by his men and the army, and loved by the people. So not only does he get someone to blow the pride of the empire up he does it to create chaos. It is more than likely that Prince Heolbus and his accomplice knew the chests were no longer on board, let's face it no one is stupid enough to get close to the chests with those officers around. But it also marks the end of an era. Prince Taigor's Scavenger had prowess amongst the seas. If Prince Heolbus' plan was always to come back and take the throne he needed to start picking at his brother's strengths, show him who the real king is,' said Mëdez.

'So, it's a diversionary tactic again, except from the other side? To show his brother that he knows he has the chests and will get them no matter what? Including taking the crown that he never wanted in the first place?' asked Phæ'enor.

Archä and Mëdez both shrugged their shoulders, 'Well who knows, but it will be exciting to watch it all unfold,' said Archä, his eyes twinkling with delight at the idea of a fight between the two princes.

Mëdez continued, 'The problem you have Rasia, is that your brother was framed for the break in at the garrisons, even though we all know that was Archä and me. But it gets worse when evidence is placed in the wreckage of The Scavenger. The wolfskin. Your wolfskin Rasia.'

'He wore it to remind him of me. Whilst I was overseas. I'm grateful Captain Alba gave it back to me,' said Master Rasia. He looked even more sad, staring at the table in front of him.

'Anyway, your brother was just a means to an end for Prince Heolbus. The prince used him to tie up all of his and his accomplices' loose ends.'

'And so, we have a new king in the palace, and his new queen to be. Prince Taigor will need all the help from the rat king,' smiled Archä. 'Then we have you Master Wolf Rasia, will you turn to the high seas or take your brother's place in Benaghar, king of the rooftops and the night?' Archä and Mëdez eyes glinted with excitement. It was clear this was just another crime to add to their collection.

They were all silent. Phæ'enor realised how much had changed in such a short space of time. She had come from peace in the east to chaos in the west and the new king looked to keep it that way. Then she thought of what Archä had just said about the accomplice on The Scavenger. They had all thought it was her. Admiral Gull and Captain Alba questioned Phæ'enor, O'Starr Consta and O'tila, even Rasia.

'Do you know who Prince Heolbus' accomplice was on The Scavenger then?'

'Oh yes,' they both said. All of them looked at Archä and Mëdez in anticipation of the answer.

'Well, who was it then, everyone has been questioned?' asked Phæ'enor.

'Lady Amia of course. Your new queen!' said Archä, smiling through his teeth. 'What fun we are all going to have!'

No wonder she tried to label me as mad when I informed Prince Taigor I had seen her down on the gun deck, thought Phæ'enor to herself. She was afraid of getting caught, of ruining hers and Prince Heolbus' plans.

With that Archä and Mëdez digressed into another fit of laughter. O'sea, disgusted, got up from his chair and turned to the others.

'Come on, it's time we all got back. Simi take Phæ'enor home. Wolf, I don't know what I can do but I'll speak to Prince Taigor again. In the meantime, good luck.'

Chapter Twenty

Gilbä

Two by two the four of them separated outside of Polstor & Polstor. O'sea made sure the coast was clear and beckoned Phæ'enor and Simi to leave. Both put their large lace umbrellas up, linked arms and strolled off down Newtown Promenade, as though they were young ladies about town without a care in the world.

Phæ'enor glimpsed back briefly. O'sea and Rasia were facing each other, still talking. They shook hands and departed. Rasia walked in the direction of the secret passage into Old Town, his cat jumping off his shoulders and slinking off ahead of him; O'sea, picked up speed and eventually passed Simi and Phæ'enor. He ignored them, walking past as though he had never seen them before.

The two girls made their way back to No 09 Grand Alboreum Circus as fast as they could, unnoticed under the cover of their umbrellas and blending in with the rest of the white dressed women of the city. As they reached the cobbled circus they slowed down. There was still a lot of activity outside the house, guards coming and going.

'Let's go around the back,' suggested Simi.

Phæ'enor nodded in agreement as they turned their backs on the front entrance. They made their way around the back of the circus terraces, finally coming to a stop at the end of No 09's garden. It was long and quiet and only really the servants of the house used this entrance.

Phæ'enor opened the gate letting themselves in, it creaked gently. They then made their way up the garden path. They could not see from this far back and hoped no one would spot them and come charging out.

They approached the house moving slowly and quietly down the external steps to the basement. Phæ'enor could hear talking and the sound of pots and pans being moved, the smell of hot meat on the cook's stove. Simi tried to open the door, but it was locked. The noise inside stopped, pans stood still, and the chatter died.

'Who is it?' cried the familiar voice of the old housemaid, Mrs Hally Bride.

Simi and Phæ'enor looked at each other, not wanting to say out loud who they were, for fear of drawing too much attention to themselves. Phæ'enor leaned past her cousin and knocked on the door.

'Let me,' came a voice from inside. 'Who goes there?'

Phæ'enor looked back at Simi raising her eyebrows in laughter at the ridiculousness of Mimi's dramatics. Simi rolled her eyes back and leant in at the keyhole, whispering:

'It is I, your sister, you fool! Open the door!'

'Sssh!' came the response and the door opened to reveal Mimi, the cook Mrs Tibba, the young maid Florin, Mrs Bride and the footman Mr Deke who all proceeded to dance and clap before hugging Phæ'enor and Simi in silence. After they had all calmed down Phæ'enor spoke:

'What's happening upstairs?'

'Since you ran off, Miss, Officer Nathryn has had nearly half of the city guards watching the door. For signs of you,' said Mr Deke.

'He's awfully worried about you, Miss, and we know you don't want him, but it is lovely that he cares so much,' said Mrs Tibba, beaming at Phæ'enor.

'Father was also out looking for you, but I think we knew you would be okay,' smiled Mimi looking at her sister.

Phæ'enor noticed Mimi reach for the key necklace around her neck, Simi mirroring her, and she thought about all the questions she needed to ask her cousins and her Uncle Eron in the wake of what had happened, but right now she just felt grateful to be back home.

'Is Officer Nathryn here?' asked Phæ'enor.

'No, he left about an hour ago,' said Florin.

'Good,' she replied, relieved.

'But I'm sure he will be back later,' said Mrs Bride.

'And Mother and Grandmother?'

'As they always are,' said Mimi, 'in the sitting room. Aunt Doven has been sitting at the window looking out for you every day.'

Phæ'enor felt a pang of guilt, realising what she must have put her mother through again. Had she written to her father to tell him? She hoped not.

'Let's go then,' said Phæ'enor, resigned to the fact she may meet a barrage of screaming from both her grandmother and mother. She knew what they could both be like when upset. Simi led the way, with Mimi behind. As they made their way up the dark kitchen stairs from the basement, Phæ'enor spoke:

'I suppose Mother and Officer Nathryn know that there will be no marri-aaage! Arrgh!'

This time both cousins had pinned her up against the stairwell. Mimi had her hand placed tightly over Phæ'enor's mouth. The servants, having rushed to the bottom of the stairs to see what the noise was about, stared up in silence, agog.

'You will marry him,' she hissed, but there was a note of panic in her voice. Wide eyed she looked at her sister. Phæ'enor looked between the two.

'You have to marry him, Phæ'enor,' reiterated Simi, 'it is your only way out!' she continued to press against Phæ'enor's resistance. 'There is a good reason why you are to marry!'

'He doesn't love you, your mother, father, even grandma know this,' said Mimi.

'Look, it is the only way to get out of this city, and away from the trouble that is coming,' said Simi. 'Remember what I told you about Prince Heolbus before he was sent away, how Archä and Mëdez have told us what may happen next? The chests are the sole reason why you are to marry, Phæ'enor. Your father wrote to our father, Uncle Eron, before you and auntie even set sail for Benaghar.

Father has not told us all the details but what we do know is that the chests were not meant to be travelling so soon, definitely not on The Scavenger. Officer Nathryn and his men managed to convince Captain Alba to let them travel onboard, instead of waiting for the next ship. They were being followed and needed to get the chests back to Prince Taigor as soon and safe as possible.

Officer Nathryn did not have time to warn Prince Taigor; he only learned of it all once The Scavenger had arrived in Benaghar.'

Phæ'enor thought back to that day on the harbourside, the cry of the bird had distracted her from the party gathered; Prince Taigor and Officer Nathryn separate from the rest of the group, their heads close together in discussion, and then the ship had exploded.

'You were always meant to marry Officer Nathryn,' said Mimi, bringing her cousin out of her thoughts, 'but your mother and father thought you would have time to get to know each other, maybe even fall in love. But the early arrival of the chests changed that, and the unwanted attention they attract. Wherever they are others follow; O'tila keeping an eye on them for O'scilla, and his cousin…'

'… and Lady Amia for Prince Heolbus,' interjected Simi.

There was a knowing silence between them, then Mimi spoke again:

'This is why it has all been such a rush. No one wanted to force you into this. We would all like the opportunity to leave the city but not all of us are that lucky. And the rules are against us women, we can only leave the city if we are married first.'

Her cousins smiled gently at her, but Phæ'enor felt the anger creep up inside her at the injustice of it all. Yet her cousins were right, for a woman to leave the city, they must marry; she must marry Officer Nathryn.

The possibility of a power struggle between the new King Heolbus and Prince Taigor was not something she wanted to witness, even if it bought glee to the likes of Archä and Mëdez.

'There are only a select few who knew that Heolbus was making his way back to Benaghar. Whilst no one knew of his intentions once he got here; now it is all in the open for everyone to see. And it is not just our family making plans to leave this place, to take you away from what might happen,' said Simi. 'No one wants to live through another war.'

'You have family in the north,' said Mimi, 'we don't, plus we need to stay for Mother.'

'Whether you like it or not you have to do it. Re'av will take you there,' said Simi. 'I'm sorry cousin, but the marriage is set to take place the day after the royal wedding. You must do this. There is no other way.'

The cousins released Phæ'enor from their grip. She looked at them gutted.

'Come. Let's go upstairs,' said Mimi, turning Phæ'enor gently around to face the door and making her way up the steps. Phæ'enor felt ill and had the urge to run off again but her cousins must have sensed it. Mimi had a firm grip on her right wrist. Simi kept looking back, checking to see if she was still following.

Moments later they were all in the hallway. Phæ'enor could see two city guards chatting on the steps outside the front door. A city guard walked out of the sitting room to their right, nodded at them without recognition and walked out of the house. The sitting room door was left ajar. Phæ'enor walked towards it and pushed it open. Her mother was sat on the window seat, staring out the window. Her grandmother, sitting in her usual chair, was frantically knitting.

'We are fine. We don't need anything else for today, thank you,' she said, concentrating on her knitting needles.

'Not even your granddaughter's?' asked Phæ'enor.

'Huh, if you can bloody find them!' she said, looking up and stopping mid-knit. Mrs Doven casually looked down at her mother-in-law to see why she had stopped, then looked over to Phæ'enor.

'Oh my, where have you been?' she cried, running over to Phæ'enor and squeezing her tight. Phæ'enor braced herself for a screaming match but instead her mother just sobbed, holding Phæ'enor in her arms. Simi and Mimi affectionately each squeezed a wrist of their aunts and Phæ'enor briefly looked at them with gratitude. Mrs Doven's cry must have been very loud for the two officers at the door came hurrying into the hallway. They only stopped when Simi and Mimi glared threateningly at them to dare come closer. They bowed their heads awkwardly and backed away.

'Auntie, we should sit down,' said Mimi, 'Phæ'enor has a lot to tell you.'

'Mmm … hmm …' said Mrs Doven, still crying but nodding that they should sit, not letting go of her daughter. She made her way to the closest chair, sitting down besides Phæ'enor. Simi and Mimi made their way to the opposite one, closing the door behind them. Mrs Jemin wiped a tear from her own eye, trying to compose herself.

Aunt,' said Simi, 'about the wedding. Phæ'enor has made her decision.'

'Mmm. It's … it's okay. It's okay, darling. I understand, if you don't. I understand. If you don't … if you don't want to marry, then…'

'I will marry Officer Nathryn, Mother. I'm sorry. Simi and Mimi, they have explained everything. If only you had said earlier…'

'But … but you don't…'

'Yes, I do. You know I do.'

'He's a good man … he will take care … and …'

'Dear,' said Mrs Jemin, 'she knows what she needs to do. You have her back. For now, at least. There is no need to worry. Just enjoy her whilst you can. Mimi do your grandmother a favour. Write to Officer Nathryn and advise that his bride to be has reappeared and has accepted his offer. Send one of the other officers to deliver it to him. Simi, ask Mr Deke to bring in teas.'

The two cousins disappeared, Simi downstairs instead of ringing the bell and Mimi into the hallway to the side table where she hastily wrote a note.

'I'm sorry Mother. For disappearing like that.'

'Damn right child! You could have killed us with fright. Officer Nathryn and Prince Taigor searched for you the whole night,' said her grandmother, back to her usual moaning self.

'I know, I saw them, but they didn't see me.'

'It's true then. That you were in Old Town?'

'Yes. I ended up following Master Rasia, and then lost my way.' Phæ'enor stopped talking. She didn't think it would worry her grandmother too much, but she didn't want her mother to know about her encounter with O'scilla or Mrs Kuáng's Tea house, not just yet.

'Then, of course Simi ...'

'Went and got you on our orders,' said her grandmother, looking at her sternly. Here we go thought Phæ'enor. 'Your cousins, as dim witted as they seem on the surface, are quite resourceful when they need to be. The festivities turned into a bit of a riot, the rats and the wolves were out in droves, then it escalated across the city. I hear it was quite a light show in Old Town. Bumbling city guards. What possessed them to go in there is beyond me. Anyway, your cousin did as she was told, no fuss entailed.'

No, or course not, thought Phæ'enor bitterly, thinking of all they had discovered about the chests and how Rasia must be feeling helpless right now. She hoped O'sea would have some luck with

Prince Taigor. There was silence. Mrs Doven drained from her tears, rested her head on Phæ'enor's shoulder.

'I hear that we have a new king,' said Phæ'enor.

'Not yet we don't. With any luck he'll pop his clogs like his father. Then a man who is fit to be king will take his place,' said her grandmother.

'I didn't think you liked royalty no matter who was on the throne,' said Phæ'enor.

'I don't but what choice is there? As long as the ruler isn't a complete idiot ... although it's not looking good.'

Phæ'enor turned to her mother, 'Did you write to my father?'

'No, not this time. I thought it best not to worry them. Besides it would take months to get there and anything could have happened in the meantime.'

Phæ'enor felt slightly relieved at this; for now at least her father and brothers had no need to be concerned. Better still, she knew her mother would write later, when she had married and made her way out of the city. She wondered whether Officer Nathryn would stay with her or leave her into the north to wait for her family.

'Mother, Officer Nathryn and I, when we are married, will you join us?' There were heavy footsteps in the hallway and voices.

'You can't just go in there she has only just got back and ...' The sitting room door swung open. Standing there, looking tired was Officer Nathryn.

'You're back and safe then. Good. Good.' He sounded out of breath. He made to move over to Phæ'enor but must have thought better of it and went to stand by the window instead, 'You know, we don't have to go through with...'

'No. You made a promise to my father. I understand. I accept your offer.'

Officer Nathryn looked back at her and nodded, 'Good. Good.'

Neither of them moved. Officer Nathryn did not look relieved by Phæ'enor's reappearance or overjoyed by her decision to now go ahead with the marriage. He looked worried and concerned. Her grandmother, either oblivious or just not caring asked:

'Are the riots still troubling you Officer Nathryn?'

'Yes, you could say that. I'm just thankful that Miss Doven is back in one piece.'

'I think you can call me by my first name now. We are soon to be man and wife. Sooner than expected I am told,' said Phæ'enor.

Officer Nathryn smiled at her, 'Under the circumstances it is best that we are married soon. Thankfully King Sol gave us his blessing before he died, or you may have been luckier and would not have had to marry me after all,' he laughed nervously.

'You have to get permission from the king to marry?'

'Yes!' they all said.

'I am still a serving officer. Luckily for me Prince Taigor is a good friend and persuaded his father of the match.'

'However?'

'That may not have been the case with the new king,' said Officer Nathryn. Phæ'enor thought how much she hated the man already. Not only is he after the chests, hunting them all down like animals, framing Rasia's brother in his place, but he also gets to say whether someone can marry too. 'Prince Heolbus I'm afraid to say, is nothing like his brother. I have a bad feeling about all of this.' Officer Nathryn stared out of the window. 'I was hoping to bring the marriage forward.'

'Oh, okay,' said Phæ'enor, 'when?'

'I said I was hoping,' he said with a smile at Phæ'enor's willingness to go ahead with the plan, it was a practicality to her now. 'But he has already decreed a ban on all other weddings taking place until he is married to Lady Amia.'

'Gosh, I'd forgotten about her.' Phæ'enor stopped talking, thinking of how Lady Amia was far from nice, Prince Heolbus' accomplice on the ship and now soon to be his wife and queen. It had all been planned that way.

Officer Nathryn's countenance darkened, 'I wouldn't worry about her. Prince Heolbus and her go back a long way. By all accounts she will be the perfect wife for him. For Benaghar and the empire, she will make the worst queen.'

'How do you mean?' asked Mrs Doven.

'You did not hear this from me. King Sol, although old was a healthy man, but lately he became unwell, confined to his rooms and only Lady Amia could attend to him. Yet he only got worse. He should have lived for a couple more decades at least.'

'You think Lady Amia may have poisoned him?' asked Phæ'enor, remembering the less than pleased look Lady Amia had given her at the palace after being found wandering off. How King Sol was well and happy at the harbourside, but at the palace she had glimpsed him with his eldest son. He was ill and had deteriorated in appearance.

'I think you already knew what she was capable of,' he replied.

Phæ'enor looked at Officer Nathryn, tired and anxious, 'You wanted to get out of the city before their marriage was even announced, didn't you?' she asked.

'No,' he said shaking his head, 'I was hoping it would have happened before Prince Heolbus had even put one foot back in Benaghar.' He stopped, looking out of the window. 'Someone has just arrived,' he said suddenly. He turned to the sitting room door. Phæ'enor glimpsed a shadow fly by the window. They heard the voices of Simi and Mimi in the hallway:

'Yes, thank you!'

'We are not idiots, you can leave it with us.'

'Okay, you can leave now.'

'Ugh, city guards are such idiots!' said Mimi, walking into the sitting room. She held a tray of tea in her hands. Simi followed close behind her with a familiar cloak in hers. It was Officer Nathryn's birthday gift to Phæ'enor. Rich yellow, thick and bound by some ribbon.

'I believe this is yours,' said Simi, handing it over.

Phæ'enor placed it on her lap. Underneath the ribbon was a small blue envelope. She took it out and turned it over. Officer Nathryn peered over the top of her.

'It's from the palace,' said Officer Nathryn, immediately alert.

'But I left this in Old Town, it was never at the palace…' said Phæ'enor going quiet. They all looked at him, then back at Phæ'enor. It had a gold seal of the king on it, just like the invitation they had received last time for Lady Amia's private party. She opened it roughly with her fingers and pulled out a short letter.

'Read it aloud, please,' asked Officer Nathryn. They all looked at him then back at Phæ'enor who started to read:

Dear Miss Phæ'enor Doven,

I believe we had the misfortune of missing each other. I am disappointed but nonetheless I did come across our mutual friend O'scilla…

At this Phæ'enor's mother put her hand over her mouth. Mrs Jemin dropped her sewing, but the two cousins did not flinch. Officer Nathryn however did not look happy and was about to ask a question when Phæ'enor hurriedly continued reading the letter:

…he was helpful, up to a point, but gave me incorrect information on where to find you. Luckily, for you, at least, things have turned out well. For our friend, I cannot say the same. Why he misled us both is a mystery to me and therefore he has been reprimanded. Playing games with the future king and with the daughter of an officer of the Benagharian army, and I am led to believe a future officer's wife, will

351

not be tolerated. However, you are now safe,
thanks to the ingenuity of your family.

Simi and Mimi went rigid at the mention of this.

> *I hope that you are well and not traumatised by*
> *the events and whilst we may have missed each*
> *other on this occasion, I am not too disappointed,*
> *for I know I shall see you at my own coming*
> *nuptials. I enclose invitations for all your family.*
> *Your new king, and your dear friend and future*
> *queen, will be delighted to celebrate with you in*
> *just a few days' time.*
>
> *His Royal Highness,*
>
> *King Heolbus.*
>
> *P.S. What a beautiful cloak you have. Make sure*
> *you keep it on next time. The vibrant colour will*
> *make it easier to find you, if you should ever get*
> *lost again.*

Phæ'enor felt her hairs stand on end and her skin crawl with invisible insects. By the looks on everyone else's faces they had the same sensation.

'You were with O'scilla?' asked her mother astounded.

'Not by choice Mother! I'll explain in a moment. What I want to know is what he means by he has "reprimanded" O'scilla?'

'Why do you care?' asked Officer Nathryn.

'Because they are working together!' said Simi and Phæ'enor together. Phæ'enor proceeded to tell all of them what they had learned including the deliberate set up of Wolf Canis to take the blame for all the recent crimes since she had arrived. Alarmed, Officer Nathryn got to his feet.

'Do not leave this house again unless you are with me. No one else, do you hear? I'm disappointed to say that the city guards cannot be fully trusted.' Phæ'enor looked at him, understanding his concern. The morning after O'sea had intruded into their home the city guards had swarmed the place, turning everything over, never once checking to see if the inhabitants were okay, until Officer Nathryn had turned up and shouted at all of them to leave. It was clear to Phæ'enor now they were looking for the chests, just as O'sea had been.

'You mean they have been working for Prince Heolbus all along?' she asked.

Officer Nathryn nodded in reply then turned to Simi and Mimi, 'I shall send for your father to come and get you. I need to report back to Prince Taigor and I'm sorry if you don't hear from me for a while but … hang on … wait here.'

He left the room. Moments later he returned. On his left arm was the big black bird that Phæ'enor had seen fly over The Scavenger and out of the harbour, pecked at their windows, and had followed them to Polstor & Polstor.

This time, Mimi did not bat an eyelid at it, let alone start screaming that she hated birds. My cousins are not what they seem, thought Phæ'enor.

'If you need to find me, or send word, then use Gilbä,' said Officer Nathryn, continuing where he had left off before he had disappeared out of the room. The bird puffed up its wings. It was so big that they all ducked but it still managed to cuff Phæ'enor over the back of her head, shaking its feathers and its long silver hooked beak chattering away.

'He's a frigate bird, a giant one. He can't stay indoors…'

'I should think not!' snapped Mrs Jemin, who was astounded by his nerve to bring it indoors in the first place. 'You can't keep a bloody big thing like that in here!'

'No. You can't. I'll make sure he stays outside. But he will be near. So, if you need anything just call him down, like this,' with that Officer Nathryn whistled three calls in a row. The bird began to flap. 'They are not really made for land, only when they nest. He's much better in the air, but he knows his home well, and will find me quite quickly. Certainly, quicker than anyone else could. I need to get back now. I shall keep you informed of the wedding preparations, but I may not see you until the royal wedding. I'm sorry.' At that he left No 09 Grand Alboreum Circus with the frigate bird, which spread its wings ready to take flight once more.

Chapter Twenty-One

The Royal Wedding

Officer Nathryn had kept his word. In the days before the royal wedding he sent word of their upcoming nuptials to Phæ'enor. It was to be held in Hightown, a modest gathering at a small temple. It would mean that they were closer to the northern city gates and could leave straight after the ceremony. No further celebrations.

As predicted Officer Nathryn was too busy tending to preparations for the royal celebrations, and therefore did not come by the house. Phæ'enor also kept to her word. She stayed indoors, and not one for being interested in dresses and shoes, let Simi and Mimi take the lead in choosing her wedding attire, whilst she kept to the house.

Besides, there was no Wolf Rasia to escort her anywhere and maybe that was for the best as they both seemed to attract trouble. The Doven's current guard was Gilbä, the giant frigate bird, who could be seen soaring above the house.

Phæ'enor had had no word from Rasia since they had separated outside of Polstor & Polstor a few days prior. When Simi and Mimi had returned from town one day they both shook their heads. No news. They hadn't seen him and word on the street was that Wolf Canis was set to be sentenced within the week. Knowing how much Rasia cared for his brother, Phæ'enor thought he was probably down in the labyrinth of the city walls visiting him. Maybe by some chance O'sea had been able to help, but he would probably be distracted by his own troubles; no one had set eyes on his cousin, O'tila, since his encounter with Simi in Old Town.

The only comfort Phæ'enor had to distract her and take her mind off what was going on in the outside world, as well as the boredom of keeping to the house, was packing. Both her grandmother and mother, along with the old housemaid Mrs Bride had started to fold away the clothes she would need for her journey north. Winter shoes, summer shoes; her cloak she would wear, but a summer travelling cloak was also packed. Cotton clothes, fur lined clothes, it went on and on. Phæ'enor soon learned the reason for so much clothing; the seasons were not always relevant in mainland Benaghar. If you were travelling near enough to the west coast the sea air would freeze your bones, but near enough to the east you would need to keep cool.

'I know it seems a lot, but you will only need one of everything,' said Mrs Doven to her daughter, 'and it all needs to fit in tightly and compact.' She rolled up different garments, packing them firmly into two large trunks. They would be travelling by coach for the most part, staying with friends of Officer Nathryn first in the west, then making their way up through the middle country until they reached the border of the vast golden plains of Aebra. Here they would have to wait for a contact from the north until they could go any further.

The people of the Northern Aebran Territories were not very trusting of outsiders and it was better to wait for a guide than to travel without one. Phæ'enor questioned her mother on this:

'You're from the north aren't you, Mother?' She hesitated in reply,

'Yes, from one of the tribes there.'

'So, surely you don't need a guide?'

'No,' she replied smirking, 'they know me, and I them. Maybe not as well as I used to. Although, they don't know you, but I am sure you will fit right in.'

'But surely they know I am coming? You did write to them, didn't you?'

'Yes, but not about you travelling to them. We must be careful how we get information across the wall. They are not exactly favoured by the king, past or present.'

'Then how come you were allowed into Benaghar?'

'Ha!' Mrs Doven laughed out hard and kissed her daughter on the cheek. She smiled, 'It doesn't work like that. Everyone is welcome in the city, to an extent anyway. Let's just say most of the north and the south would rather not see each other. Ridiculous I know, but they are old men set in their ways, and besides, I fell in love.'

They both smiled at each other, but the smiles soon disappeared. Phæ'enor knew her mother was thinking the same as her. She would not be marrying for love, but for safety and a means to an end. It was then that it hit her. She felt a pang in her chest and realised she would be travelling alone, Officer Nathryn would be with her but her mother would not. She was the person who had made her feel like she was not alone these past weeks, like they had not really left Vanu. It had kept her calm, but now, after the wedding that would change. She would be leaving all her family behind this time, her brothers, her father and now her mother. Even her grandmother, although a constant irritation, would be missed. And she did not know how long it would be until she saw them all again. Phæ'enor would now need to put her trust in a man that at first, she could not stand, and even now still hardly knew. She just hoped that her parents' trust in him was correct.

They finished off the packing and anything left was clothing for the following couple of days; her wedding dress and clothes for the royal celebrations. Anything other than that was left for Mrs Bride and Florin to store away. It was now time to get ready for the royal wedding.

***

The wedding was to be held in the middle of the afternoon at The Grand Temple before the gathered party moved onto the palace for celebrations. Simi and Mimi, with their father, Uncle Eron, arrived

357

at No 09 Grand Alboreum Circus ahead of time, having walked all the way from Queens. It was a warm day and not one of them was appropriately dressed for it. Under strict conditions from the palace all guests were to wear evening attire but be covered during the ceremony. The future king would not allow for his dear Brotherhood to be offended by the skin and flesh of any assembled. They all knew he only meant the women. Uncle Eron turned to all of them as they sat waiting for Officer Nathryn to escort them and said:

'Try to stick together at the feast.'

'Why, what do you think is going to happen?' barked Mrs Jemin, 'he's the bloody king, he's not about to start blowing the place up on his own coronation and wedding day.'

'No, mother, but he is an unknown entity. He has been away from Benaghar for too long. Sent away on his father's orders for a reason. It was not his choice. The only people who truly know him are The Brotherhood and word is not all of them are happy with him. Let's just hope the whole thing goes smoothly.'

'I'm sure it will Father, it's just a wedding,' said Mimi.

They were all smiles but none of them looked particularly happy. Phæ'enor just wanted all the celebrations out of the way and the formalities of her own wedding completed so they could get the worst of the journey across Aebra over with. She was now impatient to leave.

***

Officer Nathryn arrived soon after with two barouche box coaches. Uncle Eron, Simi, Mimi and Mrs Jemin sat in the first coach. Phæ'enor, Mrs Doven and Officer Nathryn in the second.

'How have you all been keeping?' asked Officer Nathryn.

'Well enough. We have done as you asked. Everything is packed and ready for your journey north,' said Mrs Doven. She smiled at

Officer Nathryn and squeezed Phæ'enor's hand affectionately. Phæ'enor's stomach rolled at the thought of leaving her mother behind. Especially in a city that had become increasingly divided and where her mother would not be allowed to follow her daughter or leave without her husband.

'I'm glad that you did not have to use Gilbä, that has been a relief I can tell you, what with all the organisation and chaotic nature of today's events.' He smiled but Phæ'enor sensed he was nervous. Shadows had crept in under his eyes, his smiled strained.

'Did everything go well with Prince Taigor?' she asked.

'As well as it could. His men are doing their own investigation into what you and your cousins told me the other day. No one can find O'scilla, but Wolf Canis has confirmed everything to Prince Taigor.'

Phæ'enor thought of how awkward this would have been for the Prince, 'Has he confronted his brother?'

'How can he, Phæ'enor? They are not just brothers. Heolbus will now be king, Prince Taigor his subject. Prince Heolbus was sent away by his father at an early age and came back rarely. Prince Taigor and he are more like acquaintances. They were never close, and they do not share similar opinions or family traits.'

'They do have different mothers, don't they?' said Mrs Doven.

'Mmm … they do indeed.'

'What's wrong with their mothers?' asked Phæ'enor.

'They are both dead for starters,' said Mrs Doven. 'Queen Dannah, Prince Heolbus' mother, died quite young I believe, Officer Nathryn?'

'Yes. She took her own life. No one really knows why. However, it explains Prince Heolbus turbulent childhood. I believe it was him who found her.'

'And Prince Taigor?'

'Queen Argella died giving birth to him.'

'So, they both lost their mothers, but one turned out bad, the other good? It's hardly a good excuse to behave badly,' said Phæ'enor.

'Maybe not, but people are different, they behave differently. No matter what underlying feeling, excuse, or bond of blood they share,' said Officer Nathryn.

'So, King Sol never remarried then, after Prince Taigor's mother?'

'Oh no, he did, to Queen Phenice, of course,' said Mrs Doven.

'What happened to her?'

'Nothing. She is still Queen until Prince Heolbus and Lady Amia take the throne.' Phæ'enor was puzzled. She had not heard of Queen Phenice before.

'You have met her, albeit briefly. When you first arrived, she was the woman cloaked in black at the harbourside, alongside Prince Taigor,' said Officer Nathryn answering Phæ'enor's thoughts. 'Unable to produce an heir to King Sol's throne, he decided to remarry. To lady Amia.'

'You would think he had his fair share of children at that age,' remarked Mrs Doven, with a smile. 'He had two grown men for sons.'

'So, King Sol drove one of his wives to suicide, the second one died from childbirth and the third is no longer good enough for him. I thought you said he was a good king?'

Officer Nathryn laughed, 'He was, for the most part, just maybe not closer to home.'

'Well let us hope you and I don't drive each other to suicide,' she said sarcastically.

'Phæ'enor! That's not funny, at all!' snapped Mrs Doven.

Phæ'enor looked at Officer Nathryn who was suppressing a laugh. She too was smiling but wiped it off her face when she saw the look on her mother's.

As the coach approached The Grand Temple, Phæ'enor looked out to see Gilbä, the frigate bird soaring in the winds above. The coaches stopped, and they all got out. Phæ'enor had not been this close to the temple before. It was tall. Its many spires reaching into the skies, so much so that it looked like their tips would stretch into the beyond, its bricks sparkling in the sun's rays. Phæ'enor looked about to see other coaches and carriages arriving, with others already stationed; their passengers having departed and now walking up the path. It was lined heavily with soldiers dressed in ceremonial uniform. The large gilded wooden doors of the temple were guarded on either side. The men and women making their way along were heavily cloaked; only glimpses of silk, flashes of sparkles and colour could be seen as their cloaks were displaced momentarily by the wave of a hand or the steps of their feet.

'Phæ'enor? Phæ'enor?'

Someone tugged at her right sleeve. It was Mimi who looked at her and nodded towards the entrance of The Grand Temple. There was Wolf Rasia slowly ascending the steps, along with some of the officers that attended the meal at Lady Amia's party and her birthday celebrations; Lieutenant Hall Oleston was absent. Mimi then tugged at the sleeve of her cloak again, but this time nodded up above. At first Phæ'enor could not make out what Mimi had pointed to but then she could see them. Hundreds of them. Silhouettes lined the roofs and skyline around the temple, watching the procession of carriages and people below.

'So, it's not just the future king that has an army,' said Mimi.

Phæ'enor studied the boys and girls on the rooftop. She couldn't make them out from where she was but knew it would be the rest of the wolves scouting out the people below just as they did the night she and Rasia visited his brother, only on that occasion they were watching out for them, this time she wasn't so sure.

Phæ'cnor looked down the buildings and noticed more people on doorsteps or at the entrance to narrow streets, chatting in small groups. But they were not wolves. Dressed in brown and dirty looking clothes, they were rats.

'It looks like the wolf and the rat have put their differences aside, for the time being,' said Uncle Eron. 'Come along, we need to be inside.'

Phæ'enor had an urge to shout no! To turn and jump back inside the carriage, but before she could Officer Nathryn took her by her left arm and guided her on.

'It will be fine. Everyone wants to see the new king and his queen emerge. Whatever their reasons.'

'I don't fancy being stuck inside if any of them decide they would like to do more than celebrate,' said Phæ'enor, looking around her as they walked behind Mrs Doven who had linked arms with her Uncle Eron; Simi and Mimi were in front leading the way.

***

Once inside The Grand Temple the wedding ceremony took place first. It was long, dull and very hot. The guests, having not been allowed to take off their cloaks, were using feathers from their hats and prayer books to fan their faces. The only thing that kept Phæ'enor from falling asleep was Lady Amia's wedding dress. Jewels glittered from all over it, blinding half the guests whilst the train stretched nearly the entire length of the aisle. Phæ'enor had to quiet her grandmother who on more than one occasion commented on the preposterousness of it:

'I bet there are several children in Sulam who have gone blind from making the lace for that alone.'

'Ssshh, Grandmother.'

There were more than a few stifled laughs from the surrounding pews. Clearly others shared her view.

Then came the coronation of both King Heolbus and Queen Quenna. This was even longer and felt like a marriage taking place between the new king and Benaghar; a procession of the priests of The Brotherhood took turns to anoint the new king with oils, perfumes, powders and incense. The head priest, a solemn looking man by the name of Colla Anwir, read to the new king the vows he must promise to take:

'Do you Heolbus Bor Rothian vow to serve Benaghar and Benaghar only?'

'I Heolbus Bor Rothian, vow to serve Benaghar and only Benaghar.'

Another priest handed the king a golden staff, before turning to Lady Amia.

'Do you Quenna Addan Amia vow to fight for Benaghar and only Benaghar?'

'I Quenna Addan Amia vow to fight for Benaghar, and only Benaghar.'

Another priest handed Queen Quenna a large golden sword, and so the ceremony continued for what seemed like hours. Phæ'enor, becoming more bored of the proceedings, began to look around the temple and noticed she was not the only guest whose eyes were wandering to the architecture, or watching other guests, their mannerisms and their dress. On the row furthest away, she spotted Wolf Rasia looking dead ahead, he did not blink or smile. It was as though he was there but not in spirit.

A few pews ahead Phæ'enor glimpsed Cort Rohgah, rocking backwards and forwards, his hands clasped, and eyes closed with a smile upon his face. He was clearly enjoying himself. Next to him, was the astronomer Mr O'Starr Consta, with his usual snotty expression. His arms were clearly folded beneath his cloak, his left eyebrow raised at the new king being crowned. The boredom was not concealed from his face.

Phæ'enor glanced towards the front row and could see Prince Taigor, adorned with the cloak of a prince; the fur of some exotic animal and a thin crown of silver. His face was turned away, but his body was still, intent on the proceedings ahead. Next to him sat a young woman, also cloaked in furs, her dark hair cascading down her back and glimpses of turquoise above the neckline. She raised a silk cloth to her face, silently wiping away tears.

'That is Queen Phenice,' whispered Mrs Doven, in her daughter's ear.

Phæ'enor continued to stare at her. She had a feeling that the tears where not tears of joy. She then turned her attention away from Queen Phenice and continued to look around absently, anything to not have to listen to the drone of the priests.

Her eyes came to rest on the row of pews on her right. At the end two small black cloaked figures sat. They laughed in silence; their bodies shaking uncontrollably with mirth. Suddenly they stopped and turned toward Phæ'enor's gaze. Two faces appeared from underneath their hoods. It was Archä and Mëdez. Archä winked at her, Mëdez smiled as though he could not believe his luck that he was at the ceremony. Phæ'enor had a feeling that neither of them had been given an invite. She shook her head and turned back to face the front, just as the head priest placed the crown on King Heolbus' head. He stepped back and announced:

'All hail King Rothian V!' All the guest's shouted out the same in reply, Phæ'enor did not, noticing others said it dispiritedly under their breaths. Then the priest placed a smaller crown on Lady Amia, stepped back and announced:

'All hail Queen Rothian VII. Again, the gathered repeated the priest's words. He then stepped down between the king and queen, joined them by holding them together with his own hands and announced: 'Benaghar! Hail your new king and queen, Emperor and Empress of Aebra!'

At the palace all the guests from The Grand Temple slowly meandered into the King's Hall, a large circular stone room situated below a glass dome. Archä and Mëdez were nowhere to be seen amongst them. They must have had their share of the fun in the temple, thought Phæ'enor, but would not go unnoticed in the palace.

The tables were tiered from the top down to the back so that the new king and queen could see all their guests. The only space that was not filled was a circular space in the middle; a beautiful mosaic of moons and stars in the centre, directly below the dome. The new King Rothian and Queen Quenna made their way to the top table, smiling, laughing and joking with guests along the way. They took their seats, Prince Taigor to the left of the queen, the Queen Dowager Phenice Rothian to the right of the new king and either side of them sat five priests from the Brotherhood, the head priest Colla Anwir closest to the king.

Phæ'enor, seated next to Officer Nathryn and her mother, watched on as the other quests took their places. She spotted Cort Rohgah bumbling between the chairs and tables, trying to squeeze past the other guests; O'Starr Consta unimpressed with the unwanted attention his friend was attracting. Wolf Rasia sat down solemnly with some other guests, staring into the space in front of him; Officer Nathryn's men did not join him or appear at the reception. Once all the guests had found their places the king stood up and addressed his guests:

'Ambassadors, Officers, Ladies and gentlemen, welcome and thank you all for coming.' His voice carried, steady and well spoken, friendly even. He had practised this or had experience of addressing a crowd before, thought Phæ'enor. 'Your new Queen Rothian and I, are so very happy and grateful that you could all come.'

Phæ'enor looked across the circular room. It was silent with everyone's attention drawn to their new king. Towards the high table, although not many, sat the ambassadors from outside the empire, already stationed in Benaghar before Heolbus had arrived in the capital. Behind them, politicians and their families including Uncle Eron, Simi and Mimi sat at the same table. The rest were filled with soldiers, higher ranking officers and general guests of the new couple. The new king continued:

'However, although we have all gathered here today to celebrate, I would like to first make a toast to my late father, King Sol Rothian.' They all stood with their glasses of red wine raised, and following the lead of their new monarch all chanted:

'To King Sol, may he rest in peace!'

'Thank you,' said King Heolbus, bowing his head in reflective sadness.

'What a bloody actor,' whispered Phæ'enor's grandmother beside her mother, and tutted. Phæ'enor glared at her to be quiet again but she did not see her, continuing to smirk in the king's direction.

'Please, please, be seated and let us all celebrate the old and the new Benaghar together!' He clapped his hands together twice. Suddenly, through six different doors, dotted across the room, entered a procession of servants all carrying plates laden with food. Boar heads, lamb, vegetables, soups and fish, were accompanied by a group of musicians on lutes, strings, harps and thimbles. The guests cheered as the food was served and the feast began. Plate after plate appeared, glass after glass of wine; no one was unattended to.

The guests became more and more inebriated, including Phæ'enor who felt slightly wobbly and was laughing at everything the other guests were talking about, even if it wasn't intended to be. As everyone became more drunk, more people began to get up and start dancing in the middle of the room, the king and the queen joining them briefly before relaxing on their thrones to watch.

As Phæ'enor danced with Officer Nathryn she looked up at the high table. The queen was clapping and laughing along to the dance, but the king's countenance was very different. He frowned as he watched, displeased with what he saw. His eyes were then averted to his left. Approaching the high table was Prince Taigor. He bowed and then kissed his brother's hand offered to him. They then hugged and kissed each other on both cheeks before Prince Taigor did the same with the new queen and returned to the other end of the table. King Heolbus then rose from his throne.

'ENOUGH!' boomed the king's voice across the room. Everyone who was dancing stopped, those seated or standing immediately looked up, confused at the king addressing them so abruptly.

'My father, the late King Sol ruled over this kingdom and this empire for a long time. Too long. Many of you have been fooled by his weaknesses, friendships developed with enemies in the east, treaties that did not benefit Benaghar and Aebra. This empire has become weak! I have seen from afar how my father has left this kingdom to disintegrate. Giving land to those who do not deserve it. Joining our forces with them to make alliances?' He spat the words.

'Entwining with the enemy, the weak and the poor. Making ourselves defenceless and at the same time all I have seen is overindulgence. My people no longer care! LOOK AT YOU! Dancing? Laughing? Dressed as you are and in public, in front of your king?

The tea houses are full of intoxication, gambling! And while this all goes on you have abandoned Tekan! You have been allowed to wander from his care. But you need him. We all do. All I can do now is apologise for my father's failings, for letting you all down. His people will be found out and dismissed from my court! Here you find not just a strong king, but your new High Priest of The

Brotherhood!' At the mention of this the High Priest of Benaghar, Colla Anwir, looked shocked. 'GUARDS! Remove him from his seat!'

The guards and all the guests, shocked at the turn of events, could not quite believe the king's change in manner. People looked at each other nervously, others sat down or stood up in confusion.

'NOW!' The king demanded.

Bumbling, three guards closest to Colla Anwir picked him up, and dragged him between the tables and chairs, making their way out through the middle of the room. They passed Wolf Rasia who was now looking up, Cort Rohgah no longer looked happy and his friend, Mr Consta, was nowhere to be seen.

'STOP! The King shouted. 'Hold him there!'

The guards, looking even more confused at each other, turned the former high priest back around to face the king. The king then spoke again, spitting his words out with disgust:

'As an old reign has died I have let you have the last of its frivolities, but to all of you I say; this is the last time! I will not tolerate the dysfunction of our society, kingdom or empire!' He glared at the room at large, then shouted to the other end of the room. 'Fool! Bring them in!'

Phæ'enor looked at Officer Nathryn, concerned. He looked back at her and shook his head, implying that they should do nothing. Not yet. They all turned towards the back of the room. Through a large double door, a colourful, three eared patchwork creature, appeared in the doorway. It was crouched down, as though ready to spring up, all the while twitching its head.

Backwards and forwards, side to side, the sound of bells jingled across the room. Gangly, it sprang up and down until it reached the centre. It reminded Phæ'enor even more of a frog. It then sprung up onto its feet and dramatically bowed to the king and queen, the bells on its hat ringing out.

'Your Majesties,' it said in a drawling voice, and it slowly raised its head smiling.

Phæ'enor gasped, realising who the fool was played by, 'It's … it's Mr…'

But she was stopped short; Officer Nathryn had placed a hand over her mouth from behind and whispered, 'Be quiet, stay still.'

Phæ'enor looked on at the scene in front of her. Gone was the snotty, aloofness and sneer of the astronomer. In his place a ghostly, springy jester. His Harq eyes even more vibrant from the white painted face surrounding them, smudged red paint smeared from one side of his face to the other, blending in his mouth.

'Well then?' demanded the King.

'Of course, of course,' said the fool meekly bowing and turning back around to face the way he had entered.

'Come in! Come in! Your king and queen await! A special surprise is in store for you today!' He chuckled manically, jumping and spinning. Phæ'enor looked on bewildered and horrified. What was wrong with him? This was not the Mr Consta they had met. He was not the astronomer.

She spotted Simi and Mimi across the room. They looked as horrified as she felt. Cort Rohgah had looked at the empty chair beside him then back to the jester, his world collapsing in front of him. Phæ'enor prised away her eyes from the mad fool and looked towards the doors. Slowly a procession of four people made their way into the centre of the room. They shuffled in; their legs were chained together, their heads covered by dark sacks of cloth.

The jester moved them around, fiddling with their chains as he danced about them, lining them up to face the king and queen. He then bowed dramatically again, stooping low and remaining there. There was nothing but silence. All staring at the five, including the former high priest of Benaghar, in the middle.

'To all you gathered here today,' rang out the king's voice, 'I will show you how this kingdom, my empire, will no longer be ruled by a soft touch. We will be strong again. The friendships that were severed by my father will be remade. Those alliances that he was ill advised to choose in their place will be undone.' At the mention of this Phæ'enor saw some of the ambassadors looking about them with worried expressions upon their faces. 'He has led you to believe that there is peace when there is still an enemy at large and work to be done. We must stop it!' He surveyed his audience. 'And routing out the evil begins here, at the heart of the empire! FOOL! Take off their sacks!'

The jester bowed again and hopped and skipped behind the four chained and Colla Anwir in the centre of the room. Everyone watched as the jester cackled and spoke:

'Number one!'

He whipped off the first sack to reveal O'scilla's son. The people closest stepped back from him in disgust.

'Number two!'

He then took off the second sack to reveal Admiral Gull. A murmur of horror and surprise spread around the room. Phæ'enor turned to see Officer Nathryn recoil. She turned her gaze upon the top table. Prince Taigor had frozen still at the bedraggled sight of the Admiral of the Fleet.

'Num-ber thaaaa-reeeee!'

He pulled the sack off the third person and Phæ'enor's stomach rolled like the sea in a storm. Without his hat on, O'tila stood with his hair on end looking around frantically. Phæ'enor thought she knew who he was looking for and turned towards the top table. Standing behind a seated Prince Taigor, with panic in his eyes, stood O'sea.

'And finally, nuuuummmmm-ber, FOUR!' Drum roll, drum roll!' he shouted. The musicians in the room started to drum at the jester's command and as they did so he ripped the sack off the last man to reveal Wolf Canis. A lump had formed in Phæ'enor's throat. He had lost even more weight, but despite this, despite the lack of meat on his bones, the callouses on his legs and arms, he looked strong. Stronger than his brother looked right now; Rasia had collapsed into a chair, tears forming in his eyes staring straight back into his brother's.

Chapter Twenty-Two

The King's Fool

The room seemed to spin. Phæ'enor could not grasp what was going on. Was this too much wine? Was this a nightmare? She closed her eyes and tapped her head but when she reopened them the four men, plus Colla Anwir who, now stripped of his station, all stood in the middle of the King's Hall. Rasia's brother, under the circumstances, looked calm; O'tila just looked angry and embarrassed. The other two and the former high priest looked utterly scared. The King brushed his cloak out from beneath him and sat back down.

'Here before you all are men that have committed crimes against your kingdom. Against me, your king!' There were murmurs, gasps across the room. 'They have committed separate crimes, yet all for the same goal. The same reason. Bring in the chest!' commanded the King.

Again, the double doors, where the four men had entered, opened. Two soldiers, one at each end carried in a single chest. They proceeded into the middle of the room. As they passed, the lock side facing Phæ'enor, she inhaled a sharp breath. Officer Nathryn reminded her to be quiet, this time by poking her sharply in the back. She tensed her back from the sudden pain, but she was too distracted by what she had seen in front of her to complain. Phæ'enor had noticed the two soldiers wore blacked lined gloves, the same as Archä and Mëdez had worn, and there was a symbol above the keyhole; the shape of a full moon. The chest was real, one of the last two still to be found.

As the two soldiers placed the chest in front of the five men, Phæ'enor caught the jester staring back at her. He was down by their feet quietly tinkering with the locks on the prisoners' chains.

He winked at her and then carried on prancing around the chest like he had never spotted her.

'That's enough, Fool!' snapped King Heolbus. The jester skulked back behind the five men. 'I'm sure you are all quite aware now that there has been a lot of trouble and crime caused because of the chest you see before you. Wolf Canis not only stole goods and money from the royal treasury, he was the mastermind behind The Scavenger's explosion. Taking the lives of some of the men on board in the process.' There was an audible gasp across the room.

'That's not true,' whispered Phæ'enor, shaking her head.

'That ship belonged to my beloved brother Prince Taigor and was in possession of MY CHESTS!' Phæ'enor looked at Prince Taigor. He had not recoiled from the brother's false declaration of love or his claim to the chests. He remained still, not giving anything away. 'He then confessed all to the high priest here!' continued the King.

'That's because you tortured him and told him too!' said Colla Anwir.

'SILENCE! snapped the King. 'And then you kept it from me! Treason!' No one gasped this time. All Phæ'enor could see was a wall of worried faces. 'Then, there is Admiral Gull. In charge of a diminishing fleet, obeying orders from King Sol to hand over land that belongs to the Aebran Empire. THAT BELONGS TO ME! And to top it all off, you let your guard slip over the protection of naval goods. First, Wolf Canis breaks in and steals whatever he can get his hands on and then secondly crown gold is taken from this chest and others! You let the garrisons be broken into? Is the Benagharian Army now that easy to defeat? They have destroyed the empire! You have disgraced me! Thankfully my dutiful brother and his men were able to recover the chests.' He then looked at O'tila and O'scilla's son.

'And lastly, two men who have knowingly and willing accepted work from O'scilla! This one,' he said as he pointed at O'tila, 'was found to have kidnapped and held hostage the daughter of one of our most prominent Officers. And this one,' he said pointing out the second man, 'well, he has done nothing particularly wrong by me; your only crime is to be the son of O'scilla Juur.' So, this was O'scilla's reprimand by the new King. He had his son to ransom for the father's failings in retrieving the chest. Phæ'enor looked at him, he was tall like O'scilla, blue and green eyes rimmed by the red of no sleep. He had cuts to his hands and to nearly every part of his skin that was on show.

'This chest, you see before you, belongs to me. The chest was carrying something special to me, a jewel of the empire, gifted to me!' Phæ'enor was shaking her head; all she could hear were lies, stories being created to ensnare the guests. 'And it has been stolen by one of these men standing before you all. WHERE IS IT?' he screamed at the five men in the middle. The five men all shook their heads, looking at each other then back at the King, bewildered. 'Very well. You leave me no other choice. As part of the celebrations, and my wedding gift to my new queen, I declare Eskymira.'

There was now an audible murmur across the room. Heads turned, shoulders shrugged. Phæ'enor racked her brains. Eskymira? Why do I recognise that? She knew she had heard this word before but where?

'This is not good,' she heard Officer Nathryn say. It was hollow, dead like. She turned to see him looking at the top table. The queen was smiling. How Phæ'enor could have liked her before, she knew not. All she could think of was how much she wanted to claw her eyes out and wipe that smile off her face.

'My dear queen, this is an old tradition. One which should never have died out.'

An old tradition, Eskymira? Phæ'enor still racked her brain for where she had heard of it before.

'The rules are as follows! On either the coronation of a new king or queen, or on their wedding day, Eskymira would be performed. It's a ritual. One that cleanses the old king or queen's reign, symbolising the new life of a marriage, bringing in a new era.'

Cleanse? Thought Phæ'enor, and then she remembered where she had heard of it, read about it; in the book Benaghar: The Heart of an Empire. She looked up horrified, knowing what surely must come next.

'The new King and Queen, instead of trials or sentencing of our over populated prisons, get to choose, at random, a prisoner. They don't need to know the particulars of the crime. The one they choose is then sentenced to death.' Phæ'enor watched as the new queen's eyes lit up in delight. The men and women that enclosed the inner circle surrounding the five men visibly started to retreat from the edges. 'My Queen, please, choose which one you would like to die.'

'One?' said the new queen, looking disappointed. 'Just one?'

'Yes, my dear.'

'But, why just one? I know you said this is a tradition, but you also said we are bringing in a new era.'

'And?'

'So, new reign, new rules my darling king.' He smiled back at her. They kissed. The queen then turned towards the five men and addressed the jester. 'Fool,' she commanded, 'kill them! All of them!'

The fool's head appeared by the shoulders of Wolf Canis and O'tila's, wide eyed and still playing his part.

'All, my Queen?'

'That's what I said,' she replied, 'or are you as stupid as you look?' she laughed out loud.

'But … but my Queen …'

'But … but … but WHAT?' she shouted back at him.

'I – I only came prepared for one death this evening.'

'Then you best find other methods than the one you came with …'

'Hmmm … oh, very well. Very, good …' he said as he pranced around the five men and landed at the back of the chest. He then looked up; sneering at the top table, slowly he put on the black gloves, and opened the wooden chest from behind. He reached in with both hands, his tongue sticking out in concentration, and then jumped up in delight. In each hand he held a large three barrelled, golden plated, flintlock pistol. His legs were spread apart, his body straight and tight and the guns facing straight ahead of him towards the top table. He then turned slowly around the room and shouted to all the guests:

'Ladies and gentlemen! Tonight, I shall perform Eskymira! The King and Queen would like these five men dead!' He spun around and faced the king and queen as he said this, 'Yet, they have forgotten one little thing,' he giggled manically, nearly doubled over with laughter. The smiles of the King and Queen had disappeared.

'What are you doing, Fool?' demanded the King, 'has someone let him drink?'

'HA, HA, HA, HA!' The jester cackled louder, slowly pulling himself upright, wiping the saliva off his mouth with his sleeve and faced the King; the guns now dangling at his side, the white cream dried and cracked on his face.

It seemed that it was not only the King and Queen who had started to become alarmed with his behaviour. Nearly all the soldiers in the room had reached for their weapons; swords, guns and knives.

'You may be the new monarch, but I was employed under the old!' He laughed hysterically again. 'And under the rules of Eskymira, if you pick the old King's fool to carry out your work then it is he that gets to choose who dies. So, I have one last thing to say about your treasure … it is gone … poof! All gone! Many, many, years ago! POOF!'

Everything after this happened quickly. The jester pulled his guns up and shouted:

'I – CHOOSE – YOU!' As quick as a flash he had drawn his guns up and started to shoot at the King and Queen. The shots missed, ricocheting off tables and hitting the guests gathered instead. The five men behind him disappeared; O'tila ran as did Wolf Canis, but as Phæ'enor watched from the floor, where Officer Nathryn had thrown her out of the way of the bullets, Wolf Canis fell, landing on his face and did not move. O'scilla's boy was also lying on the floor, blood spooling out from beneath his body. The former high priest was propped up against a chair, clutching at his chest and arm, trying to breathe. Phæ'enor looked back towards the jester, who was still shooting but with shots coming back his way.

'AAAGGH! I've been shot, I've been shot!' He cried dramatically, still laughing as he fell to the floor, crawling back to the chest. People were running everywhere trying to get out or ducking from the fire. The jester put his bloodied hand back in the chest. Blood pouring from his mouth, he spotted Phæ'enor, still on the floor looking back at him.

'Run,' he mouthed, 'run, run, run!'

Officer Nathryn was behind her, 'We need to move!' said Phæ'enor.

'No, stay here!'

NO! We need to move, we need to move! Mother, Grandmother!'

'Phæ'enor, wait!'

But she did not listen and pulling her grandmother and mother up they started to run. Behind them, the jester waited for them to move. Officer Nathryn had followed. With their backs to the jester and the chest, halfway down the room to the door, there was a thunderous noise, a blast of heat and they were all thrown into the wall.

***

Phæ'enor raised her pounding head. Buzzing noises rang in her ear. Someone was shaking her. Her mother was stood over her. All Phæ'enor could do was watch her mouth move. She heard no sound come out and looked around. Her clothes, hands and arms were all covered in dust, and the debris fell densely down around them. The building tremored violently. Glass from up above sprayed all over her. Officer Nathryn appeared and shook her as the building oscillated before a wall of sound hit them.

BOOM!

People were screaming, running, crawling. Others lay motionless on the floor.

'Phæ'enor!' shouted Officer Nathryn. 'Get up! We need to move!'

The building shook again and following it flames poured in like lava through the glass dome above. It looked like people were coming down through it. Was that rope?

Officer Nathryn had pulled her onto her feet, supporting her and moving her out through the hole in the wall where the double doors once stood. She turned to look back into the middle of the room. There was no sign of O'Starr Consta. They kept moving. Phæ'enor thought she could see Mrs Doven guiding Mrs Jemin though the corridors and rooms up ahead. Eventually, the building shaking around them, they made their way out onto the grass of the island and over the King Vane bridge. They were in Parliament Square.

'Where are we going?' asked Phæ'enor. 'Should we not be heading back to help? There are bodies everywhere.'

'No, we need to get somewhere safe. We are on the wrong side of the river, we need to be north, heading to Hightown,' said Officer Nathryn.

Phæ'enor looked about, they were alone, her mother and grandmother nowhere to be seen. But she thought they had got out, she had seen them in front of her, hadn't she? She looked back at Officer Nathryn. He was clearly agitated and trying to hurry them along through the crowd.

'Where are we going?' she asked.

'Yes, where are you going in such a hurry?'

Out of the shadows of one of the buildings emerged a familiar figure, tall, wide and monstrous.

'O'scilla,' it was a statement not a question by Officer Nathryn. More of his men appeared from out of the shadows. Phæ'enor looked around wildly. Her mother and grandmother were still nowhere to be seen.

'Mother? Mother?' she screamed. 'Grandmother?'

'Ha, ha, ha! Miss Phæ'enor Doven have you gone mad?' O'scilla moved closer to them. 'You're alone. I didn't see anyone else with you but him!' He pointed, disgusted at the sight of Officer Nathryn.

'What do you want O'scilla?' said Officer Nathryn fiercely.

'What – do – I - want? Now let me see …' he tapped his chin with his large fat fingers, feigning thought. 'I think I want what is owed to me!'

'And what is that?' asked Officer Nathryn.

'She owes me my gold,' he sneered back. 'And I'm quite sure she knows where it is. Ah, ah, aaah, I don't think so,' he finished, as he saw Officer Nathryn reach for his sword. O'scilla nodded in the direction of his men, five of whom set upon Officer Nathryn. They disarmed him of his weapon and dragged Phæ'enor away from him.

'Leave him alone!' shouted Phæ'enor.

'Ha!' O'scilla laughed. His men joined in. Phæ'enor thought he would not be laughing if he had seen the body of his son under the dome of the King's Hall, still and unmoving. Two men were holding Officer Nathryn tightly.

'That King may be an idiot but I'm not. I know that chest wasn't real, nor was there ever any gold in it, because that fool produced something else entirely different, didn't he? It's fake like the rest of them. But then why go to all that trouble, all those decoys and false trails. That's because Prince Taigor and King Heolbus were working together all along! And you!' he pushed at Officer Nathryn's chest with a finger, 'you, Prince Taigor's favourite officer, his confidant, you, and her!' he spat in Phæ'enor's direction, 'the daughter of Captain Doven have been in it together from the start, hiding it all along for you. That idiot King was just trying to get rid of me, the wolves and the rats in the process. But I don't care what he does, I don't care. All I want is what is owed to me! And you know exactly where it is don't you?'

'Why would I know that?' snapped Officer Nathryn.

O'scilla laughed once more, then nodded again to the shadows. More of his men appeared, but this time they were each holding something large. O'scilla continued:

'Because I asked all your fellow officers and none of them could tell me anything other than repeat your name.'

Phæ'enor looked back at his men. They weren't just carrying something. It was someone. Each of O'scilla's men carried a body in their arms, unrecognizable, but for their uniforms. It was Officer Nathryn's fellow officers from The Scavenger and from the dinner at the palace, amongst them the officers in attendance at the wedding and Lieutenant Hall Oleston's lifeless body.

'NO!' Officer Nathryn's scream travelled far on the wind. Phæ'enor looked about her and spotted men and soldiers appearing on the bridge. Officer Nathryn made to break free; screaming at the sight of his men's bloody, and torn bodies. As the men on the bridge moved closer, O'scilla's men dropped the bodies and reached for their weapons.

'No! No, Taigor run!' shouted Officer Nathryn.

Phæ'enor looked back again to see Prince Taigor leading a group of soldiers, their weapons also drawn, over the bridge.

Bang! Whoosh! Bang! Whoosh!

Shots were fired everywhere. Phæ'enor threw herself to the ground. She tried to see where Officer Nathryn was, but he was no longer on his knees being held. Had he moved? Men where rushing past her, over her.

'Not the girl!' shouted O'scilla from somewhere to her right. 'Not the girl!' suddenly she was picked off her feet. It was O'scilla, 'I still need you, you owe me that gold!'

'No, she doesn't!' shouted Officer Nathryn, who from out of nowhere, raging like a mad man, knocked the gun from O'scilla's hand with his sword. Phæ'enor fell to the ground. The two men began to fight. Phæ'enor picked herself up and tried to move away but they kept veering near to her. A sword and long knife clanged as they clashed.

'Miss Doven! Miss Doven, this way!' It was Prince Taigor who had appeared amongst the bodies of some of O'scilla's fallen men.

Phæ'enor tried to reach him. Tried to get out of range of O'scilla and Officer Nathryn's weapons. There was a gap and she took her chance, running through and jumping over the bodies on the ground.

'Araaagh!' came a blood curdling cry from behind her. Phæ'enor swung around. She could see O'scilla, with a triumphant smile and a gun in his right hand. There, on the ground in front of him was Officer Nathryn, still moving but clearly wounded, the blood visible around him.

'Go! Go! Go!' shouted O'scilla to his men. They all stopped, some still dodging bullets and the tips of swords, some of them unable to escape. More soldiers were making their way over the bridge towards them. O'scilla pointed the gun at Phæ'enor. She froze but stared straight back at him.

'You owe me remember! You-owe-me!' He pointed the gun over her shoulder and started to shoot, retreating as he did. Phæ'enor averted her attention back to Officer Nathryn. She ran over to him and knelt by his side.

'Re'av.'

'Don't ... don't waste time ...' he replied barely able to breathe. He placed a finger to her lips. She nodded that she would be quiet for him to speak.

'You ... you need to leave this city. Get on the other side ... of the wall ... use any means. Promise me?' Phæ'enor looked at him. 'Promise me!'

She nodded hastily, 'Yes, yes I will, I promise!'

'Your cloak ...'

'Yes?'

'Take it ... you must take it with you, always ... my gift to you.'

Phæ'enor thought Officer Nathryn, in his last breaths was in a state of delirium, but she agreed all the same. 'Yes of course but let me go and get help.'

He shook his head violently and choked, blood spitting out where he lay, 'No! You can't!' And he pointed to his chest. Phæ'enor slowly opened his jacket, soaked in blood, more gushed out, 'Promise me ... find a way out ... promise me.'

'Yes, yes I will,' she said. Tears fell down her face. She did not love the man in her arms. Not like she should. But her heart sank for a man that had looked out for her, went looking for her even when she had dismissed him. He was a good man, trying to help her and it had come to this. She grabbed his hand and moved her legs underneath his head to support him, to comfort him. They looked at each other.

'I promise, I promise,' said Phæ'enor now crying. She stroked his head as he smiled back at her. Bullets and fire blazed around them. He squeezed tight on her other hand, and moved it to the left of his chest, heavily it rested over his medals.

At that moment Phæ'enor felt a gust of air upon them, it started to rain heavily. She could still see people running around shouting but amongst them one stood out. Emerging through the curtain of rain, the tall brown and tattoo skinned man walked slowly towards her. This time Phæ'enor did not panic, she was not scared of the man. Too tired and upset to move she just watched on as the man, wide eyed at the scene in front of him, started to talk to someone, someone Phæ'enor could not see. He gestured for them to look to, pointing at Phæ'enor, Officer Nathryn in her lap. But Phæ'enor could not see anyone else, and the man continued to look on at her confused.

Officer Nathryn took one more breath, he shuddered, and was gone. Phæ'enor shook; taking Officer Nathryn in her arms she wept. 'I promise. I promise,' she kept repeating as the fires raged and soldiers and men fought around her. Bodies littered the street in front of the palace now in a blaze of fire, and all the while the tall tattooed man looked on.

Epilogue

Prince Taigor made his way back through the ruins of the King's Hall. There were still fires to be put out but most of the soldiers were busy trying to cover and remove the bodies from the building. He walked past and over them, not stopping to linger. This was urgent.

He made his way around the head table, no longer occupied by his brother the King or his new Queen. He made sure they were removed to safety. He disliked his brother. Even more so now but he could not afford to turn sides, not yet. Not when there was more work to be done. There would be repercussions from last night's event, and he would pay dearly for it when his brother knew how involved he had become.

But for now, the consequences could wait, for him at least. He needed to do this now. It could not wait.

As the prince made his way to the south tower he checked behind him. No one had followed. He opened the door to the spiral stairs and made his way to the top. His legs heavy from the hours of fighting and running. Even when he picked up speed, to get to the top faster, it felt like they held him back. Eventually he came to the top of the stairs and opened the dark wooden door in front of him. The room was warm and dimly lit like it always had been. The windowless tower, heated all day long by the sun, only stayed cool from the occasional breeze that passed through and by the heavy curtains that remained drawn together. A lone candle flame flickered by a dark and empty fireplace. In the middle of the room was a bed in shadow; the covers moved gently but the occupant had not been woken by his entering.

He moved over to the window ledge, peering out through the curtains. A gust of wind blew in the smell of smoke and death and dying embers from the fires. Behind him, the bed covers stirred again.

The city was black, tarred with ash and soaked in blood. He was no different; his armour had broken in several places, scorched by flame in others. Dried blood clung to his skin. He breathed in to steady his nerves, his mouth was dry. No one must see me he thought. He moved back towards the middle of the room. At the end of the bed he bent down and clawing with his fingers he removed a flagstone. It was heavy, made heavier by his tired arms.

He placed it to the side and reached into the revealed space, lifting out a small box. It was wooden, dark and smooth, with symbols engraved on it. He opened it up, taking out some parchment, an old quill and a small pot of purple ink. A small leather cylinder remained inside. He hesitated before setting the quill to paper, using the symbols to write his message:

> *My friend,*
>
> *You must come and come quickly. Our chance has passed to safely escort the Sydula to the north. Both the Maeiniku Wind and Black Taai are dead. The Icean Knights are all but gone. I cannot guarantee its safety on my own. There is no one in the city that can help us now. I have sent The Saeward and The Meang Wind to take the news back to the others. Please come, but come alone. Do not attract attention to yourself. The new King has already ordered tougher restrictions at the borders. Find a way in, I cannot help you, but you must come quickly. The Sydula must be taken to the north to await its true master. I will take care of it until then, but I don't know for how much longer.*

He stopped writing, the quill poised above the parchment and with his left hand reached under the armour of his left breast plate. Pulling it back out, he unravelled his armoured gloved fingers to reveal a medal. It flashed copper and then gold as it caught the light. Prince Taigor smiled to himself, he had always been fascinated by the colour of emaz gold. He moved it slightly and the light of the rising sun made it flash back to copper again. The medal was plain in decoration but unlike the real medals of the Benagharian Army it was much heavier. He thought of Re'av then, carrying the weight of it upon his person for so long, before placing it back inside the breast of his armour. Then continued to write:

> *'It is well disguised for now. My friend, take counsel if you must in this decision but take care in who you confide in, what you choose to say to them. Do not reply to this letter. I write in the hope that I will see you soon. I can see no other way open to us. Good luck.'*

Instead of signing it with his name, he drew a symbol:

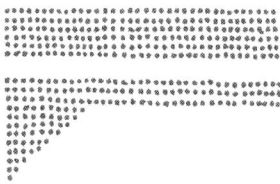

He placed the letter on the floor beside him and put the quill and ink pot back into the box, and took out the small leather cylinder, before concealing the box again with the flagstone. He then made his way back to the window and putting his fingers to his mouth whistled three times into the red sky above.

He looked back out at the city, still smothered by smoke. Hurriedly, he rolled the parchment up tight and carefully placed it into the leather cylinder. Just as he finished a shadow flew above. Silently, the frigate bird flew through the window just like it had been trained to.

'Gilbä,' he said quietly, 'here'. The bird hopped about, spreading it wings out awkwardly. It was too big for the space of the tower. Prince Taigor hurriedly tied the cylinder to the bird's feet. He then gestured for Gilbä to hop onto his wrist. 'Gilbä, my friend, take this to Bensax, where the north winds rise above the Pink Mountains. Take the path of the sea winds only. Stay as far away from land as possible until you are much closer to your destination.' He took the bird, now growing restless, to the window.

'Good luck my friend,' said Prince Taigor, as he thrust his left arm into the space beyond the window. The frigate bird flapped its large wings and soared low, then higher and higher into the currents above. Prince Taigor watched it fly off into the distance, out to sea, until the speck disappeared against a red dawn sky. He knew that all he could do now was wait. Wait in hope that the shadows that grew around him would not close in too quickly, not before he could deliver his promise first.

TO BE CONTINUED...

42129676R00228

Printed in Poland
by Amazon Fulfillment
Poland Sp. z o.o., Wrocław